AF541022

The yellowbacks... classics of popular fiction

The yellowjackets or yellowbacks were a great series of bestselling adventure and crime thrillers that had its origins in the mid to late 19th century following on from the 'penny dreadfuls'. They virtually began the mass market revolution of the early 20th century with a clear standard format and imprint/series livery (what would today be called branding). Hodder & Stoughton published the yellowjackets in two main series with series run dates of: 1923-1939 and later 1949-1957.

As the tagline ('where thrillers really began') on the back cover implies, the imprint and series focused on thrillers that were the bestsellers of their time. This current reissue or retro revival if you will, brings back many of these masterpieces, now classics in their own way and extends it further by including key titles from that period that were either great crime or thriller or even general commercial fiction (including sub-genres of noir, horror, gothic, romance, westerns, etc.) influences of their time. There are some perennial favourites and many rarities either lost or not easily available being revived in the current series. Writers and characters ranged from adventure heroes like Bulldog Drummond, Allan Quatermain, Richard Hannay or the Saint through thriller grandmasters Edgar Wallace and E. Phillips Oppenheim, crime and mystery maestros like Patricia Wentworth, GK Chesterton, Agatha Christie and the Detection club, to western and swashbucklers like Zane Grey, Max Brand, Captain Blood and even romance or general fiction classics like Hermina Black, Denise Robins, Marie Corelli or Stella Morton. These were books that had storytelling at their heart and always entertained.

The yellowbacks had both hardback (with varying design elements) and paperback (which built the series look) versions with the latter still carrying the imprint 'yellowjacket'. The current reissues pay tribute to both and use an amalgam of elements from both editions while retaining the complete yellow (or 'mustard-plaster') livery with the author's name in blue beveled type with a 'simulated emboss' effect and a white outer 'outline', and the book title in black. These reissues retain the distinctive size of the original mass market paperback and follow the three main category variations—the thrillers (crime, westerns, mystery, adventure) had blue lettering for the author's name, while Romance and softer general fiction had red; and other categories like humour had green.

For more detail and a full list of titles visit https://www.hachetteindia.com/home/yellowbacks

THE A.A. MILNE MYSTERY OMNIBUS

THE A.A. MILNE MYSTERY OMNIBUS

Alan Alexander Milne was an English writer best known for Winnie-the-Pooh, as well as for children's poetry. Milne was primarily a playwright before the mega success of Winnie-the-Pooh overshadowed all his previous work. Milne served in both World Wars, as a lieutenant in the Royal Warwickshire Regiment in the First World War and as a captain in the Home Guard in the Second World War.

Milne was the father of bookseller Christopher Robin Milne, upon whom the character Christopher Robin is based. It was during a visit to London Zoo, where Christopher became enamoured with the tame and amiable bear Winnipeg, that Milne was inspired to write the story of Winnie-the-Pooh for his son.

THE A.A. MILNE MYSTERY OMNIBUS

A. A. Milne

The Red House Mystery
Four Days' Wonder

hachette

The A.A. Milne Mystery Omnibus
First published by Methuen (UK) & E.P. Dutton (USA) in 1922
(The Red House Mystery); and 1933 (Four Days Wonder)

1

The texts in these editions in most cases have been reprinted as is, with minimal editorial changes and by and large no bowdlerizing for political correctness; though in some editions, a few words and phrases considered archaic, or those considered offensive now, along with archaic punctuation may have been modified in places to make the text more accessible to today's readers. The narratives, language, beliefs, social mores and/or cultural depictions, in these volumes are a reflection of their times and must be viewed as such. They may also contain certain cultural, racial and gender prejudices and stereotypes that may be outdated or clearly wrong then and wrong today; but their removal would be tantamount to claiming these prejudices never existed. The Publisher does not endorse or support those depictions or stereotypes; and these books have been made available for a discerning audience that will read it for entertainment value and a chronicle/record of popular fiction of past times.

Cover design by Priya Singh adapted from the original classic yellowjacket by Hodder & Stoughton.

Image of the house by Lyna Lutch (Unsplash)

Series note: Some of the books in the series (unless otherwise credited) may have cover or inside illustrations from the original yellowbacks or early editions, and while full restoration has been attempted, some images may be grainy or faded due to the condition of the original material. The end notes or bonus material or blurb details may have been sourced from the public domain or free use publications such as Wikipedia and attribution is hereby made also allowing similar free use reproduction from here. Sources requiring further specific attribution may write in and further detailing and/or corrections shall be made in subsequent printings/editions.

Reprint specifications may be subject to change including but not limited to finishes, paper, colour sections.

ISBN: 978-93-5731-242-4

Hachette Book Publishing India Pvt. Ltd.
4th & 5th Floors, Corporate Centre,
Plot No. 94, Sector 44, Gurugram - 122 003, India

Typeset in Electra LT STD 10/12.5 pt by Manipal Technologies Limited, Manipal

Printed and bound in India by Manipal Technologies Limited, Manipal

CONTENTS

TO
JOHN VINE MILNE
MY DEAR FATHER,

Like all really nice people, you have a weakness for detective stories, and feel that there are not enough of them. So, after all that you have done for me, the least that I can do for you is to write you one. Here it is: with more gratitude and affection than I can well put down here.

A.A.M.

The Red House Mystery

CONTENTS

1

MRS STEVENS IS FRIGHTENED

In the drowsy heat of the summer afternoon the Red House was taking its siesta. There was a lazy murmur of bees in the flower-borders, a gentle cooing of pigeons in the tops of the elms. From distant lawns came the whir of a mowing-machine, that most restful of all country sounds; making ease the sweeter in that it is taken while others are working.

It was the hour when even those whose business it is to attend to the wants of others have a moment or two for themselves. In the housekeeper's room Audrey Stevens, the pretty parlourmaid, re-trimmed her best hat, and talked idly to her aunt, the cook-housekeeper of Mr Mark Ablett's bachelor home.

"For Joe?" said Mrs Stevens placidly, her eye on the hat. Audrey nodded. She took a pin from her mouth, found a place in the hat for it, and said, "He likes a bit of pink."

"I don't say I mind a bit of pink myself," said her aunt. "Joe Turner isn't the only one."

"It isn't everybody's colour," said Audrey, holding the hat out at arm's length, and regarding it thoughtfully. "Stylish, isn't it?"

"Oh, it'll suit you all right, and it would have suited me at your age. A bit too dressy for me now, though wearing better than some other people, I daresay. I was never the one to pretend to be what I wasn't. If I'm fifty-five, I'm fifty-five – that's what I say."

"Fifty-eight, isn't it, auntie?"

"I was just giving that as an example," said Mrs Stevens with great dignity.

Audrey threaded a needle, held her hand out and looked at her nails critically for a moment, and then began to sew.

"Funny thing that about Mr Mark's brother. Fancy not seeing your brother for fifteen years." She gave a self-conscious laugh and went on, "Wonder what I should do if I didn't see Joe for fifteen years."

"As I told you all this morning," said her aunt, "I've been here five years, and never heard of a brother. I could say that before everybody if I was going to die tomorrow. There's been no brother here while I've been here."

"You could have knocked me down with a feather when he spoke about him at breakfast this morning. I didn't hear what went before, naturally, but they was all talking about the brother when I went in – now what was it I went in for – hot milk, was it, or toast? – well, they was all talking, and Mr Mark turns to me, and says – you know his way – 'Stevens,' he says, 'my brother is coming to see me this afternoon; I'm expecting him about three,' he says. 'Show him into the office,' he says, just like that. 'Yes, sir,' I says quite quietly, but I was never so surprised in my life, not knowing he had a brother. 'My brother from Australia,' he says – there, I'd forgotten that. From Australia."

"Well, he may have been in Australia," said Mrs Stevens, judicially; "I can't say for that, not knowing the country; but what I do say is he's never been here. Not while I've been here, and that's five years."

"Well, but, auntie, he hasn't been here for fifteen years. I heard Mr Mark telling Mr Cayley. 'Fifteen years,' he says. Mr Cayley having arst him when his brother was last in England. Mr Cayley knew of him, I heard him telling Mr Beverley, but didn't know when he was last in England – see? So that's why he arst Mr Mark."

"I'm not saying anything about fifteen years, Audrey. I can only speak for what I know, and that's five years Whitsuntide. I can take my oath he's not set foot in the house since five years Whitsuntide. And if he's been in Australia, as you say, well, I daresay he's had his reasons."

"What reasons?" said Audrey lightly.

"Never mind what reasons. Being in the place of a mother to you, since your poor mother died, I say this, Audrey – when a gentleman goes to Australia, he has his reasons. And when he stays in Australia fifteen years, as Mr Mark says, and as I know for myself for five years, he has his reasons. And a respectably brought-up girl doesn't ask what reasons."

"Got into trouble, I suppose," said Audrey carelessly. "They were saying at breakfast he'd been a wild one. Debts. I'm glad Joe isn't like that. He's got fifteen pounds in the post-office savings' bank. Did I tell you?"

But there was not to be any more talk of Joe Turner that afternoon. The ringing of a bell brought Audrey to her feet – no longer Audrey, but now Stevens. She arranged her cap in front of the glass.

"There, that's the front door," she said. "That's him. 'Show him into the office,' said Mr Mark. I suppose he doesn't want the other ladies and gentlemen to see him. Well, they're all out at their golf, anyhow – Wonder if he's going to stay – P'raps he's brought back a lot of gold from Australia – I might hear something about Australia, because if anybody can get gold there, then I don't say but what Joe and I – "

"Now, now, get on, Audrey."

"Just going, darling." She went out.

To anyone who had just walked down the drive in the August sun, the open door of the Red House revealed a delightfully inviting hall, of which even the mere sight was cooling. It was a big low-roofed, oak-beamed place, with cream-washed walls and diamond-paned windows, blue-curtained. On the right and left were doors leading into other living-rooms, but on the side which faced you as you came in were windows again, looking on to a small grass court, and from open windows to open windows such air as there was played gently. The staircase went up in broad, low steps along the right-hand wall, and, turning to the left, led you along a gallery, which ran across the width of the hall, to your bedroom. That is, if you were going to stay the night. Mr Robert Ablett's intentions in this matter were as yet unknown.

As Audrey came across the hall she gave a little start as she saw Mr Cayley suddenly, sitting unobtrusively in a seat beneath one of the front windows, reading. No reason why he shouldn't be there; certainly a much cooler place than the golf-links on such a day; but somehow there was a deserted air about the house that afternoon, as if all the guests were outside, or – perhaps the wisest place of all – up in their bedrooms, sleeping. Mr Cayley, the master's cousin, was a surprise; and, having given a little exclamation as she came suddenly upon him, she blushed, and said, "Oh, I beg your pardon, sir, I didn't see you at first," and he looked up from his book and smiled at her. An attractive smile it was on that big ugly face. "Such a gentleman, Mr Cayley," she thought to herself as she went on, and wondered what the master would do without him. If this brother, for instance, had to be bundled back to Australia, it was Mr Cayley who would do most of the bundling.

"So this is Mr Robert," said Audrey to herself, as she came in sight of the visitor.

She told her aunt afterwards that she would have known him anywhere for Mr Mark's brother, but she would have said that in any event. Actually she was surprised. Dapper little Mark, with his neat pointed beard and his carefully curled moustache; with his quick-darting eyes, always moving from one to the other of any company he was in, to register one more smile to his credit when he had said a good thing, one more expectant look when he was only waiting his turn to say it; he was a very different man from this rough-looking, ill-dressed colonial, staring at her so loweringly.

"I want to see Mr Mark Ablett," he growled. It sounded almost like a threat.

Audrey recovered herself and smiled reassuringly at him. She had a smile for everybody.

"Yes, sir. He is expecting you, if you will come this way."

"Oh! So you know who I am, eh?"

"Mr Robert Ablett?"

"Ay, that's right. So he's expecting me, eh? He'll be glad to see me, eh?"

"If you will come this way, sir," said Audrey primly.

She went to the second door on the left, and opened it.

"Mr Robert Ab – " she began, and then broke off. The room was empty. She turned to the man behind her. "If you will sit down, sir, I will find the master. I know he's in, because he told me that you were coming this afternoon."

"Oh!" He looked round the room. "What d'you call this place, eh?"

"The office, sir."

"The office?"

"The room where the master works, sir."

"Works, eh? That's new. Didn't know he'd ever done a stroke of work in his life."

"Where he writes, sir," said Audrey, with dignity. The fact that Mr Mark "wrote," though nobody knew what, was a matter of pride in the housekeeper's room.

"Not well-dressed enough for the drawing-room, eh?"

"I will tell the master you are here, sir," said Audrey decisively.

She closed the door and left him there.

Well! Here was something to tell auntie! Her mind was busy at once, going over all the things which he had said to her and she had said to him – quiet-like. "Directly I saw him I said to myself – " Why, you could have knocked her over with a feather. Feathers, indeed, were a perpetual menace to Audrey.

However, the immediate business was to find the master. She walked across the hall to the library, glanced in, came back a little uncertainly, and stood in front of Cayley.

"If you please, sir," she said in a low, respectful voice, "can you tell me where the master is? It's Mr Robert called."

"What?" said Cayley, looking up from his book. "Who?"

Audrey repeated her question.

"I don't know. Isn't he in the office? He went up to the Temple after lunch. I don't think I've seen him since."

"Thank you, sir. I will go up to the Temple."

Cayley returned to his book.

The "Temple" was a brick summer-house, in the gardens at the back of the house, about three hundred yards away. Here Mark meditated sometimes before retiring to the "office" to put his thoughts upon paper. The thoughts were not of any great value; moreover, they were given off at the dinner-table more often than they got on to paper, and got on to paper more often than they got into print. But that did not prevent the master of The Red House from being a little pained when a visitor treated the Temple carelessly, as if it had been erected for the ordinary purposes of flirtation and cigarette-smoking. There had been an occasion when two of his guests had been found playing fives in it. Mark had said nothing at the time, save to ask with a little less than his usual point – whether they couldn't find anywhere else for their game, but the offenders were never asked to The Red House again.

Audrey walked slowly up to the Temple, looked in and walked slowly back. All that walk for nothing. Perhaps the master was upstairs in his room. "Not well-dressed enough for the drawing-room." Well, now, Auntie, would you like anyone in your drawing-room with a red handkerchief round his neck and great big dusty boots, and – listen! One of the men shooting rabbits. Auntie was partial to a nice rabbit, and onion sauce. How hot it was; she wouldn't say no to a cup of tea. Well, one thing, Mr Robert wasn't staying the night; he hadn't any luggage. Of course Mr Mark could lend him things; he had clothes enough for six. She would have known him anywhere for Mr Mark's brother.

She came into the house. As she passed the housekeeper's room on her way to the hall, the door opened suddenly, and a rather frightened face looked out.

"Hallo, Aud," said Elsie. "It's Audrey," she said, turning into the room.

"Come in, Audrey," called Mrs Stevens.

"What's up?" said Audrey, looking in at the door.

"Oh, my dear, you gave me such a turn. Where have you been?"

"Up to the Temple."

"Did you hear anything?"

"Hear what?"

"Bangs and explosions and terrible things."

"Oh!" said Audrey, rather relieved. "One of the men shooting rabbits. Why, I said to myself as I came along, 'Auntie's partial to a nice rabbit,' I said, and I shouldn't be surprised if – "

"Rabbits!" said her aunt scornfully. "It was inside the house, my girl."

"Straight it was," said Elsie. She was one of the housemaids. "I said to Mrs Stevens – didn't I, Mrs Stevens? – 'That was in the house,' I said."

Audrey looked at her aunt and then at Elsie.

"Do you think he had a revolver with him?" she said in a hushed voice.

"Who?" said Elsie excitedly.

"That brother of his. From Australia. I said as soon as I set eyes on him, 'You're a bad lot, my man!' That's what I said, Elsie. Even before he spoke to me. Rude!" She turned to her aunt. "Well, I give you my word."

"If you remember, Audrey, I always said there was no saying with anyone from Australia." Mrs Stevens lay back in her chair, breathing rather rapidly. "I wouldn't go out of this room now, not if you paid me a hundred thousand pounds."

"Oh, Mrs Stevens!" said Elsie, who badly wanted five shillings for a new pair of shoes, "I wouldn't go as far as that, not myself, but – "

"There!" cried Mrs Stevens, sitting up with a start. They listened anxiously, the two girls instinctively coming closer to the older woman's chair.

A door was being shaken, kicked, rattled.

"Listen!"

Audrey and Elsie looked at each other with frightened eyes.

They heard a man's voice, loud, angry.

"Open the door!" it was shouting. "Open the door! I say, open the door!"

"Don't open the door!" cried Mrs Stevens in a panic, as if it was her door which was threatened. "Audrey! Elsie! Don't let him in!"

"Damn it, open the door!" came the voice again.

"We're all going to be murdered in our beds," she quavered. Terrified, the two girls huddled closer, and with an arm round each, Mrs Stevens sat there, waiting.

2

MR GILLINGHAM GETS OUT AT THE WRONG STATION

Whether Mark Ablett was a bore or not depended on the point of view, but it may be said at once that he never bored his company on the subject of his early life. However, stories get about. There is always somebody who knows. It was understood – and this, anyhow, on Mark's own authority – that his father had been a country clergyman. It was said that, as a boy, Mark had attracted the notice, and patronage, of some rich old spinster of the neighbourhood, who had paid for his education, both at school and university. At about the time when he was coming down from Cambridge, his father had died; leaving behind him a few debts, as a warning to his family, and a reputation for short sermons, as an example to his successor. Neither warning nor example seems to have been effective. Mark went to London, with an allowance from his patron, and (it is generally agreed) made acquaintance with the money-lenders. He was supposed, by his patron and any others who inquired, to be "writing"; but what he wrote, other than letters asking for more time to pay, has never been discovered. However, he attended the theatres and music halls very regularly – no doubt with a view to some serious articles in the "Spectator" on the decadence of the English stage.

Fortunately (from Mark's point of view) his patron died during his third year in London, and left him all the money he wanted. From that moment his life loses its legendary character, and becomes more a matter of history. He settled accounts with the money-lenders, abandoned his crop of wild oats to the harvesting of others, and became in his turn a patron. He patronized the Arts. It was not only usurers who discovered that Mark Ablett no longer wrote for money; editors were now offered free contributions as well as free lunches; publishers were given agreements for an occasional slender volume, in which the author paid all expenses and waived all royalties; promising young painters and poets dined with him; and he even took a theatrical company on tour, playing host and "lead" with equal lavishness.

He was not what most people call a snob. A snob has been defined carelessly as a man who loves a lord; and, more carefully, as a mean lover of mean things – which would be a little unkind to the peerage if the first definition were true. Mark had his vanities undoubtedly, but he would sooner have met an actor-manager than an earl; he would have spoken of his friendship with Dante – had that been possible – more glibly than of his friendship with the Duke. Call him a snob if you like, but not the worst kind of snob; a hanger-on, but to the skirts of Art, not Society; a climber, but in the neighbourhood of Parnassus, not Hay Hill.

His patronage did not stop at the Arts. It also included Matthew Cayley, a small cousin of thirteen, whose circumstances were as limited as had been Mark's own before his patron had rescued him. He sent the Cayley cousin to school and Cambridge. His motives, no doubt, were unworldly enough at first; a mere repaying to his account in the Recording Angel's book of the generosity which had been lavished on himself; a laying-up of treasure in heaven. But it is probable that, as the boy grew up, Mark's designs for his future were based on his own interests as much as those of his cousin, and that a suitably educated Matthew Cayley of twenty-three was felt by him to be a useful property for a man in his position; a man, that is to say, whose vanities left him so little time for his affairs.

Cayley, then, at twenty-three, looked after his cousin's affairs. By this time Mark had bought the Red House and the considerable amount of land which went with it. Cayley superintended the necessary staff. His duties, indeed, were many. He was not quite secretary, not quite land-agent, not quite business-adviser, not quite companion, but something of all four. Mark leant upon him and called him "Cay," objecting quite rightly in the circumstances to the name of Matthew. Cay, he felt was, above all, dependable; a big, heavy-jawed, solid fellow, who didn't bother you with unnecessary talk – a boon to a man who liked to do most of the talking himself.

Cayley was now twenty-eight, but had all the appearance of forty, which was his patron's age. Spasmodically they entertained a good deal at the Red House, and Mark's preference – call it kindliness or vanity, as you please – was for guests who were not in a position to repay his hospitality. Let us have a look at them as they came down to that breakfast, of which Stevens, the parlour-maid, has already given us a glimpse.

The first to appear was Major Rumbold, a tall, grey-haired, grey-moustached, silent man, wearing a Norfolk coat and grey flannel trousers, who lived on his retired pay and wrote natural history articles for the papers. He inspected the dishes on the side-table, decided carefully on kedgeree, and got to work on it. He had passed on to a sausage by the time of the next arrival. This was Bill Beverley, a cheerful young man in white flannel trousers and a blazer.

"Hallo, Major," he said as he came in, "how's the gout?"

"It isn't gout," said the Major gruffly.

"Well, whatever it is."

The Major grunted.

"I make a point of being polite at breakfast," said Bill, helping himself largely to porridge. "Most people are so rude. That's why I asked you. But don't tell me if it's a secret. Coffee?" he added, as he poured himself out a cup.

"No, thanks. I never drink till I've finished eating."

"Quite right, Major; it's only manners." He sat down opposite to the other. "Well, we've got a good day for our game. It's going to be dashed hot, but that's where Betty and I score. On the fifth green, your old wound, the one you got in that frontier skirmish in '43, will begin to trouble you; on the eighth, your liver, undermined by years of curry, will drop to pieces; on the twelfth – "

"Oh, shut up, you ass!"

"Well, I'm only warning you. Hallo; good morning, Miss Norris. I was just telling the Major what was going to happen to you and him this morning. Do you want any assistance, or do you prefer choosing your own breakfast?"

"Please don't get up," said Miss Norris. "I'll help myself. Good morning, Major." She smiled pleasantly at him. The Major nodded.

"Good morning. Going to be hot."

"As I was telling him," began Bill, "that's where – Hallo, here's Betty. Morning, Cayley."

Betty Calladine and Cayley had come in together. Betty was the eighteen-year-old daughter of Mrs John Calladine, widow of the painter, who was acting hostess on this occasion for Mark. Ruth Norris took herself seriously as an actress and, on her holidays, seriously as a golfer. She was quite competent as either. Neither the Stage Society nor Sandwich had any terrors for her.

"By the way, the car will be round at 10.30," said Cayley, looking up from his letters. "You're lunching there, and driving back directly afterwards. Isn't that right?"

"I don't see why we shouldn't have two rounds," said Bill hopefully.

"Much too hot in the afternoon," said the Major. "Get back comfortably for tea."

Mark came in. He was generally the last. He greeted them and sat down to toast and tea. Breakfast was not his meal. The others chattered gently while he read his letters.

"Good God!" said Mark suddenly.

There was an instinctive turning of heads towards him. "I beg your pardon, Miss Norris. Sorry, Betty."

Miss Norris smiled her forgiveness. She often wanted to say it herself, particularly at rehearsals.

"I say, Cay!" He was frowning to himself – annoyed, puzzled. He held up a letter and shook it. "Who do you think this is from?"

Cayley, at the other end of the table, shrugged his shoulders. How could he possibly guess?

"Robert," said Mark.

"Robert?" It was difficult to surprise Cayley. "Well?"

"It's all very well to say 'well?' like that," said Mark peevishly. "He's coming here this afternoon."

"I thought he was in Australia, or somewhere."

"Of course. So did I." He looked across at Rumbold. "Got any brothers, Major?"

"No."

"Well, take my advice, and don't have any."

"Not likely to now," said the Major.

Bill laughed. Miss Norris said politely: "But you haven't any brothers, Mr Ablett?"

"One," said Mark grimly. "If you're back in time you'll see him this afternoon. He'll probably ask you to lend him five pounds. Don't."

Everybody felt a little uncomfortable.

"I've got a brother," said Bill helpfully, "but I always borrow from him."

"Like Robert," said Mark.

"When was he in England last?" asked Cayley.

"About fifteen years ago, wasn't it? You'd have been a boy, of course."

"Yes, I remember seeing him once about then, but I didn't know if he had been back since."

"No. Not to my knowledge." Mark, still obviously upset, returned to his letter.

"Personally," said Bill, "I think relations are a great mistake."

"All the same," said Betty a little daringly, "it must be rather fun having a skeleton in the cupboard."

Mark looked up, frowning.

"If you think it's fun, I'll hand him over to you, Betty. If he's anything like he used to be, and like his few letters have been – well, Cay knows."

Cayley grunted.

"All I knew was that one didn't ask questions about him."

It may have been meant as a hint to any too curious guest not to ask more questions, or a reminder to his host not to talk too freely in front of strangers, although he gave it the sound of a mere statement of fact. But the subject dropped, to be succeeded by the more fascinating one of the coming foursome. Mrs Calladine was driving over with the players in order to lunch with an old friend who lived near the links, and Mark and Cayley were remaining at home – on affairs. Apparently "affairs" were now to include a prodigal brother. But that need not make the foursome less enjoyable.

At about the time when the Major (for whatever reasons) was fluffing his tee-shot at the sixteenth, and Mark and his cousin were at their business at the Red House, an attractive gentleman of the name of Antony Gillingham was handing up his ticket at Woodham station and asking the way to the village. Having received directions, he left his bag with the station-master and walked off leisurely. He is an important person to this story, so that it is as well we should know something about him before letting him loose in it. Let us stop him at the top of the hill on some excuse, and have a good look at him.

The first thing we realize is that he is doing more of the looking than we are. Above a clean-cut, clean-shaven face, of the type usually associated with the Navy, he carries a pair of grey eyes which seem to be absorbing every detail of our person. To strangers this look is almost alarming at first, until they discover that his mind is very often elsewhere; that he has, so to speak, left his eyes on guard, while he himself follows a train of thought in another direction. Many people do this, of course; when, for instance, they are talking to one person and trying to listen to another; but their eyes betray them. Antony's never did.

He had seen a good deal of the world with those eyes, though never as a sailor. When at the age of twenty-one he came into his mother's money, 400 pounds a year, old Gillingham looked up from the "Stockbreeders' Gazette" to ask what he was going to do.

"See the world," said Antony.

"Well, send me a line from America, or wherever you get to."

"Right," said Antony.

Old Gillingham returned to his paper. Antony was a younger son, and, on the whole, not so interesting to his father as the cadets of certain other families; Champion Birket's, for instance. But, then, Champion Birket was the best Hereford bull he had ever bred.

Antony, however, had no intention of going further away than London. His idea of seeing the world was to see, not countries, but people; and to see them from as many angles as possible. There are all sorts in London if you know how to look at them. So Antony looked at them – from various strange corners; from the view-point of the valet, the newspaper-reporter, the waiter, the shop-assistant. With the independence of 400 pounds a year behind him, he enjoyed it immensely. He never stayed long in one job, and generally closed his connection with it by telling his employer (contrary to all etiquette as understood between master and servant) exactly what he thought of him. He had no difficulty in finding a new profession. Instead of experience and testimonials he offered his personality and a sporting bet. He would take no wages the first month, and – if he satisfied his employer – double wages the second. He always got his double wages.

He was now thirty. He had come to Waldheim for a holiday, because he liked the look of the station. His ticket entitled him to travel further, but he had always intended to please himself in the matter. Waldheim attracted him, and he had a suitcase in the carriage with him and money in his pocket. Why not get out?

The landlady of 'The George' was only too glad to put him up, and promised that her husband would drive over that afternoon for his luggage.

"And you would like some lunch, I expect, sir."

"Yes, but don't give yourself any trouble about it. Cold anything-you've-got."

"What about beef, sir?" she asked, as if she had a hundred varieties of meat to select from, and was offering him her best.

"That will do splendidly. And a pint of beer."

While he was finishing his lunch, the landlord came in to ask about the luggage. Antony ordered another pint, and soon had him talking.

"It must be rather fun to keep a country inn," he said, thinking that it was about time he started another profession.

"I don't know about fun, sir. It gives us a living, and a bit over."

"You ought to take a holiday," said Antony, looking at him thoughtfully.

"Funny thing your saying that," said the landlord, with a smile. "Another gentleman, over from the Red House, was saying that only yesterday. Offered to take my place 'n all." He laughed rumblingly.

"The Red House? Not the Red House, Stanton?"

"That's right, sir. Stanton's the next station to Waldheim. The Red House is about a mile from here – Mr Ablett's."

Antony took a letter from his pocket. It was addressed from "The Red House, Stanton," and signed "Bill."

"Good old Bill," he murmured to himself. "He's getting on."

Antony had met Bill Beverley two years before in a tobacconist's shop. Gillingham was on one side of the counter and Mr Beverley on the other. Something about Bill, his youth and freshness, perhaps, attracted Antony; and when cigarettes had been ordered, and an address given to which they were to be sent, he remembered that he had come across an aunt of Beverley's once at a country-house. Beverley and he met again a little later at a restaurant. Both of them were in evening-dress, but they did different things with their napkins, and Antony was the more polite of the two. However, he still liked Bill. So on one of his holidays, when he was unemployed, he arranged an introduction through a mutual friend. Beverley was a little inclined to be shocked when he was reminded of their previous meetings, but his uncomfortable feeling soon wore off, and he and Antony quickly became intimate. But Bill generally addressed him as "Dear Madman" when he happened to write.

Antony decided to stroll over to the Red House after lunch and call upon his friend. Having inspected his bedroom which was not quite the lavender-smelling country-inn bedroom of fiction, but sufficiently clean and comfortable, he set out over the fields.

As he came down the drive and approached the old red-brick front of the house, there was a lazy murmur of bees in the flower-borders, a gentle cooing of pigeons in the tops of the elms, and from distant lawns the whir of a mowing-machine, that most restful of all country sounds...

And in the hall a man was banging at a locked door, and shouting, "Open the door, I say; open the door!"

"Hallo!" said Antony in amazement.

3

TWO MEN AND A BODY

Cayley looked round suddenly at the voice.

"Can I help?" said Antony politely.

"Something's happened," said Cayley. He was breathing quickly. "I heard a shot – it sounded like a shot – I was in the library. A loud bang – I didn't know what it was. And the door's locked." He rattled the handle again, and shook it. "Open the door!" he cried. "I say, Mark, what is it? Open the door!"

"But he must have locked the door on purpose," said Antony. "So why should he open it just because you ask him to?"

Cayley looked at him in a bewildered way. Then he turned to the door again. "We must break it in," he said, putting his shoulder to it. "Help me."

"Isn't there a window?"

Cayley turned to him stupidly.

"Window? Window?"

"So much easier to break in a window," said Antony with a smile. He looked very cool and collected, as he stood just inside the hall, leaning on his stick, and thinking, no doubt, that a great deal of fuss was being made about nothing. But then, he had not heard the shot.

"Window – of course! What an idiot I am."

He pushed past Antony, and began running out into the drive. Antony followed him. They ran along the front of the house, down a path to the left, and then to the left again over the grass, Cayley in front, the other close behind him. Suddenly Cayley looked over his shoulder and pulled up short.

"Here," he said.

They had come to the windows of the locked room, French windows which opened on to the lawns at the back of the house. But now they were closed. Antony couldn't help feeling a thrill of excitement as he followed Cayley's example, and put his face close up to the glass. For the first time he wondered if there really had been a revolver shot in this mysterious room. It had all seemed so absurd and melodramatic from the other side of the door. But if there had been one shot, why should there not be two more? – at the careless fools who were pressing their noses against the panes, and asking for it.

"My God, can you see it?" said Cayley in a shaking voice. "Down there. Look!"

The next moment Antony saw it. A man was lying on the floor at the far end of the room, his back towards them. A man? Or the body of a man?

"Who is it?" said Antony.

"I don't know," the other whispered.

"Well, we'd better go and see." He considered the windows for a moment. "I should think, if you put your weight into it, just where they join, they'll give all right. Otherwise, we can kick the glass in."

Without saying anything, Cayley put his weight into it. The window gave, and they went into the room. Cayley walked quickly to the body, and dropped on his knees by it. For the moment he seemed to hesitate; then with an effort he put a hand on to its shoulder and pulled it over.

"Thank God!" he murmured, and let the body go again.

"Who is it?" said Antony.

"Robert Ablett."

"Oh!" said Antony. "I thought his name was Mark," he added, more to himself than to the other.

"Yes, Mark Ablett lives here. Robert is his brother." He shuddered, and said, "I was afraid it was Mark."

"Was Mark in the room too?"

"Yes," said Cayley absently. Then, as if resenting suddenly these questions from a stranger, "Who are you?"

But Antony had gone to the locked door, and was turning the handle. "I suppose he put the key in his pocket," he said, as he came back to the body again.

"Who?"

Antony shrugged his shoulders.

"Whoever did this," he said, pointing to the man on the floor. "Is he dead?"

"Help me," said Cayley simply.

They turned the body on to its back, nerving themselves to look at it. Robert Ablett had been shot between the eyes. It was not a pleasant sight, and with his horror Antony felt a sudden pity for the man beside him, and a sudden remorse for the careless, easy way in which he had treated the affair. But then one always went about imagining that these things didn't happen – except to other people. It was difficult to believe in them just at first, when they happened to yourself.

"Did you know him well?" said Antony quietly. He meant, "Were you fond of him?"

"Hardly at all. Mark is my cousin. I mean, Mark is the brother I know best."

"Your cousin?"

"Yes." He hesitated, and then said, "Is he dead? I suppose he is. Will you – do you know anything about – about that sort of thing? Perhaps I'd better get some water."

There was another door opposite to the locked one, which led, as Antony was to discover for himself directly, into a passage from which opened two more rooms. Cayley stepped into the passage, and opened the door on the right. The door from the office, through which he had gone, remained open. The door, at the end of the short passage was shut. Antony, kneeling by the body, followed Cayley with his eyes, and, after he had disappeared, kept his eyes on the blank wall of the passage, but he was not conscious of that at which he was looking, for his mind was with the other man, sympathizing with him.

"Not that water is any use to a dead body," he said to himself, "but the feeling that you're doing something, when there's obviously nothing to be done, is a great comfort."

Cayley came into the room again. He had a sponge in one hand, a handkerchief in the other. He looked at Antony. Antony nodded. Cayley murmured something, and knelt down to bathe the dead man's face. Then he placed the handkerchief over it. A little sigh escaped Antony, a sigh of relief.

They stood up and looked at each other.

"If I can be of any help to you," said Antony, "please let me."

"That's very kind of you. There will be things to do. Police, doctors – I don't know. But you mustn't let me trespass on your kindness. Indeed, I should apologise for having trespassed so much already."

"I came to see Beverley. He is an old friend of mine."

"He's out playing golf. He will be back directly." Then, as if he had only just realized it, "They will all be back directly."

"I will stay if I can be of any help."

"Please do. You see, there are women. It will be rather painful. If you would – " He hesitated, and gave Antony a timid little smile, pathetic in so big and self-reliant a man. "Just your moral support, you know. It would be something."

"Of course." Antony smiled back at him, and said cheerfully, "Well, then, I'll begin by suggesting that you should ring up the police."

"The police? Y-yes." He looked doubtfully at the other. "I suppose – "

Antony spoke frankly.

"Now, look here, Mr – er – "

"Cayley. I'm Mark Ablett's cousin. I live with him."

"My name's Gillingham. I'm sorry, I ought to have told you before. Well now, Mr Cayley, we shan't do any good by pretending. Here's a man been shot – well, somebody shot him."

"He might have shot himself," mumbled Cayley.

"Yes, he might have, but he didn't. Or if he did, somebody was in the room at the time, and that somebody isn't here now. And that somebody took a revolver away with him. Well, the police will want to say a word about that, won't they?"

Cayley was silent, looking on the ground.

"Oh, I know what you're thinking, and believe me I do sympathize with you, but we can't be children about it. If your cousin Mark Ablett was in the room with this" – he indicated the body – "this man, then – "

"Who said he was?" said Cayley, jerking his head up suddenly at Antony.

"You did."

"I was in the library. Mark went in – he may have come out again – I know nothing. Somebody else may have gone in – "

"Yes, yes," said Antony patiently, as if to a little child. "You know your cousin; I don't. Let's agree that he had nothing to do with it. But somebody was in the room when this man was shot, and – well, the police will have to know. Don't you think – " He looked at the telephone. "Or would you rather I did it?"

Cayley shrugged his shoulders and went to the telephone.

"May I – er – look round a bit?" Antony nodded towards the open door.

"Oh, do. Yes." He sat down and drew the telephone towards him. "You must make allowances for me, Mr Gillingham. You see, I've known Mark for a very long time. But, of course, you're quite right, and I'm merely being stupid." He took off the receiver.

Let us suppose that, for the purpose of making a first acquaintance with this "office," we are coming into it from the hall, through the door which is now locked, but which, for our special convenience, has been magically unlocked for us. As we stand just inside the door, the length of the room runs right and left; or, more accurately, to the right only, for the left-hand wall is almost within our reach. Immediately opposite to us, across the breadth of the room (some fifteen feet), is that other door, by which Cayley went out and returned a few minutes ago. In the right-hand wall, thirty feet away from us, are the French windows. Crossing the room and going out by the opposite door, we come into a passage, from which two rooms lead. The one on the right, into which Cayley went, is less than half the length of the office, a small, square room, which has evidently been used some time or other as a bedroom. The bed is no longer there, but there is a basin, with hot and cold taps, in a corner; chairs; a cupboard or two, and a chest of drawers. The window faces the same way as the French windows in the next room; but anybody looking out of the bedroom window has his view on the immediate right shut off by the outer wall of the office, which projects, by reason of its greater length, fifteen feet further into the lawn.

The room on the other side of the bedroom is a bathroom. The three rooms together, in fact, form a sort of private suite; used, perhaps, during the occupation of the previous owner, by some invalid, who could not manage the stairs, but allowed by Mark to fall into disuse, save for the living-room. At any rate, he never slept downstairs.

Antony glanced at the bathroom, and then wandered into the bedroom, the room into which Cayley had been. The window was open, and he looked out at the well-kept grass beneath him, and the peaceful stretch of park beyond; and he felt very sorry for the owner of it all, who was now mixed up in so grim a business.

"Cayley thinks he did it," said Antony to himself. "That's obvious. It explains why he wasted so much time banging on the door. Why should he try to break a lock when it's so much easier to break a window? Of course he might just have lost his head; on the other hand, he might – well, he might have wanted to give his cousin a chance of getting away. The same about the police, and – oh, lots of things. Why, for instance, did we run all the way round the house in order to get to the windows? Surely there's a back way out through the hall. I must have a look later on."

Antony, it will be observed, had by no means lost his head.

There was a step in the passage outside, and he turned round, to see Cayley in the doorway. He remained looking at him for a moment, asking himself a question. It was rather a curious question. He was asking himself why the door was open.

Well, not exactly why the door was open; that could be explained easily enough. But why had he expected the door to be shut? He did not remember shutting it, but somehow he was surprised to see it open now, to see Cayley through the doorway, just coming into the room. Something working subconsciously in his brain had told him that it was surprising. Why?

He tucked the matter away in a corner of his mind for the moment; the answer would come to him later on. He had a wonderfully retentive mind. Everything which he saw or heard seemed to make its corresponding impression somewhere in his brain; often without his being conscious of it; and these photographic impressions were always there ready for him when he wished to develop them.

Cayley joined him at the window.

"I've telephoned," he said. "They're sending an inspector or someone from Middleston, and the local police and doctor from Stanton." He shrugged his shoulders. "We're in for it now."

"How far away is Middleston?" It was the town for which Antony had taken a ticket that morning – only six hours ago. How absurd it seemed.

"About twenty miles. These people will be coming back soon."

"Beverley, and the others?"

"Yes. I expect they'll want to go away at once."

"Much better that they should."

"Yes." Cayley was silent for a little. Then he said, "You're staying near here?"

"I'm at 'The George,' at Waldheim."

"If you're by yourself, I wish you'd put up here. You see," he went on awkwardly, "you'll have to be here – for the – the inquest and – and so on. If I may offer you my cousin's hospitality in his – I mean if he doesn't – if he really has – "

Antony broke in hastily with his thanks and acceptance.

"That's good. Perhaps Beverley will stay on, if he's a friend of yours. He's a good fellow."

Antony felt quite sure, from what Cayley had said and had hesitated to say, that Mark had been the last to see his brother alive. It didn't follow that Mark Ablett was a murderer. Revolvers go off accidentally; and when they have gone off, people lose their heads and run away, fearing that their story will not be believed. Nevertheless, when people run away, whether innocently or guiltily, one can't help wondering which way they went.

"I suppose this way," said Antony aloud, looking out of the window.

"Who?" said Cayley stubbornly.

"Well, whoever it was," said Antony, smiling to himself. "The murderer. Or, let us say, the man who locked the door after Robert Ablett was killed."

"I wonder."

"Well, how else could he have got away? He didn't go by the windows in the next room, because they were shut."

"Isn't that rather odd?"

"Well, I thought so at first, but – " He pointed to the wall jutting out on the right. "You see, you're protected from the rest of the house if you get out here, and you're quite close to the shrubbery. If you go out at the French windows, I imagine you're much more visible. All that part of the house – " he waved his right hand – "the west, well, north-west almost, where the kitchen parts are – you see, you're hidden from them here. Oh, yes! he knew the house, whoever it was, and he was quite right to come out of this window. He'd be into the shrubbery at once."

Cayley looked at him thoughtfully.

"It seems to me, Mr Gillingham, that you know the house pretty well, considering that this is the first time you've been to it."

Antony laughed.

"Oh, well, I notice things, you know. I was born noticing. But I'm right, aren't I, about why he went out this way?"

"Yes, I think you are." Cayley looked away – towards the shrubbery. "Do you want to go noticing in there now?" He nodded at it.

"I think we might leave that to the police," said Antony gently. "It's – well, there's no hurry."

Cayley gave a little sigh, as if he had been holding his breath for the answer, and could now breathe again.

"Thank you, Mr Gillingham," he said.

4

THE BROTHER FROM AUSTRALIA

Guests at the Red House were allowed to do what they liked within reason – the reasonableness or otherwise of it being decided by Mark. But when once they (or Mark) had made up their minds as to what they wanted to do, the plan had to be kept. Mrs Calladine, who knew this little weakness of their host's, resisted, therefore, the suggestion of Bill that they should have a second round in the afternoon, and drive home comfortably after tea. The other golfers were willing enough, but Mrs Calladine, without actually saying that Mr Ablett wouldn't like it, was firm on the point that, having arranged to be back by four, they should be back by four.

"I really don't think Mark wants us, you know," said the Major. Having played badly in the morning, he wanted to prove to himself in the afternoon that he was really better than that. "With this brother of his coming, he'll be only too glad to have us out of the way."

"Of course he will, Major." This from Bill. "You'd like to play, wouldn't you, Miss Norris?"

Miss Norris looked doubtfully at the hostess.

"Of course, if you want to get back, dear, we mustn't keep you here. Besides, it's so dull for you, not playing."

"Just nine holes, mother," pleaded Betty.

"The car could take you back, and you could tell them that we were having another round, and then it could come back for us," said Bill brilliantly.

"It's certainly much cooler here than I expected," put in the Major.

Mrs Calladine fell. It was very pleasantly cool outside the golf-house, and of course Mark would be rather glad to have them out of the way. So she consented to nine holes; and the match having ended all-square, and everybody having played much better than in the morning, they drove back to the Red House, very well pleased with themselves.

"Halo," said Bill to himself, as they approached the house, "isn't that old Tony?"

Antony was standing in front of the house, waiting for them. Bill waved, and he waved back. Then as the car drew up, Bill, who was in front with the chauffeur, jumped down and greeted him eagerly.

"Hallo, you madman, have you come to stay, or what?" He had a sudden idea. "Don't say you're Mark Ablett's long-lost brother from Australia, though I could quite believe it of you." He laughed boyishly.

"Hallo, Bill," said Antony quietly. "Will you introduce me? I'm afraid I've got some bad news."

Bill, rather sobered by this, introduced him. The Major and Mrs Calladine were on the near side of the car, and Antony spoke to them in a low voice.

"I'm afraid I'm going to give you rather a shock," he said. "Robert Ablett, Mr Mark Ablett's brother, has been killed." He jerked a thumb over his shoulder. "In the house."

"Good God!" said the Major.

"Do you mean that he has killed himself?" asked Mrs Calladine. "Just now?"

"It was about two hours ago. I happened to come here," – he half-turned to Beverley and explained – "I was coming to see you, Bill, and I arrived just after the – the death. Mr Cayley and I found the body. Mr Cayley being busy just now – there are police and doctors and so on in the house – he asked me to tell you. He says that no doubt you would prefer, the house-party having been broken up in this tragic way, to leave as soon as possible." He gave a pleasant apologetic little smile and went on, "I am putting it badly, but what he means, of course, is that you must consult your own feelings in the matter entirely, and please make your own arrangements about ordering the car for whatever train you wish to catch. There is one this evening, I understand, which you could go by if you wished it."

Bill gazed with open mouth at Antony. He had no words in his vocabulary to express what he wanted to say, other than those the Major had already used. Betty was leaning across to Miss Norris and saying, "Who's killed?" in an awestruck voice, and Miss Norris, who was instinctively looking as tragic as she looked on the stage when a messenger announced the death of one of the cast, stopped for a moment in order to explain. Mrs Calladine was quietly mistress of herself.

"We shall be in the way, yes, I quite understand," she said; "but we can't just shake the dust of the place off our shoes because something terrible has happened there. I must see Mark, and we can arrange later what to do. He must know how very deeply we feel for him. Perhaps we – " she hesitated.

"The Major and I might be useful anyway," said Bill. "Isn't that what you mean, Mrs Calladine?"

"Where is Mark?" said the Major suddenly, looking hard at Antony.

Antony looked back unwaveringly – and said nothing.

"I think," said the Major gently, leaning over to Mrs Calladine, "that it would be better if you took Betty back to London tonight."

"Very well," she agreed quietly. "You will come with us, Ruth?"

"I'll see you safely there," said Bill in a meek voice. He didn't quite know what was happening, and, having expected to stay at the Red House for another week, he had nowhere to go to in London, but London seemed to be the place that everyone was going to, and when he could get Tony alone for a moment, Tony no doubt would explain.

"Cayley wants you to stay, Bill. You have to go anyhow, tomorrow, Major Rumbold?"

"Yes. I'll come with you, Mrs Calladine."

"Mr Cayley would wish me to say again that you will please not hesitate to give your own orders, both as regard the car and as regard any telephoning or telegraphing that you want done." He smiled again and added, "Please forgive me if I seem to have taken a good deal upon myself, but I just happened to be handy as a mouthpiece for Cayley." He bowed to them and went into the house.

"Well!" said Miss Norris dramatically.

As Antony re-entered the hall, the Inspector from Middleston was just crossing into the library with Cayley. The latter stopped and nodded to Antony.

"Wait a moment, Inspector. Here's Mr Gillingham. He'd better come with us." And then to Antony, "This is Inspector Birch."

Birch looked inquiringly from one to the other.

"Mr Gillingham and I found the body together," explained Cayley.

"Oh! Well, come along, and let's get the facts sorted out a bit. I like to know where I am, Mr Gillingham."

"We all do."

"Oh!" He looked at Antony with interest. "D'you know where you are in this case?"

"I know where I'm going to be."

"Where's that?"

"Put through it by Inspector Birch," said Antony with a smile.

The inspector laughed genially.

"Well, I'll spare you as much as I can. Come along."

They went into the library. The inspector seated himself at a writing-table, and Cayley sat in a chair by the side of it. Antony made himself comfortable in an armchair and prepared to be interested.

"We'll start with the dead man," said the Inspector. "Robert Ablett, didn't you say?" He took out his notebook.

"Yes. Brother of Mark Ablett, who lives here."

"Ah!" He began to sharpen a pencil. "Staying in the house?"

"Oh, no!"

Antony listened attentively while Cayley explained all that he knew about Robert. This was news to him. "I see. Sent out of the country in disgrace. What had he done?"

"I hardly know. I was only about twelve at the time. The sort of age when you're told not to ask questions."

"Inconvenient questions?"

"Exactly."

"So you don't really know whether he had been merely wild or – or wicked?"

"No. Old Mr Ablett was a clergyman," added Cayley. "Perhaps what might seem wicked to a clergyman might seem only wild to a man of the world."

"I daresay, Mr Cayley," smiled the Inspector. "Anyhow, it was more convenient to have him in Australia?"

"Yes."

"Mark Ablett never talked about him?"

"Hardly ever. He was very much ashamed of him, and – well, very glad he was in Australia."

"Did he write Mark sometimes?"

"Occasionally. Perhaps three or four times in the last five years."

"Asking for money?"

"Something of the sort. I don't think Mark always answered them. As far as I know, he never sent any money."

"Now your own private opinion, Mr Cayley. Do you think that Mark was unfair to his brother? Unduly hard on him?"

"They'd never liked each other as boys. There was never any affection between them. I don't know whose fault it was in the first place – if anybody's."

"Still, Mark might have given him a hand?"

"I understand," said Cayley, "that Robert spent his whole life asking for hands."

The inspector nodded.

"I know that sort. Well, now, we'll go on to this morning. This letter that Mark got – did you see it?"

"Not at the time. He showed it to me afterwards."

"Any address?"

"No. A half-sheet of rather dirty paper."

"Where is it now?"

"I don't know. In Mark's pocket, I expect."

"Ah!" He pulled at his beard. "Well, we'll come to that. Can you remember what it said?"

"As far as I remember, something like this: 'Mark, your loving brother is coming to see you tomorrow, all the way from Australia. I give you warning so that you will be able to conceal your surprise, but not I hope, your pleasure. Expect him at three, or thereabouts.'"

"Ah!" The inspector copied it down carefully. "Did you notice the postmark?"

"London."

"And what was Mark's attitude?"

"Annoyance, disgust – " Cayley hesitated.

"Apprehension?"

"N-no, not exactly. Or, rather, apprehension of an unpleasant interview, not of any unpleasant outcome for himself."

"You mean that he wasn't afraid of violence, or blackmail, or anything of that sort?"

"He didn't appear to be."

"Right... Now then, he arrived, you say, about three o'clock?"

"Yes, about that."

"Who was in the house then?"

"Mark and myself, and some of the servants. I don't know which. Of course, you will ask them directly, no doubt."

"With your permission. No guests?"

"They were out all day playing golf," explained Cayley. "Oh, by the way," he put in, "if I may interrupt a moment, will you want to see them at all? It isn't very pleasant for them now, naturally, and I suggested – " he turned to Antony, who nodded back to him. "I understand that they want to go back to London this evening. There's no objection to that, I suppose?"

"You will let me have their names and addresses in case I want to communicate with them?"

"Of course. One of them is staying on, if you would like to see him later, but they only came back from their golf as we crossed the hall."

"That's all right, Mr Cayley. Well, now then, let's go back to three o'clock. Where were you when Robert arrived?"

Cayley explained how he had been sitting in the hall, how Audrey had asked him where the master was, and how he had said that he had last seen him going up to the Temple.

"She went away, and I went on with my book. There was a step on the stairs, and I looked up to see Mark coming down. He went into the office, and I went on with my book again. I went into the library for a moment, to refer to another book, and when I was in there I heard a shot. At least, it was a loud bang, I wasn't sure if it was a shot. I stood and listened. Then I came slowly to the door and looked out. Then I went back again, hesitated a bit, you know, and finally decided to go across to the office, and make sure that it was all right. I turned the handle of the door and found it was locked. Then I got frightened, and I banged at the door, and shouted, and – well, that was when Mr Gillingham arrived." He went on to explain how they had found the body.

The inspector looked at him with a smile.

"Yes, well, we shall have to go over some of that again, Mr Cayley. Mr Mark, now. You thought he was in the Temple. Could he have come in, and gone up to his room, without your seeing him?"

"There are back stairs. He wouldn't have used them in the ordinary way, of course. But I wasn't in the hall all afternoon. He might easily have gone upstairs without my knowing anything about it."

"So that you weren't surprised when you saw him coming down?"

"Oh, not a bit."

"Well, did he say anything?"

"He said, 'Robert's here?' or something of the sort. I suppose he'd heard the bell, or the voices in the hall."

"Which way does his bedroom face? Could he have seen him coming down the drive?"

"He might have, yes."

"Well?"

"Well, then, I said 'Yes,' and he gave a sort of shrug, and said, 'Don't go too far away, I might want you'; and then went in."

"What did you think he meant by that?"

"Well, he consults me a good deal, you know. I'm his sort of unofficial solicitor in a kind of way."

"This was a business meeting rather than a brotherly one?"

"Oh, yes. That's how he regarded it, I'm sure."

"Yes. How long was it before you heard the shot?"

"Very soon. Two minutes, perhaps."

The inspector finished his writing, and then regarded Cayley thoughtfully. Suddenly he said:

"What is your theory of Robert's death?"

Cayley shrugged his shoulders.

"You've probably seen more than I've seen," he answered. "It's your job. I can only speak as a layman – and Mark's friend."

"Well?"

"Then I should say that Robert came here meaning trouble, and bringing a revolver with him. He produced it almost at once, Mark tried to get it from him, there was a little struggle perhaps, and it went off. Mark lost his head, finding himself there with a revolver in his hand and a dead man at his feet. His one idea was to escape. He locked the door almost instinctively, and then, when he heard me hammering at it, went out of the window."

"Y-yes. Well, that sounds reasonable enough. What do you say, Mr Gillingham?"

"I should hardly call it 'reasonable' to lose your head," said Antony, getting up from his chair and coming towards them.

"Well, you know what I mean. It explains things."

"Oh, yes. Any other explanation would make them much more complicated."

"Have you any other explanation?"

"Not I."

"Are there any points on which you would like to correct Mr Cayley? – anything that he left out after you arrived here?"

"No, thanks. He described it all very accurately."

"Ah! Well now, about yourself. You're not staying in the house, I gather?"

Antony explained his previous movements.

"Yes. Did you hear the shot?"

Antony put his head on one side, as if listening. "Yes. Just as I came in sight of the house. It didn't make any impression at the time, but I remember it now."

"Where were you then?"

"Coming up the drive. I was just in sight of the house."

"Nobody left the house by the front door after the shot?"

Antony closed his eyes and considered.

"Nobody," he said. "No."

"You're certain of that?"

"Absolutely," said Antony, as though rather surprised that he could be suspected of a mistake.

"Thank you. You're at 'The George,' if I want you?"

"Mr Gillingham is staying here until after the inquest," explained Cayley.

"Good. Well now, about these servants?"

5

MR GILLINGHAM CHOOSES A NEW PROFESSION

As Cayley went over to the bell, Antony got up and moved to the door.

"Well, you won't want me, I suppose, inspector," he said.

"No, thank you, Mr Gillingham. You'll be about, of course?"

"Oh, yes."

The inspector hesitated.

"I think, Mr Cayley, it would be better if I saw the servants alone. You know what they are; the more people about, the more they get alarmed. I expect I can get at the truth better by myself."

"Oh, quite so. In fact, I was going to ask you to excuse me. I feel rather responsible towards these guests of ours. Although Mr Gillingham very kindly – " He smiled at Antony, who was waiting at the door, and left his sentence unfinished.

"Ah, that reminds me," said the Inspector. "Didn't you say that one of your guests – Mr Beverley was it? – a friend of Mr Gillingham's, was staying on?"

"Yes; would you like to see him?"

"Afterwards, if I may."

"I'll warn him. I shall be up in my room, if you want me. I have a room upstairs where I work – any of the servants will show you. Ah, Stevens, Inspector Birch would like to ask you a few questions."

"Yes, sir," said Audrey primly, but inwardly fluttering. The housekeeper's room had heard something of the news by this time, and Audrey had had a busy time explaining to other members of the staff exactly what he had said, and what she had said. The details were not quite established yet, but this much at least was certain: that Mr Mark's brother had shot himself and spirited Mr Mark away, and that Audrey had seen at once that he was that sort of man when she opened the door to him. She had passed the remark to Mrs Stevens. And Mrs Stevens – if you remember, Audrey – had always said that people didn't go away to Australia except for very good reasons. Elsie agreed with both of them, but she had a contribution of her own to make. She had actually heard Mr Mark in the office, threatening his brother.

"You mean Mr Robert," said the second parlour-maid. She had been having a little nap in her room, but she had heard the bang. In fact, it had woken her up – just like something going off, it was.

"It was Mr Mark's voice," said Elsie firmly.

"Pleading for mercy," said an eager-eyed kitchen-maid hopefully from the door, and was hurried out again by the others, wishing that she had not given her presence away. But it was hard to listen in silence when she knew so well from her novelettes just what happened on these occasions.

"I shall have to give that girl a piece of my mind," said Mrs Stevens. "Well, Elsie?"

"He said, I heard him say it with my own ears, 'It's my turn now,' he said, triumphant-like."

"Well, if you think that's a threat, dear, you're very particular, I must say."

But Audrey remembered Elsie's words when she was in front of Inspector Birch. She gave her own evidence with the readiness of one who had already repeated it several times, and was examined and cross-examined by the Inspector with considerable skill. The temptation to say, "Never mind about what you said to him," was strong, but he resisted it, knowing that in this way he would discover best what he said to her. By this time both his words and the looks he gave her were getting their full value from Audrey, but the general meaning of them seemed to be well-established.

"Then you didn't see Mr Mark at all."

"No, sir; he must have come in before and gone up to his room. Or come in by the front door, likely enough, while I was going out by the back."

"Yes. Well, I think that's all that I want to know, thank you very much. Now what about the other servants?"

"Elsie heard the master and Mr Robert talking together," said Audrey eagerly. "He was saying – Mr Mark, I mean – "

"Ah! Well, I think Elsie had better tell me that herself. Who is Elsie, by the way?"

"One of the housemaids. Shall I send her to you, sir?"

"Please."

Elsie was not sorry to get the message. It interrupted a few remarks from Mrs Stevens about Elsie's conduct that afternoon which were (Elsie thought) much better interrupted. In Mrs Stevens' opinion any crime committed that afternoon in the office was as nothing to the double crime committed by the unhappy Elsie.

For Elsie realized too late that she would have done better to have said nothing about her presence in the hall that afternoon. She was bad at concealing the truth and Mrs Stevens was good at discovering it. Elsie knew perfectly well that she had no business to come down the front stairs, and it was no excuse to say that she happened to come out of Miss Norris' room just at the head of the stairs, and didn't think it would matter, as there was nobody in the hall, and what was she doing anyhow in Miss

Norris' room at that time? Returning a magazine? Lent by Miss Norris, might she ask? Well, not exactly lent. Really, Elsie! – and this in a respectable house! In vain for poor Elsie to plead that a story by her favourite author was advertised on the cover, with a picture of the villain falling over the cliff. "That's where you'll go to, my girl, if you aren't careful," said Mrs Stevens firmly.

But, of course, there was no need to confess all these crimes to Inspector Birch. All that interested him was that she was passing through the hall, and heard voices in the office.

"And stopped to listen?"

"Certainly not," said Elsie with dignity, feeling that nobody really understood her. "I was just passing through the hall, just as you might have been yourself, and not supposing they was talking secrets, didn't think to stop my ears, as no doubt I ought to have done." And she sniffed slightly.

"Come, come," said the Inspector soothingly, "I didn't mean to suggest – "

"Everyone is very unkind to me," said Elsie between sniffs, "and there's that poor man lying dead there, and sorry they'd have been, if it had been me, to have spoken to me as they have done this day."

"Nonsense, we're going to be very proud of you. I shouldn't be surprised if your evidence were of very great importance. Now then, what was it you heard? Try to remember the exact words."

"Something about working in a passage," thought Elsie.

"Yes, but who said it?"

"Mr Robert."

"How do you know it was Mr Robert? Had you heard his voice before?"

"I don't take it upon myself to say that I had had any acquaintance with Mr Robert, but seeing that it wasn't Mr Mark, nor yet Mr Cayley, nor any other of the gentlemen, and

Miss Stevens had shown Mr Robert into the office not five minutes before – "

"Quite so," said the Inspector hurriedly. "Mr Robert, undoubtedly. Working in a passage?"

"That was what it sounded like, sir."

"H'm. Working a passage over – could that have been it?"

"That's right, sir," said Elsie eagerly. "He'd worked his passage over."

"Well?"

"And then Mr Mark said loudly – sort of triumphant-like – 'It's my turn now. You wait.'"

"Triumphantly?"

"As much as to say his chance had come."

"And that's all you heard?"

"That's all, sir – not standing there listening, but just passing through the hall, as it might be any time."

"Yes. Well, that's really very important, Elsie. Thank you."

Elsie gave him a smile, and returned eagerly to the kitchen. She was ready for Mrs Stevens or anybody now.

Meanwhile Antony had been exploring a little on his own. There was a point which was puzzling him. He went through the hall to the front of the house and stood at the open door, looking out on to the drive. He and Cayley had run round the house to the left. Surely it would have been quicker to have run round to the right? The front door was not in the middle of the house, it was to the end. Undoubtedly they went the longest way round. But perhaps there was something in the way, if one went to the right – a wall, say. He strolled off in that direction, followed a path round the house and came in sight of the office windows. Quite simple, and about half the distance of the other way. He went on a little farther, and came to a door, just beyond the broken-in windows. It opened easily, and he found himself in a passage. At the end of the passage was another door. He opened it and found himself in the hall again.

"And, of course, that's the quickest way of the three," he said to himself. "Through the hall, and out at the back; turn to the left and there you are. Instead of which, we ran the longest way round the house. Why? Was it to give Mark more time in which to escape? Only, in that case – why run? Also, how did Cayley know then that it was Mark who was trying to escape? If he had guessed – well, not guessed, but been afraid – that one had shot the other, it was much more likely that Robert had shot Mark. Indeed, he had admitted that this was what he thought. The first thing he had said when he turned the body over was, 'Thank God! I was afraid it was Mark.' But why should he want to give Robert time in which to get away? And again – why run, if he did want to give him time?"

Antony went out of the house again to the lawns at the back, and sat down on a bench in view of the office windows.

"Now then," he said, "let's go through Cayley's mind carefully, and see what we get."

Cayley had been in the hall when Robert was shown into the office. The servant goes off to look for Mark, and Cayley goes on with his book. Mark comes down the stairs, warns Cayley to stand by in case he is wanted, and goes to meet his brother. What does Cayley expect? Possibly that he won't be wanted at all; possibly that his advice may be wanted in the matter, say, of paying Robert's debts, or getting him a passage back to Australia; possibly that his physical assistance may be wanted to get an obstreperous Robert out of the house. Well, he sits there for a moment, and then goes into the library. Why not? He is still within reach, if wanted. Suddenly he hears a pistol-shot. A pistol-shot is the last noise you expect to hear in a country-house; very natural, then, that for the moment he would hardly realize what it was. He listens – and hears nothing more. Perhaps it wasn't a pistol-shot after all. After a moment or two he goes to the library door again. The profound silence makes him uneasy now. Was it a pistol-shot? Absurd! Still – no harm in going into the office on some excuse, just to reassure himself. So he tries the door – and finds it locked!

What are his emotions now? Alarm, uncertainty. Something is happening. Incredible though it seems, it must have been a pistol-shot. He is banging at the door and calling out to Mark, and there is no answer. Alarm – yes. But alarm for whose safety? Mark's, obviously. Robert is a stranger; Mark is an intimate friend. Robert has written a letter that morning, the letter of a man in a dangerous temper. Robert is the tough customer; Mark the highly civilized gentleman. If there has been a quarrel, it is Robert who has shot Mark. He bangs at the door again.

Of course, to Antony, coming suddenly upon this scene, Cayley's conduct had seemed rather absurd, but then, just for the moment, Cayley had lost his head. Anybody else might have done the same. But, as soon as Antony suggested trying the windows, Cayley saw that that was the obvious thing to do. So he leads the way to the windows – the longest way.

Why? To give the murderer time to escape? If he had thought then that Mark was the murderer, perhaps, yes. But he thinks that Robert is the murderer. If he is not hiding anything, he must think so. Indeed he says so, when he sees the body; "I was afraid it was Mark," he says, when he finds that it is Robert who is killed. No reason, then, for wishing to gain time. On the contrary, every instinct would urge him to get into the room as quickly as possible, and seize the wicked Robert. Yet he goes the longest way round. Why? And then, why run?

"That's the question," said Antony to himself, as he filled his pipe, "and bless me if I know the answer. It may be, of course, that Cayley is just a coward. He was in no hurry to get close to Robert's revolver, and yet wanted me to think that he was bursting with eagerness. That would explain it, but then that makes Cayley out a coward. Is he? At any rate he pushed his face up against the window bravely enough. No, I want a better answer than that."

He sat there with his unlit pipe in his hand, thinking. There were one or two other things in the back of his brain, waiting to be taken out and looked at. For the moment he left them undisturbed. They would come back to him later when he wanted them.

He laughed suddenly, and lit his pipe.

"I was wanting a new profession," he thought, "and now I've found it. Antony Gillingham, our own private sleuthhound. I shall begin today."

Whatever Antony Gillingham's other qualifications for his new profession, he had at any rate a brain which worked clearly and quickly. And this clear brain of his had already told him that he was the only person in the house at that moment who was unhandicapped in the search for truth. The inspector had arrived in it to find a man dead and a man missing. It was extremely probable, no doubt, that the missing man had shot the dead man. But it was more than extremely probable, it was almost certain that the Inspector would start with the idea that this extremely probable solution was the one true solution, and that, in consequence, he would be less disposed to consider without prejudice any other solution. As regards all the rest of them – Cayley, the guests, the servants – they also were prejudiced; in favour of Mark (or possibly, for all he knew, against Mark); in favour of, or against, each other; they had formed some previous opinion, from what had been said that morning, of the sort of man Robert was. No one of them could consider the matter with an unbiased mind.

But Antony could. He knew nothing about Mark; he knew nothing about Robert. He had seen the dead man before he was told who the dead man was. He knew that a tragedy had happened before he knew that anybody was missing. Those first impressions, which are so vitally important, had been received solely on the merits of the case; they were founded on the evidence of his senses, not on the evidence of his emotions or of other people's senses. He was in a much better position for getting at the truth than was the Inspector.

It is possible that, in thinking this, Antony was doing Inspector Birch a slight injustice. Birch was certainly prepared to believe that Mark had shot his brother. Robert had been shown into the office (witness Audrey); Mark had gone in to Robert (witness Cayley); Mark and Robert had been heard talking (witness Elsie); there was a shot (witness everybody); the room had been entered and Robert's body had been found (witness Cayley and Gillingham). And Mark was missing. Obviously, then, Mark had killed his brother: accidentally, as Cayley believed, or deliberately, as Elsie's evidence seemed to suggest. There was no point in looking for a difficult solution to a problem, when the easy solution had no flaw in it. But at the same time Birch would have preferred the difficult solution, simply because there was more credit attached to it. A "sensational" arrest of somebody in the house would have given him more pleasure than a commonplace pursuit of Mark Ablett across country. Mark must be found, guilty or not guilty. But there were other possibilities. It would have interested Antony to know that, just at the time when he was feeling rather superior to the prejudiced inspector, the Inspector himself was letting his mind dwell lovingly upon the possibilities in connection with Mr Gillingham. Was it only a coincidence that Mr Gillingham had turned up just when he did? And Mr Beverley's curious answers when asked for some account of his friend. An assistant in a tobacconist's, a waiter! An odd man, Mr Gillingham, evidently. It might be as well to keep an eye on him.

6

OUTSIDE OR INSIDE?

The guests had said goodbye to Cayley, according to their different manner. The Major, gruff and simple: "If you want me, command me. Anything I can do – Goodbye"; Betty, silently sympathetic, with everything in her large eyes which she was too much overawed to tell; Mrs Calladine, protesting that she did not know what to say, but apparently finding plenty; and Miss Norris, crowding so much into one despairing gesture that Cayley's unvarying "Thank you very much" might have been taken this time as gratitude for an artistic entertainment.

Bill had seen them into the car, had taken his own farewells (with a special squeeze of the hand for Betty), and had wandered out to join Antony on his garden seat.

"Well, this is a rum show," said Bill as he sat down.

"Very rum, William."

"And you actually walked right into it?"

"Right into it," said Antony.

"Then you're the man I want. There are all sorts of rumours and mysteries about, and that inspector fellow simply wouldn't keep to the point when I wanted to ask him about the murder, or whatever it is, but kept asking me questions about where I'd met you first, and all sorts of dull things like that. Now, what really happened?"

Antony told him as concisely as he could all that he had already told the Inspector, Bill interrupting him here and there with appropriate "Good Lords" and whistles.

"I say, it's a bit of a business, isn't it? Where do I come in, exactly?"

"How do you mean?"

"Well, everybody else is bundled off except me, and I get put through it by that inspector as if I knew all about it – what's the idea?"

Antony smiled at him.

"Well, there's nothing to worry about, you know. Naturally Birch wanted to see one of you so as to know what you'd all been doing all day. And Cayley was nice enough to think that you'd be company for me, as I knew you already. And well, that's all."

"You're staying here, in the house?" said Bill eagerly. "Good man. That's splendid."

"It reconciles you to the departure of some of the others?"

Bill blushed.

"Oh, well, I shall see her again next week, anyway," he murmured.

"I congratulate you. I liked her looks. And that grey dress. A nice comfortable sort of woman."

"You fool, that's her mother."

"Oh, I beg your pardon. But anyhow, Bill, I want you more than she does just now. So try and put up with me."

"I say, do you really?" said Bill, rather flattered. He had a great admiration for Antony, and was very proud to be liked by him.

"Yes. You see, things are going to happen here soon."

"Inquests and that sort of thing?"

"Well, perhaps something before that. Hallo, here comes Cayley."

Cayley was walking across the lawn towards them, a big, heavy-shouldered man, with one of those strong, clean-shaven, ugly faces which can never quite be called plain. "Bad luck on Cayley," said Bill. "I say, ought I to tell him how sorry I am and all that sort of thing? It seems so dashed inadequate."

"I shouldn't bother," said Antony.

Cayley nodded as he came to them, and stood there for a moment.

"We can make room for you," said Bill, getting up.

"Oh, don't bother, thanks. I just came to say," he went on to Antony, "that naturally they've rather lost their heads in the kitchen, and dinner won't be till half-past eight. Do just as you like about dressing, of course. And what about your luggage?"

"I thought Bill and I would walk over to the inn directly, and see about it."

"The car can go and fetch it as soon as it comes back from the station."

"It's very good of you, but I shall have to go over myself, anyhow, to pack up and pay my bill. Besides, it's a good evening for a walk. If you wouldn't mind it, Bill?"

"I should love it."

"Well, then, if you leave the bag there, I'll send the car round for it later."

"Thanks very much."

Having said what he wanted to say, Cayley remained there a little awkwardly, as if not sure whether to go or to stay. Antony wondered whether he wanted to talk about the afternoon's happenings, or whether it was the one subject he wished to avoid. To break the silence he asked carelessly if the Inspector had gone.

Cayley nodded. Then he said abruptly, "He's getting a warrant for Mark's arrest."

Bill made a suitably sympathetic noise, and Antony said with a shrug of the shoulders, "Well, he was bound to do that, wasn't he? It doesn't follow that – well, it doesn't mean anything. They naturally want to get hold of your cousin, innocent or guilty."

"Which do you think he is, Mr Gillingham?" said Cayley, looking at him steadily.

"Mark? It's absurd," said Bill impetuously.

"Bill's loyal, you see, Mr Cayley."

"And you owe no loyalty to anyone concerned?"

"Exactly. So perhaps I might be too frank."

Bill had dropped down on the grass, and Cayley took his place on the seat, and sat there heavily, his elbows on his knees, his chin on his hands, gazing at the ground.

"I want you to be quite frank," he said at last. "Naturally I am prejudiced where Mark is concerned. So I want to know how my suggestion strikes you who have no prejudices either way."

"Your suggestion?"

"My theory that, if Mark killed his brother, it was purely accidental as I told the Inspector."

Bill looked up with interest.

"You mean that Robert did the hold-up business," he said, "and there was a bit of a struggle, and the revolver went off, and then Mark lost his head and bolted? That sort of idea?"

"Exactly."

"Well, that seems all right." He turned to Antony. "There's nothing wrong with that, is there? It's the most natural explanation to anyone who knows Mark."

Antony pulled at his pipe.

"I suppose it is," he said slowly. "But there's one thing that worries me rather."

"What's that?" Bill and Cayley asked the question simultaneously.

"The key."

"The key?" said Bill.

Cayley lifted his head and looked at Antony. "What about the key?" he asked.

"Well, there may be nothing in it; I just wondered. Suppose Robert was killed as you say, and suppose Mark lost his head and thought of nothing but getting away before anyone could see him. Well, very likely he'd lock the door and put the key in his pocket. He'd do it without thinking, just to gain a moment's time."

"Yes, that's what I suggest."

"It seems sound enough," said Bill. "Sort of thing you'd do without thinking. Besides, if you are going to run away, it gives you more of a chance."

"Yes, that's all right if the key is there. But suppose it isn't there?"

The suggestion, made as if it were already an established fact, startled them both. They looked at him wonderingly.

"What do you mean?" said Cayley.

"Well, it's just a question of where people happen to keep their keys. You go up to your bedroom, and perhaps you like to lock your door in case anybody comes wandering in when you've only got one sock and a pair of braces on. Well, that's natural enough. And if you look round the bedrooms of almost any house, you'll find the keys all ready, so that you can lock yourself in at a moment's notice. But downstairs people don't lock themselves in. It's really never done at all. Bill, for instance, has never locked himself into the dining-room in order to be alone with the sherry. On the other hand, all women, and particularly servants, have a horror of burglars. And if a burglar gets in by the window, they like to limit his activities to that particular room. So they keep the keys on the outside of the doors, and lock the doors when they go to bed." He knocked the ashes out of his pipe, and added, "At least, my mother always used to."

"You mean," said Bill excitedly, "that the key was on the outside of the door when Mark went into the room?"

"Well, I was just wondering."

"Have you noticed the other rooms – the billiard-room, and library, and so on?" said Cayley.

"I've only just thought about it while I've been sitting out here. You live here – haven't you ever noticed them?"

Cayley sat considering, with his head on one side.

"It seems rather absurd, you know, but I can't say that I have." He turned to Bill. "Have you?"

"Good Lord, no. I should never worry about a thing like that."

"I'm sure you wouldn't," laughed Antony. "Well, we can have a look when we go in. If the other keys are outside, then this one was probably outside too, and in that case well, it makes it more interesting."

Cayley said nothing. Bill chewed a piece of grass, and then said, "Does it make much difference?"

"It makes it more hard to understand what happened in there. Take your accidental theory and see where you get to. No instinctive turning of the key now, is there? He's got to open the door to get it, and opening the door means showing his head to anybody in the hall – his cousin, for instance, whom he left there two minutes ago. Is a man in Mark's state of mind, frightened to death lest he should be found with the body, going to do anything so foolhardy as that?"

"He needn't have been afraid of me," said Cayley.

"Then why didn't he call for you? He knew you were about. You could have advised him; Heaven knows he wanted advice. But the whole theory of Mark's escape is that he was afraid of you and of everybody else, and that he had no other idea but to get out of the room himself, and prevent you or the servants from coming into it. If the key had been on the inside, he would probably have locked the door. If it were on the outside, he almost certainly wouldn't."

"Yes, I expect you're right," said Bill thoughtfully. "Unless he took the key in with him, and locked the door at once."

"Exactly. But in that case you have to build up a new theory entirely."

"You mean that it makes it seem more deliberate?"

"Yes; that, certainly. But it also seems to make Mark out an absolute idiot. Just suppose for a moment that, for urgent reasons which neither of you know anything about, he had wished to get rid of his brother. Would he have done it like that? Just killed him and then run away? Why, that's practically suicide – suicide whilst of unsound mind. No. If you really wanted to remove an undesirable brother, you would do it a little bit more cleverly than that. You'd begin by treating him as a friend, so as to avoid suspicion, and when you did kill him at last, you would try to make it look like an accident, or suicide, or the work of some other man. Wouldn't you?"

"You mean you'd give yourself a bit of a run for your money?"

"Yes, that's what I mean. If you were going to do it deliberately, that is to say, and lock yourself in before you began."

Cayley had been silent, apparently thinking over this new idea. With his eyes still on the ground, he said now: "I hold to my opinion that it was purely accidental, and that Mark lost his head and ran away."

"But what about the key?" asked Bill.

"We don't know yet that the keys were outside. I don't at all agree with Mr Gillingham that the keys of the downstairs rooms are always outside the doors. Sometimes they are, no doubt; but I think we shall probably find that these are inside."

"Oh, well, of course, if they are inside, then your original theory is probably the correct one. Having often seen them outside, I just wondered, that's all. You asked me to be quite frank, you know, and tell you what I thought. But no doubt you're right, and we shall find them inside, as you say.

"Even if the key was outside," went on Cayley stubbornly, "I still think it might have been accidental. He might have taken it in with him, knowing that the interview would be an unpleasant one, and not wishing to be interrupted."

"But he had just told you to stand by in case he wanted you; so why should he lock you out? Besides, I should think that if a man were going to have an unpleasant interview with a threatening relation, the last thing he would do would be to barricade himself in with him. He would want to open all the doors and say, 'Get out of it'"

Cayley was silent, but his mouth looked obstinate. Antony gave a little apologetic laugh and stood up.

"Well, come on, Bill," he said; "we ought to be stepping." He held out a hand and pulled his friend up. Then, turning to Cayley, he went on, "You must forgive me if I have let my thoughts run on rather. Of course, I was considering the matter purely as an outsider; just as a problem, I mean, which didn't concern the happiness of any of my friends."

"That's all right, Mr Gillingham," said Cayley, standing up too. "It is for you to make allowances for me. I'm sure you will. You say that you're going up to the inn now about your bag?"

"Yes." He looked up at the sun and then round the parkland stretching about the house. "Let me see; it's over in that direction, isn't it?" He pointed southwards. "Can we get to the village that way, or must we go by the road?"

"I'll show you, my boy," said Bill.

"Bill will show you. The park reaches almost as far as the village. Then I'll send the car round in about half an hour."

"Thanks very much."

Cayley nodded and turned to go into the house. Antony took hold of Bill's arm and walked off with him in the opposite direction.

7

PORTRAIT OF A GENTLEMAN

They walked in silence for a little, until they had left the house and gardens well behind them. In front of them and to the right the park dipped and then rose slowly, shutting out the rest of the world. A thick belt of trees on the left divided them from the main road.

"Ever been here before?" said Antony suddenly.

"Oh, rather. Dozens of times."

"I meant just here where we are now. Or do you stay indoors and play billiards all the time?"

"Oh Lord, no!"

"Well, tennis and things. So many people with beautiful parks never by any chance use them, and all the poor devils passing by on the dusty road think how lucky the owners are to have them, and imagine them doing all sorts of jolly things inside." He pointed to the right. "Ever been over there?"

Bill laughed, as if a little ashamed.

"Well, not very much. I've often been along here, of course, because it's the short way to the village."

"Yes... All right; now tell me something about Mark."

"What sort of things?"

"Well, never mind about his being your host, or about your being a perfect gentleman, or anything like that. Cut out the

Manners for Men, and tell me what you think of Mark, and how you like staying with him, and how many rows your little house-party has had this week, and how you get on with Cayley, and all the rest of it."

Bill looked at him eagerly.

"I say, are you being the complete detective?"

"Well, I wanted a new profession," smiled the other.

"What fun! I mean," he corrected himself apologetically, "one oughtn't to say that, when there's a man dead in the house, and one's host – " He broke off a little uncertainly, and then rounded off his period by saying again, "By Jove, what a rum show it is. Good Lord!"

"Well?" said Antony. "Carry on. Mark."

"What do I think of him?"

"Yes."

Bill was silent, wondering how to put into words thoughts which had never formed themselves very definitely in his own mind. What did he think of Mark? Seeing his hesitation, Antony said:

"I ought to have warned you that nothing that you say will be taken down by the reporters, so you needn't bother about a split infinitive or two. Talk about anything you like, how you like. Well, I'll give you a start. Which do you enjoy more, a week-end here or at the Barrington's, say?"

"Well; of course, that would depend – "

"Take it that she was there in both cases."

"Ass," said Bill, putting an elbow into Antony's ribs. "It's a little difficult to say," he went on. "Of course they do you awfully well here."

"Yes."

"I don't think I know any house where things are so comfortable. One's room – the food – drinks – cigars – the way everything's arranged: All that sort of thing. They look after you awfully well."

"Yes?"

"Yes." He repeated it slowly to himself, as if it had given him a new idea: "They look after you awfully well. Well, that's just what it is about Mark. That's one of his little ways. Weaknesses. Looking after you."

"Arranging things for you?"

"Yes. Of course, it's a delightful house, and there's plenty to do, and opportunities for every game or sport that's ever been invented, and, as I say, one gets awfully well done; but with it all, Tony, there's a faint sort of feeling that well, that one is on parade, as it were. You've got to do as you're told."

"How do you mean?"

"Well, Mark fancies himself rather at arranging things. He arranges things, and it's understood that the guests fall in with the arrangement. For instance, Betty – Miss Calladine – and I were going to play a single just before tea, the other day. Tennis. She's frightfully hot stuff at tennis, and backed herself to take me on level. I'm rather erratic, you know. Mark saw us going out with our rackets and asked us what we were going to do. Well, he'd got up a little tournament for us after tea – handicaps all arranged by him, and everything ruled out neatly in red and black ink – prizes and all – quite decent ones, you know. He'd had the lawn specially cut and marked for it. Well, of course Betty and I wouldn't have spoilt the court, and we'd have been quite ready to play again after tea – I had to give her half-fifteen according to his handicap – but somehow – " Bill stopped and shrugged his shoulders.

"It didn't quite fit in?"

"No. It spoilt the effect of his tournament. Took the edge off it just a little, I suppose he felt. So we didn't play." He laughed, and added, "It would have been as much as our place was worth to have played."

"Do you mean you wouldn't have been asked here again?"

"Probably. Well, I don't know. Not for some time, anyway."

"Really, Bill?"

"Oh, rather! He's a devil for taking offence. That Miss Norris, did you see her? She's done for herself. I don't mind betting what you like that she never comes here again."

"Why?"

Bill laughed to himself.

"We were all in it, really – at least, Betty and I were. There's supposed to be a ghost attached to the house. Lady Anne Patten. Ever heard of her?"

"Never."

"Mark told us about her at dinner one night. He rather liked the idea of there being a ghost in his house, you know; except that he doesn't believe in ghosts. I think he wanted all of us to believe in her, and yet he was annoyed with Betty and Mrs Calladine for believing in ghosts at all. Rum chap. Well, anyhow, Miss Norris – she's an actress, some actress too – dressed up as the ghost and played the fool a bit. And poor Mark was frightened out of his life. Just for a moment, you know."

"What about the others?"

"Well, Betty and I knew; in fact, I'd told her – Miss Norris I mean – not to be a silly ass. Knowing Mark. Mrs Calladine wasn't there – Betty wouldn't let her be. As for the Major, I don't believe anything would frighten him."

"Where did the ghost appear?"

"Down by the bowling-green. That's supposed to be its haunt, you know. We were all down there in the moonlight, pretending to wait for it. Do you know the bowling-green?"

"No."

"I'll show it to you after dinner."

"I wish you would.... Was Mark very angry afterwards?"

"Oh, Lord, yes. Sulked for a whole day. Well, he's just like that."

"Was he angry with all of you?"

"Oh, yes sulky, you know."

"This morning?"

"Oh, no. He got over it – he generally does. He's just like a child. That's really it, Tony; he's like a child in some ways. As a matter of fact, he was unusually bucked with himself this morning. And yesterday."

"Yesterday?"

"Rather. We all said we'd never seen him in such form."

"Is he generally in form?"

"He's quite good company, you know, if you take him the right way. He's rather vain and childish...well, like I've been telling you and self-important; but quite amusing in his way, and – " Bill broke off suddenly. "I say, you know, it really is the limit, talking about your host like this."

"Don't think of him as your host. Think of him as a suspected murderer with a warrant out against him."

"Oh! But that's all rot, you know."

"It's the fact, Bill."

"Yes, but I mean, he didn't do it. He wouldn't murder anybody. It's a funny thing to say, but well, he's not big enough for it. He's got his faults, like all of us, but they aren't on that scale."

"One can kill anybody in a childish fit of temper."

Bill grunted assent, but without prejudice to Mark. "All the same," he said, "I can't believe it. That he would do it deliberately, I mean."

"Suppose it was an accident, as Cayley says, would he lose his head and run away?"

Bill considered for a moment.

"Yes, I really think he might, you know. He nearly ran away when he saw the ghost. Of course, that's different, rather."

"Oh, I don't know. In each case it's a question of obeying your instinct instead of your reason."

They had left the open land and were following a path through the bordering trees. Two abreast was uncomfortable, so Antony dropped behind, and further conversation was postponed until they were outside the boundary fence and in the high road. The road sloped gently down to the village of Waldheim – a few red-roofed cottages, and the grey tower of a church showing above the green.

"Well, now," said Antony, as they stepped out more quickly, "what about Cayley?"

"How do you mean, what about him?"

"I want to see him. I can see Mark perfectly, thanks to you, Bill. You were wonderful. Now let's have Cayley's character. Cayley from within."

Bill laughed in pleased embarrassment, and protested that he was not a blooming novelist.

"Besides," he added, "Mark's easy. Cayley's one of these heavy, quiet people, who might be thinking about anything. Mark gives himself away.... Ugly, black-jawed devil, isn't he?"

"Some women like that type of ugliness."

"Yes, that's true. Between ourselves, I think there's one here who does. Rather a pretty girl at Jallands" – he waved his left hand – "down that way."

"What's Jallands?"

"Well, I suppose it used to be a farm, belonging to a bloke called Jalland, but now it's a country cottage belonging to a widow called Norbury. Mark and Cayley used to go there a good deal together. Miss Norbury – the girl – has been here once or twice for tennis; seemed to prefer Cayley to the rest of us. But of course he hadn't much time for that sort of thing."

"What sort of thing?"

"Walking about with a pretty girl and asking her if she's been to any theatres lately. He nearly always had something to do."

"Mark kept him busy?"

"Yes. Mark never seemed quite happy unless he had Cayley doing something for him. He was quite lost and helpless without him. And, funnily enough, Cayley seemed lost without Mark."

"He was fond of him?"

"Yes, I should say so. In a protective kind of way. He'd sized Mark up, of course his vanity, his self-importance, his amateurishness and all the rest of it, but he liked looking after him. And he knew how to manage him."

"Yes... What sort of terms was he on with the guests – you and Miss Norris and all of them?"

"Just polite and rather silent, you know. Keeping himself to himself. We didn't see so very much of him, except at meals. We were here to enjoy ourselves, and well, he wasn't."

"He wasn't there when the ghost walked?"

"No. I heard Mark calling for him when he went back to the house. I expect Cayley stroked down his feathers a bit, and told him that girls will be girls – Hallo, here we are."

They went into the inn, and while Bill made himself pleasant to the landlady, Antony went upstairs to his room. It appeared that he had not very much packing to do, after all. He returned his brushes to his bag, glanced round to see that nothing else had been taken out, and went down again to settle his bill. He had decided to keep on his room for a few days; partly to save the landlord and his wife the disappointment of losing a guest so suddenly, partly in case he found it undesirable later on to remain at the Red House. For he was taking himself seriously as a detective; indeed, he took himself seriously (while getting all the fun out of it which was possible) at every new profession he adopted; and he felt that there might come a time – after the inquest – say when he could not decently remain at the Red House as a guest, a friend of Bill's, enjoying the hospitality of Mark or Cayley, whichever was to be regarded as his host, without forfeiting his independent attitude towards the events of that afternoon. At present he was staying in the house merely as a necessary witness, and, since he was there, Cayley could not object to him using his eyes; but if, after the inquest, it appeared that there was still work for a pair of independent and very keen eyes to do, then he must investigate, either with his host's approval or from beneath the roof of some other host; the landlord of 'The George,' for instance, who had no feelings in the matter.

For of one thing Antony was certain. Cayley knew more than he professed to know. That is to say, he knew more than he wanted other people to know he knew. Antony was one of the "other people"; if, therefore, he was for trying to find out what it was that Cayley knew, he could hardly expect Cayley's approval of his labours. It would be 'The George,' then, for Antony after the inquest.

What was the truth? Not necessarily discreditable to Cayley, even though he was hiding something. All that could be said against him at the moment was that he had gone the longest way round to get into the locked office and that this did not fit in with what he had told the Inspector. But it did fit in with the theory that he had been an accessory after the event, and that he wanted (while appearing to be in a hurry) to give his cousin as much time as possible in which to escape. That might not be the true solution, but it was at least a workable one. The theory which he had suggested to the Inspector was not.

However, there would be a day or two before the inquest, in which Antony could consider all these matters from within The Red House. The car was at the door. He got in with Bill, the landlord put his bag on the front seat next to the chauffeur, and they drove back.

8

"DO YOU FOLLOW ME, WATSON?"

Antony's bedroom looked over the park at the back of the house. The blinds were not yet drawn while he was changing his clothes for dinner, and at various stages of undress he would pause and gaze out of the window, sometimes smiling to himself, sometimes frowning, as he turned over in his mind all the strange things that he had seen that day. He was sitting on his bed, in shirt and trousers, absently smoothing down his thick black hair with his brushes, when Bill shouted an "Hallo!" through the door, and came in.

"I say, buck up, old boy, I'm hungry," he said.

Antony stopped smoothing himself and looked up at him thoughtfully.

"Where's Mark?" he said.

"Mark? You mean Cayley."

Antony corrected himself with a little laugh. "Yes, I mean Cayley. Is he down? I say, I shan't be a moment, Bill." He got up from the bed and went on briskly with his dressing. "Oh, by the way," said Bill, taking his place on the bed, "your idea about the keys is a wash-out."

"Why, how do you mean?"

"I went down just now and had a look at them. We were asses not to have thought of it when we came in. The library key is outside, but all the others are inside."

"Yes, I know."

"You devil, I suppose you did think of it, then?"

"I did, Bill," said Antony apologetically.

"Bother! I hoped you'd forgotten. Well, that knocks your theory on the head, doesn't it?"

"I never had a theory. I only said that if they were outside, it would probably mean that the office key was outside, and that in that case Cayley's theory was knocked on the head."

"Well, now, it isn't, and we don't know anything. Some were outside and some inside, and there you are. It makes it much less exciting. When you were talking about it on the lawn, I really got quite keen on the idea of the key being outside and Mark taking it in with him."

"It's going to be exciting enough," said Antony mildly, as he transferred his pipe and tobacco into the pocket of his black coat. "Well, let's come down; I'm ready now."

Cayley was waiting for them in the hall. He made some polite inquiry as to the guest's comfort, and the three of them fell into a casual conversation about houses in general and The Red House in particular.

"You were quite right about the keys," said Bill, during a pause. He was less able than the other two, perhaps because he was younger than they, to keep away from the subject which was uppermost in the minds of them all.

"Keys?" said Cayley blankly.

"We were wondering whether they were outside or inside."

"Oh! Oh, yes!" He looked slowly round the hall, at the different doors, and then smiled in a friendly way at Antony. "We both seem to have been right, Mr Gillingham. So we don't get much farther."

"No." He gave a shrug. "I just wondered, you know. I thought it was worth mentioning."

"Oh, quite. Not that you would have convinced me, you know. Just as Elsie's evidence doesn't convince me."

"Elsie?" said Bill excitedly. Antony looked inquiringly at him, wondering who Elsie was.

"One of the housemaids," explained Cayley. "You didn't hear what she told the Inspector? Of course, as I told Birch, girls of that class make things up, but he seemed to think she was genuine."

"What was it?" said Bill.

Cayley told them of what Elsie had heard through the office door that afternoon.

"You were in the library then, of course," said Antony, rather to himself than to the other. "She might have gone through the hall without your hearing."

"Oh, I've no doubt she was there, and heard voices. Perhaps heard those very words. But – " He broke off, and then added impatiently, "It was accidental. I know it was accidental. What's the good of talking as if Mark was a murderer?" Dinner was announced at that moment, and as they went in, he added, "What's the good of talking about it at all, if it comes to that?"

"What, indeed?" said Antony, and to Bill's great disappointment they talked of books and politics during the meal.

Cayley made an excuse for leaving them as soon as their cigars were alight. He had business to attend to, as was natural. Bill would look after his friend. Bill was only too willing. He offered to beat Antony at billiards, to play him at piquet, to show him the garden by moonlight, or indeed to do anything else with him that he required.

"Thank the Lord you're here," he said piously. "I couldn't have stood it alone."

"Let's go outside," suggested Antony. "It's quite warm. Somewhere where we can sit down, right away from the house. I want to talk to you."

"Good man. What about the bowling-green?"

"Oh, you were going to show me that, anyhow, weren't you? Is it somewhere where we can talk without being overheard?"

"Rather. The ideal place. You'll see."

They came out of the front door and followed the drive to the left. Coming from Waldheim, Antony had approached the house that afternoon from the other side. The way they were going now would take them out at the opposite end of the park, on the high road to Stanton, a country town some three miles away. They passed by a gate and a gardener's lodge, which marked the limit of what auctioneers like to call "the ornamental grounds of the estate," and then the open park was before them.

"Sure we haven't missed it?" said Antony. The park lay quietly in the moonlight on either side of the drive, wearing a little way ahead of them a deceptive air of smoothness which retreated always as they advanced.

"Rum, isn't it?" said Bill. "An absurd place for a bowling green, but I suppose it was always here."

"Yes, but always where? It's short enough for golf, perhaps, but – Hallo!"

They had come to the place. The road bent round to the right, but they kept straight on over a broad grass path for twenty yards, and there in front of them was the green. A dry ditch, ten feet wide and six feet deep, surrounded it, except in the one place where the path went forward. Two or three grass steps led down to the green, on which there was a long wooden bench for the benefit of spectators.

"Yes, it hides itself very nicely," said Antony. "Where do you keep the bowls?"

"In a sort of summer house place. Round here."

They walked along the edge of the green until they came to it – a low wooden bunk which had been built into one wall of the ditch.

"H'm. Jolly view."

Bill laughed.

"Nobody sits there. It's just for keeping things out of the rain."

They finished their circuit of the green "Just in case anybody's in the ditch," said Antony and then sat down on the bench.

"Now then," said Bill, "We are alone. Fire ahead."

Antony smoked thoughtfully for a little. Then he took his pipe out of his mouth and turned to his friend.

"Are you prepared to be the complete Watson?" he asked.

"Watson?"

"Do-you-follow-me-Watson; that one. Are you prepared to have quite obvious things explained to you, to ask futile questions, to give me chances of scoring off you, to make brilliant discoveries of your own two or three days after I have made them myself – all that kind of thing? Because it all helps."

"My dear Tony," said Bill delightedly, "need you ask?" Antony said nothing, and Bill went on happily to himself, "I perceive from the strawberry-mark on your shirt-front that you had strawberries for dessert. Holmes, you astonish me. Tut, tut, you know my methods. Where is the tobacco? The tobacco is in the Persian slipper. Can I leave my practice for a week? I can."

Antony smiled and went on smoking. After waiting hopefully for a minute or two, Bill said in a firm voice:

"Well then, Holmes, I feel bound to ask you if you have deduced anything. Also whom do you suspect?"

Antony began to talk.

"Do you remember," he said, "one of Holmes's little scores over Watson about the number of steps up to the Baker Street lodging? Poor old Watson had been up and down them a thousand times, but he had never thought of counting them, whereas Holmes had counted them as a matter of course, and knew that there were seventeen. And that was supposed to be the difference between observation and non-observation. Watson was crushed again, and Holmes appeared to him more amazing than ever. Now, it always seemed to me that in that matter Holmes was the ass, and Watson the sensible person. What on earth is the point of keeping in your head an unnecessary fact like that? If you really want to know at any time the number of steps to your lodging, you can ring up your landlady and ask her. I've been up and down the steps of the club a thousand times, but if you asked me to tell you at this moment how many steps there are I couldn't do it. Could you?"

"I certainly couldn't," said Bill.

"But if you really wanted to know," said Antony casually, with a sudden change of voice, "I could find out for you without even bothering to ring up the hall-porter."

Bill was puzzled as to why they were talking about the club steps, but he felt it his duty to say that he did want to know how many they were.

"Right," said Antony. "I'll find out."

He closed his eyes.

"I'm walking up St. James' Street," he said slowly. "Now I've come to the club and I'm going past the smoking-room – windows-one-two-three-four. Now I'm at the steps. I turn in and begin going up them. One-two-three-four-five-six, then a broad step; six-seven-eight-nine, another broad step; nine-ten-eleven. Eleven – I'm inside. Good morning, Rogers. Fine day again." With a little start he opened his eyes and came back again to his present surroundings. He turned to Bill with a smile. "Eleven," he said. "Count them the next time you're there. Eleven and now I hope I shall forget it again."

Bill was distinctly interested.

"That's rather hot," he said. "Expound."

"Well, I can't explain it, whether it's something in the actual eye, or something in the brain, or what, but I have got rather an uncanny habit of recording things unconsciously. You know that game where you look at a tray full of small objects for three minutes, and then turn away and try to make a list of them. It means a devil of a lot of concentration for the ordinary person, if he wants to get his list complete, but in some odd way I manage to do it without concentration at all. I mean that my eyes seem to do it without the brain consciously taking any part. I could look at the tray, for instance, and talk to you about golf at the same time, and still get my list right."

"I should think that's rather a useful gift for an amateur detective. You ought to have gone into the profession before."

"Well, it is rather useful. It's rather surprising, you know, to a stranger. Let's surprise Cayley with it, shall we?"

"How?"

"Well, let's ask him – " Antony stopped and looked at Bill comically, "let's ask him what he's going to do with the key of the office."

For a moment Bill did not understand.

"Key of the office?" he said vaguely. "You don't mean – Tony! What do you mean? Good God! Do you mean that Cayley – But what about Mark?"

"I don't know where Mark is – that's another thing I want to know – but I'm quite certain that he hasn't got the key of the office with him. Because Cayley's got it."

"Are you sure?"

"Quite."

Bill looked at him wonderingly.

"I say," he said, almost pleadingly, "don't tell me that you can see into people's pockets and all that sort of thing as well."

Antony laughed and denied it cheerfully.

"Then how do you know?"

"You're the perfect Watson, Bill. You take to it quite naturally. Properly speaking, I oughtn't to explain till the last chapter, but I always think that that's so unfair. So here goes. Of course, I don't really know that he's got it, but I do know that he had it. I know that when I came on him this afternoon, he had just locked the door and put the key in his pocket."

"You mean you saw him at the time, but that you've only just remembered it – reconstructed it in the way you were explaining just now?"

"No. I didn't see him. But I did see something. I saw the key of the billiard-room."

"Where?

"Outside the billiard-room door."

"Outside? But it was inside when we looked just now."

"Exactly."

"Who put it there?"

"Obviously Cayley."

"But – "

"Let's go back to this afternoon. I don't remember noticing the billiard-room key at the time; I must have done so without knowing. Probably when I saw Cayley banging at the door I may have wondered subconsciously whether the key of the room next to it would fit. Something like that, I daresay. Well, when I was sitting out by myself on that seat just before you came along, I went over the whole scene in my mind, and I suddenly saw the billiard-room key there outside. And I began to wonder if the office-key had been outside too. When Cayley came up, I told you my idea and you were both interested. But Cayley was just a shade too interested. I daresay you didn't notice it, but he was."

"By Jove!"

"Well, of course that proved nothing; and the key business didn't really prove anything, because whatever side of the door the other keys were, Mark might have locked his own private room from the inside sometimes. But I piled it on, and pretended that it was enormously important, and quite altered the case altogether, and having got Cayley thoroughly anxious about it, I told him that we should be well out of the way for the next hour or so, and that he would be alone in the house to do what he liked about it. And, as I expected, he couldn't resist it. He altered the keys and gave himself away entirely."

"But the library key was still outside. Why didn't he alter that?"

"Because he's a clever devil. For one thing, the Inspector had been in the library, and might possibly have noticed it already. And for another – " Antony hesitated.

"What?" said Bill, after waiting for him to go on.

"It's only guesswork. But I fancy that Cayley was thoroughly upset about the key business. He suddenly realized that he had been careless, and he hadn't got time to think it all over. So he didn't want to commit himself definitely to the statement that the key was either outside or inside. He wanted to leave it vague. It was safest that way."

"I see," said Bill slowly.

But his mind was elsewhere. He was wondering suddenly about Cayley. Cayley was just an ordinary man – like himself. Bill had had little jokes with him sometimes; not that Cayley was much of a hand at joking. Bill had helped him to sausages, played tennis with him, borrowed his tobacco, lent him a putter.... and here was Antony saying that he was what? Well, not an ordinary man, anyway. A man with a secret. Perhaps a murderer. No, not a murderer; not Cayley. That was rot, anyway. Why, they had played tennis together.

"Now then, Watson," said Antony suddenly. "It's time you said something."

"I say, Tony, do you really mean it?"

"Mean what?"

"About Cayley."

"I mean what I said, Bill. No more."

"Well, what does it amount to?"

"Simply that Robert Ablett died in the office this afternoon, and that Cayley knows exactly how he died. That's all. It doesn't follow that Cayley killed him."

"No. No, of course it doesn't." Bill gave a sigh of relief. "He's just shielding Mark, what?"

"I wonder."

"Well, isn't that the simplest explanation?"

"It's the simplest if you're a friend of Cayley and want to let him down lightly. But then I'm not, you see."

"Why isn't it simple, anyhow?"

"Well, let's have the explanation then, and I'll undertake to give you a simpler one afterwards. Go on. Only remember the key is on the outside of the door to start with."

"Yes; well, I don't mind that. Mark goes in to see his brother, and they quarrel and all the rest of it, just as Cayley was saying. Cayley hears the shot, and in order to give Mark time to get away, locks the door, puts the key in his pocket and pretends that Mark has locked the door, and that he can't get in. How's that?"

"Hopeless, Watson, hopeless."

"Why?"

"How does Cayley know that it is Mark who has shot Robert, and not the other way round?"

"Oh!" said Bill, rather upset. "Yes." He thought for a moment, "All right. Say that Cayley has gone into the room first, and seen Robert on the ground."

"Well?"

"Well, there you are."

"And what does he say to Mark? That it's a fine afternoon; and could he lend him a pocket-handkerchief? Or does he ask him what's happened?"

"Well, of course, I suppose he asks what happened," said Bill reluctantly.

"And what does Mark say?"

"Explains that the revolver went off accidentally during a struggle."

"Whereupon Cayley shields him by doing what, Bill? Encouraging him to do the damn silliest thing that any man could possibly do – confess his guilt by running away!"

"No, that's rather hopeless, isn't it?" Bill thought again. "Well," he said reluctantly, "suppose Mark confessed that he'd murdered his brother?"

"That's better, Bill. Don't be afraid of getting away from the accident idea. Well then, your new theory is this. Mark confesses to Cayley that he shot Robert on purpose, and Cayley decides, even at the risk of committing perjury, and getting into trouble himself, to help Mark to escape. Is that right?"

Bill nodded.

"Well then, I want to ask you two questions. First, is it possible, as I said before dinner, that any man would commit such an idiotic murder – a murder that puts the rope so very tightly round his neck? Secondly, if Cayley is prepared to perjure himself for Mark (as he has to, anyway, now), wouldn't it be simpler for him to say that he was in the office all the time, and that Robert's death was accidental?"

Bill considered this carefully, and then nodded slowly again.

"Yes, my simple explanation is a wash-out," he said. "Now let's have yours."

Antony did not answer him. He had begun to think about something quite different.

9

POSSIBILITIES OF A CROQUET SET

"What's the matter?" said Bill sharply.

Antony looked round at him with raised eyebrows.

"You've thought of something suddenly," said Bill. "What is it?"

Antony laughed.

"My dear Watson," he said, "you aren't supposed to be as clever as this."

"Oh, you can't take me in!"

"No... Well, I was wondering about this ghost of yours, Bill. It seems to me – "

"Oh, that!" Bill was profoundly disappointed. "What on earth has the ghost got to do with it?"

"I don't know," said Antony apologetically. "I don't know what anything has got to do with it. I was just wondering. You shouldn't have brought me here if you hadn't wanted me to think about the ghost. This is where she appeared, isn't it?"

"Yes." Bill was distinctly short about it.

"How?"

"What?"

"I said, 'How?'"

"How? How do ghosts appear? I don't know. They just appear."

"Over four or five hundred yards of open park?"

"Well, but she had to appear here, because this is where the original one – Lady Anne, you know – was supposed to walk."

"Oh, never mind Lady Anne! A real ghost can do anything. But how did Miss Norris appear suddenly over five hundred yards of bare park?"

Bill looked at Antony with open mouth.

"I – I don't know," he stammered. "We never thought of that."

"You would have seen her long before, wouldn't you, if she had come the way we came?"

"Of course we should."

"And that would have spoilt it rather. You would have had time to recognize her walk."

Bill was interested now.

"That's rather funny, you know, Tony. We none of us thought of that."

"You're sure she didn't come across the park when none of you were looking?"

"Quite. Because, you see, Betty and I were expecting her, and we kept looking round in case we saw her, so that we should all be playing with our backs to her."

"You and Miss Calladine were playing together?"

"I say, however do you know that?"

"Brilliant deductive reasoning. Well, then you suddenly saw her?"

"Yes, she walked across that side of the lawn." He indicated the opposite side, nearer to the house.

"She couldn't have been hiding in the ditch? Do you call it the moat, by the way?"

"Mark does. We don't among ourselves. No, she couldn't. Betty and I were here before the others, and walked round a bit. We should have seen her."

"Then she must have been hiding in the shed. Or do you call

it the summer-house?"

"We had to go there for the bowls, of course. She couldn't have been there."

"Oh!"

"It's dashed funny," said Bill, after an interval for thought. "But it doesn't matter, does it? It has nothing to do with Robert."

"Hasn't it?"

"I say, has it?" said Bill, getting excited again.

"I don't know. We don't know what has, or what hasn't. But it has got something to do with Miss Norris. And Miss Norris – " He broke off suddenly.

"What about her?"

"Well, you're all in it in a kind of way. And if something unaccountable happens to one of you a day or two before something unaccountable happens to the whole house, one is well, interested." It was a good enough reason, but it wasn't the reason he had been on the point of giving.

"I see. Well?"

Antony knocked out his pipe and got up slowly.

"Well then, let's find the way from the house by which Miss Norris came."

Bill jumped up eagerly.

"By Jove! Do you mean there's a secret passage?"

"A secluded passage, anyway. There must be."

"I say, what fun! I love secret passages. Good Lord, and this afternoon I was playing golf just like an ordinary merchant! What a life! Secret passages!"

They made their way down into the ditch. If an opening was to be found which led to the house, it would probably be on the house side of the green, and on the outside of the ditch. The most obvious place at which to begin the search was the shed where the bowls were kept. It was a tidy place as anything in Mark's establishment would be. There were two boxes of croquet things, one of them with the lid open, as if the balls and mallets and hoops (neatly enough put away, though) had been recently used; a box of bowls, a small lawn-mower, a roller and so forth. A seat ran along the back of it, whereon the bowls-players could sit when it rained.

Antony tapped the wall at the back.

"This is where the passage ought to begin. It doesn't sound very hollow, does it?"

"It needn't begin here at all, need it?" said Bill, walking round with bent head, and tapping the other walls. He was just too tall to stand upright in the shed.

"There's only one reason why it should, and that is that it would save us the trouble of looking anywhere else for it. Surely Mark didn't let you play croquet on his bowling-green?" He pointed to the croquet things.

"He didn't encourage it at one time, but this year he got rather keen about it. There's really nowhere else to play. Personally I hate the game. He wasn't very keen on bowls, you know, but he liked calling it the bowling-green, and surprising his visitors with it."

Antony laughed.

"I love you on Mark," he said. "You're priceless."

He began to feel in his pockets for his pipe and tobacco, and then suddenly stopped and stiffened to attention. For a moment he stood listening, with his head on one side, holding up a finger to bid Bill listen too.

"What is it?" whispered Bill.

Antony waved him to silence, and remained listening. Very quietly he went down on his knees, and listened again. Then he put his ear to the floor. He got up and dusted himself quickly, walked across to Bill and whispered in his ear:

"Footsteps. Somebody coming. When I begin to talk, back me up."

Bill nodded. Antony gave him an encouraging pat on the

back, and stepped firmly across to the box of bowls, whistling loudly to himself. He took the bowls out, dropped one with a loud bang on the floor, said, "Oh, Lord!" and went on:

"I say, Bill, I don't think I want to play bowls, after all."

"Well, why did you say you did?" grumbled Bill.

Antony flashed a smile of appreciation at him.

"Well, I wanted to when I said I did, and now I don't want to."

"Then what do you want to do?"

"Talk."

"Oh, right-o!" said Bill eagerly.

"There's a seat on the lawn – I saw it. Let's bring these things along in case we want to play, after all."

"Right-o!" said Bill again. He felt safe with that, not wishing to commit himself until he knew what he was wanted to say.

As they went across the lawn, Antony dropped the bowls and took out his pipe.

"Got a match?" he said loudly.

As he bent his head over the match, he whispered, "There'll be somebody listening to us. You take the Cayley view," and then went on in his ordinary voice, "I don't think much of your matches, Bill," and struck another. They walked over to the seat and sat down.

"What a heavenly night!" said Antony.

"Ripping."

"I wonder where that poor devil Mark is now."

"It's a rum business."

"You agree with Cayley that it was an accident?"

"Yes. You see, I know Mark."

"H'm." Antony produced a pencil and a piece of paper and began to write on his knee, but while he wrote, he talked. He said that he thought Mark had shot his brother in a fit of anger, and that Cayley knew, or anyhow guessed, this and had tried to give his cousin a chance of getting away.

"Mind you, I think he's right. I think it's what any of us would do. I shan't give it away, of course, but somehow there are one or two little things which make me think that Mark really did shoot his brother – I mean other than accidentally."

"Murdered him?"

"Well, manslaughtered him, anyway. I may be wrong. Anyway, it's not my business."

"But why do you think so? Because of the keys?"

"Oh, the keys are a wash-out. Still, it was a brilliant idea of mine, wasn't it? And it would have been rather a score for me if they had all been outside."

He had finished his writing, and now passed the paper over to Bill. In the clear moonlight the carefully printed letters could easily be read:

"GO ON TALKING AS IF I WERE HERE. AFTER A MINUTE OR TWO, TURN ROUND AS IF I WERE SITTING ON THE GRASS BEHIND YOU, BUT GO ON TALKING."

"I know you don't agree with me," Antony went on as Bill read, "but you'll see that I'm right."

Bill looked up and nodded eagerly. He had forgotten golf and Betty and all the other things which had made up his world lately. This was the real thing. This was life. "Well," he began deliberately, "the whole point is that I know Mark. Now, Mark – "

But Antony was off the seat and letting himself gently down into the ditch. His intention was to crawl round it until the shed came in sight. The footsteps which he had heard seemed to be underneath the shed; probably there was a trap-door of some kind in the floor. Whoever it was would have heard their voices, and would probably think it worthwhile to listen to what they were saying. He might do this merely by opening the door a little without showing himself, in which case Antony would have found the entrance to the passage without any trouble to himself. But when Bill turned his head and talked over the back of the seat, it was probable that the listener would find it necessary to put his head outside in order to hear, and then Antony would be able to discover who it was. Moreover, if he should venture out of his hiding-place altogether and peep at them over the top of the bank, the fact that Bill was talking over the back of the seat would mislead the watcher into thinking that Antony was still there, sitting on the grass, no doubt, behind the seat, swinging his legs over the side of the ditch.

He walked quickly but very silently along the half-length of the bowling-green to the first corner, passed cautiously round, and then went even more carefully along the width of it to the second corner. He could hear Bill hard at it, arguing from his knowledge of Mark's character that this, that and the other must have happened, and he smiled appreciatively to himself. Bill was a great conspirator worth a hundred Watsons. As he approached the second corner he slowed down, and did the last few yards on hands and knees. Then, lying at full length, inch by inch his head went round the corner.

The shed was two or three yards to his left, on the opposite side of the ditch. From where he lay he could see almost entirely inside it. Everything seemed to be as they left it. The bowls-box, the lawn-mower, the roller, the open croquet-box, the –

"By Jove!" said Antony to himself, "That's neat."

The lid of the other croquet-box was open, too. Bill was turning round now; his voice became more difficult to hear. "You see what I mean," he was saying. "If Cayley – "

And out of the second croquet-box came Cayley's black head.

Antony wanted to shout his applause. It was neat, devilish neat. For a moment he gazed, fascinated, at that wonderful new kind of croquet-ball which had appeared so dramatically out of the box, and then reluctantly wriggled himself back. There was nothing to be gained by staying there, and a good deal to be lost, for Bill showed signs of running down. As quickly as he could Antony hurried round the ditch and took up his place at the back of the seat. Then he stood up with a yawn, stretched himself and said carelessly, "Well, don't worry yourself about it, Bill, old man. I daresay you're right. You know Mark, and I don't; and that's the difference. Shall we have a game or shall we go to bed?"

Bill looked at him for inspiration, and, receiving it, said, "Oh, just let's have one game, shall we?"

"Right you are," said Antony.

But Bill was much too excited to take the game which followed very seriously. Antony, on the other hand, seemed to be thinking of nothing but bowls. He played with great deliberation for ten minutes, and then announced that he was going to bed. Bill looked at him anxiously.

"It's all right," laughed Antony. "You can talk if you want to. Just let's put 'em away first, though."

They made their way down to the shed, and while Bill was putting the bowls away, Antony tried the lid of the closed croquet-box. As he expected, it was locked.

"Now then," said Bill, as they were walking back to the house again, "I'm simply bursting to know. Who was it?"

"Cayley."

"Good Lord! Where?"

"Inside one of the croquet-boxes."

"Don't be an ass."

"It's quite true, Bill." He told the other what he had seen.

"But aren't we going to have a look at it?" asked Bill, in great disappointment. "I'm longing to explore. Aren't you?"

"Tomorrow and tomorrow and tomorrow. We shall see Cayley coming along this way directly. Besides, I want to get in from the other end, if I can. I doubt very much if we can do it this end without giving ourselves away. Look,there's Cayley."

They could see him coming along the drive towards them. When they were a little closer, they waved to him and he waved back.

"I wondered where you were," he said, as he got up to them. "I rather thought you might be along this way. What about bed?"

"Bed it is," said Antony.

"We've been playing bowls," added Bill, "and talking, and – and playing bowls. Ripping night, isn't it?"

But he left the rest of the conversation, as they wandered back to the house, to Antony. He wanted to think. There seemed to be no doubt now that Cayley was a villain. Bill had never been familiar with a villain before. It didn't seem quite fair of Cayley, somehow; he was taking rather a mean advantage of his friends. Lot of funny people there were in the world – funny people with secrets. Look at Tony, that first time he had met him in a tobacconist's shop. Anybody would have thought he was a tobacconist's assistant. And Cayley. Anybody would have thought that Cayley was an ordinary decent sort of person. And Mark. Dash it! One could never be sure of anybody. Now, Robert was different. Everybody had always said that Robert was a shady fellow.

But what on earth had Miss Norris got to do with it? What had Miss Norris got to do with it? This was a question which Antony had already asked himself that afternoon, and it seemed to him now that he had found the answer. As he lay in bed that night he reassembled his ideas, and looked at them in the new light which the events of the evening threw upon the dark corners in his brain.

Of course it was natural that Cayley should want to get rid of his guests as soon as the tragedy was discovered. He would want this for their own sake as well as for his. But he had been a little too quick about suggesting it, and about seeing the suggestion carried out. They had been bustled off as soon as they could be packed. The suggestion that they were in his hands, to go or stay as he wished, could have been left safely to them. As it was, they had been given no alternative, and Miss Norris, who had proposed to catch an after-dinner train at the junction, in the obvious hope that she might have in this way a dramatic cross-examination at the hands of some keen-eyed detective, was encouraged tactfully, but quite firmly, to travel by the earlier train with the others. Antony had felt that Cayley, in the tragedy which had suddenly befallen the house, ought to have been equally indifferent to her presence or absence. But he was not; and Antony assumed from this that Cayley was very much alive to the necessity for her absence.

Why?

Well, that question was not to be answered off-hand. But the fact that it was so had made Antony interested in her; and it was for this reason that he had followed up so alertly Bill's casual mention of her in connection with the dressing-up business. He felt that he wanted to know a little more about Miss Norris and the part she had played in the Red House circle. By sheer luck, as it seemed to him, he had stumbled on the answer to his question.

Miss Norris was hurried away because she knew about the secret passage.

The passage, then, had something to do with the mystery of Robert's death. Miss Norris had used it in order to bring off her dramatic appearance as the ghost. Possibly she had discovered it for herself; possibly Mark had revealed it to her secretly one day, never guessing that she would make so unkind a use of it later on; possibly Cayley, having been let into the joke of the dressing-up, had shown her how she could make her appearance on the bowling-green even more mysterious and supernatural. One way or another, she knew about the secret passage. So she must be hurried away.

Why? Because if she stayed and talked, she might make some innocent mention of it. And Cayley did not want any mention of it.

Why, again? Obviously because the passage, or even the mere knowledge of its existence, might provide a clue.

"I wonder if Mark's hiding there," thought Antony; and he went to sleep.

10

MR GILLINGHAM TALKS NONSENSE

Antony came down in a very good humour to breakfast next morning, and found that his host was before him. Cayley looked up from his letters and nodded.

"Any word of Mr Ablett – of Mark?" said Antony, as he poured out his coffee.

"No. The inspector wants to drag the lake this afternoon."

"Oh! Is there a lake?"

There was just the flicker of a smile on Cayley's face, but it disappeared as quickly as it came.

"Well, it's really a pond," he said, "but it was called 'the lake.'"

"By Mark," thought Antony. Aloud he said, "What do they expect to find?"

"They think that Mark – " He broke off and shrugged his shoulders.

"May have drowned himself, knowing that he couldn't get away? And knowing that he had compromised himself by trying to get away at all?"

"Yes; I suppose so," said Cayley slowly.

"I should have thought he would have given himself more of a run for his money. After all, he had a revolver. If he was determined not to be taken alive, he could always have prevented that. Couldn't he have caught a train to London before the police knew anything about it?"

"He might just have managed it. There was a train. They would have noticed him at Waldheim, of course, but he might have managed it at Stanton. He's not so well-known there, naturally. The inspector has been inquiring. Nobody seems to have seen him."

"There are sure to be people who will say they did, later on. There was never a missing man yet but a dozen people come forward who swear to have seen him at a dozen different places at the same time."

Cayley smiled.

"Yes. That's true. Anyhow, he wants to drag the pond first." He added dryly, "From what I've read of detective stories, inspectors always do want to drag the pond first."

"Is it deep?"

"Quite deep enough," said Cayley as he got up. On his way to the door he stopped, and looked at Antony. "I'm so sorry that we're keeping you here like this, but it will only be until tomorrow. The inquest is tomorrow afternoon. Do amuse yourself how you like till then. Beverley will look after you."

"Thanks very much. I shall really be quite all right."

Antony went on with his breakfast. Perhaps it was true that inspectors liked dragging ponds, but the question was, did Cayleys like having them dragged? Was Cayley anxious about it, or quite indifferent? He certainly did not seem to be anxious, but he could hide his feelings very easily beneath that heavy, solid face, and it was not often that the real Cayley peeped out. Just a little too eager once or twice, perhaps, but there was nothing to be learnt from it this morning. Perhaps he knew that the pond had no secrets to give up. After all, inspectors were always dragging ponds.

Bill came in noisily.

Bill's face was an open book. Excitement was written all over it.

"Well," he said eagerly, as he sat down to the business of the meal, "what are we going to do this morning?"

"Not talk so loudly, for one thing," said Antony. Bill looked about him apprehensively. Was Cayley under the table, for example? After last night one never knew.

"Is er – " He raised his eyebrows.

"No. But one doesn't want to shout. One should modulate the voice, my dear William, while breathing gently from the lips. Thus one avoids those chest-notes which have betrayed many a secret. In other words, pass the toast."

"You seem bright this morning."

"I am. Very bright. Cayley noticed it. Cayley said, 'Were it not that I have other business, I would come gathering nuts and may with thee. Fain would I gyrate round the mulberry-bush and hop upon the little hills. But the waters of Jordan encompass me and Inspector Birch tarries outside with his shrimping-net. My friend William Beverley will attend thee anon. Farewell, a long farewell to all – thy grape-nuts.' He then left up-centre. Enter W. Beverley, R."

"Are you often like this at breakfast?"

"Almost invariably. Said he with his mouth full. 'Exit W. Beverley, L."

"It's a touch of the sun, I suppose," said Bill, shaking his head sadly.

"It's the sun and the moon and the stars, all acting together on an empty stomach. Do you know anything about the stars, Mr Beverley? Do you know anything about Orion's Belt, for instance? And why isn't there a star called Beverley's Belt? Or a novel? Said he masticating. Re-enter W. Beverley through trap-door."

"Talking about trap-doors – "

"Don't," said Antony, getting up. "Some talk of Alexander and some of Hercules, but nobody talks about – what's the Latin for trap-door? – Mensa a table; you might get it from that.

Well, Mr Beverley," – and he slapped him heartily on the back as he went past him – "I shall see you later. Cayley says that you will amuse me, but so far you have not made me laugh once. You must try and be more amusing when you have finished your breakfast. But don't hurry. Let the upper mandibles have time to do the work." With those words Mr Gillingham then left the spacious apartment.

Bill continued his breakfast with a slightly bewildered air. He did not know that Cayley was smoking a cigarette outside the windows behind him; not listening, perhaps; possibly not even overhearing; but within sight of Antony, who was not going to take any risks. So he went on with his breakfast, reflecting that Antony was a rum fellow, and wondering if he had dreamed only of the amazing things which had happened the day before.

Antony went up to his bedroom to fetch his pipe. It was occupied by a housemaid, and he made a polite apology for disturbing her. Then he remembered.

"Is it Elsie?" he asked, giving her a friendly smile.

"Yes, sir," she said, shy but proud. She had no doubts as to why it was that she had achieved such notoriety.

"It was you who heard Mr Mark yesterday, wasn't it? I hope the inspector was nice to you?"

"Yes, thank you, sir."

"'It's my turn now. You wait,'" murmured Antony to himself.

"Yes, sir. Nasty-like. Meaning to say his chance had come."

"I wonder."

"Well, that's what I heard, sir. Truly."

Antony looked at her thoughtfully and nodded.

"Yes. I wonder. I wonder why."

"Why what, sir?"

"Oh, lots of things, Elsie... It was quite an accident your being outside just then?"

Elsie blushed. She had not forgotten what Mrs Stevens had said about it.

"Quite, sir. In the general way I use the other stairs."

"Of course."

He had found his pipe and was about to go downstairs again when she stopped him.

"I beg your pardon, sir, but will there be an inquest?"

"Oh, yes. Tomorrow, I think."

"Shall I have to give my evidence, sir?"

"Of course. There's nothing to be frightened of."

"I did hear it, sir. Truly."

"Why, of course you did. Who says you didn't?"

"Some of the others, sir, Mrs Stevens and all."

"Oh, that's just because they're jealous," said Antony with a smile.

He was glad to have spoken to her, because he had recognized at once the immense importance of her evidence. To the Inspector no doubt it had seemed only of importance in that it had shown Mark to have adopted something of a threatening attitude towards his brother. To Antony it had much more significance. It was the only trustworthy evidence that Mark had been in the office at all that afternoon.

For who saw Mark go into the office? Only Cayley. And if Cayley had been hiding the truth about the keys, why should he not be hiding the truth about Mark's entry into the office? Obviously all Cayley's evidence went for nothing. Some of it no doubt was true; but he was giving it, both truth and falsehood, with a purpose. What the purpose was Antony did not know as yet – to shield Mark, to shield himself – even to betray Mark – it might be any of these. But since his evidence was given for his own ends, it was impossible that it could be treated as the evidence of an impartial and trustworthy onlooker. Such, for instance, as Elsie appeared to be.

Elsie's evidence, however, seemed to settle the point. Mark had gone into the office to see his brother; Elsie had heard them both talking; and then Antony and Cayley had found the body of Robert... and the Inspector was going to drag the pond.

But certainly Elsie's evidence did not prove anything more than the mere presence of Mark in the room. "It's my turn now; you wait." That was not an immediate threat; – it was a threat for the future. If Mark had shot his brother immediately afterwards it must have been an accident, the result of a struggle, say, provoked by that "nasty-like" tone of voice. Nobody would say "You wait" to a man who was just going to be shot. "You wait" meant "You wait, and see what's going to happen to you later on." The owner of the Red House had had enough of his brother's sponging, his brother's blackmail; now it was Mark's turn to get a bit of his own back. Let Robert just wait a bit, and he would see. The conversation which Elsie had overheard might have meant something like this. It couldn't have meant murder. Anyway not murder of Robert by Mark.

"It's a funny business," thought Antony. "The one obvious solution is so easy and yet so wrong. And I've got a hundred things in my head, and I can't fit them together. And this afternoon will make a hundred and one. I mustn't forget this afternoon."

He found Bill in the hall and proposed a stroll. Bill was only too ready. "Where do you want to go?" he asked.

"I don't mind much. Show me the park."

"Righto."

They walked out together.

"Watson, old man," said Antony, as soon as they were away from the house, "you really mustn't talk so loudly indoors. There was a gentleman outside, just behind you, all the time."

"Oh, I say," said Bill, going pink. "I'm awfully sorry. So that's why you were talking such rot."

"Partly, yes. And partly because I do feel rather bright this morning. We're going to have a busy day."

"Are we really? What are we going to do?"

"They're going to drag the pond – beg its pardon, the lake. Where is the lake?"

"We're on the way to it now, if you'd like to see it."

"We may as well look at it. Do you haunt the lake much in the ordinary way?"

"Oh, no, rather not. There's nothing to do there."

"You can't bathe?"

"Well, I shouldn't care to. Too dirty."

"I see.... This is the way we came yesterday, isn't it? The way to the village?"

"Yes. We go off a bit to the right directly. What are they dragging it for?"

"Mark."

"Oh, rot," said Bill uneasily. He was silent for a little, and then, forgetting his uncomfortable thoughts in his sudden remembrance of the exciting times they were having, said eagerly, "I say, when are we going to look for that passage?"

"We can't do very much while Cayley's in the house."

"What about this afternoon when they're dragging the pond? He's sure to be there."

Antony shook his head.

"There's something I must do this afternoon," he said. "Of course we might have time for both."

"Has Cayley got to be out of the house for the other thing too?"

"Well, I think he ought to be."

"I say, is it anything rather exciting?"

"I don't know. It might be rather interesting. I daresay I could do it at some other time, but I rather fancy it at three o'clock, somehow. I've been specially keeping it back for then."

"I say, what fun! You do want me, don't you?"

"Of course I do. Only, Bill don't talk about things inside the house, unless I begin. There's a good Watson."

"I won't. I swear I won't."

They had come to the pond – Mark's lake – and they walked silently round it. When they had made the circle, Antony sat down on the grass, and relit his pipe. Bill followed his example.

"Well, Mark isn't there," said Antony.

"No," said Bill. "At least, I don't quite see why you know he isn't."

"It isn't 'knowing,' it's 'guessing,'" said Antony rapidly. "It's much easier to shoot yourself than to drown yourself, and if Mark had wanted to shoot himself in the water, with some idea of not letting the body be found, he'd have put big stones in his pockets, and the only big stones are near the water's edge, and they would have left marks, and they haven't, and therefore he didn't, and oh, bother the pond; that can wait till this afternoon. Bill, where does the secret passage begin?"

"Well, that's what we've got to find out, isn't it?"

"Yes. You see, my idea is this."

He explained his reasons for thinking that the secret of the passage was concerned in some way with the secret of Robert's death, and went on:

"My theory is that Mark discovered the passage about a year ago – the time when he began to get keen on croquet. The passage came out into the floor of the shed, and probably it was Cayley's idea to put a croquet-box over the trap-door, so as to hide it more completely. You know, when once you've discovered a secret yourself, it always seems as if it must be so obvious to everybody else. I can imagine that Mark loved having this little secret all to himself and to Cayley, of course, but Cayley wouldn't count and they must have had great fun fixing it up, and making it more difficult for other people to find out. Well then, when Miss Norris was going to dress-up, Cayley gave it away. Probably he told her that she could never get down to the bowling-green without being discovered, and then perhaps showed that he knew there was one way in which she could do it, and she wormed the secret out of him somehow."

"But this was two or three days before Robert turned up."

"Exactly. I am not suggesting that there was anything sinister about the passage in the first place. It was just a little private bit of romance and adventure for Mark, three days ago. He didn't even know that Robert was coming. But somehow the passage has been used since, in connection with Robert. Perhaps Mark escaped that way; perhaps he's hiding there now. And if so, then the only person who could give him away was Miss Norris. And she of course would only do it innocently not knowing that the passage had anything to do with it."

"So it was safer to have her out of the way?"

"Yes."

"But, look here, Tony, why do you want to bother about this end of it? We can always get in at the bowling-green end."

"I know, but if we do that we shall have to do it openly. It will mean breaking open the box, and letting Cayley know that we've done it. You see, Bill, if we don't find anything out for ourselves in the next day or two, we've got to tell the police what we have found out, and then they can explore the passage for themselves. But I don't want to do that yet."

"Rather not."

"So we've got to carry on secretly for a bit. It's the only way." He smiled and added, "And it's much more fun."

"Rather!" Bill chuckled to himself.

"Very well. Where does the secret passage begin?"

11

THE REVEREND THEODORE USSHER

"There's one thing, which we have got to realize at once," said Antony, "and that is that if we don't find it easily, we shan't find it at all."

"You mean that we shan't have time?"

"Neither time nor opportunity. Which is rather a consoling thought to a lazy person like me."

"But it makes it much harder, if we can't really look properly."

"Harder to find, yes, but so much easier to look. For instance, the passage might begin in Cayley's bedroom. Well, now we know that it doesn't."

"We don't know anything of the sort," protested Bill.

"We – know for the purposes of our search. Obviously we can't go tailing into Cayley's bedroom and tapping his wardrobes; and obviously, therefore, if we are going to look for it at all, we must assume that it doesn't begin there."

"Oh, I see." Bill chewed a piece of grass thoughtfully. "Anyhow, it wouldn't begin on an upstairs floor, would it?"

"Probably not. Well, we're getting on."

"You can wash out the kitchen and all that part of the house," said Bill, after more thought. "We can't go there."

"Right. And the cellars, if there are any."

"Well, that doesn't leave us much."

"No. Of course it's only a hundred-to-one chance that we find it, but what we want to consider is which is the most likely place of the few places in which we can look safely."

"All it amounts to," said Bill, "is the living-rooms downstairs – dining-room, library, hall, billiard-room and the office rooms."

"Yes, that's all."

"Well, the office is the most likely, isn't it?"

"Yes. Except for one thing."

"What's that?"

"Well, it's on the wrong side of the house. One would expect the passage to start from the nearest place to which it is going. Why make it longer by going under the house first?"

"Yes, that's true. Well, then, you think the dining-room or the library?"

"Yes. And the library for choice. I mean for our choice. There are always servants going into dining-rooms. We shouldn't have much of a chance of exploring properly in there. Besides, there's another thing to remember. Mark has kept this a secret for a year. Could he have kept it a secret in the dining-room? Could Miss Norris have got into the dining-room and used the secret door just after dinner without being seen? It would have been much too risky."

Bill got up eagerly.

"Come along," he said, "let's try the library. If Cayley comes in, we can always pretend we're choosing a book."

Antony got up slowly, took his arm and walked back to the house with him.

The library was worth going into, passages or no passages. Antony could never resist another person's bookshelves. As soon as he went into the room, he found himself wandering round it to see what books the owner read, or (more likely) did not read, but kept for the air which they lent to the house. Mark had prided himself on his library. It was a mixed collection of books. Books which he had inherited both from his father and from his patron; books which he had bought because he was interested in them or, if not in them, in the authors to whom he wished to lend his patronage; books which he had ordered in beautifully bound editions, partly because they looked well on his shelves, lending a noble colour to his rooms, partly because no man of culture should ever be without them; old editions, new editions, expensive books, cheap books, a library in which everybody, whatever his taste, could be sure of finding something to suit him.

"And which is your particular fancy, Bill?" said Antony, looking from one shelf to another. "Or are you always playing billiards?"

"I have a look at 'Badminton' sometimes," said Bill. "It's over in that corner there." He waved a hand.

"Over here?" said Antony, going to it.

"Yes." He corrected himself suddenly. – "Oh, no, it's not. It's over there on the right now. Mark had a grand re-arrangement of his library about a year ago. It took him more than a week, he told us. He's got such a frightful lot, hasn't he?"

"Now that's very interesting," said Antony, and he sat down and filled his pipe again.

There was indeed a "frightful lot" of books. The four walls of the library were plastered with them from floor to ceiling, save only where the door and the two windows insisted on living their own life, even though an illiterate one. To Bill it seemed the most hopeless room of any in which to look for a secret opening.

"We shall have to take every blessed book down," he said, "before we can be certain that we haven't missed it."

"Anyway," said Antony, "if we take them down one at a time, nobody can suspect us of sinister designs. After all, what does one go into a library for, except to take books down?"

"But there's such a frightful lot."

Antony's pipe was now going satisfactorily, and he got up and walked leisurely to the end of the wall opposite the door.

"Well, let's have a look," he said, "and see if they are so very frightful. Hallo, here's your 'Badminton.' You often read that, you say?"

"If I read anything."

"Yes." He looked down and up the shelf. "Sport and Travel chiefly. I like books of travel, don't you?"

"They're pretty dull as a rule."

"Well, anyhow, some people like them very much," said Antony, reproachfully. He moved on to the next row of shelves. "The Drama. The Restoration dramatists. You can have most of them. Still, as you well remark, many people seem to love them. Shaw, Wilde, Robertson – I like reading plays, Bill. There are not many people who do, but those who do are usually very keen. Let us pass on."

"I say, we haven't too much time," said Bill restlessly.

"We haven't. That's why we aren't wasting any. Poetry. Who reads poetry nowadays? Bill, when did you last read 'Paradise Lost'?"

"Never."

"I thought not. And when did Miss Calladine last read 'The Excursion' aloud to you?"

"As a matter of fact, Betty – Miss Calladine – happens to be jolly keen on – what's the beggar's name?"

"Never mind his name. You have said quite enough. We pass on."

He moved on to the next shelf.

"Biography. Oh, lots of it. I love biographies. Are you a member of the Johnson Club? I bet Mark is. 'Memories of Many Courts' – I'm sure Mrs Calladine reads that. Anyway, biographies are just as interesting as most novels, so why linger? We pass on." He went to the next shelf, and then gave a sudden whistle. "Hallo, hallo!"

"What's the matter?" said Bill rather peevishly.

"Stand back there. Keep the crowd back, Bill. We are getting amongst it. Sermons, as I live. Sermons. Was Mark's father a clergyman, or does Mark take to them naturally?"

"His father was a parson, I believe. Oh, yes, I know he was."

"Ah, then these are Father's books. 'Half-Hours with the Infinite' – I must order that from the library when I get back. 'The Lost Sheep,' 'Jones on the Trinity,' 'The Epistles of St. Paul Explained.' Oh, Bill, we're amongst it. 'The Narrow Way, being Sermons by the Rev. Theodore Ussher' – hal-LO!"

"What is the matter?"

"William, I am inspired. Stand by." He took down the Reverend Theodore Ussher's classic work, looked at it with a happy smile for a moment, and then gave it to Bill.

"Here, hold Ussher for a bit."

Bill took the book obediently.

"No, give it me back. Just go out into the hall, and see if you can hear Cayley anywhere. Say 'Hallo' loudly, if you do."

Bill went out quickly, listened, and came back.

"It's all right."

"Good." He took the book out of its shelf again. "Now then, you can hold Ussher. Hold him in the left hand so. With the right or dexter hand, grasp this shelf firmly so. Now, when I say 'Pull,' pull gradually. Got that?"

Bill nodded, his face alight with excitement.

"Good." Antony put his hand into the space left by the stout Ussher, and fingered the back of the shelf. "Pull," he said.

Bill pulled.

"Now just go on pulling like that. I shall get it directly. Not hard, you know, but just keeping up the strain."

His fingers went at it again busily.

And then suddenly the whole row of shelves, from top to bottom, swung gently open towards them.

"Good Lord!" said Bill, letting go of the shelf in his amazement.

Antony pushed the shelves back, extracted Ussher from Bill's fingers, replaced him, and then, taking Bill by the arm, led him to the sofa and deposited him in it. Standing in front of him, he bowed gravely.

"Child's play, Watson," he said; "child's play."

"How on earth – "

Antony laughed happily and sat down on the sofa beside him.

"You don't really want it explained," he said, smacking him on the knee; "you're just being Watsonish. It's very nice of you, of course, and I appreciate it."

"No, but really, Tony."

"Oh, my dear Bill!" He smoked silently for a little, and then went on, "It's what I was saying just now – a secret is a secret until you have discovered it, and as soon as you have discovered it, you wonder why everybody else isn't discovering it, and how it could ever have been a secret at all. This passage has been here for years, with an opening at one end into the library, and at the other end into the shed. Then Mark discovered it, and immediately he felt that everybody else must discover it. So he made the shed end more difficult by putting the croquet-box there, and this end more difficult by – " he stopped and looked at the other "by what, Bill?"

But Bill was being Watsonish.

"What?"

"Obviously by re-arranging his books. He happened to take out 'The Life of Nelson' or 'Three Men in a Boat,' or whatever it was, and by the merest chance discovered the secret. Naturally he felt that everybody else would be taking down 'The Life of Nelson' or 'Three Men in a Boat.' Naturally he felt that the secret would be safer if nobody ever interfered with that shelf at all. When you said that the books had been re-arranged a year ago – just about the time the croquet-box came into existence – of course, I guessed why. So I looked about for the dullest books I could find, the books nobody ever read. Obviously the collection of sermon-books of a mid-Victorian clergyman was the shelf we wanted."

"Yes, I see. But why were you so certain of the particular place?"

"Well, he had to mark the particular place by some book. I thought that the joke of putting 'The Narrow Way' just over the entrance to the passage might appeal to him. Apparently it did."

Bill nodded to himself thoughtfully several times. "Yes, that's very neat," he said. "You're a clever devil, Tony."

Tony laughed.

"You encourage me to think so, which is bad for me, but very delightful."

"Well, come on, then," said Bill, and he got up, and held out a hand.

"Come on where?"

"To explore the passage, of course."

Antony shook his head.

"Why ever not?"

"Well, what do you expect to find there?"

"I don't know. But you seemed to think that we might find something that would help."

"Suppose we find Mark?" said Antony quietly.

"I say, do you really think he's there?"

"Suppose he is?"

"Well, then, there we are."

Antony walked over to the fireplace, knocked out the ashes of his pipe, and turned back to Bill. He looked at him gravely without speaking.

"What are you going to say to him?" he said at last.

"How do you mean?"

"Are you going to arrest him, or help him to escape?"

"I – I – well, of course, I – " began Bill, stammering, and then ended lamely, "Well, I don't know."

"Exactly. We've got to make up our minds, haven't we?"

Bill didn't answer. Very much disturbed in his mind, he walked restlessly about the room, frowning to himself, stopping now and then at the newly discovered door and looking at it as if he were trying to learn what lay behind it. Which side was he on, if it came to choosing sides – Mark's or the Law's?

"You know, you can't just say, 'Oh er hallo!' to him," said Antony, breaking rather appropriately into his thoughts.

Bill looked up at him with a start.

"Nor," went on Antony, "can you say, 'This is my friend Mr Gillingham, who is staying with you. We were just going to have a game of bowls.'"

"Yes, it's dashed difficult. I don't know what to say. I've been rather forgetting about Mark." He wandered over to the window and looked out on to the lawns. There was a gardener clipping the grass edges. No reason why the lawn should be untidy just because the master of the house had disappeared. It was going to be a hot day again. Dash it, of course he had forgotten Mark. How could he think of him as an escaped murderer, a fugitive from justice, when everything was going on just as it did yesterday, and the sun was shining just as it did when they all drove off to their golf, only twenty-four hours ago? How could he help feeling that this was not real tragedy, but merely a jolly kind of detective game that he and Antony were playing?

He turned back to his friend.

"All the same," he said, "you wanted to find the passage, and now you've found it. Aren't you going into it at all?"

Antony took his arm.

"Let's go outside again," he said. "We can't go into it now, anyhow. It's too risky, with Cayley about. Bill, I feel like you

– just a little bit frightened. But what I'm frightened of I don't quite know. Anyway, you want to go on with it, don't you?"

"Yes," said Bill firmly. "We must."

"Then we'll explore the passage this afternoon, if we get the chance. And if we don't get the chance, then we'll try it tonight."

They walked across the hall and out into the sunlight again.

"Do you really think we might find Mark hiding there?" asked Bill.

"It's possible," said Antony. "Either Mark or – " He pulled himself up quickly. "No," he murmured to himself, "I won't let myself think that – not yet, anyway. It's too horrible."

12

A SHADOW ON THE WALL

In the twenty hours or so at his disposal Inspector Birch had been busy. He had telegraphed to London a complete description of Mark in the brown flannel suit which he had last been seen wearing; he had made inquiries at Stanton as to whether anybody answering to this description had been seen leaving by the 4.20; and though the evidence which had been volunteered to him had been inconclusive, it made it possible that Mark had indeed caught that train, and had arrived in London before the police at the other end had been ready to receive him. But the fact that it was market-day at Stanton, and that the little town would be more full than usual of visitors, made it less likely that either the departure of Mark by the 4.20, or the arrival of Robert by the 2.10 earlier in the afternoon, would have been particularly noticed. As Antony had said to Cayley, there would always be somebody ready to hand the police a circumstantial story of the movements of any man in whom the police were interested.

That Robert had come by the 2.10 seemed fairly certain. To find out more about him in time for the inquest would be difficult. All that was known about him in the village where he and Mark had lived as boys bore out the evidence of Cayley. He was an unsatisfactory son, and he had been hurried off to

Australia; nor had he been seen since in the village. Whether there were any more substantial grounds of quarrel between the two brothers than that the younger one was at home and well-to-do, while the elder was poor and an exile, was not known, nor, as far as the inspector could see, was it likely to be known until Mark was captured.

The discovery of Mark was all that mattered immediately. Dragging the pond might not help towards this, but it would certainly give the impression in court tomorrow that Inspector Birch was handling the case with zeal. And if only the revolver with which the deed was done was brought to the surface, his trouble would be well repaid. "Inspector Birch produces the weapon" would make an excellent headline in the local paper.

He was feeling well-satisfied with himself, therefore, as he walked to the pond, where his men were waiting for him, and quite in the mood for a little pleasant talk with Mr Gillingham and his friend, Mr Beverley. He gave them a cheerful "Good afternoon," and added with a smile, "Coming to help us?"

"You don't really want us," said Antony, smiling back at him.

"You can come if you like."

Antony gave a little shudder.

"You can tell me afterwards what you find," he said. "By the way," he added, "I hope the landlord at 'The George' gave me a good character?"

The Inspector looked at him quickly.

"Now how on earth do you know anything about that?"

Antony bowed to him gravely.

"Because I guessed that you were a very efficient member of the Force."

The inspector laughed.

"Well, you came out all right, Mr Gillingham. You got a clean bill. But I had to make certain about you."

"Of course you did. Well, I wish you luck. But I don't think you'll find much at the pond. It's rather out of the way, isn't it, for anybody running away?"

"That's just what I told Mr Cayley, when he called my attention to the pond. However, we shan't do any harm by looking. It's the unexpected that's the most likely in this sort of case."

"You're quite right, Inspector. Well, we mustn't keep you. Good afternoon," and Antony smiled pleasantly at him.

"Good afternoon, sir."

"Good afternoon," said Bill.

Antony stood looking after the Inspector as he strode off, silent for so long that Bill shook him by the arm at last, and asked him rather crossly what was the matter.

Antony shook his head slowly from side to side.

"I don't know; really I don't know. It's too devilish what I keep thinking. He can't be as cold-blooded as that."

"Who?"

Without answering, Antony led the way back to the garden-seat on which they had been sitting. He sat there with his head in his hands.

"Oh, I hope they find something," he murmured. "Oh, I hope they do."

"In the pond?"

"Yes."

"But what?"

"Anything, Bill; anything."

Bill was annoyed. "I say, Tony, this won't do. You really mustn't be so damn mysterious. What's happened to you suddenly?"

Antony looked up at him in surprise.

"Didn't you hear what he said?"

"What, particularly?"

"That it was Cayley's idea to drag the pond."

"Oh! Oh, I say!" Bill was rather excited again. "You mean that he's hidden something there? Some false clue which he wants the police to find?"

"I hope so," said Antony earnestly, "but I'm afraid – " He stopped short.

"Afraid of what?"

"Afraid that he hasn't hidden anything there. Afraid that – "

"Well?"

"What's the safest place in which to hide anything very important?"

"Somewhere where nobody will look."

"There's a better place than that."

"What?"

"Somewhere where everybody has already looked."

"By Jove! You mean that as soon as the pond has been dragged, Cayley will hide something there?"

"Yes, I'm afraid so."

"But why afraid?"

"Because I think that it must be something very important, something which couldn't easily be hidden anywhere else."

"What?" asked Bill eagerly.

Antony shook his head.

"No, I'm not going to talk about it yet. We can wait and see what the Inspector finds. He may find something – I don't know what – something that Cayley has put there for him to find. But if he doesn't, then it will be because Cayley is going to hide something there tonight."

"What?" asked Bill again.

"You will see what, Bill," said Antony; "because we shall be there."

"Are we going to watch him?"

"Yes, if the Inspector finds nothing."

"That's good," said Bill.

If it were a question of Cayley or the Law, he was quite decided as to which side he was taking. Previous to the tragedy of yesterday he had got on well enough with both of the cousins, without being in the least intimate with either. Indeed, of the two he preferred, perhaps, the silent, solid Cayley to the more volatile Mark. Cayley's qualities, as they appeared to Bill, may have been chiefly negative; but even if this merit lay in the fact that he never exposed whatever weaknesses he may have had, this is an excellent quality in a fellow-guest (or, if you like, fellow-host) in a house where one is continually visiting. Mark's weaknesses, on the other hand, were very plain to the eye, and Bill had seen a good deal of them.

Yet, though he had hesitated to define his position that morning in regard to Mark, he did not hesitate to place himself on the side of the Law against Cayley. Mark, after all, had done him no harm, but Cayley had committed an unforgivable offence. Cayley had listened secretly to a private conversation between himself and Tony. Let Cayley hang, if the Law demanded it.

Antony looked at his watch and stood up.

"Come along," he said. "It's time for that job I spoke about."

"The passage?" said Bill eagerly.

"No; the thing which I said that I had to do this afternoon."

"Oh, of course. What is it?"

Without saying anything, Antony led the way indoors to the office.

It was three o'clock, and at three o'clock yesterday Antony and Cayley had found the body. At a few minutes after three, he had been looking out of the window of the adjoining room, and had been surprised suddenly to find the door open and Cayley behind him. He had vaguely wondered at the time why he had expected the door to be shut, but he had had no time then to worry the thing out, and he had promised himself to look into it at his leisure afterwards. Possibly it meant nothing; possibly, if it meant anything, he could have found out its meaning by a visit to the office that morning. But he had felt that he would be more likely to recapture the impressions of yesterday if he chose as far as possible the same conditions for his experiment. So he had decided that three o'clock that afternoon should find him once more in the office.

As he went into the room, followed by Bill, he felt it almost as a shock that there was now no body of Robert lying there between the two doors. But there was a dark stain which showed where the dead man's head had been, and Antony knelt down over it, as he had knelt twenty-four hours before.

"I want to go through it again," he said. "You must be Cayley. Cayley said he would get some water. I remember thinking that water wasn't much good to a dead man, and that probably he was only too glad to do anything rather than nothing. He came back with a wet sponge and a handkerchief. I suppose he got the handkerchief from the chest of drawers. Wait a bit."

He got up and went into the adjoining room; looked round it, pulled open a drawer or two, and, after shutting all the doors, came back to the office.

"The sponge is there, and there are handkerchiefs in the top right-hand drawer. Now then, Bill, just pretend you're Cayley. You've just said something about water, and you get up."

Feeling that it was all a little uncanny, Bill, who had been kneeling beside his friend, got up and walked out. Antony, as he had done on the previous day, looked up after him as he went. Bill turned into the room on the right, opened the drawer and got the handkerchief, damped the sponge and came back.

"Well?" he said wonderingly.

Antony shook his head.

"It's all different," he said. "For one thing, you made a devil of a noise and Cayley didn't."

"Perhaps you weren't listening when Cayley went in?"

"I wasn't. But I should have heard him if I could have heard him, and I should have remembered afterwards."

"Perhaps Cayley shut the door after him."

"Wait!"

He pressed his hand over his eyes and thought. It wasn't anything which he had heard, but something which he had seen. He tried desperately hard to see it again.... He saw Cayley getting up, opening the door from the office, leaving it open and walking into the passage, turning to the door on the right, opening it, going in, and then – What did his eyes see after that? If they would only tell him again!

Suddenly he jumped up, his face alight. "Bill, I've got it!" he cried.

"What?"

"The shadow on the wall! I was looking at the shadow on the wall. Oh, ass, and ten times ass!"

Bill looked uncomprehendingly at him. Antony took his arm and pointed to the wall of the passage.

"Look at the sunlight on it," he said. "That's because you've left the door of that room open. The sun comes straight in through the windows. Now, I'm going to shut the door. Look! D'you see how the shadow moves across? That's what I saw – the shadow moving across as the door shut behind him. Bill, go in and shut the door behind you – quite naturally. Quick!"

Bill went out and Antony knelt, watching eagerly.

"I thought so!" he cried. "I knew it couldn't have been that."

"What happened?" said Bill, coming back.

"Just what you would expect. The sunlight came, and the shadow moved back again – all in one movement."

"And what happened yesterday?"

"The sunlight stayed there; and then the shadow came very slowly back, and there was no noise of the door being shut."

Bill looked at him with startled eyes.

"By Jove! You mean that Cayley closed the door afterwards as an afterthought – and very quietly – so that you couldn't hear?"

Antony nodded.

"Yes. That explains why I was surprised afterwards when I went into the room to find the door open behind me. You know how those doors with springs on them close?"

"The sort which old gentlemen have to keep out draughts?"

"Yes. Just at first they hardly move at all, and then very, very slowly they swing to – well, that was the way the shadow moved, and subconsciously I must have associated it with the movement of that sort of door. By Jove!" He got up, and dusted his knees. "Now, Bill, just to make sure, go in and close the door like that. As an afterthought, you know; and very quietly, so that I don't hear the click of it."

Bill did as he was told, and then put his head out eagerly to hear what had happened.

"That was it," said Antony, with absolute conviction. "That was just what I saw yesterday." He came out of the office, and joined Bill in the little room.

"And now," he said, "let's try and find out what it was that Mr Cayley was doing in here, and why he had to be so very careful that his friend Mr Gillingham didn't overhear him."

13

THE OPEN WINDOW

Anthony's first thought was that Cayley had hidden something; something, perhaps, which he had found by the body, but that was absurd. In the time at his disposal, he could have done no more than put it away in a drawer, where it would be much more open to discovery by Antony than if he had kept it in his pocket. In any case he would have removed it by this time, and hidden it in some more secret place. Besides, why in this case bother about shutting the door?

Bill pulled open a drawer in the chest, and looked inside.

"Is it any good going through these, do you think?" he asked.

Antony looked over his shoulder.

"Why did he keep clothes here at all?" he asked. "Did he ever change down here?"

"My dear Tony, he had more clothes than anybody in the world. He just kept them here in case they might be useful, I expect. When you and I go from London to the country we carry our clothes about with us. Mark never did. In his flat in London he had everything all over again which he has here. It was a hobby with him, collecting clothes. If he'd had half a dozen houses, they would all have been full of a complete gentleman's town and country outfit."

"I see."

"Of course, it might be useful sometimes, when he was busy in the next room, not to have to go upstairs for a handkerchief or a more comfortable coat."

"I see. Yes." He was walking round the room as he answered, and he lifted the top of the linen basket which stood near the wash basin and glanced in. "He seems to have come in here for a collar lately."

Bill peered in. There was one collar at the bottom of the basket.

"Yes. I daresay he would," he agreed. "If he suddenly found that the one he was wearing was uncomfortable or a little bit dirty, or something. He was very finicky."

Antony leant over and picked it out.

"It must have been uncomfortable this time," he said, after examining it carefully. "It couldn't very well be cleaner." He dropped it back again. "Anyway, he did come in here sometimes?"

"Oh, yes, rather."

"Yes, but what did Cayley come in for so secretly?"

"What did he want to shut the door for?" said Bill. "That's what I don't understand. You couldn't have seen him, anyhow."

"No. So it follows that I might have heard him. He was going to do something which he didn't want me to hear."

"By Jove, that's it!" said Bill eagerly.

"Yes; but what?"

Bill frowned hopefully to himself, but no inspiration came.

"Well, let's have some air, anyway," he said at last, exhausted by the effort, and he went to the window, opened it, and looked out. Then, struck by an idea, he turned back to Antony and said, "Do you think I had better go up to the pond to make sure that they're still at it? Because – "

He broke off suddenly at the sight of Antony's face.

"Oh, idiot, idiot!" Antony cried. "Oh, most super-excellent of Watsons! Oh, you lamb, you blessing! Oh, Gillingham, you incomparable ass!"

"What on earth – "

"The window, the window!" cried Antony, pointing to it.

Bill turned back to the window, expecting it to say something. As it said nothing, he looked at Antony again.

"He was opening the window!" cried Antony.

"Who?"

"Cayley, of course." Very gravely and slowly he expounded. "He came in here in order to open the window. He shut the door so that I shouldn't hear him open the window. He opened the window. I came in here and found the window open. I said, 'This window is open. My amazing powers of analysis tell me that the murderer must have escaped by this window.' 'Oh,' said Cayley, raising his eyebrows. 'Well,' said he, 'I suppose you must be right.' Said I proudly, 'I am. For the window is open,' I said. Oh, you incomparable ass!"

He understood now. It explained so much that had been puzzling him.

He tried to put himself in Cayley's place – Cayley, when Antony had first discovered him, hammering at the door and crying, "Let me in!" Whatever had happened inside the office, whoever had killed Robert, Cayley knew all about it, and knew that Mark was not inside, and had not escaped by the window. But it was necessary to Cayley's plans – to Mark's plans if they were acting in concert – that he should be thought so to have escaped. At some time, then, while he was hammering (the key in his pocket) at the locked door, he must suddenly have remembered – with what a shock! – that a mistake had been made. A window had not been left open!

Probably it would just have been a horrible doubt at first. Was the office window open? Surely it was open! Was it?.... Would he have time now to unlock the door, slip in, open the French windows and slip out again? No. At any moment the servants might come. It was too risky. Fatal, if he were discovered. But servants were stupid. He could get the windows safely open while they were crowding round the body. They wouldn't notice. He could do it somehow.

And then Antony's sudden appearance! Here was a complication. And Antony suggesting that they should try the window! Why, the window was just what he wanted to avoid. No wonder he had seemed dazed at first.

Ah, and here at last was the explanation why they had gone the longest way round and yet run. It was Cayley's only chance of getting a start on Antony, of getting to the windows first, of working them open somehow before Antony caught him up. Even if that were impossible, he must get there first, just to make sure. Perhaps they were open. He must get away from Antony and see. And if they were shut, hopelessly shut, then he must have a moment to himself, a moment in which to think of some other plan, and avoid the ruin which seemed so suddenly to be threatening.

So he had run. But Antony had kept up with him. They had broken in the window together, and gone into the office. But Cayley was not done yet. There was the dressing-room window! But quietly, quietly. Antony mustn't hear.

And Antony didn't hear. Indeed, he had played up to Cayley splendidly. Not only had he called attention to the open window, but he had carefully explained to Cayley why Mark had chosen this particular window in preference to the office window. And Cayley had agreed that probably that was the reason. How he must have chuckled to himself! But he was still a little afraid. Afraid that Antony would examine the shrubbery. Why? Obviously because there was no trace of anyone having broken through the shrubbery. No doubt Cayley had provided the necessary traces since, and had helped the Inspector to find them. Had he even gone as far as footmarks in Mark's shoes?

But the ground was very hard. Perhaps footmarks were not necessary. Antony smiled as he thought of the big Cayley trying to squeeze into the dapper little Mark's shoes. Cayley must have been glad that footmarks were not necessary.

No, the open window was enough; the open window and a broken twig or two. But quietly, quietly. Antony mustn't hear. And Antony had not heard... But he had seen a shadow on the wall.

They were outside on the lawn again now, Bill and Antony, and Bill was listening open-mouthed to his friend's theory of yesterday's happenings. It fitted in, it explained things, but it did not get them any further. It only gave them another mystery to solve.

"What's that?" said Antony.

"Mark. Where's Mark? If he never went into the office at all, then where is he now?"

"I don't say that he never went into the office. In fact, he must have gone. Elsie heard him." He stopped and repeated slowly, "She heard him, at least she says she did. But if he was there, he came out again by the door."

"Well, but where does that lead you?"

"Where it led Mark. The passage."

"Do you mean that he's been hiding there all the time?" Antony was silent until Bill had repeated his question, and then with an effort he came out of his thoughts and answered him.

"I don't know. But look here. Here is a possible explanation. I don't know if it is the right one – I don't know, Bill; I'm rather frightened. Frightened of what may have happened, of what may be going to happen. However, here is an explanation. See if you can find any fault with it."

With his legs stretched out and his hands deep in his pockets, he lay back on the garden-seat, looking up to the blue summer sky above him, and just as if he saw up there the events of yesterday being enacted over again, he described them slowly to Bill as they happened.

"We'll begin at the moment when Mark shoots Robert. Call it an accident; probably it was. Mark would say it was, anyhow. He is in a panic, naturally. But he doesn't lock the door and run away. For one thing, the key is on the outside of the door; for another, he is not quite such a fool as that. But he is in a horrible position. He is known to be on bad terms with his brother; he has just uttered some foolish threat to him, which may possibly have been overheard. What is he to do? He does the natural thing, the thing which Mark would always do in such circumstances. He consults Cayley, the invaluable, inevitable Cayley.

"Cayley is just outside, Cayley must have heard the shot, Cayley will tell him what to do. He opens the door just as Cayley is coming to see what is the matter. He explains rapidly. 'What's to be done, Cay? What's to be done? It was an accident. I swear it was an accident. He threatened me. He would have shot me if I hadn't. Think of something, quick!'

"Cayley has thought of something. 'Leave it to me,' he says. 'You clear out altogether. I shot him, if you like. I'll do all the explaining. Get away. Hide. Nobody saw you go in. Into the passage, quick. I'll come to you there as soon as I can.'

"Good Cayley. Faithful Cayley! Mark's courage comes back. Cayley will explain all right. Cayley will tell the servants that it was an accident. He will ring up the police. Nobody will suspect Cayley – Cayley has no quarrel with Robert. And then Cayley will come into the passage and tell him that it is all right, and Mark will go out by the other end, and saunter slowly back to the house. He will be told the news by one of the servants. Robert accidentally shot? Good Heavens!

"So, greatly reassured, Mark goes into the library. And Cayley goes to the door of the office.... and locks it. And then he bangs on the door and shouts, 'Let me in!'"

Antony was silent. Bill looked at him and shook his head.

"Yes, Tony, but that doesn't make sense. What's the point of Cayley behaving like that?"

Antony shrugged his shoulders without answering.

"And what has happened to Mark since?"

Antony shrugged his shoulders again.

"Well, the sooner we go into that passage, the better," said Bill.

"You're ready to go?"

"Quite," said Bill, surprised.

"You're quite ready for what we may find?"

"You're being dashed mysterious, old boy."

"I know I am." He gave a little laugh, and went on, "Perhaps I'm being an ass, just a melodramatic ass. Well, I hope I am." He looked at his watch.

"It's safe, is it? They're still busy at the pond?"

"We'd better make certain. Could you be a sleuthhound, Bill – one of those that travel on their stomachs very noiselessly? I mean, could you get near enough to the pond to make sure that Cayley is still there, without letting him see you?"

"Rather!" He got up eagerly. "You wait."

Antony's head shot up suddenly. "Why, that was what Mark said," he cried.

"Mark?"

"Yes. What Elsie heard him say."

"Oh, that."

"Yes I suppose she couldn't have made a mistake, Bill? She did hear him?"

"She couldn't have mistaken his voice, if that's what you mean."

"Oh?"

"Mark had an extraordinary characteristic voice."

"Oh!"

"Rather high-pitched, you know, and well, one can't explain, but – "

"Yes?"

"Well, rather like this, you know, or even more so if anything." He rattled these words off in Mark's rather monotonous, high-pitched voice, and then laughed, and added in his natural voice, "I say, that was really rather good."

Antony nodded quickly. "That was like it?" he said.

"Exactly."

"Yes." He got up and squeezed Bill's arm. "Well just go and see about Cayley, and then we'll get moving. I shall be in the library."

"Right."

Bill nodded and walked off in the direction of the pond. This was glorious fun; this was life. The immediate programme could hardly be bettered. First of all he was going to stalk Cayley. There was a little copse above the level of the pond, and about a hundred yards away from it. He would come into this from the back, creep cautiously through it, taking care that no twigs cracked, and then, drawing himself on his stomach to the edge, peer down upon the scene below him. People were always doing that sort of thing in books, and he had been filled with a hopeless envy of them; well, now he was actually going to do it himself. What fun!

And then, when he had got back unobserved to the house and reported to Antony, they were going to explore the secret passage! Again, what fun! Unfortunately there seemed to be no chance of buried treasure, but there might be buried clues. Even if you found nothing, you couldn't get away from the fact that a secret passage was a secret passage, and anything might happen in it. But even that wasn't the end of this exciting day. They were going to watch the pond that night; they were going to watch Cayley under the moonlight, watch him as he threw into the silence of the pond what? The revolver? Well, anyhow, they were going to watch him. What fun!

To Antony, who was older and who realized into what deep waters they were getting, it did not seem fun. But it was amazingly interesting. He saw so much, and yet somehow it was all out of focus. It was like looking at an opal, and discovering with every movement of it some new colour, some new gleam of light reflected, and yet never really seeing the opal as a whole. He was too near it, or too far away; he strained his eyes and he relaxed his eyes; it was no good. His brain could not get hold of it.

But there were moments when he almost had it...and then turned away from it. He had seen more of life than Bill, but he had never seen murder before, and this which was in his mind now, and to which he was afraid to listen, was not just the hot-blooded killing which any man may come to if he lose control. It was something much more horrible. Too horrible to be true. Then let him look again for the truth. He looked again but it was all out of focus.

"I will not look again," he said aloud, as he began to walk towards the house. "Not yet, anyway." He would go on collecting facts and impressions. Perhaps the one fact would come along, by itself which would make everything clear.

14

MR BEVERLEY QUALIFIES FOR THE STAGE

Bill had come back, and had reported, rather breathless, that Cayley was still at the pond.

"But I don't think they're getting up much except mud," he said. "I ran most of the way back so as to give us as much time as possible."

Antony nodded.

"Well, come along, then," he said. "The sooner, the quicker."

They stood in front of the row of sermons. Antony took down the Reverend Theodore Ussher's famous volume, and felt for the spring. Bill pulled. The shelves swung open towards them.

"By Jove!" said Bill, "It is a narrow way."

There was an opening about a yard square in front of them, which had something the look of a brick fireplace, a fireplace raised about two feet from the ground. But, save for one row of bricks in front, the floor of it was emptiness. Antony took a torch from his pocket and flashed it down into the blackness.

"Look," he whispered to the eager Bill. "The steps begin down there. Six feet down."

He flashed his torch up again. There was a handhold of iron, a sort of large iron staple, in the bricks in front of them.

"You swing off from there," said Bill. "At least, I suppose you do. I wonder how Ruth Norris liked doing it."

"Cayley helped her, I should think... It's funny."

"Shall I go first?" asked Bill, obviously longing to do so. Antony shook his head with a smile.

"I think I will, if you don't mind very much, Bill. Just in case."

"In case of what?"

"Well, in case."

Bill, had to be content with that, but he was too much excited to wonder what Antony meant.

"Righto," he said. "Go on."

"Well, we'll just make sure we can get back again, first. It really wouldn't be fair on the Inspector if we got stuck down here for the rest of our lives. He's got enough to do trying to find Mark, but if he has to find you and me as well – "

"We can always get out at the other end."

"Well, we're not certain yet. I think I'd better just go down and back. I promise faithfully not to explore."

"Right you are."

Antony sat down on the ledge of bricks, swung his feet over, and sat there for a moment, his legs dangling. He flashed his torch into the darkness again, so as to make sure where the steps began; then returned it to his pocket, seized the staple in front of him and swung himself down. His feet touched the steps beneath him, and he let go.

"Is it all right?" said Bill anxiously.

"All right. I'll just go down to the bottom of the steps and back. Stay there."

The light shone down by his feet. His head began to disappear. For a little while Bill, craning down the opening, could still see faint splashes of light, and could hear slow uncertain footsteps; for a little longer he could fancy that he saw and heard them; then he was alone...

Well, not quite alone. There was a sudden voice in the hall outside.

"Good Lord!" said Bill, turning round with a start, "Cayley!"

If he was not so quick in thought as Antony, he was quick enough in action. Thought was not demanded now. To close the secret door safely but noiselessly, to make sure that the books were in the right places, to move away to another row of shelves so as to be discovered deep in "Badminton" or "Baedeker" or whomever the kind gods should send to his aid; the difficulty was not to decide what to do, but to do all this in five seconds rather than in six.

"Ah, there you are," said Cayley from the doorway.

"Hallo!" said Bill, in surprise, looking up from the fourth volume of "The Life and Works of Samuel Taylor Coleridge." "Have they finished?"

"Finished what?"

"The pond," said Bill, wondering why he was reading Coleridge on such a fine afternoon. Desperately he tried to think of a good reason... Verifying a quotation – an argument with Antony – that would do. But what quotation?

"Oh, no. They're still at it. Where's Gillingham?"

'The Ancient Mariner' – water, water, everywhere – or was that something else? And where was Gillingham? Water, water everywhere...

"Tony? Oh, he's about somewhere. We're just going down to the village. They aren't finding anything at the pond, are they?"

"No. But they like doing it. Something off their minds when they can say they've done it."

Bill, deep in his book, looked up and said "Yes," and went back to it again. He was just getting to the place.

"What's the book?" said Cayley, coming up to him. Out of the corner of his eye he glanced at the shelf of sermons as he came. Bill saw that glance and wondered. Was there anything there to give away the secret?

"I was just looking up a quotation," he drawled. "Tony and I had a bet about it. You know that thing about – er water, water everywhere, and – er – not a drop to drink." (But what on earth, he wondered to himself, were they betting about?)

"'Nor any drop to drink,' to be accurate."

Bill looked at him in surprise. Then a happy smile came on his face.

"Quite sure?" he said.

"Of course."

"Then you've saved me a lot of trouble. That's what the bet was about." He closed the book with a slam, put it back in its shelf, and began to feel for his pipe and tobacco. "I was a fool to bet with Tony," he added. "He always knows that sort of thing."

So far, so good. But here was Cayley still in the library, and there was Antony, all unsuspecting, in the passage. When Antony came back he would not be surprised to find the door closed, because the whole object of his going had been to see if he could open it easily from the inside. At any moment, then, the bookshelf might swing back and show Antony's head in the gap. A nice surprise for Cayley!

"Come with us?" he said casually, as he struck a match. He pulled vigorously at the flame as he waited for the answer, hoping to hide his anxiety, for if Cayley assented, he was done.

"I've got to go into Stanton."

Bill blew out a great cloud of smoke with an expiration which covered also a heartfelt sigh of relief.

"Oh, a pity. You're driving, I suppose?"

"Yes. The car will be here directly. There's a letter I must write first." He sat down at a writing table, and took out a sheet of notepaper.

He was facing the secret door; if it opened he would see it. At any moment now it might open.

Bill dropped into a chair and thought. Antony must be warned. Obviously. But how? How did one signal to anybody?

By code. Morse code. Did Antony know it? Did Bill know it himself, if it came to that? He had picked up a bit in the Army – not enough to send a message, of course. But a message was impossible, anyhow; Cayley would hear him tapping it out. It wouldn't do to send more than a single letter. What letters did he know? And what letter would convey anything to Antony? He pulled at his pipe, his eyes wandering from Cayley at his desk to the Reverend Theodore Ussher in his shelf. What letter?

C for Cayley. Would Antony understand? Probably not, but it was just worth trying. What was C? Long, short, long, short. Umpty-iddy-umpty-iddy. Was that right? C yes, that was C. He was sure of that. C. Umpty-iddy-umpty-iddy.

Hands in pockets, he got up and wandered across the room, humming vaguely to himself, the picture of a man waiting for another man (as it might be his friend Gillingham) to come in and take him away for a walk or something. He wandered across to the books at the back of Cayley, and began to tap absent-mindedly on the shelves, as he looked at the titles. Umpty-iddy-umpty-iddy. Not that it was much like that at first; he couldn't get the rhythm of it.... Umpt-y-iddy-umpt-y-iddy. That was better. He was back at Samuel Taylor Coleridge now. Antony would begin to hear him soon. Umpt-y-iddy-umpt-y-iddy; just the aimless tapping of a man who is wondering what book he will take out with him to read on the lawn. Would Antony hear? One always heard the man in the next flat knocking out his pipe. Would Antony understand? Umpt-y-iddy-umpt-y-iddy. C. for Cayley, Antony. Cayley's here. For God's sake, wait.

"Good Lord! Sermons!" said Bill, with a loud laugh. (Umpt-y-iddy-umpt-y-iddy) "Ever read 'em, Cayley?"

"What?" Cayley looked up suddenly. Bill's back moved slowly along, his fingers beating a tattoo on the shelves as he walked.

"Er, no," said Cayley, with a little laugh. An awkward, uncomfortable little laugh, it seemed to Bill.

"Nor do I." He was past the sermons now past the secret door but still tapping in the same aimless way.

"Oh, for God's sake sit down," burst out Cayley. "Or go outside if you want to walk about."

Bill turned round in astonishment.

"Hallo, what's the matter?"

Cayley was slightly ashamed of his outburst.

"Sorry, Bill," he apologized. "My nerves are on edge. Your constant tapping and fidgeting about – "

"Tapping?" said Bill with an air of complete surprise.

"Tapping on the shelves, and humming. Sorry. It got on my nerves."

"My dear old chap, I'm awfully sorry. I'll go out in the hall."

"It's all right," said Cayley, and went on with his letter. Bill sat down in his chair again. Had Antony understood? Well, anyhow, there was nothing to do now but wait for Cayley to go. "And if you ask me," said Bill to himself, much pleased, "I ought to be on the stage. That's where I ought to be. The complete actor."

A minute, two minutes, three minutes.... five minutes. It was safe now. Antony had guessed.

"Is the car there?" asked Cayley, as he sealed up his letter.

Bill strolled into the hall, called back "Yes," and went out to talk to the chauffeur. Cayley joined him, and they stood there for a moment.

"Hallo," said a pleasant voice behind them. They turned round and saw Antony.

"Sorry to keep you waiting, Bill."

With a tremendous effort Bill restrained his feelings, and said casually enough that it was all right.

"Well, I must be off," said Cayley. "You're going down to the village?"

"That's the idea."

"I wonder if you'd take this letter to Jallands for me?"

"Of course."

"Thanks very much. Well, I shall see you later."

He nodded and got into the car.

As soon as they were alone Bill turned eagerly to his friend.

"Well?" he said excitedly.

"Come into the library."

They went in, and Tony sank down into a chair.

"You must give me a moment," he panted. "I've been running."

"Running?"

"Well, of course. How do you think I got back here?"

"You don't mean you went out at the other end?"

Antony nodded.

"I say, did you hear me tapping?"

"I did, indeed. Bill, you're a genius."

Bill blushed.

"I knew you'd understand," he said. "You guessed that I meant Cayley?"

"I did. It was the least I could do after you had been so brilliant. You must have had rather an exciting time."

"Exciting? Good Lord, I should think it was."

"Tell me about it."

As modestly as possible, Mr Beverley explained his qualifications for a life on the stage.

"Good man," said Antony at the end of it. "You are the most perfect Watson that ever lived. Bill, my lad," he went on dramatically, rising and taking Bill's hand in both of his, "There is nothing that you and I could not accomplish together, if we gave our minds to it."

"Silly old ass."

"That's what you always say when I'm being serious. Well, anyway, thanks awfully. You really saved us this time."

"Were you coming back?"

"Yes. At least I think I was. I was just wondering when I heard you tapping. The fact of the door being shut was rather surprising. Of course the whole idea was to see if it could be opened easily from the other side, but I felt somehow that you wouldn't shut it until the last possible moment – until you saw me coming back. Well, then I heard the taps, and I knew it must mean something, so I sat tight. Then when C began to come along I said, 'Cayley, b'Jove' – bright, aren't I? – and I simply hared to the other end of the passage for all I was worth. And hared back again. Because I thought you might be getting rather involved in explanations – about where I was, and so on."

"You didn't see Mark, then?"

"No. Nor his – No, I didn't see anything."

"Nor what?"

Antony was silent for a moment.

"I didn't see anything, Bill. Or rather, I did see something; I saw a door in the wall, a cupboard. And it's locked. So if there's anything we want to find, that's where it is."

"Could Mark be hiding there?"

"I called through the keyhole in a whisper 'Mark, are you there?' he would have thought it was Cayley. There was no answer."

"Well, let's go down and try again. We might be able to get the door open."

Antony shook his head.

"Aren't I going at all?" said Bill in great disappointment.

When Antony spoke, it was to ask another question:

"Can Cayley drive a car?"

"Yes, of course. Why?"

"Then he might easily drop the chauffeur at his lodge and go off to Stanton, or wherever he wanted to, on his own?"

"I suppose so if he wanted to."

"Yes." Antony got up. "Well, look here, as we said we were going into the village, and as we promised to leave that letter, I almost think we'd better do it."

"Oh! Oh, very well."

"Jallands. What were you telling me about that? Oh, yes; the Widow Norbury."

"That's right. Cayley used to be rather keen on the daughter. The letter's for her."

"Yes; well, let's take it. Just to be on the safe side."

"Am I going to be done out of that secret passage altogether?" asked Bill fretfully.

"There's nothing to see, really, I promise you."

"You're very mysterious. What's upset you? You did see something down there, I'm certain of it."

"I did and I've told you about it."

"No, you haven't. You only told me about the door in the wall."

"That's it, Bill. And it's locked. And I'm frightened of what's behind it."

"But then we shall never know what's there if we aren't going to look."

"We shall know tonight," said Antony, taking Bill's arm and leading him to the hall, "when we watch our dear friend Cayley dropping it into the pond."

15

MRS NORBURY CONFIDES IN DEAR MR GILLINGHAM

They left the road, and took the path across the fields which sloped gently downwards towards Jallands. Antony was silent, and since it is difficult to keep up a conversation with a silent man for any length of time, Bill had dropped into silence too. Or rather, he hummed to himself, hit at thistles in the grass with his stick and made uncomfortable noises with his pipe. But he noticed that his companion kept looking back over his shoulder, almost as if he wanted to remember for a future occasion the way by which they were coming. Yet there was no difficulty about it, for they remained all the time in view of the road, and the belt of trees above the long park wall which bordered its further side stood out clearly against the sky.

Antony, who had just looked round again, turned back with a smile.

"What's the joke?" said Bill, glad of the more social atmosphere.

"Cayley. Didn't you see?"

"See what?"

"The car. Going past on the road there."

"So that's what you were looking for. You've got jolly good eyes, my boy, if you recognize the car at this distance after only seeing it twice."

"Well, I have got jolly good eyes."

"I thought he was going to Stanton."

"He hoped you'd think so obviously."

"Then where is he going?"

"The library, probably. To consult our friend Ussher. After making quite sure that his friends Beverley and Gillingham really were going to Jallands, as they said."

Bill stopped suddenly in the middle of the path.

"I say, do you think so?"

Antony shrugged his shoulders.

"I shouldn't be surprised. We must be devilishly inconvenient for him, hanging about the house. Any moment he can get, when we're definitely somewhere else, must be very useful to him."

"Useful for what?"

"Well, useful for his nerves, if for nothing else. We know he's mixed up in this business; we know he's hiding a secret or two. Even if he doesn't suspect that we're on his tracks, he must feel that at any moment we might stumble on something."

Bill gave a grunt of assent, and they went slowly on again.

"What about tonight?" he said, after a lengthy blow at his pipe.

"Try a piece of grass," said Antony, offering it to him. Bill pushed it through the mouthpiece, blew again, said, "That's better," and returned the pipe to his pocket.

"How are we going to get out without Cayley knowing?"

"Well, that wants thinking over. It's going to be difficult. I wish we were sleeping at the inn... Is this Miss Norbury, by any chance?"

Bill looked up quickly. They were close to Jallands now, an old thatched farmhouse which, after centuries of sleep, had woken up to a new world, and had forthwith sprouted wings;

wings, however, of so discreet a growth that they had not brought with them any obvious change of character, and Jallands even with a bathroom was still Jallands. To the outward view, at any rate. Inside, it was more clearly Mrs Norbury's.

"Yes – Angela Norbury," murmured Bill. "Not bad-looking, is she?"

The girl who stood by the little white gate of Jallands was something more than "not bad-looking," but in this matter Bill was keeping his superlatives for another. In Bill's eyes she must be judged, and condemned, by all that distinguished her from Betty Calladine. To Antony, unhampered by these standards of comparison, she seemed, quite simply, beautiful.

"Cayley asked us to bring a letter along," explained Bill, when the necessary handshakings and introductions were over. "Here you are."

"You will tell him, won't you, how dreadfully sorry I am about what has happened? It seems so hopeless to say anything; so hopeless even to believe it. If it is true what we've heard."

Bill repeated the outline of events of yesterday.

"Yes... And Mr Ablett hasn't been found yet?" She shook her head in distress. "It still seems to have happened to somebody else; somebody we didn't know at all." Then, with a sudden grave smile which included both of them, "But you must come and have some tea."

"It's awfully decent of you," said Bill awkwardly, "but we – er – "

"You will, won't you?" she said to Antony.

"Thank you very much."

Mrs Norbury was delighted to see them, as she always was to see any man in her house who came up to the necessary standard of eligibility. When her life-work was completed, and summed up in those beautiful words: "A marriage has been arranged, and will shortly take place, between Angela, daughter of the late John Norbury..." then she would utter a grateful Nunc dimittis and depart in peace to a better world, if Heaven insisted, but preferably to her new son-in-law's more dignified establishment. For there was no doubt that eligibility meant not only eligibility as a husband.

But it was not as "eligibles" that the visitors from the Red House were received with such eagerness today, and even if her special smile for "possibles" was there, it was instinctive rather than reasoned. All that she wanted at this moment was news – news of Mark. For she was bringing it off at last; and, if the engagement columns of the "Morning Post" were preceded, as in the case of its obituary columns, by a premonitory bulletin, the announcement of yesterday would have cried triumphantly to the world, or to such part of the world as mattered: "A marriage has very nearly been arranged (by Mrs Norbury), and will certainly take place, between Angela, only daughter of the late John Norbury, and – Mark Ablett of the Red House." And, coming across it on his way to the sporting page, Bill would have been surprised. For he had thought that, if anybody, it was Cayley.

To the girl it was neither. She was often amused by her mother's ways; sometimes ashamed of them; sometimes distressed by them. The Mark Ablett affair had seemed to her particularly distressing, for Mark was so obviously in league with her mother against her. Other suitors, upon whom her mother had smiled, had been embarrassed by that championship; Mark appeared to depend on it as much as on his own attractions; great though he thought these to be. They went a-wooing together. It was a pleasure to turn to Cayley, that hopeless ineligible.

But alas! Cayley had misunderstood her. She could not imagine Cayley in love until she saw it, and tried, too late, to stop it. That was four days ago. She had not seen him since, and now here was this letter. She dreaded opening it. It was a relief to feel that at least she had an excuse for not doing so while her guests were in the house.

Mrs Norbury recognized at once that Antony was likely to be the more sympathetic listener; and when tea was over, and Bill and Angela had been dispatched to the garden with the promptness and efficiency of the expert, dear Mr Gillingham found himself on the sofa beside her, listening to many things which were of even greater interest to him than she could possibly have hoped.

"It is terrible, terrible," she said. "And to suggest that dear Mr Ablett – "

Antony made suitable noises.

"You've seen Mr Ablett for yourself. A kinder, more warmhearted man – "

Antony explained that he had not seen Mr Ablett.

"Of course, yes, I was forgetting. But, believe me, Mr Gillingham, you can trust a woman's intuition in these matters."

Antony said that he was sure of this.

"Think of my feelings as a mother."

Antony was thinking of Miss Norbury's feelings as a daughter, and wondering if she guessed that her affairs were now being discussed with a stranger. Yet what could he do? What, indeed, did he want to do except listen, in the hope of learning? Mark engaged, or about to be engaged! Had that any bearing on the events of yesterday? What, for instance, would Mrs Norbury have thought of brother Robert, that family skeleton? Was this another reason for wanting brother Robert out of the way?

"I never liked him, never!"

"Never liked?" said Antony, bewildered.

"That cousin of his, Mr Cayley."

"Oh!"

"I ask you, Mr Gillingham, am I the sort of woman to trust my little girl to a man who would go about shooting his only brother?"

"I'm sure you wouldn't, Mrs Norbury."

"If there has been any shooting done, it has been done by somebody else."

Antony looked at her inquiringly.

"I never liked him," said Mrs Norbury firmly. "Never." However, thought Antony to himself, that didn't quite prove that Cayley was a murderer.

"How did Miss Norbury get on with him?" he asked cautiously.

"There was nothing in that at all," said Miss Norbury's mother emphatically. "Nothing. I would say so to anybody."

"Oh, I beg your pardon. I never meant – "

"Nothing. I can say that for dear Angela with perfect confidence. Whether he made advances – " She broke off with a shrug of her plump shoulders.

Antony waited eagerly.

"Naturally they met. Possibly he might have – I don't know. But my duty as a mother was clear, Mr Gillingham."

Mr Gillingham made an encouraging noise.

"I told him quite frankly that – how shall I put it? – that he was trespassing. Tactfully, of course. But frankly."

"You mean," said Antony, trying to speak calmly, "that you told him that – er – Mr Ablett and your daughter – ?"

Mrs Norbury nodded several times.

"Exactly, Mr Gillingham. I had my duty as a mother."

"I am sure, Mrs Norbury, that nothing would keep you from doing your duty. But it must have been disagreeable. Particularly if you weren't quite sure – "

"He was attracted, Mr Gillingham. Obviously attracted."

"Who would not be?" said Antony, with a charming smile. "It must have been something of a shock to him to – "

"It was just that which made me so glad that I had spoken. I saw at once that I had not spoken a moment too soon."

"There must have been a certain awkwardness about the next meeting," suggested Antony.

"Naturally, he has not been here since. No doubt they would have been bound to meet up at the Red House sooner or later."

"Oh, – this was only quite lately?"

"Last week, Mr Gillingham. I spoke just in time."

"Ah!" said Antony, under his breath. He had been waiting for it.

He would have liked now to have gone away, so that he might have thought over the new situation by himself; or, perhaps preferably, to have changed partners for a little while with Bill. Miss Norbury would hardly be ready to confide in a stranger with the readiness of a mother, but he might have learnt something by listening to her. For which of them had she the greater feeling, Cayley or Mark? Was she really prepared to marry Mark? Did she love him or the other – or neither? Mrs Norbury was only a trustworthy witness in regard to her own actions and thoughts; he had learnt all that was necessary of those, and only the daughter now had anything left to tell him. But Mrs Norbury was still talking.

"Girls are so foolish, Mr Gillingham," she was saying. "It is fortunate that they have mothers to guide them. It was so obvious to me from the beginning that dear Mr Ablett was just the husband for my little girl. You never knew him?"

Antony said again that he had not seen Mr Ablett.

"Such a gentleman. So nice-looking, in his artistic way. A regular Velasquez – I should say Van Dyck. Angela would have it that she could never marry a man with a beard. As if that mattered, when – " She broke off, and Antony finished her sentence for her.

"The Red House is certainly charming," he said.

"Charming. Quite charming. And it is not as if Mr Ablett's appearance were in any way undistinguished. Quite the contrary. I'm sure you agree with me?"

Antony said that he had never had the pleasure of seeing Mr Ablett.

"Yes. And quite the centre of the literary and artistic world. So desirable in every way."

She gave a deep sigh, and communed with herself for a little. Antony was about to snatch the opportunity of leaving, when Mrs Norbury began again.

"And then there's this scapegrace brother of his. He was perfectly frank with me, Mr Gillingham. He would be. He told me of this brother, and I told him that I was quite certain it would make no difference to my daughter's feelings for him.... After all, the brother was in Australia."

"When was this? Yesterday?" Antony felt that, if Mark had only mentioned it after his brother's announcement of a personal call at the Red House, this perfect frankness had a good deal of wisdom behind it.

"It couldn't have been yesterday, Mr Gillingham. Yesterday – " she shuddered, and shook her head.

"I thought perhaps he had been down here in the morning."

"Oh, no! There is such a thing, Mr Gillingham, as being too devoted a lover. Not in the morning, no. We both agreed that dear Angela – Oh, no. No; the day before yesterday, when he happened to drop in about tea-time."

It occurred to Antony that Mrs Norbury had come a long way from her opening statement that Mark and Miss Norbury were practically engaged. She was now admitting that dear Angela was not to be rushed, that dear Angela had, indeed, no heart for the match at all.

"The day before yesterday. As it happened, dear Angela was out. Not that it mattered. He was driving to Middleston. He hardly had time for a cup of tea, so that even if she had been in – "

Antony nodded absently. This was something new. Why did Mark go to Middleston the day before yesterday? But, after all, why shouldn't he? A hundred reasons unconnected with the death of Robert might have taken him there.

He got up to go. He wanted to be alone – alone, at least, with Bill. Mrs Norbury had given him many things to think over, but the great outstanding fact which had emerged was this: that Cayley had reason to hate Mark – Mrs. Norbury had given him that reason. To hate? Well, to be jealous, anyhow. But that was enough.

"You see," he said to Bill, as they walked back, "we know that Cayley is perjuring himself and risking himself over this business, and that must be for one of two reasons. Either to save Mark or to endanger him. That is to say, he is either wholeheartedly for him or wholeheartedly against him. Well, now we know that he is against him, definitely against him."

"But, I say, you know," protested Bill, "one doesn't necessarily try to ruin one's rival in love."

"Doesn't one?" said Antony, turning to him with a smile.

Bill blushed.

"Well, of course, one never knows, but I mean – "

"You mightn't try to ruin him, Bill, but you wouldn't perjure yourself in order to get him out of a trouble of his own making."

"Lord! No."

"So that of the two alternatives the other is the more likely."

They had come to the gate into the last field which divided them from the road, and having gone through it, they turned round and leant against it, resting for a moment, and looking down at the house which they had left.

"Jolly little place, isn't it?" said Bill.

"Very. But rather mysterious."

"In what way?"

"Well, where's the front door?"

"The front door? Why, you've just come out of it."

"But isn't there a drive, or a road or anything?"

Bill laughed.

"No; that's the beauty of it to some people. And that's why it's so cheap, and why the Norburys can afford it, I expect. They're not too well off."

"But what about luggage and tradesmen and that kind of thing?"

"Oh, there's a cart-track, but motor-cars can't come any nearer than the road," he turned round and pointed, "up there. So the weekend millionaire people don't take it. At least, they'd have to build a road and a garage and all the rest of it, if they did."

"I see," said Antony carelessly, and they turned round and continued their walk up to the road. But later on he remembered this casual conversation at the gate, and saw the importance of it.

16

GETTING READY FOR THE NIGHT

What was it which Cayley was going to hide in that pond that night? Antony thought that he knew now. It was Mark's body.

From the beginning he had seen this answer coming and had drawn back from it. For, if Mark had been killed, it seemed such a cold-blooded killing. Was Cayley equal to it? Bill would have said "No," but that was because he had had breakfast with Cayley, and lunch with him, and dinner with him; had ragged him and played games with him. Bill would have said "No," because Bill wouldn't have killed anybody in cold blood himself, and because he took it for granted that other people behaved pretty much as he did. But Antony had no such illusions. Murders were done; murder had actually been done here, for there was Robert's dead body. Why not another murder?

Had Mark been in the office at all that afternoon? The only evidence (other than Cayley's, which obviously did not count) was Elsie's. Elsie was quite certain that she had heard his voice. But then Bill had said that it was a very characteristic voice – an easy voice, therefore, to imitate. If Bill could imitate it so successfully, why not Cayley?

But perhaps it had not been such a cold-blooded killing, after all. Suppose Cayley had had a quarrel with his cousin that afternoon over the girl whom they were both wooing. Suppose Cayley had killed Mark, either purposely, in sudden passion, or accidentally, meaning only to knock him down. Suppose that this had happened in the passage, say about two o'clock, either because Cayley had deliberately led him there, or because Mark had casually suggested a visit to it. (One could imagine Mark continually gloating over that secret passage.) Suppose Cayley there, with the body at his feet, feeling already the rope round his neck; his mind darting this way and that in frantic search for a way of escape; and suppose that suddenly and irrelevantly he remembers that Robert is coming to the house at three o'clock that afternoon – automatically he looks at his watch – in half an hour's time... In half an hour's time. He must think of something quickly, quickly. Shall he bury the body in the passage and let it be thought that Mark ran away, frightened at the mere thought of his brother's arrival? But there was the evidence of the breakfast table. Mark had seemed annoyed at this resurrection of the black sheep, but certainly not frightened. No; that was much too thin a story. But suppose Mark had actually seen his brother and had a quarrel with him; suppose it could be made to look as if Robert had killed Mark –

Antony pictured to himself Cayley in the passage, standing over the dead body of his cousin, and working it out. How could Robert be made to seem the murderer, if Robert were alive to deny it? But suppose Robert were dead, too?

He looks at his watch again. (Only twenty-five minutes now.) Suppose Robert were dead, too? Robert dead in the office, and Mark dead in the passage, how does that help? Madness! But if the bodies were brought together somehow and Robert's death looked like suicide? Was it possible?

Madness again. Too difficult. (Only twenty minutes now.) Too difficult to arrange in twenty minutes. Can't arrange a suicide. Too difficult... Only nineteen minutes...

And then the sudden inspiration! Robert dead in the office, Mark's body hidden in the passage – impossible to make Robert seem the murderer, but how easy to make Mark! Robert dead and Mark missing; why, it jumped to the eye at once. Mark had killed Robert – accidentally; yes, that would be more likely – and then had run away. Sudden panic... (He looks at his watch again. Fifteen minutes, but plenty of time now. The thing arranges itself.)

Was that the solution, Antony wondered. It seemed to fit in with the facts as they knew them; but then, so did that other theory which he had suggested to Bill in the morning.

"Which one?" said Bill.

They had come back from Jallands through the park and were sitting in the copse above the pond, from which the Inspector and his fishermen had now withdrawn. Bill had listened with open mouth to Antony's theory, and save for an occasional "By Jove!" had listened in silence. "Smart man, Cayley," had been his only comment at the end.

"Which other theory?"

"That Mark had killed Robert accidentally and had gone to Cayley for help, and that Cayley, having hidden him in the passage, locked the office door from the outside and hammered on it."

"Yes, but you were so dashed mysterious about that. I asked you what the point of it was, and you wouldn't say anything." He thought for a little, and then went on, "I suppose you meant that Cayley deliberately betrayed Mark, and tried to make him look like a murderer?"

"I wanted to warn you that we should probably find Mark in the passage, alive or dead."

"And now you don't think so?"

"Now I think that his dead body is there."

"Meaning that Cayley went down and killed him afterwards – after you had come, after the police had come?"

"Well, that's what I shrink from, Bill. It's so horribly cold-blooded. Cayley may be capable of it, but I hate to think of it."

"But, dash it all, your other way is cold-blooded enough. According to you, he goes up to the office and deliberately shoots a man with whom he has no quarrel, whom he hasn't seen for fifteen years!"

"Yes, but to save his own neck. That makes a difference. My theory is that he quarrelled violently with Mark over the girl, and killed him in sudden passion. Anything that happened after that would be self-defence. I don't mean that I excuse it, but that I understand it. And I think that Mark's dead body is in the passage now, and has been there since, say, half-past two yesterday afternoon. And tonight Cayley is going to hide it in the pond."

Bill pulled at the moss on the ground beside him, threw away a handful or two, and said slowly, "You may be right, but it's all guesswork, you know."

Antony laughed.

"Good Lord, of course it is," he said. "And tonight we shall know if it's a good guess or a bad one."

Bill brightened up suddenly.

"Tonight," he said. "I say, tonight's going to be rather fun. How do we work it?"

Antony was silent for a little.

"Of course," he said at last, "we ought to inform the police, so that they can come here and watch the pond tonight."

"Of course," grinned Bill.

"But I think that perhaps it is a little early to put our theories before them."

"I think perhaps it is," said Bill solemnly.

Antony looked up at him with a sudden smile.

"Bill, you old bounder."

"Well, dash it, it's our show. I don't see why we shouldn't get our little bit of fun out of it."

"Neither do I. All right, then, we'll do without the police tonight."

"We shall miss them," said Bill sadly, "but 'tis better so."

There were two problems in front of them: first, the problem of getting out of the house without being discovered by Cayley, and secondly, the problem of recovering whatever it was which Cayley dropped into the pond that night.

"Let's look at it from Cayley's point of view," said Antony. "He may not know that we're on his track, but he can't help being suspicious of us. He's bound to be suspicious of everybody in the house, and more particularly of us, because we're presumably more intelligent than the others."

He stopped for a moment to light his pipe, and Bill took the opportunity of looking more intelligent than Mrs Stevens.

"Now, he has got something to hide tonight, and he's going to take good care that we aren't watching him. Well, what will he do?"

"See that we are asleep first, before he starts out."

"Yes. Come and tuck us up, and see that we're nice and comfortable."

"Yes, that's awkward," said Bill. "But we could lock our doors, and then he wouldn't know that we weren't there."

"Have you ever locked your door?"

"Never."

"No. And you can bet that Cayley knows that. Anyway, he'd bang on it, and you wouldn't answer, and then what would he think?"

Bill was silent; crushed.

"Then I don't see how we're going to do it," he said, after deep thought. "He'll obviously come to us just before he starts out, and that doesn't give us time to get to the pond in front of him."

"Let's put ourselves in his place," said Antony, puffing slowly at his pipe. "He's got the body, or whatever it is, in the passage. He won't come up the stairs, carrying it in his arms, and look in at our doors to see if we're awake. He'll have to make sure about us first, and then go down for the body afterwards. So that gives us a little time."

"Y-yes," said Bill doubtfully. "We might just do it, but it'll be a bit of a rush."

"But wait. When he's gone down to the passage and got the body, what will he do next?"

"Come out again," said Bill helpfully.

"Yes; but which end?"

Bill sat up with a start.

"By Jove, you mean that he will go out at the far end by the bowling-green?"

"Don't you think so? Just imagine him walking across the lawn in full view of the house, at midnight, with a body in his arms. Think of the awful feeling he would have in the back of the neck, wondering if anybody, any restless sleeper, had chosen just that moment to wander to the window and look out into the night. There's still plenty of moonlight, Bill. Is he going to walk across the park in the moonlight, with all those windows staring at him? Not if he can help it. But he can get out by the bowling green, and then come to the pond without ever being in sight of the house, at all."

"You're right. And that will just about give us time. Good. Now, what's the next thing?"

"The next thing is to mark the exact place in the pond where he drops whatever he drops."

"So that we can fish it out again."

"If we can see what it is, we shan't want to. The police can have a go at it tomorrow. But if it's something we can't identify from a distance, then we must try and get it out. To see whether it's worth telling the police about."

"Y-yes," said Bill, wrinkling his forehead. "Of course, the trouble with water is that one bit of it looks pretty much like the next bit. I don't know if that had occurred to you.

"It had," smiled Antony. "Let's come and have a look at it."

They walked to the edge of the copse, and lay down there in silence, looking at the pond beneath them.

"See anything?" said Antony at last.

"What?"

"The fence on the other side."

"What about it?"

"Well, it's rather useful, that's all."

"Said Sherlock Holmes enigmatically," added Bill. "A moment later, his friend Watson had hurled him into the pond."

Antony laughed.

"I love being Sherlocky," he said. "It's very unfair of you not to play up to me."

"Why is that fence useful, my dear Holmes?" said Bill obediently.

"Because you can take a bearing on it. You see – "

"Yes, you needn't stop to explain to me what a bearing is."

"I wasn't going to. But you're lying here" – he looked up – "underneath this pine tree. Cayley comes out in the old boat and drops his parcel in. You take a line from here on to the boat, and mark it off on the fence there. Say it's the fifth post from the end. Well, then I take a line from my tree – we'll find one for me directly – and it comes on to the twentieth post, say. And where the two lines meet, there shall the eagles be gathered together. Q.E.D. And there, I almost forgot to remark, will the taller eagle, Beverley by name, do his famous diving act. As performed nightly at the Hippodrome."

Bill looked at him uneasily.

"I say, really? It's beastly dirty water, you know."

"I'm afraid so, Bill. So it is written in the book of Jasher."

"Of course I knew that one of us would have to, but I hoped... well, it's a warm night."

"Just the night for a bathe," agreed Antony, getting up. "Well now, let's have a look for my tree."

They walked down to the margin of the pond and then looked back. Bill's tree stood up and took the evening, tall and unmistakable, fifty feet nearer to heaven than its neighbours. But it had its fellow at the other end of the copse, not quite so tall, perhaps, but equally conspicuous.

"That's where I shall be," said Antony, pointing to it. "Now, for the Lord's sake, count your posts accurately."

"Thanks very much, but I shall do it for my own sake," said Bill with feeling. "I don't want to spend the whole night diving."

"Fix on the post in a straight line with you and the splash, and then count backwards to the beginning of the fence."

"Right, old boy. Leave it to me. I can do this on my head."

"Well, that's how you will have to do the last part of it," said Antony with a smile.

He looked at his watch. It was nearly time to change for dinner. They started to walk back to the house together.

"There's one thing which worries me rather," said Antony. "Where does Cayley sleep?"

"Next door to me. Why?"

"Well, it's just possible that he might have another look at you after he's come back from the pond. I don't think he'd bother about it in the ordinary way, but if he is actually passing your door, I think he might glance in."

"I shan't be there. I shall be at the bottom of the pond, sucking up mud."

"Yes... Do you think you could leave something in your bed that looked vaguely like you in the dark? A bolster with a pyjama-coat round it, and one arm outside the blanket, and a pair of socks or something for the head. You know the kind of thing. I think it would please him to feel that you were still sleeping peacefully."

Bill chuckled to himself.

"Rather. I'm awfully good at that. I'll make him up something really good. But what about you?"

"I'm at the other end of the house; he's hardly likely to bother about me a second time. And I shall be so very fast asleep at his first visit. Still, I may as well to be on the safe side."

They went into the house. Cayley was in the hall as they came in. He nodded, and took out his watch.

"Time to change?" he said.

"Just about," said Bill.

"You didn't forget my letter?"

"I did not. In fact, we had tea there."

"Ah!" He looked away and said carelessly, "How were they all?"

"They sent all sorts of sympathetic messages to you, and – and all that sort of thing."

"Oh, yes."

Bill waited for him to say something more, and then, as nothing was coming, he turned round, said, "Come on, Tony," and led the way upstairs.

"Got all you want?" he said at the top of the stairs.

"I think so. Come and see me before you go down."

"Righto."

Antony shut his bedroom door behind him and walked over to the window. He pushed open a casement and looked out. His bedroom was just over the door at the back of the house. The side wall of the office, which projected out into the lawn beyond the rest of the house, was on his left. He could step out on to the top of the door, and from there drop easily to the ground. Getting back would be little more difficult. There was a convenient water-pipe which would help.

He had just finished his dressing when Bill came in. "Final instructions?" he asked, sitting down on the bed. "By the way, how are we amusing ourselves after dinner? I mean immediately after dinner."

"Billiards?"

"Righto. Anything you like."

"Don't talk too loud," said Antony in a lower voice. "We're more or less over the hall, and Cayley may be there." He led the way to the window. "We'll go out this way tonight. Going downstairs is too risky. It's easy enough; better put on tennis-shoes."

"Right. I say, in case I don't get another chance alone with you, what do I do when Cayley comes to tuck me up?"

"It's difficult to say. Be as natural as you can. I mean, if he just knocks lightly and looks in, be asleep. Don't overdo the snoring. But if he makes a hell of a noise, you'll have to wake up and rub your eyes, and wonder what on earth he's doing in your room at all. You know the sort of thing."

"Right. And about the dummy figure. I'll make it up directly we come upstairs, and hide it under the bed."

"Yes... I think we'd better go completely to bed ourselves. We shan't take a moment dressing again, and it will give him time to get safely into the passage. Then come into my room."

"Right... Are you ready?"

"Yes."

They went downstairs together.

17

MR BEVERLEY TAKES THE WATER

Cayley seemed very fond of them that night. After dinner was over, he suggested a stroll outside. They walked up and down the gravel in front of the house, saying very little to each other, until Bill could stand it no longer. For the last twenty turns he had been slowing down hopefully each time they came to the door, but the hint had always been lost on his companions, and each time another turn had been taken. But in the end he had been firm.

"What about a little billiards?" he said, shaking himself free from the others.

"Will you play?" said Antony to Cayley.

"I'll watch you," he said, and he had watched them resolutely until the game, and then another game after that, had been played.

They went into the hall and attacked the drinks.

"Well, thank heaven for bed," said Bill; putting down his glass. "Are you coming?"

"Yes," said Antony, and finished his drink. He looked at Cayley.

"I've just got one or two little things to do," said Cayley. "I shan't be long following you."

"Well, good night, then."

"Good night."

"Good night," called Bill from half-way up the stairs. "Good night, Tony."

"Good night."

Bill looked at his watch. Half-past eleven. Not much chance of anything happening for another hour. He pulled open a drawer and wondered what to wear on their expedition. Grey flannel trousers, flannel shirt, and a dark coat; perhaps a sweater, as they might be lying out in the copse for some time. And good idea a towel. He would want it later on, and meanwhile he could wear it round his waist.

Tennis-shoes... There. Everything was ready. Now then for the dummy figure.

He looked at his watch again before getting into bed. Twelve-fifteen. How long to wait before Cayley came up? He turned out the light, and then, standing by the door in his pyjamas, waited for his eyes to become accustomed to the new darkness... He could only just make out the bed in the corner of the room. Cayley would want more light than that if he were to satisfy himself from the door that the bed was occupied. He pulled the curtains a little way back. That was about right. He could have another look later on, when he had the dummy figure in the bed.

How long would it be before Cayley came up? It wasn't that he wanted his friends, Beverley and Gillingham, to be asleep before he started on his business at the pond; all that he wanted was to be sure that they were safely in their bedrooms. Cayley's business would make no noise, give no sign, to attract the most wakeful member of the household, so long as the household was really inside the house. But if he wished to reassure himself about his guests, he would have to wait until they were far enough on their way to sleep not to be disturbed by him as he came up to reassure himself. So it amounted to the same thing, really. He would wait until they were asleep... until they were asleep... asleep...

With a great effort Bill regained the mastery over his wandering thoughts and came awake again. This would never do. It would be fatal if he went to sleep... if he went to sleep... to sleep... And then, in an instant, he was intensely awake. Suppose Cayley never came at all!

Suppose Cayley was so unsuspicious that, as soon as they had gone upstairs, he had dived down into the passage and set about his business. Suppose, even now, he was at the pond, dropping into it that secret of his. Good heavens, what fools they had been! How could Antony have taken such a risk? Put yourself in Cayley's place, he had said. But how was it possible? They weren't Cayley. Cayley was at the pond now. They would never know what he had dropped into it.

Listen!... Somebody at the door. He was asleep. Quite naturally now. Breathe a little more loudly, perhaps. He was asleep... The door was opening. He could feel it opening behind him... Good Lord, suppose Cayley really was a murderer! Why, even now he might be – no, he mustn't think of that. If he thought of that, he would have to turn round. He mustn't turn round. He was asleep; just peacefully asleep. But why didn't the door shut? Where was Cayley now? Just behind him? And in his hand... No, he mustn't think of that. He was asleep. But why didn't the door shut?

The door was shutting. There was a sigh from the sleeper in the bed, a sigh of relief which escaped him involuntarily. But it had a very natural sound – a deep breath from a heavy sleeper. He added another one to it to make it seem more natural. The door was shut.

Bill counted a hundred slowly and then got up. As quickly and as noiselessly as possible he dressed himself in the dark. He put the dummy figure in the bed, arranged the clothes so that just enough but not too much of it was showing, and stood by the door looking at it. For a casual glance the room was just about light enough. Then very quietly, very slowly he opened the door. All was still. There was no light from beneath the door of Cayley's room. Very quietly, very carefully he crept along the passage to Antony's room. He opened the door and went in.

Antony was still in bed. Bill walked across to wake him up, and then stopped rigid, and his heart thumped against his ribs. There was somebody else in the room.

"All right, Bill," said a whispering voice, and Antony stepped out from the curtains.

Bill gazed at him without saying anything.

"Rather good, isn't it?" said Antony, coming closer and pointing to the bed. "Come on; the sooner we get out now, the better."

He led the way out of the window, the silent Bill following him. They reached the ground safely and noiselessly, went quickly across the lawn and so, over the fence, into the park. It was not until they were out of sight of the house that Bill felt it safe to speak.

"I quite thought it was you in bed," he said.

"I hoped you would. I shall be rather disappointed now if Cayley doesn't call again. It's a pity to waste it."

"He came all right just now?"

"Oh, rather. What about you?"

Bill explained his feelings picturesquely.

"There wouldn't have been much point in his killing you," said Antony prosaically. "Besides being too risky."

"Oh!" said Bill. And then, "I had rather hoped that it was his love for me which restrained him."

Antony laughed.

"I doubt it... You didn't turn up your light when you dressed?"

"Good Lord, no. Did you want me to?"

Antony laughed again and took him by the arm.

"You're a splendid conspirator, Bill. You and I could take on anything together."

The pond was waiting for them, more solemn in the moonlight. The trees which crowned the sloping bank on the far side of it were mysteriously silent. It seemed that they had the world very much to themselves.

Almost unconsciously Antony spoke in a whisper.

"There's your tree, there's mine. As long as you don't move, there's no chance of his seeing you. After he's gone, don't come out till I do. He won't be here for a quarter of an hour or so, so don't be impatient."

"Righto," whispered Bill.

Antony gave him a nod and a smile, and they walked off to their posts.

The minutes went by slowly. To Antony, lying hidden in the undergrowth at the foot of his tree, a new problem was presenting itself. Suppose Cayley had to make more than one journey that night? He might come back to find them in the boat; one of them, indeed, in the water. And if they decided to wait in hiding, on the chance of Cayley coming back again, what was the least time they could safely allow? Perhaps it would be better to go round to the front of the house and watch for his return there, the light in his bedroom, before conducting their experiments at the pond. But then they might miss his second visit in this way, if he made a second visit. It was difficult.

His eyes were fixed on the boat as he considered these things, and suddenly, as if materialized from nowhere, Cayley was standing by the boat. In his hand was a small brown bag.

Cayley put the bag in the bottom of the boat, stepped in, and using an oar as a punt-pole, pushed slowly off. Then, very silently, he rowed towards the middle of the pond.

He had stopped. The oars rested on the water. He picked up the bag from between his feet, leant over the nose of the boat, and rested it lightly on the water for a moment. Then he let go. It sank slowly. He waited there, watching; afraid, perhaps, that it might rise again. Antony began to count...

And now Cayley was back at his starting-place. He tied up the boat, looked carefully round to see that he had left no traces behind him, and then turned to the water again. For a long time, as it seemed to the watchers, he stood there, very big, very silent, in the moonlight. At last he seemed satisfied. Whatever his secret was, he had hidden it; and so with a gentle sigh, as unmistakable to Antony as if he had heard it, Cayley turned away and vanished again as quietly as he had come.

Antony gave him three minutes, and stepped out from the trees. He waited there for Bill to join him.

"Six," whispered Bill.

Antony nodded.

"I'm going round to the front of the house. You get back to your tree and watch, in case Cayley comes again. Your bedroom is the left-hand end one, and Cayley's the end but one? Is that right?"

Bill nodded.

"Right. Wait in hiding till I come back. I don't know how long I shall be, but don't be impatient. It will seem longer than it is." He patted Bill on the shoulder, and with a smile and a nod of the head he left him there.

What was in the bag? What could Cayley want to hide other than a key or a revolver? Keys and revolvers sink of themselves; no need to put them in a bag first. What was in the bag? Something which wouldn't sink of itself; something which needed to be helped with stones before it would hide itself safely in the mud.

Well, they would find that out. There was no object in worrying about it now. Bill had a dirty night's work in front of him. But where was the body which Antony had expected so confidently or, if there were no body, where was Mark?

More immediately, however, where was Cayley? As quickly as he could Antony had got to the front of the house and was now lying in the shrubbery which bordered the lawn, waiting for the light to go up in Cayley's window. If it went up in Bill's window, then they were discovered. It would mean that Cayley had glanced into Bill's room, had been suspicious of the dummy figure in the bed, and had turned up the light to make sure. After that, it was war between them. But if it went up in Cayley's room –

There was a light. Antony felt a sudden thrill of excitement. It was in Bill's room. War!

The light stayed there, shining vividly, for a wind had come up, blowing the moon behind a cloud, and casting a shadow over the rest of the house. Bill had left his curtains undrawn. It was careless of him; the first stupid thing he had done, but –

The moon slipped out again... and Antony laughed to himself in the bushes. There was another window beyond Cayley's, and there was no light in it. The declaration of war was postponed.

Antony lay there, watching Cayley into bed. After all it was only polite to return Cayley's own solicitude earlier in the night. Politeness demanded that one should not disport oneself on the pond until one's friends were comfortably tucked up.

Meanwhile Bill was getting tired of waiting. His chief fear was that he might spoil everything by forgetting the number "six." It was the sixth post. Six. He broke off a twig and divided it into six pieces. These he arranged on the ground in front of him. Six. He looked at the pond, counted up to the sixth post, and murmured "six" to himself again. Then he looked down at his twigs. One-two-three-four-five-six-seven. Seven! Was it seven? Or was that seventh bit of a twig an accidental bit which had been on the ground anyhow? Surely it was six! Had he said "six" to Antony? If so, Antony would remember, and it was all right. Six. He threw away the seventh twig and collected the other six together. Perhaps they would be safer in his pocket. Six. The height of a tall man – well, his own height. Six feet. Yes, that was the way to remember it. Feeling a little safer on the point, he began to wonder about the bag, and what Antony would say to it, and the possible depth of the water and of the mud at the bottom; and was still so wondering, and saying, "Good Lord, what a life!" to himself, when Antony reappeared.

Bill got up and came down the slope to meet him.

"Six," he said firmly. "Sixth post from the end."

"Good," smiled Antony. "Mine was the eighteenth – a little way past it."

"What did you go off for?"

"To see Cayley into bed."

"Is it all right?"

"Yes. Better hang your coat over the sixth post, and then we shall see it more easily. I'll put mine on the eighteenth. Are you going to undress here or in the boat?"

"Some here, and some in the boat. You're quite sure that you wouldn't like to do the diving yourself?"

"Quite, thanks."

They had walked round to the other side of the pond. Coming to the sixth post of the fence, Bill took off his coat and put it in position, and then finished his undressing, while Antony went off to mark the eighteenth post. When they were ready, they got into the boat, Antony taking the oars.

"Now, Bill, tell me as soon as I'm in a line with your two marks."

He rowed slowly towards the middle of the pond.

"You're about there now," said Bill at last.

Antony stopped rowing and looked about him.

"Yes, that's pretty well right." He turned the boat's nose round until it was pointing to the pine tree under which Bill had lain. "You see my tree and the other coat?"

"Yes," said Bill.

"Right. Now then, I'm going to row gently along this line until we're dead in between the two. Get it as exact as you can – for your own sake."

"Steady!" said Bill warningly. "Back a little.... a little more .... a little more forward again.... Right." Antony left the oars on the water and looked around. As far as he could tell, they were in an exact line with each pair of landmarks.

"Now then, Bill, in you go."

Bill pulled off his shirt and trousers, and stood up.

"You mustn't dive from the boat, old boy," said Antony hastily. "You'll shift its position. Slide in gently."

Bill slid in from the stern and swam slowly round to Antony.

"What's it like?" said Antony.

"Cold. Well, here's luck to it."

He gave a sudden kick, flashed for a moment in the water, and was gone. Antony steadied the boat, and took another look at his landmarks.

Bill came up behind him with a loud explosion. "It's pretty muddy," he protested.

"Weeds?"

"No, thank the Lord."

"Well, try again."

Bill gave another kick and disappeared. Again Antony coaxed the boat back into position, and again Bill popped up, this time in front of him.

"I feel that if I threw you a sardine," said Antony, with a smile, "you'd catch it in your mouth quite prettily."

"It's awfully easy to be funny from where you are. How much longer have I got to go on doing this?"

Antony looked at his watch.

"About three hours. We must get back before daylight. But be quicker if you can, because it's rather cold for me sitting here."

Bill flicked a handful of water at him and disappeared again. He was under for almost a minute this time, and there was a grin on his face when it was visible again.

"I've got it, but it's devilish hard to get up. I'm not sure that it isn't too heavy for me."

"That's all right," said Antony. He brought out a ball of thick string from his pocket. "Get this through the handle if you can, and then we can both pull."

"Good man." He paddled to the side, took one end of the string and paddled back again. "Now then."

Two minutes later the bag was safely in the boat. Bill clambered in after it, and Antony rowed back. "Well done, Watson," he said quietly, as they landed. He fetched their two coats, and then waited, the bag in his hand, while Bill dried and dressed himself. As soon as the latter was ready, he took his arm and led him into the copse. He put the bag down and felt in his pockets.

"I shall light a pipe before I open it," he said. "What about you?"

"Yes."

With great care they filled and lit their pipes. Bill's hand was a little unsteady. Antony noticed it and gave him a reassuring smile.

"Ready?"

"Yes."

They sat down, and taking the bag between his knees, Antony pressed the catch and opened it.

"Clothes!" said Bill.

Antony pulled out the top garment and shook it out. It was a wet brown flannel coat.

"Do you recognize it?" he asked.

"Mark's brown flannel suit."

"The one he is advertised as having run away in?"

"Yes. It looks like it. Of course he had a dashed lot of clothes."

Antony put his hand in the breast-pocket and took out some letters. He considered them doubtfully for a moment.

"I suppose I'd better read them," he said. "I mean, just to see – " He looked inquiringly at Bill, who nodded. Antony turned on his torch and glanced at them. Bill waited anxiously.

"Yes. Mark.... Hallo!"

"What is it?"

"The letter that Cayley was telling the Inspector about. From Robert. 'Mark, your loving brother is coming to see you – ' Yes, I suppose I had better keep this. Well, that's his coat. Let's have out the rest of it." He took the remaining clothes from the bag and spread them out.

"They're all here," said Bill. "Shirt, tie, socks, underclothes, shoes – yes, all of them."

"All that he was wearing yesterday?"

"Yes."

"What do you make of it?"

Bill shook his head, and asked another question.

"Is it what you expected?"

Antony laughed suddenly.

"It's too absurd," he said. "I expected – well, you know what I expected. A body. A body in a suit of clothes. Well, perhaps it would be safer to hide them separately. The body here, and the clothes in the passage, where they would never betray themselves. And now he takes a great deal of trouble to hide the clothes here, and doesn't bother about the body at all." He shook his head. "I'm a bit lost for the moment, Bill, and that's the fact."

"Anything else there?"

Antony felt in the bag.

"Stones and – yes, there's something else." He took it out and held it up. "There we are, Bill."

It was the office key.

"By Jove, you were right."

Antony felt in the bag again, and then turned it gently upside down on the grass. A dozen large stones fell out – and something else. He flashed down his torch.

"Another key," he said.

He put the two keys in his pocket, and sat there for a long time in silence, thinking. Bill was silent, too, not liking to interrupt his thoughts, but at last he said:

"Shall I put these things back?"

Antony looked up with a start.

"What? Oh, yes. No, I'll put them back. You give me a light, will you?"

Very slowly and carefully he put the clothes back in the bag, pausing as he took up each garment, in the certainty, as it seemed to Bill, that it had something to tell him if only he could read it. When the last of them was inside, he still waited there on his knees, thinking.

"That's the lot," said Bill.

Antony nodded at him.

"Yes, that's the lot," he said, "and that's the funny thing about it. You're sure it is the lot?"

"What do you mean?"

"Give me the torch a moment." He took it and flashed it over the ground between them. "Yes, that's the lot. It's funny." He stood up, the bag in his hands. "Now let's find a hiding-place for these, and then – " He said no more, but stepped off through the trees, Bill following him meekly.

As soon as they had got the bag off their hands and were clear of the copse, Antony became more communicative. He took the two keys out of his pocket.

"One of them is the office key, I suppose, and the other is the key of the passage cupboard. So I thought that perhaps we might have a look at the cupboard."

"I say, do you really think it is?"

"Well, I don't see what else it can be."

"But why should he want to throw it away?"

"Because it has now done its work, whatever it was, and he wants to wash his hands of the passage. He'd throw the passage away if he could. I don't think it matters much one way or another, and I don't suppose there's anything to find in the cupboard, but I feel that we must look."

"Do you still think Mark's body might be there?"

"No. And yet where else can it be? Unless I'm hopelessly wrong, and Cayley never killed him at all."

Bill hesitated, wondering if he dare advance his theory.

"I know you'll think me an ass – "

"My dear Bill, I'm such an obvious ass myself that I should be delighted to think you are too."

"Well, then, suppose Mark did kill Robert, and Cayley helped him to escape, just as we thought at first. I know you proved afterwards that it was impossible, but suppose it happened in a way we don't know about and for reasons we don't know about. I mean, there are such a lot of funny things about the whole show that – well, almost anything might have happened."

"You're quite right. Well?"

"Well, then, this clothes business. Doesn't that seem rather to bear out the escaping theory? Mark's brown suit was known to the police. Couldn't Cayley have brought him another one in the passage, to escape in, and then have had the brown one on his hands? And thought it safest to hide it in the pond?"

"Yes," said Anthony thoughtfully. Then: "Go on."

Bill went on eagerly:

"It all seems to fit in, you know. I mean even with your first theory – that Mark killed him accidentally and then came to Cayley for help. Of course, if Cayley had played fair, he'd have told Mark that he had nothing to be afraid of. But he isn't playing fair; he wants to get Mark out of the way because of the girl. Well, this is his chance. He makes Mark as frightened as possible, and tells him that his only hope is to run away. Well, naturally, he does all he can to get him well away, because if Mark is caught, the whole story of Cayley's treachery comes out."

"Yes. But isn't it overdoing it rather to make him change his underclothes and everything? It wastes a good deal of time, you know."

Bill was pulled up short, and said, "Oh!" in great disappointment.

"No, it's not as bad as that, Bill," said Antony with a smile. "I daresay the underclothes could be explained. But here's the difficulty. Why did Mark need to change from brown to blue, or whatever it was, when Cayley was the only person who saw him in brown?"

"The police description of him says that he is in a brown suit."

"Yes, because Cayley told the police. You see, even if Mark had had lunch in his brown suit, and the servants had noticed it, Cayley could always have pretended that he had changed into blue after lunch, because only Cayley saw him afterwards. So if Cayley had told the Inspector that he was wearing blue, Mark could have escaped quite comfortably in his brown, without needing to change at all."

"But that's just what he did do," cried Bill triumphantly. "What fools we are!"

Antony looked at him in surprise, and then shook his head.

"Yes, yes!" insisted Bill. "Of course! Don't you see? Mark did change after lunch, and, to give him more of a chance of getting away, Cayley lied and said that he was wearing the brown suit in which the servants had seen him. Well, then he was afraid that the police might examine Mark's clothes and find the brown suit still there, so he hid it, and then dropped it in the pond afterwards."

He turned eagerly to his friend, but Antony said nothing. Bill began to speak again, and was promptly waved into silence.

"Don't say anything more, old boy; you've given me quite enough to think about. Don't let's bother about it tonight. We'll just have a look at this cupboard and then get to bed."

But the cupboard had not much to tell them that night. It was empty save for a few old bottles.

"Well, that's that," said Bill.

But Antony, on his knees with the torch in his hand, continued to search for something.

"What are you looking for?" asked Bill at last.

"Something that isn't there," said Antony, getting up and dusting his trousers. And he locked the door again.

18

GUESSWORK

The inquest was at three o'clock; thereafter Antony could have no claim on the hospitality of the Red House. By ten o'clock his bag was packed, and waiting to be taken to 'The George.' To Bill, coming upstairs after a more prolonged breakfast, this early morning bustle was a little surprising.

"What's the hurry?" he asked.

"None. But we don't want to come back here after the inquest. Get your packing over now and then we can have the morning to ourselves."

"Righto." He turned to go to his room, and then came back again. "I say, are we going to tell Cayley that we're staying at 'The George'?"

"You're not staying at 'The George,' Bill. Not officially. You're going back to London."

"Oh!"

"Yes. Ask Cayley to have your luggage sent in to Stanton, ready for you when you catch a train there after the inquest. You can tell him that you've got to see the Bishop of London at once. The fact that you are hurrying back to London to be confirmed will make it seem more natural that I should resume my interrupted solitude at 'The George' as soon as you have gone."

"Then where do I sleep tonight?"

"Officially, I suppose, in Fulham Place; unofficially, I suspect, in my bed, unless they've got another spare room at 'The George.' I've put your confirmation robe – I mean your pyjamas and brushes and things – in my bag, ready for you. Is there anything else you want to know? No? Then go and pack. And meet me at ten-thirty beneath the blasted oak or in the hall or somewhere. I want to talk and talk and talk, and I must have my Watson."

"Good," said Bill, and went off to his room.

An hour later, having communicated their official plans to Cayley, they wandered out together into the park.

"Well?" said Bill, as they sat down underneath a convenient tree. "Talk away."

"I had many bright thoughts in my bath this morning," began Antony. "The brightest one of all was that we were being damn fools, and working at this thing from the wrong end altogether."

"Well, that's helpful."

"Of course it's very hampering being a detective, when you don't know anything about detecting, and when nobody knows that you're doing detection, and you can't have people up to cross-examine them, and you have neither the energy nor the means to make proper inquiries; and, in short, when you're doing the whole thing in a thoroughly amateur, haphazard way."

"For amateurs I don't think we're doing at all badly," protested Bill.

"No; not for amateurs. But if we had been professionals, I believe we should have gone at it from the other end. The Robert end. We've been wondering about Mark and Cayley all the time. Now let's wonder about Robert for a bit."

"We know so little about him."

"Well, let's see what we do know. First of all, then, we know vaguely that he was a bad lot – the sort of brother who is hushed up in front of other people."

"Yes."

"We know that he announced his approaching arrival to Mark in a rather unpleasant letter, which I have in my pocket."

"Yes."

"And then we know rather a curious thing. We know that Mark told you all that this black sheep was coming. Now, why did he tell you?"

Bill was thoughtful for a moment.

"I suppose," he said slowly, "that he knew we were bound to see him, and thought that the best way was to be quite frank about him."

"But were you bound to see him? You were all away playing golf."

"We were bound to see him if he stayed in the house that night."

"Very well, then. That's one thing we've discovered. Mark knew that Robert was staying in the house that night. Or shall we put it this way – he knew that there was no chance of getting Robert out of the house at once."

Bill looked at his friend eagerly.

"Go on," he said. "This is getting interesting."

"He also knew something else," went on Antony. "He knew that Robert was bound to betray his real character to you as soon as you met him. He couldn't pass him off on you as just a travelled brother from the Dominions, with perhaps a bit of an accent; he had to tell you at once, because you were bound to find out, that Robert was a wastrel."

"Yes. That's sound enough."

"Well, now, doesn't it strike you that Mark made up his mind about all that rather quickly?"

"How do you mean?"

"He got this letter at breakfast. He read it; and directly he had read it he began to confide in you all. That is to say, in about one second he thought out the whole business and came to a decision – to two decisions. He considered the possibility of getting Robert out of the way before you came back, and decided that it was impossible. He considered the possibility of Robert's behaving like an ordinary decent person in public, and decided that it was very unlikely. He came to those two decisions instantaneously, as he was reading the letter. Isn't that rather quick work?"

"Well, what's the explanation?"

Antony waited until he had refilled and lighted his pipe before answering.

"What's the explanation? Well, let's leave it for a moment and take another look at the two brothers. In conjunction, this time, with Mrs Norbury."

"Mrs Norbury?" said Bill, surprised.

"Yes. Mark hoped to marry Miss Norbury. Now, if Robert really was a blot upon the family honour, Mark would want to do one of two things. Either keep it from the Norburys altogether, or else, if it had to come out, tell them himself before the news came to them indirectly. Well, he told them. But the funny thing is that he told them the day before Robert's letter came. Robert came, and was killed, the day before yesterday – Tuesday. Mark told Mrs Norbury about him on Monday. What do you make of that?"

"Coincidence," said Bill, after careful thought. "He'd always meant to tell her; his suit was prospering, and just before it was finally settled, he told her. That happened to be Monday. On Tuesday he got Robert's letter, and felt jolly glad that he'd told her in time."

"Well, it might be that, but it's rather a curious coincidence. And here is something which makes it very curious indeed. It only occurred to me in the bath this morning. Inspiring place, a bathroom. Well, it's this – he told her on Monday morning, on his way to Middleston in the car."

"Well?"

"Well."

"Sorry, Tony; I'm dense this morning."

"In the car, Bill. And how near can the car get to Jallands?"

"About six hundred yards."

"Yes. And on his way to Middleston, on some business or other, Mark stops the car, walks six hundred yards down the hill to Jallands, says, 'Oh, by the way, Mrs Norbury, I don't think I ever told you that I have a shady brother called Robert,' walks six hundred yards up the hill again, gets into the car, and goes off to Middleston. Is that likely?"

Bill frowned heavily.

"Yes, but I don't see what you're getting at. Likely or not likely, we know he did do it."

"Of course he did. All I mean is that he must have had some strong reason for telling Mrs Norbury at once. And the reason I suggest is that he knew on that morning – Monday morning, not Tuesday – that Robert was coming to see him, and had to be in first with the news.

"But – but – "

"And that would explain the other point – his instantaneous decision at breakfast to tell you all about his brother. It wasn't instantaneous. He knew on Monday that Robert was coming, and decided then that you would all have to know."

"Then how do you explain the letter?"

"Well, let's have a look at it."

Antony took the letter from his pocket and spread it out on the grass between them.

"Mark, your loving brother is coming to see you tomorrow, all the way from Australia. I give you warning, so that you will be able to conceal your surprise but not I hope your pleasure. Expect him at three or thereabouts."

"No date mentioned, you see," said Antony. "Just tomorrow."

"But he got this on Tuesday."

"Did he?"

"Well, he read it out to us on Tuesday."

"Oh, yes! He read it out to you."

Bill read the letter again, and then turned it over and looked at the back of it. The back of it had nothing to say to him.

"What about the postmark?" he asked.

"We haven't got the envelope, unfortunately."

"And you think that he got this letter on Monday."

"I'm inclined to think so, Bill. Anyhow, I think – I feel almost certain – that he knew on Monday that his brother was coming."

"Is that going to help us much?"

"No. It makes it more difficult. There's something rather uncanny about it all. I don't understand it." He was silent for a little, and then added, "I wonder if the inquest is going to help us."

"What about last night? I'm longing to hear what you make of that. Have you been thinking it out at all?"

"Last night," said Antony thoughtfully to himself. "Yes, last night wants some explaining."

Bill waited hopefully for him to explain. What, for instance, had Antony been looking for in the cupboard?

"I think," began Antony slowly, "that after last night we must give up the idea that Mark has been killed; killed, I mean, by Cayley. I don't believe anybody would go to so much trouble to hide a suit of clothes when he had a body on his hands. The body would seem so much more important. I think we may take it now that the clothes are all that Cayley had to hide."

"But why not have kept them in the passage?"

"He was frightened of the passage. Miss Norris knew about it."

"Well, then, in his own bedroom, or even, in Mark's. For all you or I or anybody knew, Mark might have had two brown suits. He probably had, I should think."

"Probably. But I doubt if that would reassure Cayley. The

brown suit hid a secret, and therefore the brown suit had to be hidden. We all know that in theory the safest hiding-place is the most obvious, but in practice very few people have the nerve to risk it."

Bill looked rather disappointed.

"Then we just come back to where we were," he complained. "Mark killed his brother, and Cayley helped him to escape through the passage; either in order to compromise him, or because there was no other way out of it. And he helped him by telling a lie about his brown suit."

Antony smiled at him in genuine amusement.

"Bad luck, Bill," he said sympathetically. "There's only one murder, after all. I'm awfully sorry about it. It was my fault for – "

"Shut up, you ass. You know I didn't mean that."

"Well, you seemed awfully disappointed."

Bill said nothing for a little, and then with a sudden laugh confessed.

"It was so exciting yesterday," he said apologetically, "and we seemed to be just getting there, and discovering the most wonderful things, and now – "

"And now?"

"Well, it's so much more ordinary."

Antony gave a shout of laughter.

"Ordinary!" he cried. "Ordinary! Well, I'm dashed! Ordinary! If only one thing would happen in an ordinary way, we might do something, but everything is ridiculous." Bill brightened up again.

"Ridiculous? How?"

"Every way. Take those ridiculous clothes we found last night. You can explain the brown suit, but why the underclothes. You can explain the underclothes in some absurd way, if you like – you can say that Mark always changed his underclothes whenever he interviewed anybody from Australia – but why, in that case, my dear Watson, why didn't he change his collar?"

"His collar?" said Bill in amazement.

"His collar, Watson."

"I don't understand."

"And it's all so ordinary," scoffed Antony.

"Sorry, Tony, I didn't mean that. Tell me about the collar."

"Well, that's all. There was no collar in the bag last night. Shirt, socks, tie – everything except a collar. Why?"

"Was that what you were looking for in the cupboard?" said Bill eagerly.

"Of course. 'Why no collar?' I said. For some reason Cayley considered it necessary to hide all Mark's clothes; not just the suit, but everything which he was wearing, or supposed to be wearing, at the time of the murder. But he hadn't hidden the collar. Why? Had he left it out by mistake? So I looked in the cupboard. It wasn't there. Had he left it out on purpose? If so, why? – and where was it? Naturally I began to say to myself, 'Where have I seen a collar lately? A collar all by itself?' And I remembered – what, Bill?"

Bill frowned heavily to himself, and shook his head.

"Don't ask me, Tony. I can't – By Jove!" He threw up his head, "In the basket in the office bedroom!"

"Exactly."

"But is that the one?"

"The one that goes with the rest of the clothes? I don't know. Where else can it be? But if so, why send the collar quite casually to the wash in the ordinary way, and take immense trouble to hide everything else? Why, why, why?"

Bill bit hard at his pipe, but could think of nothing to say.

"Anyhow," said Antony, getting up restlessly, "I'm certain of one thing. Mark knew on the Monday that Robert was coming here."

19

THE INQUEST

The Coroner, having made a few commonplace remarks as to the terrible nature of the tragedy which they had come to investigate that afternoon, proceeded to outline the case to the jury. Witnesses would be called to identify the deceased as Robert Ablett, the brother of the owner of the Red House, Mark Ablett. It would be shown that he was something of a ne'er-do-well, who had spent most of his life in Australia, and that he had announced, in what might almost be called a threatening letter, his intention of visiting his brother that afternoon. There would be evidence of his arrival, of his being shown into the scene of the tragedy – a room in the Red House, commonly called "the office" – and of his brother's entrance into that room. The jury would have to form their own opinion as to what happened there. But whatever happened, happened almost instantaneously. Within two minutes of Mark Ablett's entrance, as would be shown in the evidence, a shot was heard, and when – perhaps five minutes later – the room was forced open, the dead body of Robert Ablett was found stretched upon the floor. As regards Mark Ablett, nobody had seen him from the moment of his going into the room, but evidence would be called to show that he had enough money on him at the time to take him to any other part of the country, and that a man answering to his description had been observed on the platform of Stanton station, apparently waiting to catch the 3.55 up train to London. As the jury would realize, such evidence of identity was not always reliable. Missing men had a way of being seen in a dozen different places at once. In any case, there was no doubt that for the moment Mark Ablett had disappeared.

"Seems a sound man," whispered Antony to Bill. "Doesn't talk too much."

Antony did not expect to learn much from the evidence – he knew the facts of the case so well by now – but he wondered if Inspector Birch had developed any new theories. If so, they would appear in the Coroner's examination, for the Coroner would certainly have been coached by the police as to the important facts to be extracted from each witness. Bill was the first to be put through it.

"Now, about this letter, Mr Beverley?" he was asked when his chief evidence was over. "Did you see it at all?"

"I didn't see the actual writing. I saw the back of it. Mark was holding it up when he told us about his brother."

"You don't know what was in it, then?"

Bill had a sudden shock. He had read the letter only that morning. He knew quite well what was in it. But it wouldn't do to admit this. And then, just as he was about to perjure himself, he remembered: Antony had heard Cayley telling the Inspector.

"I knew afterwards. I was told. But Mark didn't read it out at breakfast."

"You gathered, however, that it was an unwelcome letter?"

"Oh, yes!"

"Would you say that Mark was frightened by it?"

"Not frightened. Sort of bitter – and resigned. Sort of 'Oh, Lord, here we are again!'"

There was a titter here and there. The Coroner smiled, and tried to pretend that he hadn't.

"Thank you, Mr Beverley."

The next witness was summoned by the name of Andrew Amos, and Antony looked up with interest, wondering who he was.

"He lives at the inner lodge," whispered Bill to him.

All that Amos had to say was that a stranger had passed by his lodge at a little before three that afternoon, and had spoken to him. He had seen the body and recognized it as the man.

"What did he say?"

"'Is this right for the Red House?' or something like that, sir."

"What did you say?"

"I said, 'This is the Red House. Who do you want to see?' He was a bit rough-looking, you know, sir, and I didn't know what he was doing there."

"Well?"

"Well, sir, he said, 'Is Mister Mark Ablett at home?' It doesn't sound much put like that, sir, but I didn't care about the way he said it. So I got in front of him like, and said, 'What do you want, eh?' and he gave a sort of chuckle and said, 'I want to see my dear brother Mark.' Well, then I took a closer look at him, and I see that p'raps he might be his brother, so I said, 'If you'll follow the drive, sir, you'll come to the house. Of course I can't say if Mr Ablett's at home.' And he gave a sort of nasty laugh again, and said, 'Fine place Mister Mark Ablett's got here. Plenty of money to spend, eh?' Well, then I had another look at him, sir, because gentlemen don't talk like that, and if he was Mr Ablett's brother – but before I could make up my mind, he laughed and went on. That's all I can tell you, sir."

Andrew Amos stepped down and moved away to the back of the room, nor did Antony take his eyes off him until he was assured that Amos intended to remain there until the inquest was over.

"Who's Amos talking to now?" he whispered to Bill.

"Parsons. One of the gardeners. He's at the outside lodge on the Stanton road. They're all here today. Sort of holiday for 'em.

"I wonder if he's giving evidence too," thought Antony. He was. He followed Amos. He had been at work on the lawn in front of the house, and had seen Robert Ablett arrive. He didn't hear the shot – not to notice. He was a little hard of hearing. He had seen a gentleman arrive about five minutes after Mr Robert.

"Can you see him in court now?" asked the Coroner. Parsons looked round slowly. Antony caught his eye and smiled.

"That's him," said Parsons, pointing.

Everybody looked at Antony.

"That was about five minutes afterwards?"

"About that, sir."

"Did anybody come out of the house before this gentleman's arrival?"

"No, sir. That is to say I didn't see 'em."

Stevens followed. She gave her evidence much as she had given it to the Inspector. Nothing new was brought out by her examination. Then came Elsie. As the reporters scribbled down what she had overheard, they added in brackets "Sensation" for the first time that afternoon.

"How soon after you had heard this did the shot come?" asked the Coroner.

"Almost at once, sir."

"A minute?"

"I couldn't really say, sir. It was so quick."

"Were you still in the hall?"

"Oh, no, sir. I was just outside Mrs Stevens' room. The housekeeper, sir."

"You didn't think of going back to the hall to see what had happened?"

"Oh, no, sir. I just went in to Mrs Stevens, and she said, 'Oh, what was that?' frightened-like. And I said, 'That was in the house, Mrs Stevens, that was.' Just like something going off, it was."

"Thank you," said the Coroner.

There was another emotional disturbance in the room as Cayley went into the witness-box; not "Sensation" this time, but an eager and, as it seemed to Antony, sympathetic interest. Now they were getting to grips with the drama.

He gave his evidence carefully, unemotionally – the lies with the same slow deliberation as the truth. Antony watched him intently, wondering what it was about him which had this odd sort of attractiveness. For Antony, who knew that he was lying, and lying (as he believed) not for Mark's sake but his own, yet could not help sharing some of that general sympathy with him.

"Was Mark ever in possession of a revolver?" asked the Coroner.

"Not to my knowledge. I think I should have known if he had been."

"You were alone with him all that morning. Did he talk about this visit of Robert's at all?"

"I didn't see very much of him in the morning. I was at work in my room, and outside, and so on. We lunched together and he talked of it then a little."

"In what terms?"

"Well – " he hesitated, and then went on. "I can't think of a better word than 'peevishly.' Occasionally he said, 'What do you think he wants?' or 'Why couldn't he have stayed where he was?' or 'I don't like the tone of his letter. Do you think he means trouble?' He talked rather in that kind of way."

"Did he express his surprise that his brother should be in England?"

"I think he was always afraid that he would turn up one day."

"Yes... You didn't hear any conversation between the brothers when they were in the office together?"

"No. I happened to go into the library just after Mark had gone in, and I was there all the time."

"Was the library door open?"

"Oh, yes."

"Did you see or hear the last witness at all?"

"No."

"If anybody had come out of the office while you were in the library, would you have heard it?"

"I think so. Unless they had come out very quietly on purpose."

"Would you call Mark a hasty-tempered man?"

Cayley considered this carefully before answering.

"Hasty-tempered, yes," he said. "But not violent-tempered."

"Was he fairly athletic? Active and quick?"

"Active and quick, yes. Not particularly strong."

"Yes... One question more. Was Mark in the habit of carrying any considerable sum of money about with him?"

"Yes. He always had one 100 pound note on him, and perhaps ten or twenty pounds as well."

"Thank you, Mr Cayley."

Cayley went back heavily to his seat. "Damn it," said Antony to himself, "why do I like the fellow?"

"Antony Gillingham!"

Again the eager interest of the room could be felt. Who was this stranger who had got mixed up in the business so mysteriously?

Antony smiled at Bill and stepped up to give his evidence.

He explained how he came to be staying at 'The George' at Waldheim, how he had heard that the Red House was in the neighbourhood, how he had walked over to see his friend Beverley, and had arrived just after the tragedy. Thinking it over afterwards he was fairly certain that he had heard the shot, but it had not made any impression on him at the time. He had come to the house from the Waldheim end and consequently had seen nothing of Robert Ablett, who had been a few minutes in front of him. From this point his evidence coincided with Cayley's.

"You and the last witness reached the French windows together and found them shut?"

"Yes."

"You pushed them in and came to the body. Of course you had no idea whose body it was?"

"No."

"Did Mr Cayley say anything?"

"He turned the body over, just so as to see the face, and when he saw it, he said, 'Thank God.'"

Again the reporters wrote "Sensation."

"Did you understand what he meant by that?"

"I asked him who it was, and he said that it was Robert Ablett. Then he explained that he was afraid at first it was the cousin with whom he lived – Mark."

"Yes. Did he seem upset?"

"Very much so at first. Less when he found that it wasn't Mark."

There was a sudden snigger from a nervous gentleman in the crowd at the back of the room, and the Coroner put on his glasses and stared sternly in the direction from which it came. The nervous gentleman hastily decided that the time had come to do up his bootlace. The Coroner put down his glasses and continued.

"Did anybody come out of the house while you were coming up the drive?"

"No."

"Thank you, Mr Gillingham."

He was followed by Inspector Birch. The Inspector, realizing that this was his afternoon, and that the eyes of the world were upon him, produced a plan of the house and explained the situation of the different rooms. The plan was then handed to the jury.

Inspector Birch, so he told the world, had arrived at the Red House at 4.42 p.m. on the afternoon in question. He had been received by Mr Matthew Cayley, who had made a short statement to him, and he had then proceeded to examine the scene of the crime. The French windows had been forced from outside. The door leading into the hall was locked; he had searched the room thoroughly and had found no trace of a key. In the bedroom leading out of the office he had found an open window. There were no marks on the window, but it was a low one, and, as he found from experiment, quite easy to step out of without touching it with the boots. A few yards outside the window a shrubbery began. There were no recent footmarks outside the window, but the ground was in a very hard condition owing to the absence of rain. In the shrubbery, however, he found several twigs on the ground, recently broken off, together with other evidence that some body had been forcing its way through. He had questioned everybody connected with the estate, and none of them had been into the shrubbery recently. By forcing a way through the shrubbery it was possible for a person to make a detour of the house and get to the Stanton end of the park without ever being in sight of the house itself.

He had made inquiries about the deceased. Deceased had left for Australia some fifteen years ago, owing to some financial trouble at home. Deceased was not well spoken of in the village from which he and his brother had come. Deceased and his brother had never been on good terms, and the fact that Mark Ablett had come into money had been a cause of great bitterness between them. It was shortly after this that Robert had left for Australia.

He had made inquiries at Stanton station. It had been market-day at Stanton and the station had been more full of arrivals than usual. Nobody had particularly noticed the arrival of Robert Ablett; there had been a good many passengers by the 2.10 train that afternoon, the train by which Robert had undoubtedly come from London. A witness, however, would state that he noticed a man resembling Mark Ablett at the station at 3.53 p.m. that afternoon, and this man caught the 3.55 up train to town.

There was a pond in the grounds of the Red House. He had dragged this, but without result...

Antony listened to him carelessly, thinking his own thoughts all the time. Medical evidence followed, but there was nothing to be got from that. He felt so close to the truth; at any moment something might give his brain the one little hint which it wanted. Inspector Birch was just pursuing the ordinary. Whatever else this case was, it was not ordinary. There was something uncanny about it.

John Borden was giving evidence. He was on the up platform seeing a friend off by the 3.55 on Tuesday afternoon. He had noticed a man on the platform with coat collar turned up and a scarf round his chin. He had wondered why the man should do this on such a hot day. The man seemed to be trying to escape observation. Directly the train came in, he hurried into a carriage. And so on.

"There's always a John Borden at every murder case," said Antony to himself.

"Have you ever seen Mark Ablett?"

"Once or twice, sir."

"Was it he?"

"I never really got a good look at him, sir, what with his collar turned up and the scarf and all. But directly I heard of the sad affair, and that Mr Ablett was missing, I said to Mrs Borden, 'Now I wonder if that was Mr Ablett I saw at the station?' So then we talked it over and decided that I ought to come and tell Inspector Birch. It was just Mr Ablett's height, sir."

Antony went on with his thoughts....

The Coroner was summing up. The jury, he said, had now heard all the evidence and would have to decide what had happened in that room between the two brothers. How had the deceased met his death? The medical evidence would probably satisfy them that Robert Ablett had died from the effects of a bullet-wound in the head. Who had fired that bullet? If Robert Ablett had fired it himself, no doubt they would bring in a verdict of suicide, but if this had been so, where was the revolver which had fired it, and what had become of Mark Ablett? If they disbelieved in this possibility of suicide, what remained? Accidental death, justifiable homicide, and murder. Could the deceased have been killed accidentally? It was possible, but then would Mark Ablett have run away? The evidence that he had run away from the scene of the crime was strong. His cousin had seen him go into the room, the servant Elsie Wood had heard him quarrelling with his brother in the room, the door had been locked from the inside, and there were signs that outside the open window someone had pushed his way very recently through the shrubbery. Who, if not Mark? They would have then to consider whether he would have run away if he had been guiltless of his brother's death. No doubt innocent people lost their heads sometimes. It was possible that if it were proved afterwards that Mark Ablett had shot his brother, it might also be proved that he was justified in so doing, and that when he ran away from his brother's corpse he had really nothing to fear at the hands of the Law. In this connection he need hardly remind the jury that they were not the final tribunal, and that if they found Mark Ablett guilty of murder it would not prejudice his trial in any way if and when he was apprehended... The jury could consider their verdict.

They considered it. They announced that the deceased had died as the result of a bullet-wound, and that the bullet had been fired by his brother Mark Ablett.

Bill turned round to Antony at his side. But Antony was gone. Across the room he saw Andrew Amos and Parsons going out of the door together, and Antony was between them.

20

MR BEVERLEY IS TACTFUL

The inquest had been held at the "Lamb" at Stanton; at Stanton Robert Ablett was to be buried next day. Bill waited about outside for his friend, wondering where he had gone. Then, realizing that Cayley would be coming out to his car directly, and that a farewell talk with Cayley would be a little embarrassing, he wandered round to the yard at the back of the inn, lit a cigarette, and stood surveying a torn and weather-beaten poster on the stable wall. "GRAND THEATRICAL ENTER" it announced, to take place on "Wednesday, Decem." Bill smiled to himself as he looked at it, for the part of Joe, a loquacious postman, had been played by "William B. Beverl," as the remnants of the poster still maintained, and he had been much less loquacious than the author had intended, having forgotten his words completely, but it had all been great fun. And then he stopped smiling, for there would be no more fun now at the Red House.

"Sorry to keep you waiting," said the voice of Antony behind him. "My old friends Amos and Parsons insisted on giving me a drink."

He slipped his hand into the crook of Bill's arm, and smiled happily at him.

"Why were you so keen about them?" asked Bill a little resentfully. "I couldn't think where on earth you had got to."

Antony didn't say anything. He was staring at the poster.

"When did this happen?" he asked.

"What?"

Antony waved to the poster.

"Oh, that? Last Christmas. It was rather fun."

Antony began to laugh to himself.

"Were you good?"

"Rotten. I don't profess to be an actor."

"Mark good?"

"Oh, rather. He loves it."

"Rev. Henry Stutters – Mr Matthew Cay," read Antony.

"Was that our friend Cayley?"

"Yes."

"Any good?"

"Well, much better than I expected. He wasn't keen, but Mark made him."

"Miss Norris wasn't playing, I see."

"My dear Tony, she's a professional. Of course she wasn't."

Antony laughed again.

"A great success, was it?"

"Oh, rather!"

"I'm a fool, and a damned fool," Antony announced solemnly. "And a damned fool," he said again under his breath, as he led Bill away from the poster, and out of the yard into the road. "And a damned fool. Even now – " He broke off and then asked suddenly, "Did Mark ever have much trouble with his teeth?"

"He went to his dentist a good deal. But what on earth – "

Antony laughed a third time.

"What luck!" he chuckled. "But how do you know?"

"We go to the same man; Mark recommended him to me. Cartwright, in Wimpole Street."

"Cartwright in Wimpole Street," repeated Antony thoughtfully. "Yes, I can remember that. Cartwright in Wimpole Street. Did Cayley go to him too, by any chance?"

"I expect so. Oh, yes, I know he did. But what on earth – "

"What was Mark's general health like? Did he see a doctor much?"

"Hardly at all, I should think. He did a lot of early morning exercises which were supposed to make him bright and cheerful at breakfast. They didn't do that, but they seemed to keep him pretty fit. Tony, I wish you'd – "

Antony held up a hand and hushed him into silence.

"One last question," he said. "Was Mark fond of swimming?"

"No, he hated it. I don't believe he could swim. Tony, are you mad, or am I? Or is this a new game?"

Antony squeezed his arm.

"Dear old Bill," he said. "It's a game. What a game! And the answer is Cartwright in Wimpole Street."

They walked in silence for half a mile or so along the road to Waldheim. Bill tried two or three times to get his friend to talk, but Antony had only grunted in reply. He was just going to make another attempt, when Antony came to a sudden stop and turned to him anxiously.

"I wonder if you'd do something for me," he said, looking at him with some doubt.

"What sort of thing?"

"Well, it's really dashed important. It's just the one thing I want now."

Bill was suddenly enthusiastic again.

"I say, have you really found it all out?"

Antony nodded.

"At least, I'm very nearly there, Bill. There's just this one thing I want now. It means your going back to Stanton. Well, we haven't come far; it won't take you long. Do you mind?"

"My dear Holmes, I am at your service."

Antony gave him a smile and was silent for a little, thinking.

"Is there another inn at Stanton – fairly close to the station?"

"The 'Plough and Horses' – just at the corner where the road goes up to the station – is that the one you mean?"

"That would be the one. I suppose you could do with a drink, couldn't you?"

"Rather!" said Bill, with a grin.

"Good. Then have one at the 'Plough and Horses.' Have two, if you like, and talk to the landlord, or landlady, or whoever serves you. I want you to find out if anybody stayed there on Monday night."

"Robert?" said Bill eagerly.

"I didn't say Robert," said Antony, smiling. "I just want you to find out if they had a visitor who slept there on Monday night. A stranger. If so, then any particulars you can get of him, without letting the landlord know that you are interested – "

"Leave it to me," broke in Bill. "I know just what you want."

"Don't assume that it was Robert – or anybody else. Let them describe the man to you. Don't influence them unconsciously by suggesting that he was short or tall, or anything of that sort. Just get them talking. If it's the landlord, you'd better stand him a drink or two."

"Right you are," said Bill confidently. "Where do I meet you again?"

"Probably at 'The George.' If you get there before me, you can order dinner for eight o'clock. Anyhow we'll meet at eight, if not before."

"Good." He nodded to Antony and strode off back to Stanton again.

Antony stood watching him with a little smile at his enthusiasm. Then he looked round slowly, as if in search of something. Suddenly he saw what he wanted. Twenty yards farther on a lane wandered off to the left, and there was a gate a little way up on the right-hand side of it. Antony walked to the gate, filling his pipe as he went. Then he lit his pipe, sat on the gate, and took his head in his hands.

"Now then," he said to himself, "let's begin at the beginning."

It was nearly eight o'clock when William Beverley, the famous sleuthhound, arrived, tired and dusty, at 'The George,' to find Antony, cool and clean, standing bare-headed at the door, waiting for him.

"Is dinner ready?" were Bill's first words.

"Yes."

"Then I'll just have a wash. Lord, I'm tired."

"I never ought to have asked you," said Antony penitently.

"That's all right. I shan't be a moment." Half-way up the stairs he turned round and asked, "Am I in your room?"

"Yes. Do you know the way?"

"Yes. Start carving, will you? And order lots of beer." He disappeared round the top of the staircase. Antony went slowly in.

When the first edge of his appetite had worn off, and he was able to spare a little time between the mouthfuls, Bill gave an account of his adventures. The landlord of the "Plough and Horses" had been sticky, decidedly sticky – Bill had been unable at first to get anything out of him. But Bill had been tactful; lorblessyou, how tactful he had been.

"He kept on about the inquest, and what a queer affair it had been, and so on, and how there'd been an inquest in his wife's family once, which he seemed rather proud about, and I kept saying, 'Pretty busy, I suppose, just now, what?' and then he'd say, 'Middlin',' and go on again about Susan – that was the one that had the inquest – he talked about it as if it were a disease – and then I'd try again, and say, 'Slack times, I expect, just now, eh?' and he'd say 'Middlin' again, and then it was time to offer him another drink, and I didn't seem to be getting much nearer. But I got him at last. I asked him if he knew John Borden – he was the man who said he'd seen Mark at the station. Well, he knew all about Borden, and after he'd told me all about Borden's wife's family, and how one of them had been burnt to death – after you with the beer; thanks – well, then I said carelessly that it must be very hard to remember anybody whom you had just seen once, so as to identify him afterwards, and he agreed that it would be 'middlin' hard,' and then – "

"Give me three guesses," interrupted Antony. "You asked him if he remembered everybody who came to his inn?"

"That's it. Bright, wasn't it?"

"Brilliant. And what was the result?"

"The result was a woman."

"A woman?" said Antony eagerly.

"A woman," said Bill impressively. "Of course I thought it was going to be Robert – so did you, didn't you? – but it wasn't. It was a woman. Came quite late on Monday night in a car – driving herself – went off early next morning."

"Did he describe her?"

"Yes. She was middlin'. Middlin' tall, middlin' age, middlin' colour, and so on. Doesn't help much, does it? But still – a woman. Does that upset your theory?"

Antony shook his head.

"No, Bill, not at all," he said.

"You knew all the time? At least, you guessed?"

"Wait till tomorrow. I'll tell you everything tomorrow."

"Tomorrow!" said Bill in great disappointment.

"Well, I'll tell you one thing tonight, if you'll promise not to ask any more questions. But you probably know it already."

"What is it?"

"Only that Mark Ablett did not kill his brother."

"And Cayley did?"

"That's another question, Bill. However, the answer is that Cayley didn't, either."

"Then who on earth – "

"Have some more beer," said Antony with a smile. And Bill had to be content with that.

They were early to bed that evening, for both of them were tired. Bill slept loudly and defiantly, but Antony lay awake, wondering. What was happening at the Red House now? Perhaps he would hear in the morning; perhaps he would get a letter. He went over the whole story again from the beginning – was there any possibility of a mistake? What would the police do? Would they ever find out? Ought he to have told them? Well, let them find out; it was their job. Surely he couldn't have made a mistake this time. No good wondering now; he would know definitely in the morning.

In the morning there was a letter for him.

21

CAYLEY'S APOLOGY

"My Dear Mr Gillingham,

"I gather from your letter that you have made certain discoveries which you may feel it your duty to communicate to the police, and that in this case my arrest on a charge of murder would inevitably follow. Why, in these circumstances, you should give me such ample warning of your intentions I do not understand, unless it is that you are not wholly out of sympathy with me. But whether or not you sympathize, at any rate you will want to know – and I want you to know – the exact manner in which Ablett met his death and the reasons which made that death necessary. If the police have to be told anything, I would rather that they too knew the whole story. They, and even you, may call it murder, but by that time I shall be out of the way. Let them call it what they like.

"I must begin by taking you back to a summer day fifteen years ago, when I was a boy of thirteen and Mark a young man of twenty-five. His whole life was make-believe, and just now he was pretending to be a philanthropist. He sat in our little drawing-room, flicking his gloves against the back of his left hand, and my mother, good soul, thought what a noble young gentleman he was, and Philip and I, hastily washed and crammed into collars, stood in front of him, nudging each other and kicking the backs of our heels and cursing him in our hearts for having interrupted our game. He had decided to adopt one of us, kind Cousin Mark. Heaven knows why he chose me. Philip was eleven; two years longer to wait. Perhaps that was why.

"Well, Mark educated me. I went to a public school and to Cambridge, and I became his secretary. Well, much more than his secretary as your friend Beverley perhaps has told you: his land agent, his financial adviser, his courier, his – but this most of all – his audience. Mark could never live alone. There must always be somebody to listen to him. I think in his heart he hoped I should be his Boswell. He told me one day that he had made me his literary executor – poor devil. And he used to write me the absurdest long letters when I was away from him, letters which I read once and then tore up. The futility of the man!

"It was three years ago that Philip got into trouble. He had been hurried through a cheap grammar school and into a London office, and discovered there that there was not much fun to be got in this world on two pounds a week. I had a frantic letter from him one day, saying that he must have a hundred at once, or he would be ruined, and I went to Mark for the money. Only to borrow it, you understand; he gave me a good salary and I could have paid it back in three months. But no. He saw nothing for himself in it, I suppose; no applause, no admiration. Philip's gratitude would be to me, not to him. I begged, I threatened, we argued; and while we were arguing, Philip was arrested. It killed my mother – he was always her favourite – but Mark, as usual, got his satisfaction out of it. He preened himself on his judgment of character in having chosen me and not Philip twelve years before!

"Later on I apologized to Mark for the reckless things I had said to him, and he played the part of a magnanimous gentleman with his accustomed skill, but, though outwardly we were as before to each other, from that day forward, though his vanity would never let him see it, I was his bitterest enemy. If that had been all, I wonder if I should have killed him? To live on terms of intimate friendship with a man whom you hate is dangerous work for your friend. Because of his belief in me as his admiring and grateful protege and his belief in himself as my benefactor, he was now utterly in my power. I could take my time and choose my opportunity. Perhaps I should not have killed him, but I had sworn to have my revenge – and there he was, poor vain fool, at my mercy. I was in no hurry.

"Two years later I had to reconsider my position, for my revenge was being taken out of my hands. Mark began to drink. Could I have stopped him? I don't think so, but to my immense surprise I found myself trying to. Instinct, perhaps, getting the better of reason; or did I reason it out and tell myself that, if he drank himself to death, I should lose my revenge? Upon my word, I cannot tell you; but, for whatever motive, I did genuinely want to stop it. Drinking is such a beastly thing, anyhow.

"I could not stop him, but I kept him within certain bounds, so that nobody but myself knew his secret. Yes, I kept him outwardly decent; and perhaps now I was becoming like the cannibal who keeps his victim in good condition for his own ends. I used to gloat over Mark, thinking how utterly he was mine to ruin as I pleased, financially, morally, whatever way would give me most satisfaction. I had but to take my hand away from him and he sank. But again I was in no hurry.

"Then he killed himself. That futile little drunkard, eaten up with his own selfishness and vanity, offered his beastliness to the truest and purest woman on this earth. You have seen her, Mr Gillingham, but you never knew Mark Ablett. Even if he had not been a drunkard, there was no chance for her of happiness with him. I had known him for many years, but never once had I seen him moved by any generous emotion.

To have lived with that shrivelled little soul would have been hell for her; and a thousand times worse hell when he began to drink.

"So he had to be killed. I was the only one left to protect her, for her mother was in league with Mark to bring about her ruin. I would have shot him openly for her sake, and with what gladness, but I had no mind to sacrifice myself needlessly. He was in my power; I could persuade him to almost anything by flattery; surely it would not be difficult to give his death the appearance of an accident.

"I need not take up your time by telling you of the many plans I made and rejected. For some days I inclined towards an unfortunate boating accident in the pond – Mark, a very indifferent swimmer, myself almost exhausted in a gallant attempt to hold him up. And then he himself gave me the idea, he and Miss Norris between them, and so put himself in my hands; without risk of discovery, I should have said, had you not discovered me.

"We were talking about ghosts. Mark had been even more vain, pompous and absurd than usual, and I could see that Miss Norris was irritated by it. After dinner she suggested dressing up as a ghost and frightening him. I thought it my duty to warn her that Mark took any joke against himself badly, but she was determined to do it. I gave way reluctantly. Reluctantly, also, I told her the secret of the passage. (There is an underground passage from the library to the bowling-green. You should exercise your ingenuity, Mr Gillingham, in trying to discover it. Mark came upon it by accident a year ago. It was a godsend to him; he could drink there in greater secrecy. But he had to tell me about it. He wanted an audience, even for his vices.)

"I told Miss Norris, then, because it was necessary for my plan that Mark should be thoroughly frightened. Without the passage she could never have got close enough to the bowling-green to alarm him properly, but as I arranged it with her she made the most effective appearance, and Mark was in just the state of rage and vindictiveness which I required. Miss Norris, you understand, is a professional actress. I need not say that to her I appeared to be animated by no other feeling than a boyish desire to bring off a good joke – a joke directed as much against the others as against Mark.

"He came to me that night, as I expected, still quivering with indignation. Miss Norris must never be asked to the house again; I was to make a special note of it; never again. It was outrageous. Had he not a reputation as a host to keep up, he would pack her off next morning. As it was, she could stay; hospitality demanded it; but never again would she come to the Red House – he was absolutely determined about that. I was to make a special note of it.

"I comforted him, I smoothed down his ruffled feathers. She had behaved very badly, but he was quite right; he must try not to show how much he disapproved of her. And of course she would never come again – that was obvious. And then suddenly I began to laugh. He looked up at me indignantly.

"Is there a joke?" he said coldly.

"I laughed gently again.

"'I was just thinking,' I said, 'that it would be rather amusing if you – well, had your revenge."

"'My revenge? How do you mean?'

"'Well, paid her back in her own coin.'

"'Do you mean try and frighten her?'

"'No, no; but dressed up and pulled her leg a bit. Made her look a fool in front of the others.' I laughed to myself again. 'Serve her jolly well right.'

"He jumped up excitedly.

"'By Jove, Cay!' he cried. 'If I could! How? You must think of a way.

"I don't know if Beverley has told you about Mark's acting. He was an amateur of all the arts, and vain of his little talents, but as an actor he seemed to himself most wonderful. Certainly he had some ability for the stage, so long as he had the stage to himself and was playing to an admiring audience. As a professional actor in a small part he would have been hopeless; as an amateur playing the leading part, he deserved all that the local papers had ever said about him. And so the idea of giving us a private performance, directed against a professional actress who had made fun of him, appealed equally to his vanity and his desire for retaliation. If he, Mark Ablett, by his wonderful acting could make Ruth Norris look a fool in front of the others, could take her in, and then join in the laugh at her afterwards, he would indeed have had a worthy revenge!

"It strikes you as childish, Mr Gillingham? Ah, you never knew Mark Ablett.

"'How, Cay, how?' he said eagerly.

"'Well, I haven't really thought it out,' I protested. 'It was just an idea.'

"He began to think it out for himself.

"'I might pretend to be a manager, come down to see her – but I suppose she knows them all. What about an interviewer?'

"'It's going to be difficult,' I said thoughtfully. 'You've got rather a characteristic face, you know. And your beard – '

"'I'd shave it off,' he snapped.

"'My dear Mark!'

"He looked away, and mumbled, 'I've been thinking of taking it off, anyhow. And besides, if I'm going to do the thing, I'm going to do it properly.'

"'Yes, you always were an artist,' I said, looking at him admiringly.

"He purred. To be called an artist was what he longed for most. Now I knew that I had him.

"'All the same,' I went on, 'even without your beard and moustache you might be recognizable. Unless, of course – ' I broke off.

"'Unless what?'

"'You pretend to be Robert.' I began to laugh to myself again. 'By Jove!' I said, 'that's not a bad idea. Pretend to be Robert, the wastrel brother, and make yourself objectionable to Miss Norris. Borrow money from her, and that sort of thing.'

"He looked at me, with his bright little eyes, nodding eagerly.

"'Robert,' he said. 'Yes. How shall we work it?'

"There was really a Robert, Mr Gillingham, as I have no doubt you and the Inspector both discovered. And he was a wastrel and he went to Australia. But he never came to the Red House on Tuesday afternoon. He couldn't have, because he died (unlamented) three years ago. But there was nobody who knew this, save Mark and myself, for Mark was the only one of the family left, his sister having died last year. Though I doubt, anyhow, if she knew whether Robert was alive or dead. He was not talked about.

"For the next two days Mark and I worked out our plans. You understand by now that our aims were not identical. Mark's endeavour was that his deception should last for, say, a couple of hours; mine that it should go to the grave with him. He had only to deceive Miss Norris and the other guests; I had to deceive the world. When he was dressed up as Robert, I was going to kill him. Robert would then be dead, Mark (of course) missing. What could anybody think but that Mark had killed Robert? But you see how important it was for Mark to enter fully into his latest (and last) impersonation. Half-measures would be fatal.

"You will say that it was impossible to do the thing thoroughly enough. I answer again that you never knew Mark. He was being what he wished most to be – an artist. No Othello ever blacked himself all over with such enthusiasm as did Mark. His beard was going anyhow – possible a chance remark of Miss Norbury's helped here. She did not like beards. But it was important for me that the dead man's hands should not be the hands of a manicured gentleman. Five minutes playing upon the vanity of the artist settled his hands. He let the nails grow and then cut them raggedly. 'Miss Norris would notice your hands at once,' I had said. 'Besides, as an artist – '

"So with his underclothes. It was hardly necessary to warn him that his pants might show above the edge of his socks; as an artist he had already decided upon Robertian pants. I bought them, and other things, in London for him. Even if I had not cut out all trace of the maker's name, he would instinctively have done it. As an Australian and an artist, he could not have an East London address on his underclothes. Yes, we were doing the thing thoroughly, both of us; he as an artist, I as a – well, you may say murderer, if you like. I shall not mind now.

"Our plans were settled. I went to London on the Monday and wrote him a letter from Robert. (The artistic touch again.) I also bought a revolver. On the Tuesday morning he announced the arrival of Robert at the breakfast-table. Robert was now alive – we had six witnesses to prove it; six witnesses who knew that he was coming that afternoon. Our private plan was that Robert should present himself at three o'clock, in readiness for the return of the golfing-party shortly afterwards. The maid would go to look for Mark, and having failed to find him, come back to the office to find me entertaining Robert in Mark's absence. I would explain that Mark must have gone out somewhere, and would myself introduce the wastrel brother to the tea-table. Mark's absence would not excite any comment, for it would be generally felt – indeed Robert would suggest it – that he had been afraid of meeting his brother. Then Robert would make himself amusingly offensive to the guests, particularly, of course, Miss Norris, until he thought that the joke had gone far enough.

"'That was our private plan. Perhaps I should say that it was Mark's private plan. My own was different.

"The announcement at breakfast went well. After the golfing-party had gone off, we had the morning in which to complete our arrangements. What I was chiefly concerned about was to establish as completely as possible the identity of Robert. For this reason I suggested to Mark that, when dressed, he should go out by the secret passage to the bowling-green, and come back by the drive, taking care to enter into conversation with the lodge-keeper. In this way I would have two more witnesses of Robert's arrival – first the lodge-keeper, and secondly one of the gardeners whom I would have working on the front lawn. Mark, of course, was willing enough. He could practise his Australian accent on the lodge-keeper. It was really amusing to see how readily he fell into every suggestion which I made. Never was a killing more carefully planned by its victim.

"He changed into Robert's clothes in the office bedroom. This was the safest way – for both of us. When he was ready, he called me in, and I inspected him. It was extraordinary how well he looked the part. I suppose that the signs of his dissipation had already marked themselves on his face, but had been concealed hitherto by his moustache and beard; for now that he was clean-shaven they lay open to the world from which we had so carefully hidden them, and he was indeed the wastrel which he was pretending to be.

"'By Jove, you're wonderful,' I said.

"He smirked, and called my attention to the various artistic touches which I might have missed.

"'Wonderful,' I said to myself again. 'Nobody could possibly guess.'

"I peered into the hall. It was empty. We hurried across to the library; he got into the passage and made off. I went back to the bedroom, collected all his discarded clothes, did them up in a bundle and returned with them to the passage. Then I sat down in the hall and waited.

"You heard the evidence of Stevens, the maid. As soon as she was on her way to the Temple in search of Mark, I stepped into the office. My hand was in my side-pocket, and in my hand was the revolver.

"He began at once in his character of Robert – some rigmarole about working his passage over from Australia; a little private performance for my edification. Then in his natural voice, gloating over his well-planned retaliation on Miss Norris, he burst out, 'It's my turn now. You wait.' It was this which Elsie heard. She had no business to be there and she might have ruined everything, but as it turned out it was the luckiest thing which could have happened. For it was the one piece of evidence which I wanted; evidence, other than my own, that Mark and Robert were in the room together.

"I said nothing. I was not going to take the risk of being heard to speak in that room. I just smiled at the poor little fool, and took out my revolver, and shot him. Then I went back into the library and waited – just as I said in my evidence.

"Can you imagine, Mr Gillingham, the shock which your sudden appearance gave me? Can you imagine the feelings of a 'murderer' who has (as he thinks) planned for every possibility, and is then confronted suddenly with an utterly new problem? What difference would your coming make? I didn't know. Perhaps none; perhaps all. And I had forgotten to open the window!

"I don't know whether you will think my plan for killing Mark a clever one. Perhaps not. But if I do deserve any praise in the matter, I think I deserve it for the way I pulled myself together in the face of the unexpected catastrophe of your arrival. Yes, I got a window open, Mr Gillingham, under your very nose; the right window too, you were kind enough to say. And the keys – yes, that was clever of you, but I think I was cleverer. I deceived you over the keys, Mr Gillingham, as I learnt when I took the liberty of listening to a conversation on the bowling-green between you and your friend Beverley. Where was I? Ah, you must have a look for that secret passage, Mr Gillingham.

"But what am I saying? Did I deceive you at all? You have found out the secret – that Robert was Mark – and that is all that matters. How have you found out? I shall never know now. Where did I go wrong? Perhaps you have been deceiving me all the time. Perhaps you knew about the keys, about the window, even about the secret passage. You are a clever man, Mr Gillingham.

"I had Mark's clothes on my hands. I might have left them in the passage, but the secret of the passage was now out. Miss Norris knew it. That was the weak point of my plan, perhaps, that Miss Norris had to know it. So I hid them in the pond, the Inspector having obligingly dragged it for me first. A couple of keys joined them, but I kept the revolver. Fortunate, wasn't it, Mr Gillingham?

"I don't think that there is any more to tell you. This is a long letter, but then it is the last which I shall write. There was a time when I hoped that there might be a happy future for me, not at the Red House, not alone. Perhaps it was never more than an idle day-dream, for I am no more worthy of her than Mark was. But I could have made her happy, Mr Gillingham. God, how I would have worked to make her happy! But now that is impossible. To offer her the hand of a murderer would be as bad as to offer her the hand of a drunkard. And Mark died for that. I saw her this morning. She was very sweet. It is a difficult world to understand.

"Well, well, we are all gone now – the Abletts and the Cayleys. I wonder what old Grandfather Cayley thinks of it all. Perhaps it is as well that we have died out. Not that there was anything wrong with Sarah – except her temper. And she had the Ablett nose – you can't do much with that. I'm glad she left no children.

"Goodbye, Mr Gillingham. I'm sorry that your stay with

us was not of a pleasanter nature, but you understand the difficulties in which I was placed. Don't let Bill think too badly of me. He is a good fellow; look after him. He will be surprised. The young are always surprised. And thank you for letting me end it my own way. I expect you did sympathize a little, you know. We might have been friends in another world – you and I, and I and she. Tell her what you like. Everything or nothing. You will know what is best. Goodbye, Mr Gillingham.

"MATTHEW CAYLEY.

"I am lonely tonight without Mark. That's funny, isn't it?"

22

MR BEVERLEY MOVES ON

"Good Lord!" said Bill, as he put down the letter.

"I thought you'd say that," murmured Antony.

"Tony, do you mean to say that you knew all this?"

"I guessed some of it. I didn't quite know all of it, of course."

"Good Lord!" said Bill again, and returned to the letter. In a moment he was looking up again. "What did you write to him? Was that last night? After I'd gone into Stanton?"

"Yes."

"What did you say? That you'd discovered that Mark was Robert?"

"Yes. At least I said that this morning I should probably telegraph to Mr Cartwright of Wimpole Street, and ask him to – "

Bill burst in eagerly on the top of the sentence. "Yes, now what was all that about? You were so damn Sherlocky yesterday all of a sudden. We'd been doing the thing together all the time, and you'd been telling me everything, and then suddenly you become very mysterious and private and talk enigmatically – is that the word? – about dentists and swimming and the 'Plough and Horses,' and – well, what was it all about? You simply vanished out of sight; I didn't know what on earth we were talking about."

Antony laughed and apologized.

"Sorry, Bill. I felt like that suddenly. Just for the last half-hour; just to end up with. I'll tell you everything now. Not that there's anything to tell, really. It seems so easy when you know it – so obvious. About Mr Cartwright of Wimpole Street. Of course he was just to identify the body."

"But whatever made you think of a dentist for that?"

"Who could do it better? Could you have done it? How could you? You'd never gone bathing with Mark; you'd never seen him stripped. He didn't swim. Could his doctor do it? Not unless he'd had some particular operation, and perhaps not then. But his dentists could – at any time, always – if he had been to his dentist fairly often. Hence Mr Cartwright of Wimpole Street."

Bill nodded thoughtfully and went back again to the letter.

"I see. And you told Cayley that you were telegraphing to Cartwright to identify the body?"

"Yes. And then of course it was all up for him. Once we knew that Robert was Mark we knew everything."

"How did you know?"

Antony got up from the breakfast table and began to fill his pipe.

"I'm not sure that I can say, Bill. You know those problems in Algebra where you say, 'Let x be the answer,' and then you work it out and find what x is. Well, that's one way; and another way, which they never give you any marks for at school, is to guess the answer. Pretend the answer is 4 – well, will that satisfy the conditions of the problem? No. Then try 6; and if 6 doesn't either, then what about 5? – and so on. Well, the Inspector and the Coroner and all that lot had guessed their answer, and it seemed to fit, but you and I knew it didn't really fit; there were several conditions in the problem which it didn't fit at all. So we knew that their answer was wrong, and we had to think of another – an answer which explained all the things which were puzzling us. Well, I happened to guess the right one. Got a match?"

Bill handed him a box, and he lit his pipe.

"Yes, but that doesn't quite do, old boy. Something must have put you on to it suddenly. By the way, I'll have my matches back, if you don't mind."

Antony laughed and took them out of his pocket.

"Sorry... Well then, let's see if I can go through my own mind again, and tell you how I guessed it. First of all, the clothes."

"Yes?"

"To Cayley the clothes seemed an enormously important clue. I didn't quite see why, but I did realize that to a man in Cayley's position the smallest clue would have an entirely disproportionate value. For some reason, then, Cayley attached this exaggerated importance to the clothes which Mark was wearing on that Tuesday morning; all the clothes, the inside ones as well as the outside ones. I didn't know why, but I did feel certain that, in that case, the absence of the collar was unintentional. In collecting the clothes he had overlooked the collar. Why?"

"It was the one in the linen-basket?"

"Yes. It seemed probable. Why had Cayley put it there? The obvious answer was that he hadn't. Mark had put it there. I remembered what you told me about Mark being finicky, and having lots of clothes and so on, and I felt that he was just the sort of man who would never wear the same collar twice." He paused, and then asked, "Is that right, do you think?"

"Absolutely," said Bill with conviction.

"Well, I guessed it was. So then I began to see an x which would fit just this part of the problem – the clothes part. I saw Mark changing his clothes; I saw him instinctively dropping the collar in the linen-basket, just as he had always dropped every collar he had ever taken off, but leaving the rest of the clothes on a chair in the ordinary way; and I saw Cayley collecting all the clothes afterwards – all the visible clothes – and not realizing that the collar wasn't there."

"Go on," said Bill eagerly.

"Well, I felt pretty sure about that, and I wanted an explanation of it. Why had Mark changed down there instead of in his bedroom? The only answer was that the fact of his changing had to be kept secret. When did he change? The only possible time was between lunch (when he would be seen by the servants) and the moment of Robert's arrival. And when did Cayley collect the clothes in a bundle? Again, the only answer was 'Before Robert's arrival.' So another x was wanted – to fit those three conditions."

"And the answer was that a murder was intended, even before Robert arrived?"

"Yes. Well now, it couldn't be intended on the strength of that letter, unless there was very much more behind the letter than we knew. Nor was it possible a murder could be intended without any more preparation than the changing into a different suit in which to escape. The thing was too childish. Also, if Robert was to be murdered, why go out of the way to announce his existence to you all – even, at the cost of some trouble, to Mrs Norbury? What did it all mean? I didn't know. But I began to feel now that Robert was an incident only; that the plot was a plot of Cayley's against Mark – either to get him to kill his brother, or to get his brother to kill him – and that for some inexplicable reason Mark seemed to be lending himself to the plot." He was silent for a little, and then said, almost to himself, "I had seen the empty brandy bottles in that cupboard."

"You never said anything about them" complained Bill.

"I only saw them afterwards. I was looking for the collar, you remember. They came back to me afterwards; I knew how Cayley would feel about it.... Poor devil!"

"Go on," said Bill.

"Well, then, we had the inquest, and of course I noticed, and I suppose you did too, the curious fact that Robert had asked his way at the second lodge and not at the first. So I talked to Amos and Parsons. That made it more curious. Amos told me that Robert had gone out of his way to speak to him; had called to him, in fact. Parsons told me that his wife was out in their little garden at the first lodge all the afternoon, and was certain that Robert had never come past it. He also told me that Cayley had put him on to a job on the front lawn that afternoon. So I had another guess. Robert had used the secret passage – the passage which comes out into the park between the first and second lodges. Robert, then, had been in the house; it was a put-up job between Robert and Cayley. But how could Robert be there without Mark knowing? Obviously, Mark knew too. What did it all mean?"

"When was this?" interrupted Bill. "Just after the inquest – after you'd seen Amos and Parsons, of course?"

"Yes. I got up and left them, and came to look for you. I'd got back to the clothes then. Why did Mark change his clothes so secretly? Disguise? But then what about his face? That was much more important than clothes. His face, his beard – he'd have to shave off his beard – and then – oh, idiot! I saw you looking at that poster. Mark acting, Mark made-up, Mark disguised. Oh, priceless idiot! Mark was Robert.... Matches, please."

Bill passed over the matches again, waited till Antony had relit his pipe, and then held out his hand for them, just as they were going into the other's pocket.

"Yes," said Bill thoughtfully. "Yes.... But wait a moment. What about the 'Plough and Horses'?" Antony looked comically at him.

"You'll never forgive me, Bill," he said. "You'll never come clue-hunting with me again."

"What do you mean?"

Antony sighed.

"It was a fake, Watson. I wanted you out of the way. I wanted to be alone. I'd guessed at my x, and I wanted to test it – to test it every way, by everything we'd discovered. I simply had to be alone just then. So – " he smiled and added, "Well, I knew you wanted a drink."

"You are a devil," said Bill, staring at him. "And your interest when I told you that a woman had been staying there – "

"Well, it was only polite to be interested when you'd taken so much trouble."

"You brute! You – you Sherlock! And then you keep trying to steal my matches. Well, go on."

"That's all. My x fitted."

"Did you guess Miss Norris and all that?"

"Well, not quite. I didn't realize that Cayley had worked for it from the beginning – had put Miss Norris up to frightening Mark. I thought he'd just seized the opportunity."

Bill was silent for a long time. Then, puffing at his pipe, he said slowly, "Has Cayley shot himself?"

Antony shrugged his shoulders.

"Poor devil," said Bill. "It was decent of you to give him a chance. I'm glad you did."

"I couldn't help liking Cayley in a kind of way, you know."

"He's a clever devil. If you hadn't turned up just when you did, he would never have been found out."

"I wonder. It was ingenious, but it's often the ingenious thing which gets found out. The awkward thing from Cayley's point of view was that, though Mark was missing, neither he nor his body could ever be found. Well, that doesn't often happen with a missing man. He generally gets discovered in the end; a professional criminal; perhaps not – but an amateur like Mark! He might have kept the secret of how he killed Mark, but I think it would have become obvious sooner or later that he had killed him."

"Yes, there's something in that.... Oh, just tell me one thing. Why did Mark tell Miss Norbury about his imaginary brother?"

"That's puzzled me rather, too, Bill. It may be that he was just doing the Othello business – painting himself black all over. I mean he may have been so full of his appearance as Robert that he had almost got to believe in Robert, and had to tell everybody. More likely, though, he felt that, having told all of you at the house, he had better tell Miss Norbury, in case she met one of you; in which case, if you mentioned the approaching arrival of Robert, she might say, 'Oh, I'm certain he has no brother; he would have told me if he had,' and so spoil his joke. Possibly, too, Cayley put him on to it; Cayley obviously wanted as many people as possible to know about Robert."

"Are you going to tell the police?"

"Yes, I suppose they'll have to know. Cayley may have left another confession. I hope he won't give me away; you see, I've been a sort of accessory since yesterday evening. And I must go and see Miss Norbury."

"I asked," explained Bill, "because I was wondering what I should say to – to Betty. Miss Calladine. You see, she's bound to ask."

"Perhaps you won't see her again for a long, long time," said Antony sadly.

"As a matter of fact, I happen to know that she will be at the Barringtons. And I go up there tomorrow."

"Well, you had better tell her. You're obviously longing to. Only don't let her say anything for a day or two. I'll write to you."

"Righto!"

Antony knocked the ashes out of his pipe and got up.

"The Barringtons," he said. "Large party?"

"Fairly, I think."

Antony smiled at his friend.

"Yes. Well, if any of 'em should happen to be murdered, you might send for me. I'm just getting into the swing of it."

Four Days' Wonder

CONTENTS

Tuesday

1

RETURN OF AUNT FANE

I

When, on a fine June morning not so long ago, Jenny Windell let herself in with her latch-key at Auburn Lodge, and, humming dreamily to herself, drifted upstairs to the drawing-room, she was surprised to see the body of her Aunt Jane lying on a rug by the open door. It had been known for years, of course, that Aunt Jane would come to a bad end. Not only was her black hair cropped short like a boy's, but she smoked cigarettes out of a long red holder, and knew the Sitwells. Moreover, she acted on Sundays in plays which either meant nothing at all, which was silly, or meant what you thought they did, which was hardly possible. And it was said that she—but of course that wasn't true. After all, her father had served his King in India and the Windells had always been gentlefolk.

It was not surprising, then, that Aunt Jane should have been cut short like this; nor was it surprising that Jenny should drift upstairs and find a body in the drawing-room. Jenny was a well-read girl, and knew that people were continually drifting upstairs and finding bodies in the drawing-room. Only last night Michael Alloway, a barrister by profession, had found the body of a well-dressed woman on his hearthrug, with a note by its side which said 'A K 17 L P K 29 Friday'. What it meant Jenny would not know until tonight. Flitting from shop window to shop window this morning, or counter to counter, she had let her mind wander over the possibilities of adventure for herself in this romantic setting, so much more easily to be called up, when one was in fact in the Brompton Road, than the saddle-bows of an Arab sheikh. The body... the handsome young detective... the Old Bailey... Jenny Windell in the box: Dramatic Evidence. *('Oh, good morning! No, I'm just looking round, thank you very much')*

No, the surprising thing was that Aunt Jane should be at Auburn Lodge at all. She had not been near them for—let me see, Jenny, it must be nearly eight years. Happy years, had thought to herself Aunt Caroline (the Good One), for it was so much better that Jane should not come near Jenny. Being what she was, she would be bad for Jenny; put all the wrong ideas into her head. It was a great mercy that Jane had left Auburn Lodge forever eight years ago.

And now Jane had come back to Auburn Lodge... had met Jenny again after eight years... was going to be very bad for Jenny, and put *all* the wrong ideas into her head.

II

'Oh!' said Jenny. And then 'Well!' And then, in surprise, 'Why, it's Aunt Jane!'

Even after eight years she never had a doubt. The sleek, black head, the absurd gipsy earrings, the ridiculously shaved eyebrows over the Chinese eyes, the sulky, over-red mouth, the notorious cigarette-holder, now lying broken on the floor, all these had been shared so long and so generously with those who read their peerage in the Sunday Papers, that any woman of them would have said at once: 'Why, it's Jane Latour!' The Sunday Papers did not come up to the drawing-room of Auburn Lodge; not the 'Sunday Papers'. Mr. Garvin of the *Observer* came up because he was patriotic, and really doing his best for England; but that was different. It was more a National Organ. For the real Sunday Papers one had to go down to the kitchen... and wait for Cook to say 'There's another little bit about yer aunt, Miss Jenny. I cut it out for you.' And from Cook's little bits, and from the illustrated papers over; which her fair head drooped for the hairdresser, and from the childish memories of eight years ago, Jenny had now in her mind as complete a picture of her Aunt Jane as any niece could wish.

It was a picture which, to Jenny, had all the attraction and repulsion of her first, and last, cocktail. That had been called a White Lady, which was something nobody would dream of calling Aunt Jane. Aunt Jane was a Red-and-black Lady. In as far as she was a well-known actress, one could say carelessly: 'Oh, yes, that's my aunt,' and wait for the envious 'Really?' In as far as she was notorious in other ways, one could say hurriedly: 'Well, actually she *is* a sort of relation, but' and wait for the reluctant change of subject. What really irritated Jenny (when she thought about it) was that she was never quite sure what Aunt Jane had *done*. Aunt Caroline had explained to her once what Jane had *not* done, but she felt that there should have been more to it than that. After all, anybody might marry a French Count, and then find that he wasn't a Count, and that you hadn't married him, and that all that was left of him was that he was undoubtedly (oh, but *undoubtedly)* French. You wouldn't go on having bits in the paper about yourself, just because of a mistake like that. Would you, Aunt Caroline?

'My dear,' said Aunt Caroline, 'that was not All.'

'All what?'

'It is not a pleasant subject for a sister to discuss; it is not a pleasant subject for a girl of sixteen to discuss. My methods of bringing you up, Jenny, may be old-fashioned, but, to use an old-fashioned word, I want you to grow up a lady. We will now talk of something else.'

'Did Aunt Jane grow up a lady?'

'Aunt Jane', said Caroline proudly, 'would always be a lady whatever she did. She is a Windell.'

It occurred to Jenny that she also was a Windell and would therefore always be a lady whatever she did, even if she did all that Aunt Jane had done, whatever that was, so why—

'Touch the bell, please, and we will have tea. Is that a ladder coming in your stocking? Let me look. Yes. You had better go and change them now, and then you can mend them afterwards.'

So it was left to Jenny and her great friend Nancy to decide (over a box of chocolates) what Aunt Jane was doing. Jenny decided that she took Snow in Large and Increasing Quantities. Nancy decided that she played the harp with nothing on before All the Crowned Heads of Europe. Then they talked about something else.

And now, two years later, Aunt Jane was in the drawing-room of Auburn Lodge, and Jenny still didn't know what she was doing.

III

Jenny's first thought was 'How exciting!'—and then remorsefully 'Oh, but poor Aunt Jane!'—and then, being a sensible girl, she thought that, if it were really all true, all that was said, perhaps it was as well that Aunt Jane should be cut off before she could take still more snow, and play the harp before still more Crowned Heads, and perhaps even Presidents, with nothing on. And she thought that, since neither of these could be nice things to do, because anything up the nose was rather sickish, and the other would be very, very embarrassing, particularly if

Presidents looked like their photographs in the papers, why, even Aunt Jane must be glad that it was now all over. So, feeling a little excited again, she looked about the floor to see if there were any messages in cipher from the heads of any of the Greatest Criminal Organizations in Europe. Because, if so...

But there were none. Worse than that (or, as one would say, fortunately) there was no evidence of any sort of crime. Aunt Jane's high heels had slipped on the parquet floor, she had fallen to the ground, and her head had hit heavily against a valuable old brass door-stop. Nobody was to blame.

Jenny's next thought was to pick up the door-stop and restore it to its usual place upon the grand piano. The door-stop, which Aunt Caroline had previously picked up in Whitstable, was a representation of a slice of Conway Castle, and, though not actually beautiful, bore enough resemblance to a slice of Conway Castle to be ostensibly attractive rather than useful, and, as such, entitled to a place upon the piano, where it could be appreciated in comfort, rather than upon the floor, where it could only be appreciated when lying down. Jenny, then, picked this up; but noticing that it was a little stained, she did not immediately return it to its place between the General and Lord Roberts (under whom he had, at one time, served), but wiped it carefully first with her pocket-handkerchief. Then, since the handkerchief was also stained now, she made a little face at it and dropped it for the moment upon a chair, while she wondered what next she ought to do.

She had no time to wonder. There was a noise of a door opening below; there was a noise of voices on the stairs; and suddenly the awful realization swept over Jenny Windell, leaving her hot and cold, and red and white, sending her heart hotly up into her throat and then coldly down into her stomach, the awful realization that she had no business to be here at all—that six months ago she, too, had left Auburn Lodge forever.

2

BEGINNINGS OF JENNY

I

General Sir Oliver Windell, K.C.B., and so forth, was too good a Victorian to wish to survive his Queen. He had died, therefore, in March 1901; a little to the relief of the War Office (which had had him on its hands all through the Boer War) and greatly to the relief of his three children. Their attitude must have appealed strongly to the General, who had always deprecated damned sentimental nonsense.

The eldest child, and presumably the most relieved, was Caroline. She was twenty-seven, and for the last four years had been chatelaine of Auburn Lodge, thus enjoying not only the privileges of a daughter, but the daytime benefits of a wife. The second child was Young Oliver, who had had the advantage of attending a boarding-school during the greater part of those four years. He was now seventeen. The third child was Jane. She was seven, an age at which one can take refuge in the nursery and be damned by proxy.

This recurring interval of ten years between their births, which gave them the air of an Arithmetical Progression, and, as such, seemed to evidence some profound, but slightly unreasonable, military design on the part of the General, was in fact inevitable. When Caroline was one, she and her mother, in accordance with precedent, were returned to England. Here they settled down at Auburn Lodge, and waited anxiously for the General to join them on leave. Their anxiety was unnecessary. His unique capacity for provoking, and subsequently quelling, outbreaks of religious enthusiasm, kept him so occupied that it was not until eight years later that he could resume family life. Even now it was not safe for him to leave the country: Elaine was ordered to put Caroline out to school and join him at Chukrapoota. She obeyed; and within two years was able to escape again to England, this time with Young Oliver. Feeling more satisfied with her now, for the thought of some future India without a Windell was repugnant to him, the General returned to duty. Another eight years of religious enthusiasm followed, and Young Oliver was of age to be put out. But Fate intervened. The General was ordered home to receive the rewards due to him. He and her ladyship spent the winter together in the South of France; and when at last the uncanny quiet of India summoned him urgently back, it was obviously unwise for her ladyship to accompany him. She remained at Auburn Lodge; she died at Auburn Lodge four years later; and a General whose genius for provoking outbreaks had outlived his capacity for quelling them hastened home to protect his motherless children.

His first duty to them was to change the name of the house from Auburn Lodge to Simla. Caroline, lacking as yet the experience of the border tribes, dared to oppose him. She asked Why? The General replied shortly that one was a damned silly name and the other wasn't. Young Oliver, essaying his first schoolboy joke in the presence of the Indian Empire, murmured that anyhow the other sounded very Simla. When this had been explained to his father and Oliver had been sent to bed, the General announced that all this damned nonsense would now stop, and that Caroline would kindly oblige him by taking down a letter to the Postmaster-General; at that time a Mr. Hanbury. Caroline obliged. The letter, a dignified compromise between the first and third persons, was dispatched; and in due course, and entirely in the third person, Mr. Hanbury regretted that it was impossible to adopt Sir Oliver's suggestion. The General, who was unaccustomed to having his commands mistaken for suggestions, then dictated a strong letter to *The Times*, but Mr. Hanbury was again too much for him. The letter was not delivered. Young Oliver, now up and back at school, did what he could for his father, without wasting a stamp, by writing every Sunday to:

Miss Windell
Simla
(*nee* Auburn Lodged)
Brompton Road, S.W.—

but this was found not to be helpful. The General, in fact, was defeated.

Caroline was twenty-three, but not beautiful. The General looked over *The Times* at her across the breakfast-table, and felt uneasily that her face was familiar in some damned way; as indeed it was, for he had shaved something like it every morning for years. She was a Windell. Jane was not; but Jane was only three, and her future was not yet written on her face. Nurse said she would be a beauty when she grew up, but the General abandoned hope afresh with every inspection of Caroline over *The Times*. The Providence which had supervised so long and so wisely the suppression of religious enthusiasm on the Frontier had betrayed him now. Here he was, with that damned bloody feller in the Government, and the whole damned country all over the place, and in ten years' time he'd just be that poor old feller with the two damned ugly daughters.

Well, he supposed he must provide for them, for God knew no husband was likely to do it. Better leave 'em the house, and they could live in it together, two old maids with a tabby and a damned canary...

He sent for Mr. Watterson, and issued his instructions. True to his tradition of never recognizing defeat, particularly when committing anything officially to paper, he bequeathed Simla to the absolute joint use and benefit of his two daughters, together with a sufficient sum for the proper upkeep of the same. Mr. Watterson was, not unnaturally, surprised at the munificence of the gift, and a little doubtful as to the validity of the title.

'Are you in fact,' he asked, 'I mean is it really—I had always understood that Simla—' and he tried to remember if anything in the lives of Warren Hastings and Clive formed a reliable precedent.

'This house', said the General coldly, 'is called Simla.'

Mr. Watterson, who had thought it was called all that messuage and hereditament known as Auburn Lodge, coughed and said: 'Quite, quite.'

'Then is that clear?' asked the General.

'Perfectly, my dear Sir Oliver,' said a greatly relieved Mr. Watterson.

So that was how Jenny's two aunts, Caroline and Jane, came to live together at Auburn Lodge. For the General's prophecy was correct; no husband ever did provide for them. But it is doubtful if, for that reason, Jane Latour could properly be regarded as an old maid.

II

Sir Oliver was not buried in the Abbey. He had expressed a wish to be put away without any of this damned flummery, and his wish was respected. All the obituary notices spoke highly of his services to the country, in some cases instancing what these were. High Commanding Officers had been under a cloud for the last eighteen months, and it was not difficult to feel enthusiasm for a General who had never been nearer to South Africa than the South of France, and now could never go. Indeed, one of the more patriotic organs said (and truthfully) that it was not generally known that Sir Oliver had been on the verge of taking up an important command in the Transvaal, and implied that any victories gained by the Boers in his now enforced absence were hardly to their credit.

Caroline was left in charge. Mr. Watterson had told her to be sure to call upon him, if in any difficulty she felt the need of a father. As she felt the need of nothing so little, she thanked him and said that she could manage quite well. She did. Oliver went to Sandhurst and then into the Hussars, where he looked extremely dashing in blue and yellow. Jane went to a succession of schools, and acquired a catholic education; not so obviously in English History (for, as Chance would have it, each school was doing Henry VIII in the term that she was there) but in matters possibly as important. At eighteen she took her *bizarre* good looks, her cat-like indifference to others, and, of course, her knowledge of Henry VIII (which was by this time considerable) to a French finishing school. At twenty she was finished; and the Great War was beginning...

With the coming of the Great Peace, there were again three Windells at Auburn Lodge.

First, Caroline. She was now the forty-five which she had always looked to her father, and the old maid which he had always known she would be. She differed from others of her age and Parliamentary status in that she refused to take advantage of the new Cosmetic Era which had arisen. By looking the same in whatever light and (within the limits of a room) from whatever distance, she achieved a distinction which no

Victorian could have foretold for her. There was only one Caroline Windell.

Then Jane. London was full of Jane Windells. She was now the twenty-five which she would have looked in any case. She had entertained the troops during the war; just how much, and in what direction, was not known. But her experiences with a Company of Players at Havre and Rouen had made it clear that the Stage gave her most scope for her natural abilities.

Lastly, the orphaned Jenny. She was five.

III

Since Edward had done so little for Jane, and George had not, in Caroline's view, been a conspicuous success with the modern girl, Jenny was brought up by Queen Victoria. She throve, under these auspices, in a world of her own.

She was the daughter of that dashing young Hussar whom she had never seen. She was glad and proud that he had been a Hussar. As she pointed out to God in one of her early prayers, he might have been in the Manchester Regiment.

Every night they talked together in bed.

'Well, Jenny, what shall we do tonight?'

Perhaps she had been reading *Robinson Crusoe*, by Mr. Daniel Defoe.

'Darling, I thought we might be wrecked together on a desert island.'

'Without the Aunts?'

'Just whatever you think, Hussar darling?'

'I don't like Aunt Jane,' said the Hussar dashingly.

Jenny called God's attention to the fact that it was the Hussar who was saying this.

'I do like Aunt Caroline, but I don't think she would be good on a desert island,' said the Hussar.

('We both like her,' explained Jenny, 'but we do *not* think she would be good on a desert island. You do see, don't you?')

'So it's just you and me, Jenny. Now the ship's breaking up, and I'm swimming to shore with you on my back. Go!'

When she was nine, she met Julian.

'Well, Jenny, what shall we do tonight?'

'Darling, I thought we might be the Dauntless Three, if you wouldn't mind very much. Do you mind very much, Hussar darling? You could be Horatius, and I could stand on your right hand.'

'But how about my left hand, Jenny?'

'I thought you might think of somebody, darling.'

'What about Julian?' said the Hussar, after racking his brain.

'Darling, what a *lovely* idea! You do think of lovely ideas.'

And then, a year later, Aunt Jane met the Comte de la Tour. At least, he said she did.

'Hussar darling?'

'Yes, Jenny?'

'Did you know about Aunt Jane running away with the French Count?'

'Yes, Jenny.'

'Why do you have to *run?*'

'He wants to get back to France quickly so as to say "*Vive la France!*" and it's a long way to go.'

'I thought that was it... Hussar darling?'

'Yes, Jenny?'

'Why mustn't I talk about her any more?'

'Because they're carrying secret dispatches to the exiled King, and nobody must know.'

'I thought that was it. But I shan't tell Julian.'

'Oh, no, you mustn't.'

'Well, I don't tell him anything now. I think he's a silly little boy.'

'I think he is too,' said the extremely intelligent Hussar.

So Aunt Jane left Auburn Lodge... and the Jane Latour who afterwards played the harp, and did other odd and exciting things, never saw Jenny again. But Jenny, as we know, saw Jane Latour.

IV

When Aunt Caroline died, Jenny was eighteen. The first thing that she did was to have her hair shingled. There was a great deal of it, parti-coloured like a straw-stack after rain, and as soon as it was safely off, she wondered if she had been unkind to her aunt's memory to proclaim her independence so quickly. Then she remembered that some tribes always shaved their heads as a sign of mourning, and if she had been one of those tribes she would have had to have had her hair shingled. This made her feel better. By the time she had called on Mr. Watterson (who was now nearly eighty) and Mr. Watterson had said nothing about her hair, because, being eighty, he hadn't noticed the difference, she felt quite comfortable again.

Mr. Watterson suggested that they should let Auburn Lodge (furnished) for a year, and that she should make her home with him and his dear wife for that time, while, as he put it, she looked round. Mr. Watterson lived in a house in St. John's Wood, with a garden, and, as he said this, he had a sudden thought of Jenny in the hammock between the two pear-trees, reading a magazine with a gay cover, while a thrush sang over her head, and beneath her on the grass lay a hat with cherry ribbons; which was how he remembered somebody in some other world; and two tears came into his two old eyes, and he knew that now nothing could ever happen, and in a little while he would be dead. Then he forgot all this just as suddenly, and remembered that there were six dozen of the port left and Victoria Falls Preferred were going up.

'You *are* kind,' said Jenny.

'You realize, my dear, that I am now your guardian?'

'Oh!' said Jenny, and thought: '*Another* guardian!' when all she really wanted was her dear Hussar.

She wondered what would be said about her hair, because Mrs. Watterson would be sure to notice it. Well, thank goodness, it couldn't go back.

'So I think that that's what we will do, my dear.'

Jenny agreed, as she always did when a guardian spoke to her.

So Auburn Lodge was let for a year (furnished) to Mr. and Mrs. George Parracot, who also wanted to look round. Mr. and Mrs. Parracot had lived for ten years at The Chestnuts, Chislehurst. They were great theatre-goers, and had missed the last five minutes of the Third Act of every play worth seeing since 1922. They had also missed in this way some five hundred renderings of the National Anthem. So when old Paul Parracot died suddenly (but not too suddenly, considering that they were only second cousins) they decided to take a house in London for a year, and see how they liked it. For whatever could be said about Chislehurst, it was not so central as the Brompton Road.

But Jane Latour knew nothing of all this. She did not even know that her sister Caroline was dead. Caroline was not News. No subeditor dropped a headline for her; in her name no vowels were wrung at Broadcasting House; and on that remote island in the South Seas at which the ex-President's yacht had just landed them, Jane Latour neither wept nor hung her harp upon the trees.

However, even ex-Presidents tire, and pleasure-cruises come to an end. Jane Latour was in London again, and, in the language of her profession, resting. She also, in a sense, was looking round. Taking stock.

In a year she would be forty—forty—forty. And now and at once and all the time she wanted money—money—money.

Forty... money...

Then, as she was lying one morning in the red-and-black bath in the red-and-black bathroom in the little red-and-black house in Stapleton Mews, corifparing, as so often now, her overdraft, which was at the National Provincial Bank, with her assets, which, at the moment, were mostly under water, she remembered suddenly her sister Caroline. Caroline and she were joint-owners of Auburn Lodge; indeed, she still had the key to which joint-ownership entitled her. It was true that Caroline paid over to her yearly a half-share of the estimated rent, but why should not Caroline buy her out altogether? The house must be worth—what? Six—eight— ten thousand? Five thousand pounds for Jane Latour! She stretched out an arm and added another handful of bath-salts to the water. She could afford it.

So it was that Aunt Jane came again to Auburn Lodge. As she clicked up the little alley-way in her absurdly high heels, she fumbled in her bag for the latch-key, so long unused. To let herself into her own house was an assertion of her rights; it was to be a gesture, a reminder to Caroline that half of all this was hers; yes, even down to half of the silver photograph-frames on the grand piano. She would stand for no nonsense from Caroline.

She fidgeted the key into the lock, smiling a little scornfully as she thought of poor Caroline. And the child Jenny. Jenny must be nearly eighteen. What sort of a mid-Victorian miss had Caroline made of her?

But she did not smile scornfully as she thought of Jenny. Jenny was eighteen.

3

OLD FELSBRIDGIAN

I

There was a noise of a door opening below; there was a noise of footsteps on the stairs; and suddenly the awful realization swept over Jenny that she had no business to be here at all!

How could she have been so silly!

The answer was that today, for the first time since she had left Auburn Lodge, she had found herself in her dear Brompton Road. Old inhabitants of the North-West do their shopping in Oxford Street. Not exclusively in Oxford Street, for they may stop short at Wigmore Street, or venture as far south as Bond Street, Regent Street or Hanover Square; but they have a marked Oxford Street manner, which will never carry them across the Park. For six months Jenny had been striving to acquire this manner, and striving in vain. She had the stamp of Brompton Road upon her.

Brompton Road was particularly sweet to her, because it was the only London street in which she and her dear Hussar had been allowed to go about together. In Brompton Road, Aunt Caroline had felt, a young girl was Safe. However noisomely Danger might lurk in the side streets, waiting to pounce upon the divergent, along the straight way of Brompton Road walked only the Loyal and the Respectable. Jenny tripped up and down it untouched; but amid the perils of Beauchamp Place there marched by the side of Jenny her Aunt Caroline, or her Aunt Caroline's maid.

In St. John's Wood it was different. Mr. Watterson had the usual views about the modern young girl, but the fact that Abduction was Illegal made him indisposed to think that it could happen to a ward of Watterson, Watterson and Hinchoe's. There was no need for Jenny to have a latch-key, but (he assured Mrs. Watterson) she could safely run about London alone in the daytime. Indeed, in this way she could take some of the housekeeping off Mrs. Watterson's shoulders.

So at eighteen Jenny had been given the freedom of London. Moreover, unknown to Mr. Watterson, she had a latch-key in her bag. Admittedly it was not the latch-key to the house in Acacia Road, and therefore did not greatly enlarge her freedom; but a latch-key, brought casually to the surface when feeling for coppers in an omnibus, could only have one meaning, and her possession of it gave Jenny, if not the conductor, an authentic thrill. In fact, it was one of those in use at Auburn Lodge, which Jenny had been allowed to borrow on a certain notable occasion. She had gone to a dance without Aunt Caroline but not the less chaperoned, and the chaperones (there were several of them) had delivered her at the door of Auburn Lodge at an hour almost Edwardian. 'We'll just see you safely in,' had said the Colonel with a hearty laugh, and they had all gathered (a little humorously) round the front door, while Jenny felt proudly for her latch-key. The fact that it had slipped down behind the lining of her bag, and was not discovered until eight months later, had spoilt the joke at the time, but had left in Jenny's possession a key which should now have been with the Parracots.

She had this key, then, in her bag, and she had there ten pounds of her quarterly allowance, and it was a fine warm day in June, and all Brompton Road was calling to her as never before.

She went. She spent. She tripped backwards and forwards, and round and about—oh, the darling Brompton Road, how glad she was to get back to it again! Her dear Hussar was with her just as he used to be, and she was telling him all about Michael Alloway, the barrister by profession, who had found the body of a well-dressed woman in his drawing-room, and they were thinking how exciting this would be, and not really looking where they were going... and, before they knew where they were, they had come to the little alley-way together and, chattering as they had always done, turned up it. And there was the latchkey in her hand, and the key had fitted so easily, and now she was in the well-known house, and going dreamily up the stairs as she had gone a hundred, a thousand times before... 'Aunt Caroline! I'm back!'

II

The footsteps, the voices, were nearer. They were just outside the door. Only one thing to do. Hide!

In a flash Jenny was into the window-seat which went round the three sides of the big window over the lawn. She was curled up behind the curtains. As a child she had hidden here from Aunt Caroline or Aunt Jane and then popped her head out and said 'Bo!'—a joke in which, somehow, no grown-up had ever seemed able to join. But now it was not a joke; it was desperate. One simply couldn't let perfect strangers know how *idiotic* one had been.

'My God!' said Mr. George Parracot.

Jenny was neither surprised nor shocked. From a hundred detective stories she knew that this was how men greeted the body of an unknown woman in the drawing-room.

'What is it?' called a voice from Aunt Caroline's bedroom.

'I say, quick!' shouted Mr. Parracot. And then commandingly: 'No—don't. Stay where you are!' Mr. Parracot had remembered that he was a Man and an Old Felsbridgian. One must keep The Women out of this sort of thing.

It was too late. Mrs. Parracot was in the doorway.

'George!' she cried.

There was just that something in her voice which made it clear that, from now onwards, whatever might happen, it was *his* body, not hers. Mr. Parracot, wearing the Club tie, recognized the note and accepted all responsibility.

'It's quite all right, old girl. You'd better go to your bedroom. Leave it all to me.'

'Is she—dead?'

'Yes.'

'Who is it?'

'Haven't the faintest. I say, old girl, you'd better—'

Mrs. Parracot came a little closer and said: 'Why, it's Jane Latour!'

'Good lord, not Jane Latour?'

'Yes. I'm sure it is.' She looked up at him. 'George?'

It was not quite an accusation, not quite a question; and it said all about Jane Latour that was not going to be said in the obituary notices.

'I've never spoken to her in my life,' said George indignantly. 'I've never—Well, we've seen her act once or twice. But that's all. How on earth did she get *here?*'

'Poor thing,' said Laura Parracot, suddenly feeling an immense envy for one who had had such an exciting life, an immense pity for one who now would have it no more. 'Did she—kill herself?'

George looked about him in a puzzled way. 'Well, but—How?'

'Veronal or whatever—Oh!' She had come still closer.

'She couldn't have hit her head, because there's nothing—'

'George!'

'It's quite all right, old girl. You go to your bedroom, and I'll ring up the police.'

'But, George, don't you *understand*, she was *murdered?*'

'Yes, that's all right, old girl. *I'll* see to that.'

'But he may be in the house still!'

'Nonsense, old girl, he's far enough off by this time.'

'But he must have known the house was empty, or he wouldn't have been here with—her. And if we hadn't come in on our way to Mary's—Oh, I wish we'd gone straight through instead of—But I had to get some thinner things, and you wanted your Brilliantine, but don't you see he might be in the house *now*, looking for—for whatever it is they came here for.'

'Now now, old girl,' said Mr. Parracot quickly, 'this won't do.' He had an uneasy feeling that Laura was getting hysterical, and that the best way to stop it was to slap her face smartly with the open hand, an action so definitely un-Felsbridgian that he could not possibly bring himself to it. He fingered his tie anxiously, and said: 'If you go into your bedroom and lock the door, and if I'm here all the time, it *must* be all right, mustn't it, old girl?'

'All right, George,' said the old girl bravely.

She went out. Jenny was left alone with Mr. Parracot. For a little while there was silence. Then a voice began to speak.

'Hallo! I want the nearest police-station, please... Auburn Lodge. Brompton Road... Thank you... Oh, hallo! I'm speaking from Auburn Lodge, just off the Brompton Road. Er—there's a— there's a—a body here ... A *body*... Yes ... A well-dressed woman ... I don't know ... I don't know... George Parracot... Yes. But we've been away, and the house has been empty... Quite sure... Right... Right... Goodbye.'

Then there was silence again. Jenny looked round the corner of the curtain. Mr. Parracot was in an arm-chair, waiting. Jenny breathed a prayer to God or her Hussar, she wasn't sure which, to think of something. For if she were found now, not even the handsomest young detective could save her.

She had done *everything* wrong! Why, the first thing they told you was not to move anything until the police came, and she had moved the one thing which she ought to have left: the door-stop! Worse still, she had cleaned it with her handkerchief! Worst of all ('Oh, Hussar *darling*, isn't it *awful*') she had left her handkerchief in a chair for everyone to see! And it had 'Jenny' on it!

And then *hiding!*

Even that wasn't all. She was Aunt Jane's only relation, and so by law she would get all Aunt Jane's money, and the police would say that that was why she had done it!

JENNY WINDELL IN THE DOCK: DRAMATIC EVIDENCE

Jenny realized that there was only one thing to do. She must escape and fly the country. But how? And, more important, *when?*

When? Before the police came. There was just one moment when it could be done. There were no servants in the house, and Mrs. Parracot was safely locked up. So Mr. Parracot would have to go downstairs to let the police in. Then would be the moment.

How? That was easy. Through the window. The ground was higher at the back of the house than at the front, and there was a flower-bed not more than eight feet below her. Then out by the garden-door into the other little alley-way, and out through the far end into Merrion Plaee…

Suppose Mrs. Parracot answered the door? *She* couldn't…

Suppose the Police came in with a skeleton-key? *They wouldn't…*

Suppose—

The front-door bell rang. There was a movement from the chair. Jenny, looking out, saw the disappearing back of Mr. Parracot, heard his 'All right, old girl, it's only the police'. She pushed open the casement window behind her, squeezed through, wriggled round and let herself down by her hands. There was only about eighteen inches to drop... just enough to give Inspector Marigold, who had the case well in hand from the start, a couple of interesting footprints.

4

ENTRY OF GLORIA HARRIS

I

In a tea-shop in Piccadilly, over a cup of coffee, half a toasted scone and two portions of honey, Jenny considered her position. It was half-past twelve. Twenty minutes ago she had escaped from Auburn Lodge, and for twenty minutes Inspector Marigold had been relentlessly finding clues. She wondered if he would stop for lunch, and hoped, if so, that he would have a nice long one.

She considered in her mind the Good and the Bad, as her old friend Robinson Crusoe would have done.

1.	*Bad.*	I've only got £2 5s. 9y2d., and if I hadn't bought that hat, it would have been £6 9s. 9^{1}/2d.
	Good.	But I might have bought the other one.
2.	*Bad.*	I've really got the wrong clothes for escaping.
	Good.	But I suppose I could buy some others.
	Bad.	But I've only got £2 5s. 9 Vid.
3.	*Bad.*	My handkerchief.
	Good.	But it's got 'Jenny' on it, and when the Inspector identifies Aunt Jane, he *might* think 'Jenny' is short for Jane.

Bad. Until somebody tells him it isn't.

4. *Bad.* Fingerprints. I must have left them all *over* the place.

Good. Still, that doesn't matter, if they don't know it's me.

5. *Bad.* I wish I could get some other clothes, and some more money and some cold cream and a tooth-brush. I wonder if I *dare* go home for them.

Good. I think I might, because Mr. and Mrs. Watterson have gone down to Bath for a wedding.

Bad. All the safte I daren't, because of the servants.

Good. I'm glad I said I would be out to lunch.

6. *Good.* It's lucky I never saw the Parracots when they were taking the house. They've simply never heard of me.

Bad. But the Inspector is sure to ask who lived there before the Parracots, and then he'll go to see Mr. Watterson.

Good. But Mr. Watterson is at Bath for the day.

7. *Good.* So I've probably got the whole of today to get away in, only I mustn't go home.

Bad. But I've only got £2 5s. 9½*d.*

8. *Good.* Still £2 5s. 9½d is quite a lot *really,* if you sleep under haystacks.

Bad. But not nearly so much as £6 9s. 9½d. when you've got to buy all sorts of things.

And then, just as she was beginning her second portion of honey, Jenny had a most wonderful idea.

9. *Really* AWFULLY *Good.* Nancy Fairbrother!
Of course!

This was that Nancy, who had supposed, mistakenly, that Aunt Jane played the harp with nothing on before all the Crowned Heads of Europe. She had been helpful and instructive in other ways, and in numerous imaginary adventures had been Jenny's sole female confederate. She had Jenny's romantic nature, very much Jenny's figure, and all of Jenny's passion for Crime. Probably she knew already what 'A K 17 L P K 29 Friday' meant.

Jenny paid for her lunch (leaving £2 5s. 1½*d.)* and walked to a telephone-box in the Piccadilly Tube station.

In her very deepest tones Jenny said: 'Hallo, is that Mr. Archibald Fenton's house?'

'Yes, Mr. Fenton's secretary speaking,' said a bright secretarial voice.

'Is that Miss Fairbrother?'

'Speaking.'

'Nancy,' said Jenny's voice urgently, 'this is Gloria Harris speaking. Do you remember? Say "Oh, yes, Miss Harris" if you do.'

'Oh, yes, Miss Harris,' said Miss Fairbrother primly.

'You sound as if you weren't alone, darling.'

'Quaite.'

'Is Mr. Fenton there?'

'Yes.'

'Listen, Nancy, it's terribly important. You mustn't see me, and you mustn't know that I've rung up, that's why I said Gloria Harris. But you *must* do something for me, if you'll be an angel. Will you be an angel, Nancy darling?'

'Of course, Miss Harris,' said Miss Fairbrother reassuringly.

'I want to go to your flat, and I want to change there, and I want to wear something of yours, something old and countryish, and I'll leave you what I'm wearing instead. It's the green georgette. And nobody must know I've been. So if I call for your key now, will you leave it addressed to Miss Harris, but not so as people will guess it's a key, and I'll tie it on a piece of string and leave it hanging inside the letterbox. And you might say what you'd like me to wear of yours. Something you were going to sell, and you'll have my green georgette, so that *will* be all right, won't it?'

'That will be *quite* all right, Miss Harris. I'll do it at once.'

'You utter angel. You do understand, don't you?'

'Why, of course, Miss Harris. I assure you we're *quite* used to this sort of thing. Goodbye.'

'Goodbye, *darling*!'

Mr. Fenton looked up inquiringly.

'Autograph,' said Miss Fairbrother with a little shrug.

Until he had written A *Flock of Sheep* two years ago, Mr. Fenton had despised both those who asked for autographs and those who granted them. In those days he had been a reviewer and publisher's reader, a combination of professions not without its advantages, one of them being, in Mr. Fenton's case, immunity from the autograph-hunter. With the success of A *Flock of Sheep*, however, he had acquired a new set of values.

'Remind me,' said Archibald Fenton graciously.

'I wonder if you would mind just doing it now,' said Miss Fairbrother. 'She's calling for it directly. It came this morning.'

'Oh, very well.'

Nancy produced an autograph-book which had come that morning, and Mr. Fenton produced a gold fountain-pen with which he wrote 'Archibald Fenton, Kind regards' on a mauve page between 'Stanley Baldwin' and 'Kaye Don'. He always chose a mauve page, and preferred to be between Rudyard Kipling and John Masefield, but this was not always possible.

'Would it be a bother', said Miss Fairbrother, 'if I just got this off, and then we shouldn't be interrupted again? I shall just have to write a letter; she wants a list of the titles of all your other books. She's ordered the new one, of course.'

'You've got some lists made out, haven't you?'

'I'm afraid I shall have to make it out again. We've run out of the last lot.'

Mr. Fenton looked at his watch.

'All right, we'll take five minutes off. I want to get this done before lunch. Who is she, by the way?'

'A Miss Gloria Harris,' said Nancy.

'Gloria? That wasn't the name in the book?'

Miss Fairbrother put a fresh sheet of paper into her typewriter, and said calmly: 'She's filling up the book for her little niece, as a surprise.'

'Oh, an Aunt,' said Mr. Fenton, losing interest, and went out of the room. It was time for a cocktail, anyhow.

At headlong speed Nancy typed the following list of titles for Miss Harris:

> 'Darling, I don't know what you've done, but it sounds as if you were leading a Hue-and-cry. Take the beige stockinette about three from the left, and the brown beret, bottom drawer. Shoes? Stockings of course. How are you underneath, or doesn't that matter? You can have the beige knickers if you like, because unless you're going to wear two lots(!) I shall have yours. Shoes. There's a pound in the bead box in the dressing-table drawer, or you could have the old *crepe* ones with a patch which leap to the eye, the only thing is, if you're going to be pursued for long, they mightn't go on fitting. So take the pound if you think you'll want it. *Disguise.* Most important. *Show your ears,* that will do it. Have you got time before you start, or must you wait till you're well away? There's a very good hairdresser in Tunbridge Wells, if you're making for the coast. Leave this stupid album in the flat, and I'll send it off tonight. All good luck, Jenny darling. You are a family, aren't you? My ridiculous Fenton will come back in a moment, and I must get this sealed up before he asks to read it. I wish I could

have spoken to you properly just now, but perhaps it's as well, because now if the police come, I can say I don't know anything. Nancy.

'P.S. Burn this.'

Nancy took out her latch-key, tied a piece of string to it, wrapped the key and the string in this letter, put the letter in the middle of the album, put the album in a suitable envelope, address the envelope *'Miss Gloria Harris, To be called for'* and hurried it down to the hall table. Then she went upstairs again, and almost immediately was joined by Mr. Archibald Fenton.

'Just let me make sure you've got that list right,' he said, holding out a hand.

'Oh, Mr. Fenton, I'm so sorry! I'm afraid it's sealed up now. I could open it if you like, but—'

'It doesn't matter. You didn't include *Lovely Lady*, of course,' said Mr. Fenton, referring to an earlier work of which he was now ashamed.

'No,' said Miss Fairbrother truthfully.

II

Jenny realized that the thing to avoid was taxis, because taxi-drivers always remembered when they had driven a fair girl in a biscuit-coloured hat and green georgette to Waterloo Station, and they nearly always heard her say to the porter: 'Bittiesham Regis, it's the three-ten, isn't it?' and then they always went to Scotland Yard and, after waiting a little while, were shown into the Inspector's room, and told him all about it. So she went to Bloomsbury by omnibus, and was very glad that omnibus drivers didn't remember so well, or want so much money.

It was wonderful of Nancy to have recognized Gloria Harris so quickly. *Gloria* (because it was the most glorious name Jenny could think of) *Harris* (as a slight tribute to Cook) and *Acetylene* (because it was a name Nancy had just heard about) *Pitt* (out of compliment to the Younger Pitt whom she was doing that term) had had their last adventure together six years ago, when they had served with Wellington in the Peninsular War, and, as far as was possible to two drummer boys, had rolled up the map of Europe at Waterloo. Now she was going to be Gloria Harris again, but not, thought Jenny, disguised as a boy. That always seemed to her so silly, because, however slim you were, you *were* different, and nobody could mistake that tight look that men's clothes gave you. Like that girl in Nancy's school in *The Young Cavalier*, all the wrong shapes and so silly. Why, the police would know at once she was escaping.

She came to Mr. Archibald Fenton's house and rang the bell. Nancy heard it, and longed to rush to the window and give one encouraging wave. But she could not. Mr. Fenton, who had been forced to the conclusion lately that success and artistic merit were not really incompatible, was dictating a kindly article on the novels of Mr. Galsworthy.

'It's Miss Harris,' said Jenny to the maid. 'I've called for a—a letter.'

'Oh yes, miss.' The envelope was shown to her. 'Would that be it?'

'That's it. Thank you very much,' said Jenny, a little surprised at the shape which Nancy's latch-key had taken. She hurried down the steps and across the square; and Mr. Fenton, carried on a slightly involved metaphor to the window, saw the back of her, and thought that, for an aunt, Miss Harris had kept her figure remarkably well.

Jenny sped round to the British Museum, and in a room where she was the youngest inhabitant by three thousand years she opened her precious envelope.

'Oh, Nancy darling,' she thought, 'oh, Acetylene Pitt, you are wonderful!'

How marvellous it would have been if they could have escaped together! If Mr. Fenton had hurt himself badly on a dictionary or something, and Suspicion had rested upon his secretary! Perhaps Nancy could join her later, taking a ticket ostensibly to Earl's Court, but slipping out at Tottenham Court Road, and doubling back to St. Pancras.

She put the letter and the latch-key into her bag, and, with the autograph album under her arm, made her way back to the omnibus country, and waited for something to take her to Victoria. But she was careful when paying for her ticket not to let the conductor see that she now had *two* latch-keys.

At Victoria she got into an omnibus for the King's Road, and all down the King's Road she was thinking to herself 'Hair'. Should she wait until she got to Tunbridge Wells, or should she get it done now? And if now, should she go into a hairdresser's and have a proper Eton crop, or should she try to cut it herself? She put two fingers at the back of her hat and snipped... Yes, she could get the curls off easily—*and* the ones over her ears—but it would look rather funny, wouldn't it?

Bad. It would look rather funny.

Good. But I shall still have £2 4s. 5½d. That settled it.

III

Gloria Harris came out of the little flat and looked cautiously round. The Inspector was obviously having his lunch. She walked into the King's Road and waited for an omnibus to take her back to Victoria.

Her plans were made. She would be a hiker. You couldn't very well start hiking in the King's Road, so she would take a train to Tunbridge Wells and start hiking from there. As far as she remembered, you either hiked in large companies or else in couples. She wouldn't be likely to find a large company, so she would have to do it by herself, but it would not really be by herself because she would always have her dear Hussar. So *that* was all right.

In the flat this letter was waiting for Miss Fairbrother:

'Darling Nancy,—

'You are an angel, darling, for understanding and everything. I have taken the stockinette, and two pairs of country stockings, and the beige knickers and chemise, but I *haven't* left you my green set because I *must* have two of everything, because I may have to wander about the country and I must have a change, and I haven't taken your pound, so I haven't very much money, so I can't afford to buy very much, and the shoes fit perfectly, darling. I am wearing the beige now, and shall dye the green later on if I can, because they might look rather funny getting over a stile, because the skirt is just the least bit short, but it doesn't matter because I shall be *hiking*, but a detective might notice and it's just the sort of *little* thing which makes them suspicious. Darling Nancy, do you mind, I've taken your pyjamas, I didn't know you wore them, I never have, are they nice, there was only one pair, the blue, which I've taken, because I suddenly remembered about that, and I must have something. I'm buying a knapsack to put them all in, and darling I've left you my watch, it's one Aunt Caroline gave me, but Mr. and Mrs. Watterson have never said anything, I mean they've never said What a pretty watch that is, so that means they've never really noticed it so as to describe it to the police, so I should think you could sell it quite easily, but not the bag, which I shan't want *hiking*, and people might remember it. So please do, Nancy, I mean the watch, because of the extra stockings and the knickers and the pyjamas and all the extra things I've taken, oh, and two handkerchiefs, and I hope you'll like the hat, it cost four guineas, so perhaps you could sell that too, I mean to a friend. Oh no, darling, I've just remembered, Mrs. Watterson *particularly* noticed the hat, so you'd better hide it altogether. Oh dear! And perhaps you oughtn't to wear the georgette either, oh *darling!* But you *will* sell the watch, won't you, and those are real little diamonds.

'I must fly, Nancy darling, because I daren't stay in London a moment longer, I've cut my hair myself, *quite* short, it looks awful, and I've found a lipstick of yours, I didn't know you used them, I *never* have, are they nice, I've put a lot on for disguise, and I've taken it with me, so *mind you sell the watch.* And do just write to Miss Gloria Harris, Poste Restante, Tunbridge Wells, to say you don't mind what I've done. Your loving, grateful Jenny.

'P.S. Burn this.'

So, with a brown-paper parcel under her arm, and mixed emotions in her bosom, Miss Gloria Harris left London for Tunbridge Wells.

5

ACTIVITY IN LONDON

I

Although Inspector James Marigold had had a long and varied career in the Police Force, he had never actually taken part in a Murder Case. It was almost the only thing in which he hadn't taken part. He had watched most of the Test Matches at Lord's from a sedentary position in front of the bowling screen, rousing himself in the intermissions to say 'Pass off the ground there, please' to those spectators who were delaying the resumption of play. He had joined hands with other members of the Force to keep back the crowd at fashionable weddings. In the Row on one occasion a horse which had suddenly caught sight of the Albert Memorial and was hurrying back to its stable was stopped by P.C. Marigold and returned to its lessee, and the fact that this gentleman was a Member of Parliament had brought the police officer a short but gratifying notice in the evening papers. On another occasion he had held the traffic up at Hyde Park Corner while a flock of sheep had transferred its grazing quarters to the Green Park; and though the photograph of him doing this (headed 'RURAL LONDON') had given the impression that it was the flock of sheep which was holding the traffic up while Sergeant Marigold went for a drink, it had all helped to fire his ambition, and to prepare him for what was to be his Greatest Case, the Auburn Lodge Mystery.

He had begun by arresting George Parracot. There were three reasons for arresting Mr. Parracot.

1. He had been the first to find the body.
2. He had called attention to Jenny's handkerchief in a Marked Manner.
3. He was obviously Concealing Something.

'There's this handkerchief, Inspector,' said Mr. Parracot almost as soon as they were in the room. 'I don't know if it has anything to do with it, but—'

'All in due course,' said the Inspector, holding up the hand which had stopped a thousand motor-omnibuses. 'We take things in order, Mr.—er '

'Parracot.'

'Mr. Parracot, and in that way we keep things orderly. Now then, over there, please, until I'm ready for you.'

The body was examined, photographed, removed. '*Right* over there,' said the Inspector to Mr. Parracot, who had already got the legs of his trousers into two photographs. 'Sit right over there in that corner, and don't move until I tell you to come out.'

'About the handkerchief,' said George a little later on. 'I didn't want you to think—'

'When the moment comes to come to the handkerchief, Mr.— er—'

'Parracot.'

'Parracot, we shall come to it.' He looked round the room. 'Now then, what were you saying about a handkerchief?'

'There's a handkerchief over there on that chair.'

'Well?'

'Well, you see, my wife—I mean it's got "Jenny" on it.'

'Well?'

'Well, I mean my wife's name is Laura.'

'We shall come to Mrs. Parracot later,' said the Inspector. 'Suppose we begin at the beginning, and try to get things into some sort of order.' He took out his notebook. 'Your name?'

'Parracot.'

'Just Parracot?'

'George Parracot.'

'Don't keep anything back. Now then, Mr. Parracot, if you would like to give some account of your movements this morning and to explain how you made this shocking discovery—'

'Well, it was like this,' said Mr. Parracot eagerly.

He gave an account. He explained. He made it perfectly clear that the responsibility was his and his alone; that though, as he maintained, he had not struck the actual blow, yet, if a Jury of his fellow-countrymen, some of them possibly Old Felsbridgians, held that the harbouring of a strange body in one's drawing-room was such bad form as to be practically indistinguishable from murder, then he was prepared to take what was coming to him, even if it meant the Supreme Penalty, so long as his dear wife, Laura—'

'Look here,' said Inspector Marigold, getting more and more suspicious, 'you say your wife's name is Laura?'

'Yes,' said George eagerly. 'Laura Mary Parracot.'

'And this,' said the Inspector, holding up the handkerchief, 'has "Jenny" on it?'

'Yes.'

'Then whose is it?'

Mr. Parracot was carried away on a wave of fine feeling. 'Mine,' he said simply, and fingered his tie.

'I thought you said your name was *George* Parracot,' said the Inspector, thumbing his way back to an earlier passage in his notebook.

Mr. Parracot returned to the surface. 'Er—yes,' he said.

'And yet you have "Jenny" on your handkerchiefs?'

'Well, I don't exactly,' said George.

'How do you mean you don't exactly?'

'Well—' George wondered what he did mean.

'You mean somebody called Jenny gave you this handkerchief, and you always carry it about with you?'

'Good Heavens, no,' said Mr. Parracot hastily, realizing that he had gone much too far. 'No, no, of course not. As a matter of fact,' he said weakly, 'it isn't really mine at all.'

'Then why do you say it was?'

'Well—'

'Are you', demanded Inspector Marigold sternly, 'endeavouring to Obstruct the Cause of Justice?'

'No, really,' said Mr. Parracot.

'Are you aware', said Inspector Marigold severely, 'that Obstructing the Cause of Justice is an Extremely Serious Offence?'

'I—I misunderstood you. It isn't my handkerchief at all.'

'Then whose is it?'

'I don't— I mean I—Why, of course!' Mr. Parracot was suddenly inspired. 'Jane Latour! Jenny!'

'And who, might I ask, is Jane Latour?'

'Why, *she* was.' He jerked his head towards the door.

The Inspector moistened his thumb again and worked his way backwards.

'Five minutes ago you told me that you had never seen the dead woman before, and had no idea who she was.'

'Well, yes, in a way, but what I meant—'

'Mr. Parracot, in your own interests I advise you to be Very, Very Careful.'

'What I meant was my wife—' He pulled himself up. 'No, no, I mean *I*—I said to my wife, who—who just happened—as I say, I happened to call her in here, she was in her bedroom as a matter of fact, I should have said it anyhow, well really I just said it to myself, "It looks rather like Jane Latour," I said, and my wife said "Like *who?*" and I said "Nobody *you* know, old girl, it's just somebody I saw on the stage once," and photographs, you know, and—'

'I think', said Inspector Marigold, 'that I had better see Mrs. Parracot now.'

'Oh, I say,' cried George, 'must you?'

'Laura Parracot, didn't you say?' He got on to a clean page of his notebook.

'I say, you will spare her as much as possible? You know what I mean? She's only a woman, and—er—rather delicate and all that.'

Inspector Marigold's old school had no club tie, but he was a sportsman and a gentleman. His whole manner altered. For the first time he became friendly, human, understanding.

'That's all right, sir,' he said, with a look in his eye which was just not a wink. In a Delicate Condition, eh?'

'Er—yes,' said Mr. Parracot helplessly.

It was when he discovered that Mr. Parracot was lying for the third time that the Inspector arrested him.

II

If George Parracot had been taken in gyves to Merrion Place police station, then (a disturbing thought to many) this story might have been written differently. For the poster

FAMOUS ACTRESS
FOUND DEAD
WELL-KNOWN CLUBMAN
ARRESTED

would certainly have caught Nancy's eye in London, if not Jenny's in Tunbridge Wells, and Jenny, however absurd the arrest had seemed to her, since he was not a relation of Aunt Jane's, would have returned to save Mr. Parracot's life.

Fortunately Inspector Marigold had not as yet committed himself to publicity. Mr. Parracot, considering himself, as requested by the Inspector, under arrest, but as yet unmanacled, was waiting in the hall with Sergeant Bagshaw until investigations in the drawing-room were finished. Bagshaw, who always exerted himself socially on these occasions, was telling him about the last moments of the Edmonton murderer, but George could manage no more in reply than an occasional 'Fancy!' as horror succeeded horror. How, he wondered, was Laura getting on upstairs?

He need not have been anxious. Once the body was out of the way, Laura was her own woman again. Having removed the first misapprehension from the Inspector's mind, and excused him for a moment while he arrested George, she then put him right on one or two other points.

The dead woman was Jane Latour, the actress, as anybody with eyes in his head could have seen for himself...

Jane Latour was *not* called Jenny. Her intimate friends called her Toto, as anybody who could read would have known for himself...

They had taken the house through Harrods. The owner had died. No, not been murdered. Just died. Watterson, Watterson and Hinchcoe were the solicitors. Young Mr. Hinchcoe had met her at the house and gone into things with her...

Mr. Parracot had never met Miss Latour. He wouldn't. Not *that* sort of woman...

Now she remembered. She knew there was *something* about Jane Latour. Of course! Her real name was Jane Windell. She was the daughter of General Sir Oliver Windell...

It had *everything* to do with it. Auburn Lodge had belonged to a Miss Windell. The one who died...

She couldn't say everything at once. If the Inspector took that sort of tone, then she wouldn't say anything at all.

Inspector Marigold apologized humbly. Mrs. Parracot smiled at him sweetly. Inspector Marigold curled his moustache and smiled back; and metaphorically tied a knot in his handkerchief to remind him to release George, who was obviously not concerned in what, it was now plain, was a Family Job. Very handsome woman, Mrs. Parracot. Would have looked well at Lord's being passed gently off the ground after the luncheon interval.

'I'll tell you something else,' said Laura archly.

'Please do, madam.'

'I've only just noticed it, so don't ask me why I didn't say so before.' She said it so charmingly that the Inspector was not offended, but he did just wonder how personal a tone the conversation was going to take. Not, of course, a crumb on the moustache, but—

'The window,' said Laura.

'The window?' He turned in his chair.

Laura gave an apologetic little laugh.

'No, I'm being silly. Of course, *you* opened it.'

'No, madam, certainly not. Why?'

'Well, it wasn't open when we came in.'

'What!' The Inspector hoisted himself up and lumbered to the window.

'Of course, George might have done it, while he was waiting for you,' said Laura, trying to spoil it all.

She was too late. The Inspector was already at the window. He looked out. He saw the footprints. He beckoned mysteriously to Mrs. Parracot.

They looked out together.

'See that?'

'Footprints!' said Laura excitedly.

'The murderess,' said the Inspector solemnly.

'Jenny,' said Laura.

'Jenny it is.'

They drew their heads in and nodded to each other.

'And now,' said Inspector Marigold with grim determination, 'to find Jenny.'

He looked at his watch, and decided that he would find her after the luncheon interval.

III

Archibald Fenton had a wife and six children, and at first he had minded this a good deal. Not only were the seven of them expensive to maintain, but they formed, he could not help feeling, the wrong background for a critic of the Advanced School. The greeting which he was accustomed to receive from the less mathematical of his friends, 'Well, how's the family?' placed him definitely among the Victorians. So might Dickens have been addressed by Wilkie Collins; so, doubtless, he often was. But with the success of A Flock of Sheep, he realized that the family was just the background which he wanted. A man who had brought back 'heartiness', 'virility', 'the smell of hops', 'something of an Elizabethan tang' and 'a Rabelaisian robustness' to the English novel (to quote from different columns of the Observer review) was living well within himself in limiting his output of children to six; and though he did not go so far as to feel grateful to Fanny, he was now so far from blaming her that he insisted on accepting all the credit for himself. She was, so to say, merely her husband's publisher.

There was, he found, another advantage to him in the large family. As a young woman Fanny had been more admirable for her bank-balance than for her figure. It was natural that the needs of all these children should reduce considerably the one, and perhaps not surprising that the provision of them should have added considerably to the other, but certainly she was now much more noticeable for her figure than for her bank-balance. In men Archibald had no objection to that heartiness of outline which could not—or, anyhow, should not—be called stoutness; indeed, he himself, to take a case, had an accommodating fullness of habit, a certain not unpleasing convexity of figure which sorted well with the robustness of his work. But Fanny was a woman; and Fanny, in any case, had gone too far altogether. It was as well, then, that the cares of the nursery should keep her so devotedly at home, at a time when her husband was, so conspicuously, going about. Even if Fanny had been slim and beautiful, yet in his new social system Archibald would have shone more brilliantly alone, the solitary focus of attention. Moreover, no real artist can preserve that mystery, that aloofness, which the laity demands from its artists, in the presence of one for whom he has lost all mystery... and from whom he was never, strictly speaking, aloof.

This excursion into Mr. Archibald Fenton's family life is bringing us to no more than the fact that the house in Bloomsbury was full. Rightly Archibald had the largest room as his work-room, but it was a pity that there was no cupboard left over, however small, for his secretary.

At 9.30 Miss Fairbrother arrived, and looked through the letters which Mr. Fenton had left for her.

At 10.15 Mr. Fenton entered the work-room. Miss Fairbrother rose, and Mr. Fenton said something about the weather or his secretary's personal appearance.

From 10.15 to 1.10 Mr. Fenton dictated.

At 1.10 Mr. Fenton left for his club.

At 1.15 Miss Fairbrother joined the family for luncheon, thus enabling Mr. Fenton to pay her slightly less, and Miss Fairbrother to get an insight into the duties of a nursery governess, should she ever wish to be one.

At two o'clock Miss Fairbrother returned, alone, to the work-room, and typed all that she had taken down in shorthand in the morning.

At 4.30 Miss Fairbrother left, generally meeting Mr. Fenton on the doorstep; in which case he said to her 'Just off?' and she said 'Yes', these being the facts.

From 5-7 Mr. Fenton, alone in his work-room, prepared, either in his mind or in rough pencillings, the next morning's instalment.

At eight o'clock, complete from eye-glass to fob, Mr. Fenton went out to dinner.

At nine o'clock Mrs. Fenton put the last of the family (excepting, of course, Mr. Fenton) to bed.

At ten o'clock, when Mr. Fenton was just joining the ladies, she went to bed herself...

At 4.30, then, on this day of late June, Nancy had begun her eager return to the Chelsea Flat. Jenny had been in her thoughts all through the long afternoon. The clack-clack of the typewriter went on; the rumble of Oxford Street, the gentler noises of the quiet square, drifted through the geranium-scented windows; but in her mind Nancy was at one moment in the heart of Kent, hiding among the hay-cocks while the pursuit went by, or fording a stream to give some blood-hound the slip... and, at the next, back in London again, bidding a reluctant farewell to her beige knickers. If only she had been with Jenny (each, of course, wearing her own, and starting the thing properly) what fun they would have had!...

Clack-clack-clack. Clack-clack. *(What* had *Jenny done?)* Clackclack-clack. Clack.

She wondered how she would look in Jenny's green georgette. Not really her colour, of course. *Clack-clack-clack* ...

At last the afternoon was over, and she was free. Her mind still full of fancies, she hurried to her omnibus, and from the top of it began to get into touch with reality. A poster bore the words:

WELL KNOWN
ACTRESS
DEAD

Nancy wondered who it was, and hoped that it wouldn't be Gladys Cooper.

The next poster was more informative:

WEST END
ACTRESS
FOUND DEAD

Nancy was relieved, because now it was almost certainly *not* Gladys Cooper, who was much too West-end to be called a West-end actress. And 'Found dead' meant that nobody was there when you died, so you had probably done it yourself. Nancy wondered what it was like... doing it yourself. Anyhow Gladys Cooper wouldn't.

WEST END
MURDER MYSTERY
LATEST

That was that one at Notting Hill, wasn't it? The organ-grinder with the wooden leg.

ACTRESS DEAD
IN
WEST END
MANSION

That, thought Nancy, is the West-end actress. Gladys Cooper lived at Highgate. It would look funny if you had a poster

'ACTRESS ALIVE IN NORTH END MANSION'. What a lot of funny posters you could have if you tried.

FAMOUS
ACTRESS
MURDERED

I say! thought Nancy. So it isn't the organ-grinder! I *wonder* who it is! I expect her understudy did it! They always do. So as to play the part! I suppose the theatre will shut tonight. I wonder if—

And then, as she came into Sloane Square, two more posters told her all.

BROMPTON ROAD
MYSTERY
LATEST

said the one. And the other:

JANE
LATOUR
LATEST DEVELOPMENTS

'Jenny!' cried out Nancy's heart. 'Oh, Jenny darling!' And she rushed down the stairs of the omnibus, and out into the Square.

IV

Nancy drew the second sheet from the typewriter, placed it beneath the first sheet, and settled down to read. From time to time she nodded to herself approvingly. It was a good letter. She was prepared to bet that not even Archibald Fenton himself, with all his reputation, could have written a letter so good. It did everything which it had set out, six copies ago, to do.

It is possible that her early experiences in the Peninsular War had made Acetylene Pitt unduly cautious when communicating with a friend in the presence of the enemy; but certainly caution was necessary. For though the Englishman's home may still have the integrity, and to some extent (if desired) the exterior decoration, of a castle, his correspondence has long ceased to have any privacy at all. Once a letter gets into the hands of His Majesty's Postmaster-General, it is at the mercy of a Home Secretary looking for lottery tickets or a War Office searching for traitors. What more hopeful centre for their investigations, thought Nancy, than the Tunbridge Wells Post Office? Tunbridge Wells was notoriously the home of retired Admirals, Generals and Indian Civil Servants: admirable men, with a fixed but inadequate income, and an unconquerable belief in their ability to enlarge it. Who more likely than an Admiral to enter breezily for a sweepstake, or a General to sell to some treacherous foreign power his copy of *King's Regulations*, 1886? What more likely pseudonym for them to adopt than an innocent-seeming 'Gloria Harris'?

Nancy realized, then, that her letter to Jenny was a public rather than a private communication. Yet it had to answer Jenny's extremely private letter. It had to make the following points quite clear to Jenny without giving away anything to the police.

1. I know all about it, Jenny darling, and of course I'll help you.
2. It's perfectly all right about the clothes, and I don't mind a bit about the extra things.
3. I quite understand about not wearing the green georgette and hat.

4. I'll pawn the watch, and send you most of the money, because it's much too much just for the things you've taken.

So, with this in mind, Nancy sat down to her typewriter, and after six attempts, achieved the following:

'The Menagerie, Tuesday.

'Darling Gloria,—

'How nice to hear from you. I do hope you will enjoy your holiday. I haven't much news, except that two new exhibits joined the menagerie yesterday, but I haven't seen them yet. Sisters. Of course we are all very excited about the Jane Latour Murder, because one of the girls—Bertha Holloway — did you see her that time you came?—glasses and a protruding head like a tortoise—well, Bertha saw her in all those *Russian* plays, and had rather a crush on her, and of course we've all read all *sorts* of things about her, so it isn't really surprising, I mean being murdered, but Bertha says they aren't true. Apparently she wrote for her autograph once, but I don't see that that proves it. Bertha also says that the "Jenny" the police are looking for is *not* her illegitimate daughter, I mean Jane Latour's, as people are saying, but she doesn't know *who* she is—and neither does anybody else, not even the police, I mean, not *really*. But of course they're bound to find out soon, because of the handkerchief and the footprints, and then, I suppose, they'll begin to look for her properly.

'Well, that shows what London's like, with me listening to Miss Bertha Tortoise about a stupid murder, when I long to be out in the open sunshine, like you are, and listening to the birds. I got a new georgette—*blue*—and a ducky little hat at the sales, but I shan't be able to wear them yet, so I've put them away *very carefully*, and am sticking to the brown. (Well, really in this weather, *almost!)* And I've been selling one or two things, that stockinette, do you remember, and the undies that I always used to wear with it, but *quite* good still, and one or two other things, and have got a very good price for them, *quite* satisfactory in *every* way. I haven't actually got the money yet, but it's coming tomorrow, and what with one thing and another, spare-time work and Aunt Mary sending me a postal order on my birthday, I shall be able to pay you back *five pounds* of the money you lent me, darling, and *possibly more.* So this is very important, will you give me an address where I can send it, *and where you're sure to get it safely*, because I always say you can't have too much money on a holiday, particularly the sort of wandering-about holiday you're having now. So *don't forget.*

'Goodbye, Gloria darling, I *wish* I could be with you, but I expect I'm really better where I am, if you look at it all round. I mean just now.

'Your very loving A. P.

'P.S. Wasn't I right to insist on your taking pyjamas? I never wear them in London, but I think in the country, and *of course* if you sleep out, you simply *must* have them.'

The best of this letter, thought Nancy as she put it in its envelope, was that, not only was it an absolutely natural one to be waiting for anybody at the Tunbridge Wells Post Office, but that it gave Gloria Harris what Mr. Fenton would have called a Background. It would be safe for her, indeed it would be wise for her, to leave this letter lying about, so that whoever read it would know that Gloria Harris was a real person. With a Background.

Nancy had achieved the Background with her first six copies. What had made the seventh copy necessary was the problem of the address.

To put her real address at the head of the letter was to provide a clue. If the letter came into the Wrong Hands, then one of those hands could lay itself on Nancy's shoulder (if it should so desire) and lead her wherever it willed. But to put no address, as at first she had done, was to make Gloria Harris's background too indistinct altogether. A genuine letter would surely have *some* address. A false one then? Easy enough to invent, but also, in the wrong hands, easily proved false. Also, quite possibly, confusing to Jenny. And then, brilliant inspiration, she thought of 'The Menagerie'. It could refer to so many things. A boardinghouse, a Young Women's hostel, a shop, a secretarial college, a girls' school: from any one of these A. P. might be writing in very much the words of this letter. It needed a little alteration here and there; perhaps a slight reference to the Menagerie in the body of it; just enough to make a seventh copy advisable, but so little as to make it absolutely final—the Perfect Work of Art.

She stamped the letter and took it for a walk to South Kensington. South Kensington was so safe, and so full of menageries. As she walked, she wondered about A. P. Not Acetylene Pitt, which you couldn't really be called nowadays, but Alice Pitman. Thirty-five, she thought; good, earnest, slightly perspiring; half governess (without certificate) half matron at a large kindergarten with resident mistresses. The mistresses were young enough to think of themselves as 'the girls', and Bertha Holloway was the English mistress and taught the children to act plays, and Alice Pitman (secretary, of course, to the Head, as well as the other things, because of using a typewriter) was really called Miss Pitman, but she liked to think that they called her Alice and thought of her as one of the girls too; and Gloria Harris—

But how would Miss Pitman have a friend like Gloria Harris? Oh, well, that was easy. An old pupil...

It was really quite a story...

Might write a story one day, thought Nancy. I know most of the tricks...

Why not dye the green georgette? Why ever not?

Why not?...

She would...

The letter went into the box, but, before it came to Gloria Harris, Jenny had got a new background altogether.

6

JENNY AT TUNBRIDGE WELLS

I

With two brown-paper parcels under her arm and mixed emotions in her bosom, Miss Gloria Harris left Tunbridge Wells by omnibus.

It was five o'clock in the afternoon, such a mellow, gracious June afternoon as Jenny had never known. In one of her parcels were a green set of underclothes, a pair of blue pyjamas, a pair of beige stockings, two handkerchiefs and a lipstick. In the other were a knapsack, a small towel, a cake of soap, a comb, a pair of scissors, a toothbrush, a small sponge, a tube of toothpaste, a pair of pink garters, some cold cream, a large slab of chocolate, a box of dates, and Watson's Wonderful Combination Watch-dog-and-Water-pistol. The first parcel contained all that she had taken away from Nancy's flat; the second contained all that little Mr. Sandroyd, of Sandroyd's Stores and General Depository, had sold her as soon as he heard the magic word 'knapsack'.

'A knapsack? Certainly, madam,' said Mr. Sandroyd, brushing up the cascade of his moustache with the back of his hand, as if to make himself more audible. 'Going hiking, if I may be permitted the phrase?'

'Yes,' said Jenny.

'Ah' He beamed at her through his glasses. 'Then perhaps you will allow me to bring to your notice this list which I have compiled for the convenience of our customers.' He handed her a gaudily printed bill headed: 'HIKERS. BEWARE!'

'Beware of what?' said Jenny a little nervously.

'A little ruse of mine, madam,' said Mr. Sandroyd reassuringly, 'for calling the attention of ladies and gentlemen to the articles which they so often forget to take with them. You will notice'—he leant over the counter and jabbed at the list with a stubby and reflexed thumb—'that I have ventured to divide the articles into two columns headed *Optional* and *Obligatory*. Far be it from me', said Mr. Sandroyd kindly, to dictate to ladies and gentlemen what they should take and what they should not. My only purpose—if you will allow me one moment'—he swooped down on the list, made a mark with a finger-nail against one item, and leant back | complacently—'There! Soap!' He twinkled at her. 'I am not going too far in suggesting that *soap* as an article for a young lady's toilet...? Even in the give-and-take of camp life...? Well, one I wouldn't *quite* say "*optional*", would one?' He put his head on one side and looked at her comically over his glasses.

Jenny nodded confidingly at him.

'I do want some,' she said.

'A dainty cake of freshly scented soap,' he agreed. 'Verbena, lemon, rose, sandal-wood—a matter of personal choice for the customer, but we have them all—'

'Verbena,' nodded Jenny.

'Dainty and distinguished,' said Mr. Sandroyd approvingly. 'Now suppose we decide upon the knapsack first, and then place each article as bought into its proper receptacle. I have here —excuse me one moment'—he disappeared behind the counter and came back almost at once —'I have here', said

Mr. Sandroyd, holding it up and turning it this way and that, 'a superb specimen of the knapsacker's art.'

Jenny gasped.

'Oh, I'm *sure,*' she began, 'I mean— You see, I haven't really very much money.'

'Ah!'

He put the knapsack down, and looked at her commiseratingly, holding his elbow with one hand, and scratching his ear with the other. 'Well now, let me think.' He nodded to himself. 'Yes. How would this be? We buy the soap and other articles first, and then we know how much money we have over? We can then suit the knapsack to our means. How would that be?'

Jenny agreed that that would be a very good idea, and said that she *did* want a tube of Kolynos, and in fact—er—well, perhaps a—

Mr. Sandroyd held up a kindly hand. He understood perfectly. Having the—how should he put it?—the publicity of camp life in their minds, many young ladies took this opportunity of renewing certain of their toilet accessories. A sponge, for instance, after quite a short use which had in no way impaired its properties, frequently proved to have lost its air of freshness when brought, as it were, into competition with a more newly purchased article... Quite a small sponge? Certainly... And the next?

Jenny told him...

'And that really *is* all,' she said at last.

Mr. Sandroyd held up a finger, and shook his head. 'Food, madam. What in the Army we used to call the emergency rations. My own recommendation to my clients is a packet of chocolate and a box of dates. Dates,' said Mr. Sandroyd, lovingly stroking a box, 'from Tunis. A most sustaining food, as many travellers can attest who have crossed the desert on no more than a handful of dates.'

'Oh, thank you, yes,' said Jenny. 'I did want something. And that really *is* all, thank you. How much does all that come to?'

Mr. Sandroyd pushed his spectacles on to his forehead, and involved himself in the necessary addition. He emerged, after a short struggle, with a total of 18s. 4½d.

'I see,' said Jenny, but without much hope.

'Now what would that leave us for the knapsack?'

'What is the very cheapest you have?' asked Jenny anxiously.

'I shouldn't care to let you have one for less than five and sixpence.'

Jenny tried not to show her relief, and, having asked to see a five-and-sixpenny one, said that that would do beautifully. 'That's one pound three and tenpence halfpenny, isn't it, so if I give you one pound four—' She took out her purse.

'Excuse me a moment, miss.' Mr. Sandroyd disappeared into the western recesses of his counter, and came back a little mysteriously, one hand hidden. 'Now, madam,' he went on solemnly, 'I feel bound to ask you and I trust you will forgive the liberty, are you making this pleasure-jaunt in a large company of both sexes, or, as I might say, more intimately?'

'I—I'm meeting somebody,' stammered Jenny. 'I—I mean I shall be *with* somebody,' and told herself that she would always be with her dear Hussar whatever happened.

'Far be it from me to intrude,' said Mr. Sandroyd, holding up his free hand. 'All I wish to bring home to you, madam, is that there will be times, there must be times, when you will be separated from your companion. He—or she— *or* she,' he said again, to show how little he wished to intrude, 'will have gone to a neighbouring farm for eggs, while you remain in camp and boil the kettle. Or you yourself will have gone down to the stream to fill the kettle, while she—or, as it might be, he—remains in camp. However it is, you will be separated. You will be alone. Am I not right?' He waited anxiously.

Jenny agreed that there would be times when she would be alone.

'Ah!' He gave a sigh of relief. 'Then in that case I must insist on selling you a Watson's Wonderful Combination Watch-dog-and-Water-pistol.' With which words, he whipped it out from behind his back and presented it at an imaginary enemy in the doorway.

Jenny screamed, thinking that a gang was breaking in, thinking that he was going to fire. Mr. Sandroyd, taking the scream as a tribute to the alarming appearance of Watson's Wonderful Combination Watch-dog-and-Water-pistol, turned to her with a happy smile. 'Only five and six,' he said, 'the same price as the knapsack,' as if, in some way, this made it more of a bargain.

'Oh, but I daren't,' said Jenny. 'I should be afraid—why, I might—' She remembered that she was already being held responsible for one body, and she couldn't, she simply couldn't, take the risk of having to explain another.

'It is not a real pistol, madam,' he said delightedly.

'Oh, I thought it was.'

'Precisely! Now allow me to explain.' Without waiting for permission he brushed up his moustache, took a deep breath and launched himself on his favourite recitation.

'The watch-dog. Now what is the function of the watch-dog? He has, we may say, two functions. To alarm the intruder by his bark, and to arouse the household. Watson's Wonderful Combination Watch-dog-and-Water-pistol performs these two functions. It alarms the intruder, the marauding tramp, by the volume of its explosion, an explosion of similar volume to that of an ordinary pistol, and at the same time it summons help from the passer-by. But it does more. Let us suppose that some prowling ruffian has demanded a lady's purse, or—' Mr. Sandroyd modestly closed his eyes— 'something even dearer to her. She produces her Watson, and says "Leave me or I fire!" He laughs brutally; he realizes that she will never have the courage. She fires! And now comes in the real beauty of the invention, amply meriting in my opinion the word Wonderful. She pulls the trigger again, and a thin stream of water is discharged. Now consider, as Watson has considered it, the psychology of the marauder. He sees the pistol; he hears the explosion; instinctively he closes his eyes; then suddenly he feels something streaming down his brow. *Blood!* He has been hit! He will be hit again if he stays! He flies! Watson's Wonderful Combination Watch-dog-and-Water-pistol. Invented,' added Mr. Sandroyd kindly, the recitation over, 'by a man called Watson. A Benefactor. With six cartridges and full instructions, five and sixpence.'

'Oh,' said Jenny. 'I see.'

'No daughter of mine', said Mr. Sandroyd sternly, 'should go hiking without it.'

'I hadn't thought of—of tramps and things.'

Mr. Sandroyd hesitated for a moment, and then risked all his profit from five and sixpence in one large reassuring smile. She was so young and, in spite of her painted lips, so simple.

'And ten to one you won't need to, miss,' he said comfortingly. 'But just in case?' he pleaded. And, indeed, he was going to sleep happier tonight, if he could think of her under Watson's protection.

'But where would I carry it? I mean if you had it on your back in your knapsack—'

'In the pocket, madam? As you see, it is very small and handy. Or some ladies carry it in the garter, in the Spanish fashion, strapped, as it were, to the leg.'

'Oh, but I'm wearing suspenders!' said Jenny.

'Allow me, madam.' He went away and came back with a pair of cheap pink garters.

'Oh, but—' began Jenny.

'If you will allow me,' said Mr. Sandroyd with a fatherly beam, 'we will say nothing about—let me see, it was one pound three shillings and tenpence halfpenny, and five and sixpence for the pistol. That makes one pound nine shillings and fourpence ha'penny altogether. Are we putting the knapsack on now, or shall I wrap them all up?'

'Oh, wrapped up, please. Oh, but I—oh, but are you really? Oh, but it *is* good of you. Thank you so much. . . Thank you... Good afternoon and—and *thank* you.'

Mr. Sandroyd accompanied her to the door. At the door he ventured to pat her shoulder gently—two little pats so gentle that they hardly reached her.

'Take care of yourself, my dear young lady,' he said solemnly. 'In every way.'

'Oh, I *will*,' said Jenny earnestly. 'I *promise* I will.'

II

Jenny's one idea now was to escape from Tunbridge Wells. In Tunbridge Wells there were policemen; she had just seen one. In the fields there were none. Was there anything else she wanted before she made for the fields? There was. A shop across the road was calling out CREAM ICES, and this was always a trumpet-call for Jenny. She crossed the road and went into the Olde Kent Kreamery (F. Searle, Proprietor) for what would probably be the last cream ice she would ever eat.

It was the magic hour of tea, and the Olde Kent Kreamery was full of women who could have refreshed themselves more comfortably, but less noticeably, at home. Jenny shared a table with two friends, May and Nina. May lived in Tunbridge Wells with Aunt Jane—obviously another one; Nina had come in for the day, and was coming in again next week, and would be sure to let May know, so that they could have the whole day together this time. 'I did ask you how Mrs. Anderson was?' said May, and

Nina said Yes, she had... and Mrs. Anderson was left there, so that Jenny never really knew how she was. May said that there was no doubt the busses were *awfully* convenient, whatever people said about spoiling the country, and Nina said that now that Daddy had had to give up the car, if it wasn't for the busses—but of course they did spoil the country rather, at least, when you weren't riding in one yourself. They both laughed at this, and May went into a reverie, her teaspoon idly chasing a stranger round her cup. As soon as her ideas were solidified, she said: 'Don't you think Life *is* rather like that? I mean things seem different according to how you look at them? I mean it's like looking at two sides of a wall.' Nina wrinkled her forehead, and said that she saw what May meant, and she supposed it *was* rather. Like two sides of a penny. 'Y-yes,' said May, a little doubtfully, feeling, perhaps, that Nina had not advanced the idea as much as she might have done; and then shook a dozen bangles off her wrist, and looked at her watch, and said: 'Good gracious, oh but there's plenty of time. I'll come down to the bus with you. We needn't go for five minutes yet.' Nina, looking at her watch, agreed, and asked for the bills, adding 'Separately, please,' just as May was beginning to say: 'Oh no, dear, you really mustn't.'

'Of course there's something about the country,' said May quickly, to hide her embarrassment, 'I mean the real country, that does make it different, I mean from a place like Tunbridge Wells, I mean *right* in the country, I mean like you are.'

'Well, of course,' said Nina, 'I do think you want to be one or the other. I mean—'

It was at this moment that Jenny came to a decision. Even at the cost of a pain in the forehead, she must finish her ice in four minutes so as to follow Nina into the real country, where it was different from a place like Tunbridge Wells...

The three bills were paid. May gathered herself and her bangles together and came out of her seat. There was a good deal to come, and Jenny, following her to the door, thought: 'Of course a lot of it's bone, but I believe if she *did* something, but I suppose it's too late now. Anyhow I shan't lose sight of her, which is lucky.' She lingered at the next shop window, so that she should not seem to follow, and then hurried up the hill, a little anxiously at first, but, reassured by unmistakable glimpses of May from the south, soon more leisurely, until she found herself again within earshot of the bangles and the voices, and knew that she was safe. They came to an omnibus.

'Well, we're in time all right,' said May, looking at her watch, and Nina, looking at the omnibus, agreed. Nina said: 'Don't bother to wait,' and May said that perhaps she *had* better get back, as Aunt Jane generally liked to be read to about that time. Nina asked her if she had read A *Flock of Sheep*, and May said wasn't it funny she was just going to ask Nina if *she* had. Apparently they had both read it, and thought it was lovely. May said that some friends of theirs, the Graysons, knew a great friend of Archibald Fenton's, and that he was just like that himself, and that all the Circus part was drawn from his own experiences, when he had run away from school. Nina said: 'Oh, I thought he was at Eton,' and May said she didn't *think* so, but she might be wrong. They both seemed to feel that nobody would want to run away from Eton.

Meanwhile Jenny was walking round the omnibus, to see if it would tell her where it went to. Not that she minded, so long as it went away from Tunbridge Wells; but she felt that a girl with two large parcels under her arm would not just be taking the parcels for a drive into the country, but would have some definite destination for them in her mind. She might sit next to Nina, but on the far side of the conductor, and say whatever Nina said. But then that would fix her in Nina's mind, and she didn't want to be fixed in anybody's mind. Besides, Nina might have a return ticket, if they had return tickets on country omnibuses. They didn't have them on London ones, of course.

The omnibus said that it was going to Maidstone. One of the less useful things which Jenny had learnt with her second governess was that Maidstone was the capital of Kent, and what was now proving to be one of the more useful things which she had learnt with her third governess was that the capital town of a county was where the county gaol was. So she decided not to go to Maidstone. In fact she had almost decided not to use the omnibus at all, owing to its unfortunate connexions, when a little woman in black came up to the driver and said 'Do you go through Endover?' and the driver said 'Near as may be, mother,' and she said 'Thank you' and went inside. There and then Jenny made up her mind to sit as far away from the little woman as she could, and whisper Endover to the conductor as quietly as possible, and get out at the next stopping-place after the little woman had got out, *and* (most important) pay for her ticket with half a crown to be on the safe side. Because anybody going to Endover with two parcels obviously lived at Endover, and ought to know how much the fare was.

Nina was getting in. May was saying 'Tell Mrs. Anderson I asked after her,' and Nina said 'Yes I will,' this further glimpse of Mrs. Anderson leaving Jenny much where she was. The omnibus started. May and Nina waved to each other, May with the more abandon, as befitted one in the more spacious surroundings. Then May went slowly up the hill to her Aunt Jane, jingling as she went, and telling herself that Nina wasn't exactly stuck-up, but wasn't nearly as nice as she used to be; and Nina sat in the omnibus, looking as if she had never waved at anybody, and telling herself that May wasn't a bad sort, but a little—*you* know, and perhaps it was as well that they needn't meet again... And the omnibus went on; and by and by the little woman got out, and went off down a side-lane, and a quarter of a mile farther on they came to a village. This, then, thought Jenny, must be Endover. So she got out with her parcels, looking as if she had known the village all her life, and the omnibus growled its way out of sight... and Jenny Windell stood there, watching it go, and telling herself that so far everything had worked out beautifully.

She was just preparing to take to the fields, when the dashing Hussar had one of his most dashing ideas. He whispered to Jenny, who was standing outside the village stores, and pointed to something in the window. Gurgling to herself she went in and bought it. She also bought two oranges.

7

HUSSAR'S DAUGHTER

I

Jenny sat down, not unwillingly, by the side of the little river, and unpacked her parcels. Not until everything was safely in the knapsack could she consider herself a real hiker. But with the contents of the parcels on the ground beside her, she asked herself 'What would a real Hussar do first?' and knew by instinct that the answer was: 'He would load and place in position Watson's Wonderful Combination Watch-dog-and-Water-pistol.'

She took it from its box. She followed the instructions with a solicitude which would have charmed the author of them; doubtless Watson himself. No pistol was ever more tenderly loaded. But all the instructions of the armament ring would not solve the problem which now faced her. *Which leg?* Hero and villain alike, as she well knew, drew from the hip. Hips, however, were not in the picture. If Jenny drew, it would be from the calf, or no, not the calf, since Nancy's skirt was a little short for the fashion, but from a point six inches above the knee. Which knee? The fact, impressed upon her by her second governess, that Madrid was the capital of Spain, gave her no clue to the romantic Spanish mode, but she knew (who better?) where English Hussars carried so dashingly their swords. Over the left hip. Bother! Hips again. Well, then, romance must make way for the practical. A simple trial urged the claims of the knee which came nearest. The right ... So the pistol was fixed there, and for the first time in the history of the elastic trade a pair of garters found themselves, to their surprise, upon the same leg.

It was a practical Jenny also who packed the knapsack. Change of clothes at the bottom; then the pyjamas; then the articles of toilet; then the towel; then the food. There! The knapsack was strapped up; the brown paper and string pushed down a rabbithole—('It's all right,' Jenny told herself, 'because they do have another way, because of ferrets'); the knapsack hoisted on to her shoulders; and there was Gloria Harris, complete from head to foot, from shoulder to knee, the bachelor girl on holiday.

Now to walk and walk and walk. She walked round a bend of the river, no farther, and stopped dead. A little cry escaped from her. His boots by his side, his back against a tree, the most unattractive man she had ever seen was taking his siesta.

At the noise of Jenny's cry, he opened his eyes.

'Gor',' said this unattractive man slowly, 'two ruddy females.'

Jenny stood there. Her heart was beating ridiculously, right up in her throat. It was silly, because she was the daughter of a soldier; not just a soldier in the Manchester Regiment, but a real Hussar. 'Courage, Jenny,' he was saying. Or was this Gloria Harris, to be so frightened?

She greeted him bravely.

'Good afternoon,' she said with a gulp.

'*One* ruddy female,' said the Tramp, correcting himself.

'Good afternoon,' said Jenny, but with the intonation now of one who was leaving. She took a step forward.

'What's the hurry?' said the Tramp.

Jenny knew, but thought it bad manners to explain. She smiled apologetically, and stopped.

'Fellowship ruddy road,' said the Tramp, and as a development of the theme, added 'Ships parss night.' He was silent for a little, and then explained 'Ruddy night,' in case Jenny hadn't understood.

She had seen him somewhere before: on the stage or in the pages of *Punch.* His nose and eyes were inflamed; he had a month's beard all over him; his hands were horrid, his feet showed through his socks... and yet... and yet... somehow through the mat of hair which hid him there gleamed—something. Something, as it were, alive, human, companionable; or something of this that would be there when he was sober.

'*Siddown*!' commanded the Tramp with sudden violence.

Jenny sat down shrinkingly.

'Stannup!'

Jenny stood up.

'Do what you ruddy well like,' said the Tramp, exhausted by so much authority. He closed his eyes.

Jenny sat down. It was now or never, she felt. If she were frightened now, then she might as well go back to London. But it was idiotic to be frightened. She and Hussar and Watson—three to one! She sat down and took off her hat...

'Wojjer think I've eat today?' asked the Tramp with his eyes closed. And he answered: 'Two ruddy chesnuts.'

'Is that all?' asked Jenny.

'Two ruddy 'orse-chesnuts.'

Jenny said that she had always thought that horse-chestnuts weren't ripe until September.

'*Ripe?*' said the Tramp scornfully. 'Two ruddy unripe ruddy 'orse—' he paused for a moment as if not quite sure about this, and then added 'ruddy chesnuts.'

'Would you like some chocolate?'

'No,' said the Tramp with absolute conviction.

There was another silence. It was very peaceful by the little river, and Jenny decided that she was not afraid of anybody now.

'Two ruddy 'orse-chesnuts off of a nolly-tree,' he mumbled, 'and I ses to 'er "Is this the way to Paradise?" and she ses—' He opened his eyes suddenly and shouted '*Stannup!*'

'Why?' asked Jenny bravely, not moving.

''Cos you're sitting on a ruddy wopses nest.'

Jenny jumped to her feet with a scream.

'*Siddown*,' said the Tramp, ''cos it's a false alarm.' He chuckled to himself 'Ruddy female,' and closed his eyes.

'I've a good mind to go altogether,' said Jenny severely, 'if you can't behave properly.'

She sat down again, a little farther away, having made quite sure that there were no nests of any kind underneath her.

'I've got a wife and six starving children,' said the Tramp with his eyes shut. 'Don't be 'ard on me.' He wagged a hand at her by way of withdrawal. 'Seven,' he amended. 'I was forgetting ruddy 'Orace.'

'What are the names of the others?' asked Jenny.

'Wot others?'

'The other six.'

'Six wot?'

'Six children.'

''Oose children?'

'Oh, never mind,' said Jenny.

'I don't,' said the Tramp. 'Not one ruddy barnacle.' He roused himself and came to business. ''Ow much money 'ave you got?'

'I—I haven't counted,' said Jenny. She put a hand under her skirt—ready.

'Got the price of a pint?'

'A pint of what?'

'Gor'! These ruddy females. Better 'and it all over, and I'll give you back what I don't want.'

'No,' said Jenny.

'Owjer mean No?'

'I mean, Don't be silly.'

'Look 'ere,' said the Tramp reasonably, 'jer *wornt* to be strangled?'

'No.'

'Or 'it over the 'ead with a banana-skin?'

'No.'

'Jer *wornt* to wait until I've got me boots on, so's I can jump on yer defenceless stomach?'

'No.' *(Suppose it didn't work, didn't fire properly!)*

'Then 'and over.'

'Not like that,' said Jenny bravely.

'Like wot?'

'If you ask nicely, and say "Please," I might give you sixpence. That's a penny for each of your family.'

'Wot family?'

'Oh, never mind.'

'Wot about ruddy 'Grace?'

Jenny realized that the conversation was getting them nowhere. She slipped the pistol out of her garters, and held it behind her back. Then she stood up, her hat in her left hand.

'Goodbye,' she said. 'I'm going now.'

'Well 'and over first.'

'*Please* don't be silly.'

The Tramp hoisted himself with care and dignity to his feet.

'Boots or no boots,' he said, 'I've got to strangle one ruddy female.' He spat on his hands, and shuffled towards her.

With a prayer in her heart to Hussar, to Watson, to Mr. Sandroyd, to God—'oh, *please* let it be all right'—she pointed the pistol. 'Go away,' she said, 'or I shall fire.'

('He laughs brutally. He realizes that she will never have the courage'... *Jenny waited for the brutal laugh. It didn't come.)*

'Gor',' said the Tramp, surprised, 'she's got a ruddy gun.' He took a quick step back, trod firmly on a thistle, yelled, jumped high to avoid another one, and sat down heavily. 'Now then, now then,' he said, 'none o' that.'

'I've a good mind to shoot you,' said Jenny severely.

'You can't,' said the Tramp, feeling his foot tenderly.

'Why not?'

''Cos I've trod on a thistle and 'urt the ball of me toe.'

'That's no reason.'

'Wot isn't?' He was peering at his foot.

'Lots of people get shot when they've hurt their toes.'

'Trod on a thistle and 'urt the balls of their toes?' said the Tramp surprised.

'Yes,' said Jenny.

'Their ruddy big toes?'

Jenny nodded.

'I suppose', said the Tramp, leaving it there for the moment, 'you 'aven't got a tweezies in that bag o' yours.'

'I'm afraid not.'

'Not got a tweezies?'

'No.'

'Then *'ow,'* said the Tramp, returning to his foot, 'ow does a ruddy superfellus female remove 'er ruddy superfellus 'air, if she don't twitch it out with a tweezies?'

Jenny decided not to go into this.

'I must be going now,' she said firmly.

'Bye-bye,' said the Tramp.

'Goodbye,' said Jenny.

She walked off. At the next bend of the river she looked round. The Tramp was still deep in the mysteries of his foot. Jenny turned the corner, her heart, her whole body, singing with happiness...

II

Jenny came to a haystack at about 9.30 that evening, and decided to sleep there. Almost immediately she made her second discovery of the day. The first had been that Tramps were Harmless—and this of course depends on whether or not you have Watson's Wonderful Combination Watch-dog-and-Water-pistol strapped to your leg. The second discovery was unconditionally true: being the notorious fact that it is always the other side of a haystack which affords invisibility.

As soon as Jenny saw the haystack, she decided to undress behind it. She went behind it... and found that she was visible to the whole of Kent. Realizing that, by a silly mistake, she had got, not behind, but in front of the haystack, she went round to the back, and again found herself in front of it. The remaining two sides, promising as they seemed, proved to be no more trustworthy. She realized that you cannot undress behind a haystack.

She now began to wonder what people meant when they talked about 'sleeping under a haystack'. Not only had a haystack no behind, but it had no underneath; it seemed to be strangely ill-equipped. Did they mean sleeping on the top of a haystack? She walked round it again... and there was a ladder! She sat down, caring nothing for visibility, and thought it out.

The hayfield ran down to the river, and by its banks there were still a few haycocks uncarried. The unfinished haystack meant not only that a farm was near, but that early in the morning men would be coming back to the field. It also meant, thought Jenny, that the farmer was not afraid of rain, and farmers always knew about the weather. Moreover, and this was important, they always got up very, very early. So what it came to was: she could sleep without fear of rain at the top of the haystack, but she would have to wake up very early, so as to get away before the farmer came.

Right. The Hussar's daughter began to make her plans.

1. She would get ready for bed by the side of the river. With a haycock behind her, and the stream, sheltered on the other side by trees, in front of her, she would be perfectly safe.
2. She would wash in the stream.
3. Teeth! *(She thought for a little.)* Yes. She would eat an orange for supper, and cut it with her nail-scissors, so that she had two orange-peel cups, and clean her teeth out of one of them.
4. She must be ready to start *at once* in the morning, with the knapsack already packed, so that if she suddenly saw the men coming, she could fly.
5. So she would have to sleep in her clothes. But wouldn't that be rather horrid next morning?
6. Sleep in her clothes and change into the green set as soon as she was up and away? But she didn't want to wear the green until they were dyed, because of getting over stiles.
7. Lovely idea! Sleep in the pyjamas with the stockinette over. Pack everything else in the knapsack, and have it ready by her side. As soon as she woke up, roll the pyjamas above her knees and slip on knapsack and shoes; then it would just look like the stockinette and bare legs, which anybody might wear.
8. Dress properly a little farther on after washing in the stream.

Jenny supped. The orange was good, the chocolate was good; but the dates, at close quarters, were disappointing. It seemed impossible that anybody should cross, or want to cross, the desert on a handful of dates; Mr. Sandroyd must have been misinformed about that. Jenny, licking her fingers after handling only two of them, turned with relief to her orange, and thought with pleasure of the wash which was to come. The orange cups made, she picked up her knapsack and went down to the river...

It was the hour between sunset and the dark. The flush had faded out of an innocent sky; pinks and blues were merged into a dappled grey; the world had lost its colour suddenly, its song, its laughter. Under the alders the river met the night, and began to send out tentacles of darkness towards the ghostly Jenny who leaned over it. Quickly she slipped on her clothes and hurried back to the haystack. Quickly, before the blackness was upon her, she prepared everything for the morning. Then Night came down and greeted her... enfolded her while still she knelt, a child on her castle, saying her prayers to God and her Hussar.

Wednesday

8

FURTHER ACTIVITY IN LONDON

I

It was a pity that, from the nature of them, Aunt Jane would never read the best notices of her career. Everything, of course, was in her favour. To begin with, she was an actress; and in acting, alone among the arts, a certain standard of ability is assumed, so that the artist has to be found out, rather than discovered. Partly because (for this or that reason) she had accepted few engagements, partly because most of these engagements were limited to single performances on Sunday nights, Jane Latour had never been found out. On the contrary, this obvious reluctance of hers to commercialize her art seemed a sufficient guarantee of its purity; and, taken in conjunction with her surprising death (and the fact that most of her authors had been elaborating a new technique, which would really account for anything), it more than justified the enthusiasm of the obituary notices.

In dealing with the other side of Jane Latour's life, criticism was naturally more restrained. If she did take snow in large and increasing quantities, certainly nothing more was said of it than that 'she was a well-known social figure, particularly among the younger set', and her ability as a harpist can only have been implied in the statement that 'she was always ready to offer her services on behalf of any charity'. As for her matrimonial adventure with the Count, it lost itself so easily in a summary of her distinguished father's services for the Empire that a careless reader would have supposed that she had married a Colonial Bishop.

So much for Jane Latour among the obituary notices. Jane Latour murdered had the front page to herself.

There was never any doubt that it was Murder. In inviting the co-operation of the Press and the Public, Inspector Marigold had not only been photographed in four different positions, but had put our readers in full possession of all the facts. Dr. Willoughby Hatch (the well-known expert) had yet to conduct his *post mortem*, or, at least, to communicate his findings through the Coroner to the nation. Opinion, therefore, to some extent was to be reserved. But the absence of a weapon and the presence of strange footprints and a strange handkerchief made the nature of the crime obvious.

Who was the mysterious Jenny? Was she indeed the murderess; or was she (a theory held in many well-informed quarters) another victim? Suppose (said Our Special Investigator beneath a photograph of Chukrapoota, where the dead woman's father had resided at one period), suppose Jenny had been lured by somebody engaged in the White Slave Traffic to what he had thought to be a deserted house. Suppose that the dead woman, who, as Jane Windell, had herself resided there at one time, had interrupted them. Suppose— and nobody who knew Miss Jane Latour would be surprised at this—that she had bravely intervened to save the intended victim. What happens? Callously the ruffian strikes her down. Then hastily rendering Jenny unconscious with a whiff of chloroform, he lets her out of the window, jumps after her, and half-drags, half-carries her to where his car is waiting. But he has made two little slips, just those little slips which have brought so many murderers to the gallows. Unknown to him, she has dropped the handkerchief with which she was endeavouring to stanch the injuries of the dead woman. Unknown to him, she has left her footprints in the bed. *['Flower-bed,' corrected the Night Editor, feeling that the sex-interest was getting too strong]...* This theory, held as it was in many well-informed quarters, might or might not be the correct one; but obviously, correct or not, the first thing to do was to identify the mysterious Jenny. *Who was Jenny?*

Miss Nancy Fairbrother knew the answer to that. Reading a paper on her way to Bloomsbury this morning, she saw that it would not be long before the police knew. The afternoon papers would give a full description of Miss Jenny Windell in the clothes which she was wearing on that fatal morning; the clothes which were now hidden away in Nancy's flat. Everybody would be looking for a fair girl of medium height, grey eyes, attractive appearance, in green georgette with biscuit-coloured picture-hat. Well, that wasn't going to help anybody. And even if they caught her, she could still persuade certain well-informed quarters that she was victim, not villain.

But could she? Not Jenny Windell. Jenny was too simple, too straightforward for that. If only it had been Nancy Fairbrother!

For nobody could pretend so well as Nancy. She combined the imagination of the novelist with the technique of the old-fashioned actress, transmuting herself into everything which went through her mind. She thought, as it were, in inverted commas. If, in her imagination, she met the Prince of Wales, and they talked together, then she was the Prince of Wales, talking like a Prince (of Wales) who had just met the secretary of an author, and she was Miss Nancy Fairbrother, talking like a girl who was secretary to an author, who had just met the Prince of Wales... which was all very different from the Prince of Wales just meeting Miss Nancy Fairbrother. So, had she been in Jenny's position, it would have been easy for her to have told Inspector Marigold the whole story of that terrible scene in Auburn Lodge; but she would have found it difficult, if asked for Miss Latour's actual words to the leader of the White Slave Gang, not to have given a much too brilliant impression of Miss Latour actually saying them.

Well, she was not Jenny. But she was Jenny's right hand; the girl who was to save Jenny. Also she was Mr. Archibald Fenton's private secretary, and somehow she had to pawn Jenny's watch today. Walking from the omnibus to Mr. Fenton's house she became a girl with a watch to pawn; a watch that had once belonged to her little sister Joyce.

II

Mr. Fenton was feeling pretty pleased with himself this morning. There were several reasons for this. First of all, it was his day for weighing himself, and owing to some mechanical defect in the bathroom weighing-machine, he had gone down to thirteen stone seven. Secondly, Ursula had now definitely got measles, so that her three little sisters would have to be taken by their mother to Bognor Regis to keep out of danger. Thirdly, Stephen's half-term report had just arrived, and he was top in Divinity. To one who had to leave all that sort of thing to his wife and children, this was extremely gratifying. Fourthly, the photographs in the Bookman had come out well, particularly the one of himself and Lady Claudia and Fanny at Brocken, in which Fanny, being partially obscured by the fountain round which they were grouped, looked younger than she had been for many years. Lastly, and most importantly, he began to see his way through the new book. It was going to be All Right.

'Good morning, Miss Secretary,' he said cheerily to Nancy, as he came into the work-room.

'Good morning, Mr. Fenton,' said Joyce's sister bravely.

'Hallo.'

'Yes, Mr. Fenton?'

'What's the matter with our Miss Fairbrother this bright and breezy morning?'

'Matter, Mr. Fenton?'

'Come on, let's hear all about it.'

'Really, Mr. Fenton, if you think I'm going to interrupt your morning with my own silly troubles—'

'You'll interrupt it much more, if you sit there looking like St. Agnes or St. Agatha or somebody, just before the lion came in.'

'A lion *has* just come in,' said Nancy, with a flutter of her eyes.

'That's better. Now then, what is it?'

Nancy swallowed and said: 'It's my little sister, Joyce.'

'I say, not dead? I'm terribly sorry. I wouldn't have said that, if I'd known—'

'Oh no, no!' said Nancy. She thought of saying 'Worse than death', in a sad sepulchral voice, but stopped herself just in time. If once she began like that, there was no knowing where she (and her little sister Joyce) would get to. 'But she's in trouble.'

'Ah!' said Mr. Fenton sympathetically, quite understanding. A pleasing picture of Nancy also 'in trouble', and himself the cause of it, flashed through his mind.

'Not that sort of trouble,' said Nancy primly.

'Oh!' said Mr. Fenton, disappointed. 'Well, what?'

'Money.'

'Ah!' said Mr. Fenton coldly. He might have known.

'She's sent me her watch to pawn, and I—I don't know how to do it, and—'

A revived Mr. Fenton held out his hand.

'Let's have a look at it.'

As he examined it, and noted the little 'J' in diamonds (for 'Joyce'), Nancy went on hurriedly: 'You see, she's in an office in a cathedral town, and I don't know if they do have pawnbrokers there, but Joyce daren't go to one, because she might be seen, and if once it got about, I mean her employer is so very *strict*, and besides it looks bad, doesn't it, I mean it shows that you're spending more money than you ought to, and—'

'Real diamonds?' said Mr. Fenton.

' 'm' Nancy gave another gulp. 'Uncle George gave it to her on her birthday. She was his favourite. He's dead now, so—I mean he wouldn't mind, but I've never been to a pawnbroker, and—'

'D'you know how much he paid for it?'

'I *think* twenty pounds, Joyce said Aunt Emily told her, because she was rather annoyed about it, I mean Aunt Emily, but I don't *know*. It looks very good, doesn't it, and if only she could get ten pounds, because you generally get half, don't you, and—'

'When you say "pawn", do you mean you want to redeem it later, or do you just want to sell it?'

'Sell it to a pawnbroker, I thought,' said Nancy.

Mr. Archibald Fenton was thinking. Until two years ago he had been a Realist, thus sharing with most critics and Court Painters the conviction that photography is the highest form of art. To describe with such accuracy that even the village idiot, looking over the artist's shoulder, would say 'Danged if it tident Farmer Bassett's old sow': surely authorship could go no higher than this. He discovered that it could. It could bring back a Rabelaisian robustness to the English novel; even if in so doing (as the man who looked after them in Langley's circus wrote to tell Mr. Fenton) it made three distinct errors in the toilet of a female elephant. Mr. Archibald Fenton ceased to be a realist... but at times he had misgivings. What it came to, he decided at last, was this. Elephants didn't matter because very few people knew about elephants, but with horses you would have to be careful.

Would you have to be careful with pawnbrokers? Hardly... except, of course, for the cheap editions... And serial rights... Serial rights: that settled it.

'How would it be', said Mr. Fenton, 'if I took it to a pawnbroker for you?'

'Oh, Mr. Fenton!' said Joyce's big sister.

'That's all right,' said Mr. Fenton airily. 'I'll do it this afternoon.'

'It *is* good of you. Joyce—' she gulped. 'I hardly know how to thank you.' She just touched her eyes with her handkerchief. Pretty little thing she was.

'That's all right.' He patted her shoulder encouragingly. 'Well, let's get on with Chapter Five.'

It is, of course, at the end of Chapter Five (as Nancy well knew) that Eustace Frere pawns his cuff-links.

III

Mr. Watterson's authority for what was happening in the great world had always been The Times. Mrs. Watterson's authority for what the Radicals were up to had always been Mr. Watterson. At Bath Station, on the morning after the wedding of his grandson, Mr. Watterson proposed to buy a copy of The Times and take it and Mrs. Watterson into a first-class carriage with him.

'What do you want *The Times* for, dear?' said Mrs. Watterson.

'To read,' said Mr. Watterson, in the voice of one who thought the question unnecessary.

'But it's waiting for you at home, dear. It seems a pity to have two copies.'

Mr. Watterson had been married for fifty years, and knew that the urgency for his need for *The Times* was one of those things which his wife would never understand.

'My dear, I can afford the extra twopence,' he said mildly.

'It seems such a waste. Why not get one of the other papers, dear?'

'There *are* no other papers,' said Mr. Watterson, believing it.

'Nonsense. There are plenty. Look, there's the *Morning Post.*'

From time to time Mr. Watterson had read the *Morning Post* at his club, and from time to time Mr. Watterson and the Editor of the *Morning Post* had agreed upon this or that, but not until the Editor of *The Times* and Mr. Watterson had agreed upon it first.

'Very well,' he said, 'I won't get a paper.'

'Oh, but you *must* have a *paper*, dear. Only it seems so silly to—'

'I *don't* want a paper, I don't *want* a paper, *I* don't want a paper,' said Mr. Watterson fretfully.

'Oh well, dear, you know best. Will you get me the *Illustrated London News?*'

The wedding champagne still disagreeing with him, Mr. Watterson bought two copies of the *Illustrated London News*, one for each of them. Mrs. Watterson sighed and said nothing. She had been married for fifty years, and knew that men would always go on being children. This accounted for War and Politics and Sport, and so many things.

They reached home a little after midday, and as soon as Mr. Watterson had opened the door, Cook and Hilda and Alice were in the hall. There had been an argument about this at breakfast.

Cook said that it was *her* place to break any domestic news, good or bad, to the Mistress.

Hilda said: 'When I broke that what d'you call it varse, *you* didn't break it, catch *you*.'

'Well, *you broke* it,' said Cook unanswerably.

Alice said: 'It's me the Police will want to know about what she's wearing what I put out for her being her maid as you might say.'

Cook said: 'All in good time, Alice. I'm not talking about when the Police comes, but when the Mistress comes.'

Hilda said: 'Well, I've got to be in the 'all to get the luggage in and all, 'aven't I?'

Cook said: 'I'm not saying for that.'

Alice said, sniffing slightly: 'I'm the only one as reely cares about poor Miss Jenny, being her maid, as you might say.'

Cook said: 'Alice! How *can* you sit there and say things like that, knowing what we all think about Miss Jenny, and never was a sweeter, more innocent young lady, and Dear knows what—'

Hilda said: 'Well, I've got to be in the 'all, 'aven't I, to get the luggage in and all,' just as Alice was saying: 'Well, I was the one as wanted to ring up the police, only you wouldn't let me, being her own maid, well almost.' So naturally Cook said: 'Well, if we all speak at once like that, nobody will know 'oo's missing. That's all I'm thinking of.'

'Well, I've got to be in the 'all,' said Hilda, 'that's all there is to it, and you two can do what you like.'

This was what they did; and so, as soon as the door opened, Cook and Hilda and Alice were in the hall crying: 'It's Miss Jenny, ma'am!'

'Miss Jenny?' said Mrs. Watterson. 'What?'

'She never came home, ma'am.'

'Never came home?' said Mr. Watterson, edging towards *The Times*. He picked it up, as if accidentally, and opened it, but still with the air of one listening to something else, in the middle, at the leading articles.

Cook and Hilda and Alice were explaining vociferously. They had nothing to explain, save the fact that Miss Jenny had said she would be out to lunch, and had never come back again. For, like Mr. Watterson, they had read no papers.

'Hubert,' said Mrs. Watterson, 'are you listening? Jenny went out yesterday morning and hasn't come back.'

Mr. Watterson was not listening. The name Auburn Lodge had called to him from the page opposite the leading articles, and he was reading about the death of Jane Latour...

'Hubert!'

'Yes, dear, I know.' He went to his study.

'What are you going to do?'

'Ring up the police.'

He shut the door behind him. Alice's triumphant eye caught Cook's reluctant one. 'What,' said Alice's eye, 'did I tell you?'

IV

Mr. Archibald Fenton lunched, as usual, at his club. After luncheon he found himself involved in one of those unending literary discussions, whose like he had set rolling so often and so happily in the past. Now he found them embarrassing. A man with a Fentonian reputation, particularly if he be still an occasional critic, has to be careful. As a novelist he could have afforded, and would have preferred, to be generous; to leave behind him those who would say to each other: 'What I like about Fenton is that he's always so enthusiastic about other novelists.' As an occasional critic in the monthlies his one care was not to commit himself in private to anything which might be said more cleverly in public. For instance, Blair Sturge's name was mentioned. Awkward. Sturge's book was coming out next month, and Fenton had not yet decided what he was going to say about it. It depended upon certain unknown quantities, one of them being, of course, the actual quality of the book. He might use that phrase, which had come into his mind the other day, about 'the pen of a highly certificated governess who had just learnt the facts of sex'— supposing, of course, that the new book was sufficiently like the previous one to justify it. On the other hand, Sturge and Ramsbotham were bosom friends— which made it all very difficult...

He temporized. He temporized so successfully that it was teatime before the discussion died out. The others thereupon ordered tea. Fenton felt that it was up to him, as one who had brought the smell of hops back to the English novel, to do something hearty with a tankard of beer. Never having liked beer very much, he felt depressed afterwards. London was a beastly place. Where was he dining tonight? He looked at his engagement book, and found that he wasn't. Hell!

He turned over a page or two, and saw that he had a blank week in front of him, except for next Tuesday when he was dining with the Moberleys. Oh God, he had forgotten all about that!

It was at a cocktail-party. Well, what did people do at cocktail-parties? How many hundred books had he read—well, reviewed—about cocktail-parties, in which people—And Good Heavens, it was only a kiss at most, and where else could you put your hand? Really, for a modern young girl and an art-student at that... And she had been absolutely all over him until that moment.

Damn Cynthia Moberley!

He tried to think of one or two good things for a short, stout man to say to a girl who had slapped his face the last time they'd met... There weren't any.

He tried to think of one or two good things for a man to say, who was reviewing a novel in which a young girl slapped a man's face just because he had kissed her... He thought of several. Delightfully contemptuous, ironical things ...

It looked as if life were too many-sided to be pinned down to any however realistic novel. Face-slapping in the nineteen-thirties! Who would have guessed it?

No, he couldn't dine with the Moberleys. That was certain.

He had a renewed internal awareness of what had once been a tankard of beer, and decided again that London was beastly. Why not leave it, and go down to the cottage? And really get on with the book? Authors were allowed these sudden decisions, and they always made a good paragraph for one's publishers. He would write to Mrs. Moberley. He would get away from London this evening...

It was then that Mr. Archibald Fenton remembered about the watch. Oh well, that was all right. He would pawn it now on the way home, and send the money on to Miss Fairbrother, and tell her to take a fortnight's holiday. He took out his pocket-book. Luckily, for the bank would be shut by now, he had enough. Two five-pound notes, and three ten in addition. And of course, if he sent Nancy a cheque, he would have the watch money.

He went off to find a pawnbroker, well pleased with himself as a man of sudden moods; a man also, when necessary, of decision. He returned to the house in Bloomsbury, rang up his housekeeper at the cottage, and wrote three letters.

To Fanny at Bognor Regis he wrote:

> 'Dear Fanny, Hope you all arrived safely. Chapter Five is sticking rather, and I'm just off to the cottage for a fortnight to get it cleared up.
>
> Archie.'

He read the letter through and added: *'Love to you all.'*

Fanny read the letter and said to herself: 'I wonder what *that* means.' And then aloud: 'No, darling, not marmalade *and* jam.'

To Mrs. Andrew Moberley in Seymour Street he wrote:

> 'Dear Mrs. Moberley, Will you ever forgive me? Well, yes, I am encouraged to think that you might, because you too have the artistic temperament, and know what slaves it makes of us. I have got to get down to the country, away from everybody, and wrestle with the new book in solitude. It is now or never. You know how that can be, as few women would know. Am I wrong in putting my

work first, even above courtesy to one who has shown so much kindness to me? Somehow I feel that I am not; and that you will understand why, very regretfully, I ask you to excuse me from your so charmingly hospitable table on Tuesday.

'Yours most sincerely,
'Archibald Fenton.'

He read the letter through, and regretted the unfortunate assonance of 'hospitable table'. But he was damned if he would write the thing out again.

Mrs. Moberley read the letter and passed it to her daughter. Cynthia read it and said: 'Oh well, as long as he doesn't wrestle with *me* in solitude, I don't mind.'

Mr. Fenton began his third letter. To Miss Nancy Fairbrother in Elm Park Mansions he wrote:

'Dear Miss Fairbrother, I must get away into the country and work on that chapter by myself. It is really the crucial chapter of the book. I enclose a cheque for £15 10s.—i.e. £12 10s. for your sister's watch, plus a week's salary. I suggest that you take a fortnight's holiday, on half-salary (as you have had no time to arrange anything) and perhaps in these circumstances you wouldn't mind attending to my letters, which I shall send on to you, say twice a week, with instructions. I had a job to get the £12 10s. and I doubt if anybody else would have got more than a tenner, so I hope Joyce will be properly grateful to you. You can tell her from me to be more careful in the future! Look after Miss Nancy Fairbrother while I am away, and don't let her get into mischief!

'Yours, A. F.'

He read the letter through and added: 'P.S. I sold the watch outright, as you said you wanted this.'

Nancy read the letter, and said: 'Thank the Lord *he's* out of the way. Now I can really *do* something.'

9

ARRIVAL OF NAOMI FENTON

I

Jenny had never slept out before, but she knew all about it. Lady Barbara, escaping in the guise of a boy from an unwelcome marriage, had spent many a night in a hay-stack; so had Ned Tregellis, escaping from an unwelcome prison in the guise of a girl. Both of them had spoken enthusiastically of the experience. 'By'r lady,' had said young Tregellis, 'but it shall go ill with me if ever again I spend the night within the confines of four walls'; and (on other occasion) Lady Barbara had declared: 'An I cannot pass the night beneath God's canopy, I vow I will not bed me at all.' It would have been convenient, this being so, if they had married each other, but unfortunately they were in different books. Jenny, who had been kept awake by a night-jar who went to bed at two, and, when at last she fell asleep, woken up by a blue-bottle who started the day at four, was not so enthusiastic. Long before the farmer thought of getting up, she was down from her haystack, feeling uncomfortable and unrefreshed, and telling herself that she supposed one got used to it.

Still she had done it. She had slept out— alone. How many girls could say that? And here she was, by the side of her river again, a new day beginning. However tickly and wriggly she felt, she had this confidence in herself to sustain her. She was doing a very exciting thing.

Dare she bathe? She would never feel comfortable again unless she did. Here was a little bay in the stream where the banks went steeply down to a gravelled floor. Nobody would be up so early, nobody was about. Should she? She looked all round her. She was alone. She scrambled down the bank and took off her knapsack, shoes and dress; put the towel ready. Now she was in her pyjamas, and people often went about in pyjamas. She washed. Now for it. She hurried up the bank and took a last look round. All safe. Down again. One, two, three—go!... She was down on her back in the water, the water was playing round her and over her, the sun was coming through the alders at her, birds were singing above her—By'r lady, but it shall go ill with me, an ever I lave myself again within the confines of a porcelain bath.

She lay there, exulting in the fact that it was she, the authentic Jenny, who had so escaped from Miss Windell and the world. But it was cold. She let the water go right over her head, and sat up with a gasp, and came out. In a little while she was dried and dressed. She sat on the bank in the sun, munching chocolate happily. Now she was comfortable, inside and out, and ready for anything. Oh, Hussar, *isn't* it fun? Aren't I different? Soon she was walking on again and wondering about breakfast.

It must still have been an hour before her usual breakfast-time when she met the Painter.

'Oh!' said Jenny to herself, 'Somebody sketching.'

She would have passed behind him with perhaps a 'Good morning', but he spoke to her, and his voice was nicer than the Tramp's.

He said, without looking up: 'Are you an artist's model, by any chance?'

'I'm afraid not,' said Jenny, and stopped for a moment.

'Dear, dear, how very unlucky one is.'

'Did you want an artist's model?' said Jenny, an idea suddenly coming to her.

'Well, I did rather.'

'What for? I mean what as?' She would have to earn money somehow, soon.

'A nymph or water-sprite. I suppose you wouldn't care to be a nymph or water-sprite? In other words a naiad?'

'What do they wear?'

'Nothing,' said the Painter.

'Oh, then I'm afraid I couldn't,' said Jenny reluctantly.

'I thought you probably couldn't.'

'Would an artist's model?'

'I think so. If I asked her nicely.'

'It seems funny,' mused Jenny. And then in explanation: 'I suppose you get used to it.'

'That's it. We both get used to it.'

'How funny.'

'Well, looking at it in another way, clothes are funny.'

'Well, it depends how you look at it.'

'That', said the Painter, 'is really what I mean.'

Jenny was silent for a little, and then said: 'I couldn't possibly, could I?'

'No,' said the Painter, 'not possibly.'

'All the same, it seems different in the open air somehow. I mean it's like saying "Will you marry me?" and you say "Oh, I don't think I could," and it's quite all right asking, and it's quite all right saying "No," only it just happens you can't.'

'Exactly.'

'I'm so sorry. Do you mind if I sit down and watch you?'

'Not a bit. Do you know anything about painting?'

'Nothing, I'm afraid.'

'That's good.'

He went on painting, and Jenny went on watching him.

'What a lot of things one doesn't know anything about,' she said.

'Practically everything.'

'Do you live near here?'

He dabbed with his brush over a shoulder.

'I'm at the farm there. A mile or two back.'

'Oh! How funny!'

'Why?'

'I slept on their haystack last night. Do you think they'd mind?'

'I am sure they would have been delighted, if they had known about it.'

'I thought perhaps they wouldn't mind.'

The Painter, looking in a depressed sort of way from his canvas to the river, and back again, said: 'Is that how you live?'

'How do you mean?'

'On haystacks.'

'Oh, no! I'm hiking,' said Jenny proudly.

'Just how does one do that? I've often wondered.'

'Well, you walk about with a knapsack—'

'What we used to call walking?'

'Well, yes. And you sleep in haystacks and things—'

'What we used to call sleeping out?'

'Yes. Well—well, that's about all, I suppose.'

'I see... I'm glad I know at last. And you're doing all this entirely by yourself?'

'Yes,' said Jenny. 'It's rather fun.'

'It must be. What do you call yourself when you talk to yourself?'

'Do you mean, what is my name?'

'Well, it comes to that, I suppose.'

Jenny stopped herself from saying 'Jenny Windell' just in time.

'Gloria Harris,' she said.

'You can't seriously want to be called Miss Harris,' said the Painter, after considering this for a little.

'Oh no!' agreed Jenny eagerly.

'I thought not. If it comes to that, I'm not so set on Gloria as some.'

'Isn't it funny,' said Jenny, 'I used to think it was a lovely name, and now it seems rather silly.'

'What did they call you at school?'

'I never went to school.'

'A pity. That might have given us a wider choice.'

Suddenly Jenny remembered that she had two handkerchiefs with 'N' on them. Supposing she dropped one!

'Gloria Harris isn't the whole name,' she said.

'I thought it couldn't be.'

'It's Gloria Naomi Harris. I'm really Naomi. I mean to special friends.'

'That's much better. And now,' said the Painter, 'although you have expressed no interest in the subject whatever, I shall tell you *my* name.'

'Oh, I *do* want to know. Really I do,' said Jenny earnestly. 'What is it, please?'

'Derek Fenton.'

'Oh!' said Jenny.

'Quite so.'

'Are you related to Archibald Fenton?'

'No. He's related to *me*.'

'I mean—'

'It so happens that we are brothers. I', explained the Painter, 'am the nice one.'

'How funny.'

'Not if you've seen Archibald,' said the Painter.

'I mean it's funny because—' Jenny stopped. She couldn't be sure whether Gloria Naomi Harris knew Nancy Fairbrother or not. Perhaps safer not. 'I mean, well, everybody knows Archibald Fenton. I mean A *Flock of Sheep*, and everything.'

'Have you read A *Flock of Sheep*,' asked Derek.

'Oh, yes!'

'You must tell me about it.'

'You mean you haven't *read* it?' said Jenny, in astonishment.

'No.'

'Oh, but *oughtn't* you to have?'

'Well, *he* hasn't seen this picture,' Derek pointed out.

'It's funny,' said Jenny. 'Two of the people in the bus were talking about it only yesterday.'

'About this picture?' asked Derek, surprised.

'Oh, no, I mean about the book.'

'This picture', said Derek impressively, 'will be talked about in taxi-cabs.'

It was funny, thought Jenny, that they hadn't really seen each other yet. She had been going to pass behind him; she had sat down behind him; and never once had he turned round to her. She was looking now at the back of his sunburnt neck; he was looking from the picture to the river, from the river to the picture, to the palette, to the picture, to the river again; throwing remarks to her, as it were, over his shoulder. Occasionally she saw the line of his jaw, brown and hard. His hair was very short at the back—not at all what you expect of a painter, but perhaps he wasn't a very good painter—and it went to a point in what was really rather a fascinating way. It was funny to have lived all these years—eighteen—and never to have seen the way a man's hair went at the back before.

'You're much younger than your brother, aren't you?'

'Yes.'

'Don't you ever read his books?'

'No.'

'Why not?'

'In case I might like them.'

'But—but—that's a reason *for* reading them, isn't it?'

'Well, you see, I don't like Archibald.'

'Oh!' She thought this over for a little, and then said 'Why?' It seemed so funny not to like your brother.

'Well, there are a lot of people in the world, and you can't like them all. So *I*... don't like Archibald.'

Jenny tried to think of any other brothers she had known who hadn't liked each other. She could only think of Jacob and Esau.

'Did he rob you of your inheritance?" she asked.

'Well, I suppose he did in a way.'

'How? Or don't you like talking about it?'

'I love talking about it.'

'Then how?'

'Well, you see, I inherited the name of Fenton, and he's gone and spoilt it.'

'Spoilt it?' said Jenny indignantly. 'He's made it famous.'

'That's what I mean. He's spoilt it for *me*. As soon as I mention my name, people say—well, what Gloria Naomi Harris said.'

'What did I say?' wondered Jenny, wrinkling her forehead. 'Oh, yes, I remember. Well, but you ought to be *proud*.'

'I am. Too proud to bask in the back-wash of Archibald's fame, if you follow my metaphor. I look forward', he went on in a dreamy voice, 'to the day when a complacent and hopeful Archibald is shown by a butler with a bell-like voice into a crowded ducal drawing-room, and, as soon as they hear his name, all the guests rush up to him and say: "Oh *do* tell me, *are* you any relation to *Derek* Fenton?" That', said Mr. Derek Fenton, indicating his canvas with a circling gesture of the brush, 'is why I am doing this. In private life I am in the wine-trade.'

II

At first it was a little disappointing to Jenny to find that he was in the wine-trade. A young girl whose alcoholic experience has been limited to one cocktail has not that sensitiveness which enables her to appreciate the gulf fixed between the selling of Burgundy and the selling of oatmeal biscuits. But a renewed study of the back of his neck convinced her that he couldn't be the man who actually sold the bottles, but was more probably the owner of the chateau in France where the grapes were grown—a sort of gentleman-fruit-farmer, which was rather an exciting thing to be. But she decided not to discuss the wine-trade with him, in case he wasn't.

'You won't mind my asking,' said the Fruit-farmer suddenly, after an anxious five minutes with Art, 'but in the intervals of being—or rather,' he added hastily, '*not* being a water-nymph, you live somewhere?'

'St. John's Wood,' said Jenny, without thinking.

'Oh, I see, a wood-nymph. Well, what I wanted to say was, do dryads in St. John's Wood have an occasional breakfast from time to time?'

'Well, of course,' smiled Jenny.

'Tell me', said Derek, 'all about it.'

'Do you mean what do I eat for breakfast?'

'And drink, and contemplate, and reject, and turn up the nose at, and have two helps of.'

'Well, it depends. I generally have grapefruit and toast and a scrambled egg and marmalade and an apple. *And* coffee, of course.'

'This is not my lucky day,' said Derek. 'I was hoping that you would say an orange and scones and a hard-boiled egg and butter and a banana. *And* milk, of course.'

'Oh?' said Jenny, puzzled.

'If you *had* said that, we would have opened that string-bag over there, and seen what somebody's sent us.'

'Oh!' said Jenny ecstatically. 'Are you inviting me to breakfast?'

'I certainly am, as we say in America.'

'Oh, have you been to America?'

'Yes and No,' said Derek.

'But either you've been or you haven't,' laughed Jenny. 'I mean, mustn't you?'

'No and Yes, if you follow me.'

'I don't quite, I'm afraid.'

'I started in the direction of America once, but there were sixty Americans on board who talked to me so much and so loudly about Archibald that I saw that it was hopeless to try and settle down with a hundred and fifty million of them.'

'What did you do?'

'Came back again.'

'Do you mean at once?'

'As soon as they could turn the boat round.'

'Then you never saw America at all?'

'I saw New York from the river. New York from the river,' said Mr. Derek Fenton enthusiastically, 'at a moment when the sun has just set, and no one is asking you what Archibald looked like as a child, is enough for anybody. Tell me, are you accepting my invitation?'

'To breakfast? Please!'

'Good.'

He stood up. Now they were facing each other. She tried to tell herself what he looked like; to remember what he looked like, feature by feature, so that when she went on, and saw him never again, she could think about him sometimes. Was he good-looking or ugly, tall or short? She hardly knew. All she knew was that she liked him, that you couldn't help liking him; that, if you told him about Hussar, it would be all right, that even if you told him about Aunt Jane, it would be all right. Her thoughts went back to the Tramp, and she thought that *he* was nice too, I mean *really*, if you got to know him. Derek Fenton made everybody seem nice... And then suddenly she felt herself going hot all over, and she turned away quickly to hide her face; because suddenly she remembered that they had been talking about water-nymphs, and that just for one funny moment in that early morning sunshine, when the world was so remote from all that she had ever been taught, she had felt that being a water-nymph for him to paint would not have been such a terrible thing to do, but simple and natural and beautiful. Now, suddenly, she knew that he was the one man in the world for whom she could never, never do it.

III

'This', said Derek, cracking an egg on his shoe, 'is a breakfast, not a Passport office. If I ask you anything which is inconvenient, just pass me the butter in a casual way, and I shall know that I am on slippery ground. Is that all right?'

'Yes,' said Jenny. 'Thank you.'

'Then, roughly and in a general way, where do we go from here?'

'Do you mean, where am *I* going?'

'On whose haystack are you resting tonight?'

'Well,' said Jenny guardedly, 'I'm sort of making for the coast.'

'As you were heading when we met, you would have struck it at about Northumberland. You aren't going on to Norway by any chance?'

'No. I don't think so.'

'Keep the butter handy for this one. Are you running away from anybody or anything?... Thanks. *And* the salt, if you wouldn't mind.' He buttered a scone, dipped his egg in the salt and munched.

'I'm sorry,' said Jenny, looking at him with pleading eyes.

'Perfectly all right. Now just one more question, and we can get on to the orange. How old are you, Naomi?'

'Eighteen.'

'You're sure you're not six?'

'Eighteen, *really*.'

'Or six hundred?'

'Well, eighteen and a half, actually.'

'Then who cares? Have an orange?'

'Thank you.'

'If one can't do what one likes at eighteen, when can one? The answer is, Never.'

'Can't one at thirty?'

'*I*'m thirty, and *I* can't do what I like.'

'Can't you really?' asked Jenny in surprise.

'No. I should like to paint sunlight on water, and I can't. I should like to murder Archibald, and I mustn't. I should like—' he gave her a quick glance and ended, 'oh, lots of things. Well now, listen, Dryad.'

'Yes?'

'Are you listening?'

'Yes.'

'Well now, here we are. You're going to wander from haystack to haystack, and very nice too. I'm staying at Bassetts, and very nice too. You are thinking of Mrs. Bassett entirely as a scone-baker, and you are saying to yourself that a woman who bakes scones like Mrs. Bassett has no room for any of the other virtues. You are wrong. She has all the virtues. She is a mother to those who want mothers, and an aunt to anybody who likes aunts. My portrait of her,' said Mr. Fenton, becoming enthusiastic, 'which now hangs in her parlour, depicts all these qualities. Even the scone *motif* runs through it in what I can only call—and so far only I *have* called it—a masterly way.'

'I *wish* I could see it,' said Jenny, quite carried away by this.

'Well, that's what we're working up to. In order to do this properly we must now go back to haystacks. Hay undoubtedly makes an excellent bed. The Americans, as I discovered in the course of my travels to and from that astonishing country, have an expression "to hit the hay".'

'How funny! What does it mean?'

'It means to go to bed. You, on your way to Northumberland, will hit the hay at this or that point for the next month or so. If this Northumbrian pilgrimage is merely an excuse for hay-hitting, it can be done equally well in the neighbourhood of Bassetts, as you discovered last night. We will tell Farmer Bassett not to thatch his haystack until Miss Harris has finished with it. But if one's object were simply to be out of London, or,' said Mr. Fenton carefully, 'as it might be incognito and unobserved, to fade into the landscape as the pursuit goes by, well then, again I ask you, what more eligible site than Bassetts?'

'Do you mean', said Jenny eagerly, 'that I could stay there?'

'Why not? But I suggest, in the romantic and subterfugitive way which befits a Dryad, Naiad and—and assuming you to have ascended Constitution Hill—Oread. Now listen: How would you like to take a false name?'

Miss Harris blushed.

'Rightly you are shocked,' said Derek, 'but sometimes it's rather fun.'

'Oh, it is!' said Miss Harris.

'Good. Then how would you like to be my sister?'

'Your sister?'

'I know what you are thinking. You are saying to yourself "Good Heavens, then Archibald will be *my* brother too," and you quail at the idea.'

'Oh no!' said Jenny eagerly. 'I think it's a lovely idea.'

'One of the bravest girls I ever met. But there are limits to what one can ask. You shall be my half-sister, and Archibald your half-brother only. Have you finished your breakfast?'

'Yes, thank you.'

'Do you smoke? Obviously not, if you're a Dryad?'

'No, thank you.'

'Then now I'm going to think for two minutes.'

By the time his pipe was alight, he was ready.

'You are Miss Naomi Fenton. You were going a walking-tour with a friend. Name of friend?'

Nancy Fairbrother? No, he might recognize her as his brother's secretary. Acetylene Pitt? Nobody would believe it.

'Nancy Pitt,' said Jenny.

'Good. You and Miss Pitt have walked to— where shall we say?—'

'Endover?'

Derek looked across at her quickly.

'Do you know Endover?'

'I came through it yesterday. Why?'

'I see. Could you find your way back to it?'

'Oh, I think so.' She began to think. 'Oh, I'm sure I could.'

'Splendid. Then at Endover—'

'But why did you look at me like that?'

'Did I?'

'As if you didn't like it very much.'

'You're very clever.'

Jenny's second governess, who had taught her the capitals of Europe, had said that she was industrious and full of promise, and her third, who had gone on from these to the Life of the Bee, had said that she was easily interested and that her conduct was extremely satisfactory; but nobody had called her very clever before. She glowed.

Derek explained. 'A man whom I dislike intensely has a cottage at Endover. Fortunately he isn't there now.'

'Your brother?' said Jenny cleverly.

'A relation by marriage,' said Derek guardedly, 'of the name of Archibald. To continue: at Endover your tour is interrupted.

Does Miss Pitt sprain her ankle—or is she summoned to the sick bed of her Uncle Thomas?'

'Ankle. Because how would her Uncle Thomas know she was at Endover?'

'You think of everything.' (Jenny glowed again.) 'She sprains her ankle, and returns by omnibus to Tunbridge Wells, and thence to town. She refuses to spoil your holiday, too, and insists that you shall not see her home. But you can hardly continue your walking- tour alone—'

'Why not?' interrupted Jenny.

'Why not? Because', said Mr. Fenton after deep thought, 'you had promised your half-brother Derek that you wouldn't.'

'Oh, I see.'

'Very well then. Bassetts, you will be surprised to hear, is on the telephone, but not, for which God be thanked, on the wireless. At Endover you remember that half-brother Derek is staying at Bassetts. Having seen Miss Pitt into her omnibus, you go into the post office and ring up Bassetts. Derek is out, so you speak to Mrs. Bassett. There is a lot of Bassett in all this, but no matter. You ask Mrs. B. to tell your brother that you are coming to tea, and you wonder if by any chance she has a spare bedroom, as you have been on a walking-tour with a friend who has sprained—but we needn't go through all that again. Are you keeping up with me?'

'It's easy,' said Jenny. '*Has* she got a spare room?'

'She has. Now then. We have got to get you, in a surreptitious sort of way, back to Endover. How did you come yesterday?'

'By the river after about the first mile, except when I had to leave it to go through gates and things.'

'Meet anybody?'

'Only one.'

'Man or woman?'

'Man.'

'Speak to him?'

'Yes. We—we talked a little,' said Jenny hurriedly.

'What like?'

'Rather a nice middle-aged, elderly sort of man,' said Jenny.

'Like to go back that way, or would you rather go round by the road?'

'I think I'd rather go by the road,' said Jenny. She felt in some extraordinary way that her Hussar had left her, and that she could not brave again the dangers through which, yesterday, she and he had come. Somehow she knew that, from now on, she would have to depend on the physical presence of this other man, who had taken Hussar's place. Without him there were terrifying places in the world—by the banks of streams and on haystacks.

'Safer,' nodded Derek. 'It wouldn't do if you met old Bassett down by your haystack, when you're supposed to be Tunbridge way with Miss Pitt. All right then, I'll tell you in a moment how to go. But don't hurry. You want to ring up from Endover about half-past twelve. Tell Mrs. Bassett that you are coming through the fields by the river, and will I meet you as you don't quite know the way. I'll walk along after lunch and bring you back. Meanwhile you have lunch yourself, and come the way you came yesterday. How?'

'Lovely,' said Jenny, nodding eagerly.

IV

Miss Naomi Fenton picked up the receiver.

'Is that Bassetts Farm?' she asked.

'Yes, Mrs. Bassett speaking,' said a comfortable, motherly, scone-baking voice.

'This is Miss Naomi Fenton. Could I speak to my brother, please?'

'Mr. Fenton's out at the moment, miss. Could I give him a message?'

'Oh! I'm speaking from Endover. I was wondering if I could come along this afternoon and have tea with him?'

'I'm sure he would be delighted, miss. About what time shall I tell him to expect you?'

'Well—Is that Mrs. Bassett speaking?'

'Yes, miss.'

'Well—You see, I've been on a walking-tour with a friend, and she's had to go back suddenly, and I was sort of wondering if I could stay with my brother for a few days, because I'm all alone, and I wondered if—but I suppose you haven't got a spare room—'

'That I have, miss, if it's only just the bedroom you're wanting.'

'Oh, yes, just the bedroom.'

'Mr. Fenton has the sitting-room, you see, so you could have your meals there together, and sit of an evening, and if it's just the bedroom, I've got a nice room I could get ready—'

'That would be lovely.'

'Very well, miss, then I'll tell him to expect you, and we shall look for you about teatime.'

'Oh thank you. Oh, and Mrs. Bassett?'

'Yes, miss.'

'I've been asking the way here, and they tell me if I get down to the river by the mill, and then walk along it, I can get quite close to you—'

'That's right, miss. If you follow the river, it's about six miles, but—'

'Well, will you tell Mr. Fenton I'm coming that way and ask him to meet me, and tell him I'll start from the mill about half-past one, and—'

'Yes, miss, then you'll be sure of meeting, and he can bring you back with him. It's very pretty down by the river.'

'Yes, isn't it? I mean we came along that way this morning, and then my friend sprained her ankle—"

'Oh *dear*, miss, I *am* sorry to hear that.'

'Well, sort of ricked it, so she thought she ought to go back, and then her uncle hadn't been very well, and she thought she oughtn't to be away from him any longer, and then—'

'Yes, miss. Well, I'll tell Mr. Fenton, and I'm sure we shall do our best to make you comfortable.'

'Thank you so much. Goodbye, Mrs. Bassett.'

'Goodbye, Miss Fenton. And I'll see that your room is all ready for you.'

'Thank you so much. Goodbye.'

'Goodbye, miss.'

Mrs. Bassett went back to her cooking.

10

ENTRY OF A SHORT, STOUT GENTLEMAN

I

By three o'clock that afternoon Jenny Windell, had she but known it, was cleared of the major suspicion. It was always obvious that Jane Latour had been murdered, but as the result of Dr. Willoughby Hatch's masterly post-mortem examination of the deceased, it was now certain that no woman had struck the fatal blow. On the contrary, it had been delivered from behind by a short, and probably stout, left-handed man, and there were certain subcutaneous indications that the murderer, though possessed of considerable strength, was not in the best of training. The absence of certain other indications made it quite clear that the deceased was on friendly terms with her assailant.

'Here, wait a bit,' said the Inspector. 'How d'you get that?'

'There was no sign of any struggle,' said Dr. Hatch patiently. 'On the contrary—'

'Well, but if the Shah of Persia was to walk into this room now, and I was to catch him suddenly on the head with an inkstand, that wouldn't hardly prove I was on friendly terms with him, would it? I'm not, anyway,' he added, so as to have it quite clear.

Dr. Willoughby Hatch put up an eye-glass and surveyed the Inspector dispassionately. He nodded to himself, as if he had expected to see something like that, but had thought it his duty to make sure. He stood up.

'Is there anything more you want to know?'

'Here, wait a bit, Doctor. I'm not disputing anything you say'—a faint smile curved the Doctor's lips—'but I've got to look at it all round.' He began to write. 'Short, stout man, left-handed—sedentary occupation?—' He looked up with a question in his eyes.

'That's in your department,' said the Expert, sitting down again. 'I merely state that he was stout and not in good condition. Make any deduction from the facts that you feel are justified.

'"Sedentary occupation",' wrote the Inspector, feeling that it was justified. '"*And* known to the deceased." Now can you give us anything about the girl?'

'I understood you to tell me that you knew all about her.'

'I know who she is, if that's what you mean, but that doesn't say I know what she did.'

'Ah! Well, Miss Latour and Miss Windell were engaged in conversation when the murder took place. As Miss Latour was struck she fell against the girl's shoulder, and from there to the floor.'

'Certain?'

Dr. Hatch began to feel for his eye-glass again, and the Inspector hurriedly held up a large, preventive hand.

'All right, all right,' he said. 'I just wondered how you knew, that's all.'

'There was a minute bruise on the right wall of the chest made at the moment of death. As there was nothing against which she could have fallen—'

'The floor,' said the Inspector, but not really hopefully.

'In that case the area of the bruising would have been more extensive. Moreover, the absence of any marked contusion on the knees—'

'All right, all right,' said the Inspector. 'Well, but this looks as if she might have been an accomplice, eh? Held the dead woman in talk, while the murderer—'

Dr. Willoughby Hatch shrugged. Facts, not deductions, were all that concerned him.

'Or, of course, *not* an accomplice,' said the Inspector, wishing to do himself complete justice. 'As you say, we got to look at it all round.'

The Doctor, who had said nothing of the sort, stood up.

'Inquest tomorrow,' said the Inspector. He looked at his notes. 'Well, we're getting on.'

They were indeed getting on. A complete description of Miss Jenny Windell in walking costume and picture hat was in all the evening papers. This description, in order to leave nothing to chance, was supplemented by yet another photograph of Inspector Marigold, and by a camera-study of Miss Windell, in evening costume and without a hat, showing how delightfully the curls clustered round her head and over her ears. By some sort of gentleman's agreement among the editors, however, the name 'Windell' was discarded thereafter as unhelpful, and the public was asked to look out for 'Jenny', and if it saw 'Jenny' to communicate immediately with Scotland Yard or the nearest police-station.

WHERE IS JENNY?

asked one poster, and another announced:

JENNY IDENTIFIED: WHERE IS SHE?

A more direct appeal was made by a third, which put it squarely to the passer-by:

HAVE YOU SEEN JENNY?

There was now no sort of suggestion that Jenny was an accessory to the murder. The Law being what it was, no gentleman would hint such a thing against a ward of Watterson, Watterson and Hinchcoe's. Jenny, it was assumed, was a fellow-victim, now probably on her way to the Argentine. A well-known Harley-street physician discussed the possibility of drugging (and removing to the Argentine) a girl of Jenny's build, and seemed to think that, unless she had been deceived into thinking that someone dear to her had been suddenly taken ill in the Argentine, and was calling for her, it was impossible that the trans-shipment could be effected safely, a certain amount of cooperation on Jenny's part being almost essential. On the other hand, a lady novelist of repute, in an article entitled 'Are Our Girls Safe?', gave one or two remarkable instances of what had nearly happened to the daughters of friends of hers when walking up Regent Street and passing a hospital nurse. It was obvious that, if the murderer had been disguised as a hospital nurse, almost anything might have happened.

In these circumstances it was a comfort to know that the ports were being watched...

Nancy read all this in a tea-shop in Bloomsbury. She had stayed at her work a little later than usual, so as to be sure of not missing Mr. Fenton; for Mr. Archibald Fenton was not merely returning from his club this afternoon, but from the pawnbroker's, with money in his pocket for Joyce's big sister. At five o'clock, she decided that she could wait no longer. In any case, she told herself, the money could not be sent to Tunbridge Wells, until she had heard from Jenny. She went out, bought all the papers, and settled down to them over a pot of tea and a Bath bun.

She tried to imagine herself searching for the Jenny of the description and the photograph. Hopeless, with no more knowledge of her than this, to identify the real Jenny. The photographer had caught Miss Windell in one of those unfortunate moments when one is wearing evening-dress in the afternoon, and looking at a very ugly little man in a large bow-tie, and Nancy felt that too many girls had been surprised in just this position for any one of them to excite attention. And then, reading of all the horrible things which hadn't happened to Jenny, another thought came to her. Wouldn't Mr. and Mrs. Watterson be feeling rather *anxious?*

Mr. Watterson, of course, was a Guardian and a Solicitor, thus belonging to the two classes which were most notoriously unanxious when a ward, whose money they were handling, disappeared. Moreover, he was eighty, and at nineteen Nancy felt that the only things an old gentleman of eighty would be anxious about were the conditions and prospects in the next world. Still, even so, and even though he and Mrs. Watterson were no sort of relation to Jenny, they *might* be worrying about her. Oughtn't she to relieve that anxiety?

But how? An anonymous letter in a disguised handwriting? Safer than typing, because detectives always recognized the faulty *'e'* in a typewriter, and then searched London until they found it. She wouldn't post it in Chelsea, but would buy a letter-card in the nearest post office, and send it off now.

In capital letters, written with the left hand, the message said:

> 'YR NEICE SAFE AND ZOUND CANOT SAY MORE NO FAKE RENTON FRERS IN SHOSE A FREIND'

Once more Nancy felt rather pleased with herself as a writer of letters. First the 'neice'. Nobody, by reading the papers, would suppose that Jenny was Mr. Watterson's niece, but anybody meeting Jenny, and hearing her talk of 'Uncle Hubert', might make just that mistake. Then the shoes. Jenny's shoes, bought from Renton Freres, were now in Nancy's flat. Without some sort of identification the letter might be dismissed by Mr. Watterson as the work of any half-witted humorist; with its reference to the shoes, which one of the servants could confirm, added to the mistake about the niece, it became convincingly genuine. She dropped the letter-card into the box, and made her way home. On her omnibus she wondered about A FREIND, and decided that he was the captain of a sailing-barge now making its slow way to Newcastle.

II

Alice said, 'Well! If I didn't go and forget 'er watch.'

Cook was telling them about a friend of hers called Alfred Truby, whose thumb had been taken right off by a circular saw.

'What did it look like, Mrs. Price?' asked Hilda. 'Hot, this tea is,' she added, pouring it into her saucer, and blowing on it.

'Not nice,' said Cook, shaking her head. 'Unnatural, as you might say. Well, I'm just telling you. You never know *what* may happen. Five minutes before the hour, there he was, and the last thing he was thinking of was losing his thumb—five minutes after, and there's his thumb gone, and not all the finest surgeons in the country can put it back for him.'

'Wouldn't take ten minutes for a saw to get it off, would it?' said Hilda, who had now discovered a most attractive way of blowing ripples. 'Be like in a flash. Look, Alice, see that?' She blew again. 'Like sort of little waves.'

Alice said: 'Well, fancy *me* going and forgetting 'er watch. 'Tisn't like *me*.'

'Watch?' said Cook, ready for a change of subject.

'Your telling us about that saw suddenly put it into me 'ead. Miss Jenny's watch.'

'Look, Alice, see that?' said Hilda.

'D'you mean her watch that she wears?'

'That's it. Covered with diamonds and all. And I never told that Mr. Marigold nothing about it.'

'*Now* look, Alice! I got it lovely.'

'Never mind that, Hilda,' said Cook sharply. 'This is something we've got to think about. Her watch, Alice? Well, how *could* you have been so silly?'

'It just didn't come into me 'ead.'

'What does the silly old watch matter?' said Hilda, annoyed, as any artist would be, at interruption just when perfection was reached.

'Why of course it matters.'

'Well, if you ask *me*, I should say if you can't reckernize a person by 'er hat and dress, you aren't going to do it by asking 'er the time and then taking a snoop at 'er watch.'

'It isn't that, Hilda,' explained Alice. 'It's just that if anything— if poor Miss Jenny—if she *is*—' She gulped, and had to leave it to Cook.

'First thing they'd do', said Cook impressively to Hilda, 'would be to sell that watch. He'd get a good price for a watch like that. Reel diamonds, wasn't it, Alice?'

Alice nodded.

'That's right. And what the Police would do is to send round to all the—'

'Fences,' said Alice, knowing about it from Jenny's books.

'To all the pawnbrokers, to say "'As anybody been trying to sell the aforesaid watch?" and then they get a description of him, and that's a clue, d'you see?'

'Oh, all right!' said Hilda, and drank up her tea.

So when Mr. Watterson came back from the office at six o'clock, Alice went up and told him what she had forgotten. Mr. Watterson rang up the Inspector; and then Alice told the Inspector exactly what Jenny's watch was like; and then Inspector Marigold did just what Cook had said he would do. And at about ten o'clock Mr. Watterson rang up Inspector

Marigold again, and again the Inspector went round to Acacia Road. Once more Alice went into the study, but this time only to be asked a question about Miss Jenny's shoes. When she had answered it, the Inspector and Mr. Watterson nodded solemnly at each other, and a little later Inspector Marigold left; and at eleven o'clock, under the impression that he had now cleared the ground as thoroughly as he had ever cleared it in the old days at Lord's, he went early to bed, in readiness for a full day's play tomorrow.

III

At twenty minutes to seven Mr. Archibald Fenton crossed Chelsea Bridge in his Sandeman Six on his way to Endover. As a critic had said, the success of A Flock of Sheep had raised many problems—one of them being whether one should have a chauffeur or drive the car oneself. Mr. Fenton decided against a chauffeur, on the very reasonable grounds that if one drove the car oneself, one always had it, whereas if a chauffeur drove it, one's wife might want it at some inconvenient moment; and he felt that a wife could not go on admiring a husband, if he were continually explaining to her how necessary it was for his art that he should have the car this afternoon. Of course he did not say all this to Fanny. He explained quite simply that it was necessary for his art that they should live well within their means, and that, however inconvenient to both of them, he thought that they should try to do without a chauffeur. Fanny then, rather foolishly, offered to learn to drive a car too, but her husband said that he knew it was absurd of him, but he would feel horribly nervous to think of Fanny driving about alone, particularly in London.

Mr. Fenton drove well. It was his one physical attainment, unless pure stoutness is to be reckoned as such; for, though in these last two years he had become an enthusiastic cricketer, he excelled as a bad player rather than as a good one, doing so with the air of one who preferred it this way, as being more in the literary tradition. As he drove, he thought with the pleased satisfaction which occasionally eluded him, of his negotiations with the pawnbrokers. He had been, he thought, completely in the character, even to the detail of removing his tie, but secretly, before going in, and turning up the coat of his collar. His poverty being thus apparent, he had told the story of a sick wife, Jessie, to whom he had given the watch as a wedding present, and the urgent necessity of taking her into the country for a fortnight. His name was William Makepeace Thackeray—*and,* thought Mr. Fenton, a very good name, too. The pawnbroker, who didn't seem to mind how many sick wives Mr. Thackeray had, reluctantly doled out twelve pounds ten. Mr. W. M. Thackeray left the shop, the pawn-ticket in his waistcoat pocket. He found his car. He put on his tie again and turned down his collar. And it was not until then that he remembered Julia, and the urgent necessity of taking *her* into the country for a fortnight.

Julia Treherne was an extremely beautiful and intelligent actress, who had been wedded to her Art and Mr. Allison for ten years, and had no intention of being unfaithful to either. In fact, she loved them both devotedly. But Mr. Allison and she equally recognized that an actress is not as other women, and that, within certain specified limits, it was necessary for her to be all things to all men, particularly if they were, or might be, connected with the theatre. Julia kept exactly within the limits, enjoyed herself considerably, and saw as much of her husband as was possible without being ostentatious. Mr. Archibald Fenton (who did not, however, quite know the rules) was her latest conquest, and he had just remembered that it was her birthday on Friday.

Friday. Today was Wednesday. Easy to get her a present now before he left London, but too late to make it the personal gift which, if he had remembered earlier, he would have chosen with such loving care. And now here it was waiting for him: the watch with 'J' in diamonds for Julia!

He went back to the shop. With the excuse of a suddenly remembered Uncle Makepeace from whom he had not yet borrowed, he redeemed the watch. He realized that, if he had thought of all this before, he could have bought it direct from Nancy at less expense, but he was oddly scrupulous about money matters, and was not sorry that the cheque which he was sending her had, as it were, the countersign of authority. He took the watch home with him. It was in his pocket now as he climbed up to the Crystal Palace. Tomorrow he would send it to Julia with a letter... such a letter... and then! — who knew? Even next Sunday perhaps...

As he came down River Hill he stopped thinking of this, and began to compose the letter. At Tunbridge it was almost a poem...

Thursday

11

USE FOR THE FOURTH GOVERNESS

I

Jenny, half-waking, half-sleeping, turned restlessly on to her back, and saw above her head the dim skeleton of some enormous animal.

She had seen it before somewhere... in that Natural History Museum to which she had been taken so often by her third governess. It was a mega-something. Not a megaphone, that was the other thing. 'Now this, Jenny, is one of those animals I was telling you about who lived long, long before there were any little girls in the world. They are called prehistoric animals, because they lived before history books were written. You see, history books couldn't be written because there weren't any men or women to write them!' 'Not Adam and Eve?' had asked Jenny, and the third governess, not being quite sure what to do about that, because it was all very difficult if you weren't to destroy a child's innocent faith, decided that it was now time to go home. But, before they left, they spent a few minutes with a case of humming-birds, because humming-birds were perfectly safe, and wouldn't put ideas into anybody's head...

To Jenny one skeleton more or less in the ridiculous confusion of her brain did not matter. She turned over to her left side, snuggled herself down and let herself back into her dream. In a moment she was asleep again. But not for long. The sun climbed slowly above the trees at the bottom of the meadow, and seeped through the curtains; outside the open windows starlings imitated themselves and other birds untiringly; kitchen stoves were being raked out below; animals were shifting slowly at the sound of men's voices, and a hoof would hit suddenly and restlessly upon stone. Against the new insistent day Jenny's sleep could not prevail. She woke... and wondered where she was.

Even in the daylight the centre beam and crossbeams of the ceiling looked like the backbone of a giant sole. This had been in her dreams, and adventures with tramps who were policemen, and going about in the more public places with nothing on. Now she began to remember things more sharply. Derek Fenton... Bassetts... and what was her name? Naomi Fenton. She was in a bedroom at Bassetts. It was still almost like a dream.

There was a knock at her door, and an 'Are you awake, Miss Fenton?' 'Come in,' called Jenny, and Mrs. Bassett came in.

'I've brought you a cup of tea, miss. It's a lovely morning. Shall I pull your curtains?'

'Oh, thank you. Oh yes, please. What a *lovely* day.'

'Looks like it's going to be hot. Now what would you like to do, miss? Your brother always has a bathe in the river. He's just back from his, and he said I was to say if you'd like one too, he'd show you the best place.'

'Oh.' said Jenny. 'I—I haven't got a bathing-dress.'

'Bless you, miss, that doesn't matter, there'll be nobody there to see, not at this time. I'll have some hot water ready for you by the time you get back.'

'Oh, thank you.'

'Then I'll tell Mr. Fenton you'll be ready as soon as you've drank your tea.'

'Oh, thank you.'

Mrs. Bassett bustled out.

Jenny had so many things to think about that a new problem was almost welcome, since it distracted her mind from the old ones. How did one get to the river if one hadn't a dressing-gown or anything? And how did one come back? And would Mr. Fenton— Derek—of course he wouldn't really—but would he—

There was a whistle from beneath her window —definitely not a starling—and then a call 'Na-o-mi!' She got out of bed, took her tea to the window-sill, and looked out.

'Hallo! Good morning, sister,' said Derek.

'Good morning.'

'Have you slept well?'

'Very, thank you.'

'And did you do it in a nightdress or pyjamas?'

'Do you mean what have I got on now?'

'That's what I'm leading up to.'

'Pyjamas.'

'Good. I was wondering how to get you down to the river. I've got Mrs. Bassett's second-best gum-boots for you, and there's no disguising the fact that they *don't* go with a nightdress. You're only going to meet two cows and a rabbit, but one must consider everybody. Are you more or less ready?'

'Just on,' said Jenny, and sipped her tea.

'Right. Then I'll show you the place, point out the ants' nest, and leave you to it. Here, wait a bit, I'll throw up the boots. Got anything breakable just under the window?'

'No.'

'Then withdraw yourself and cup of tea, and watch.'

Thump!... Thump!

'Well done!' cried Jenny, returning to the window.

'Tuck your trousers into those and you'll look like a musical comedy producer's idea of a midshipman. Have you got two towels?'

'One,' said Jenny, looking at the towel-horse.

'I'll have another ready for you. I've told Mrs. Bassett over and over again that the secret of a contented life is two towels. Don't be long.'

He went into the house, and Jenny finished her tea. This had suddenly become fun. She put on the boots and looked at herself. She had never seen Nancy's pyjamas in daylight. They looked rather nice. She didn't at all mind Derek or anybody seeing her like this.

She took the towel, and went downstairs.

'As I thought,' said Derek. 'Midshipman in charge of swabbing party. Here you are.' He gave her the other towel.

As they walked through the fields, Jenny said: 'I think I know the place.'

'Sure?'

'I think I passed it yesterday.'

'You must have done that, but you certainly didn't bathe there.'

'How do you know?' asked Jenny, and had the sudden thought that perhaps he had seen her yesterday. It was funny; now she felt quite different to him again now she didn't mind if he *had* seen her. It was funny that his first question to her yesterday had been 'Are you an artist's model by any chance?' Almost as if he had seen her, and thought her beautiful. 'How do you know?' she asked again.

'Intuitive deduction. I depend upon it a good deal, particularly in the wine-trade. As soon as I sip a glass of Burgundy, no matter what the vintage may be, I take one look at the bottle and say to myself "Burgundy". Sometimes it's claret, but the principle is the same.'

They came nearer the river, and Jenny pointed and said 'Is that it?'

'That is it. Here, then, I leave you, Miss Fenton. A parting word, and I am gone. Can you swim?'

'Yes,' said Jenny, for her fourth governess had insisted on this.

'It takes a good three strokes to get across the pool, *and,*' added Derek, 'a good three strokes to get back again. So husband your strength. Goodbye. We shall meet at breakfast.'...

Ten minutes later, with a towel round her waist and another over her shoulders, Jenny sat drying in the sun. If only she could let herself be quite, quite happy, how happy she would be! "True happiness', one of her governesses had said, quoting possibly from some other thinker, 'lies only in memory or anticipation.' In Jenny's case it was memory and anticipation which were troubling her present happiness.

Memory: Mr. Watterson.

Anticipation: Mrs. Bassett.

Present Happiness: Derek.

Mr. Watterson was eighty, but even at eighty you could be anxious. Besides, he was her Guardian by Law, so he was responsible for her, and would get into trouble if he lost her. She *must* let him know that she was safe...

Mrs. Bassett was—fifty? But even at fifty you wanted money for rooms. Jenny had nine-and-threepence left. Next Wednesday Mrs. Bassett would want—how much? Well, more than nine-and- threepence...

Derek was thirty. And she was safe with him, and he understood things...

It was so lovely here. If only it could go on forever...

He couldn't let her go now, could he? Not even if she told him everything?

She dropped the towel from her shoulders and stood up. He couldn't let her go now?...

It was a happy midshipman who came across the fields to the house, singing a little French nursery-song.

Frère Jacques, frère Jacques,
Dormez-vous, dormez-vous?
Sonnez la patine,
Sonnez la patine,
Bim, bom, boom!

After breakfast Derek said: 'In half an hour I am going to fish.'

'Oh, are there fish in the river?' said Jenny.

'That is what I am trying to find out.'

'What do you fish for? I mean what sort of fish?'

'There again we are in the dark. It might be mermaids and it might be eels. But I like sitting on the bank and watching nothing happen, and if you like it too, we should be certain of not missing anything.'

Jenny liked it too. She lay on the bank and watched the gay little float twisting in the eddies, and told herself that as soon as it was quite still, she would say 'Derek'... But it wasn't *quite* still... Not yet... nor yet... nor—

'Derek.'

'Naomi.'

She had called him Derek. The worst was over. She gulped down her nervousness, and said: 'Would you mind very much if you got mixed up in something?'

He understood that this was the end of the day's fishing.

'Do you mean something like marmalade?' he asked. 'Or more like a wasp's nest?'

'Murder,' said Jenny bravely.

'You mean you want me to murder somebody?' said Derek. 'I suppose', he went on wistfully, 'it couldn't be Archibald?'

Jenny shook her head.

'You see,' she said simply, 'I'm Jenny Windell.'

'*Not* Gloria Naomi Harris?'

'No.'

Derek nodded.

'I felt certain that there was some mistake. I know all the Harrises—there are only seventeen thousand of them left now—and you aren't in the least like any of them.'

'You see, it was my handkerchief.'

Derek frowned.

'Your handkerchief,' he said.

'Jenny,' she explained.

'Jenny.'

'Because of Conway Castle.'

'Conway Castle,' nodded Derek. 'Leave nothing out, however unimportant it seems. Once I have all the facts, then I can fit them together.'

'Well, of course I oughtn't to have been there at all. That's why I hid, you see.'

'That's why you hid. I must now interrupt, in order to narrate a sad story about a relation by marriage. Many years ago, before he became famous, Archibald wrote a long blank-verse poem. Or anyhow a long poem. Or anyhow,' said Derek, 'it was long. He forgot, however, to number the pages, and it so happened that they were dropped two or three times before they got to the printer. The printer then dropped them again, and the printer's boy, who was given the job of searching for, and collecting them, abstracted a page here and there so that he might make paper darts. The residue was published under the title *Ariadne in Stoke Newington*, and, I am bound to say, received high praise from Archibald's fellow-critics. *But*,' said Derek emphatically, 'and this is the point, *Archibald's poem was not what it was*. So now, Jenny Windell, *could* you get the pages of your murder story in the right order, and begin, unoriginal as it may seem, at the very beginning?'

'But haven't you read the papers?' cried Jenny.

'Not one. We get nothing but the Sunday papers. So begin by telling me who Jenny Windell is.'

Jenny told him...

When she had finished, Derek said 'Gosh!'

Jenny said: 'It is rather awful, isn't it?'

'Awful? Not a bit. It's terrific.'

'Do you mind?' asked Jenny timidly.

'Mind? O Robert Louis Stevenson, O Arthur Conan Doyle, O Freeman Hardy and Willis, I mean Freeman Wills Croft, I thank thee. I mean ye.'

'Have I been *terribly* silly?'

'You have been enchantingly wise. If there is one thing which stands out more than another in this world—and of course,' said Derek, 'one thing always *does* stand out more than another—it is that there are some things which you cannot explain to a policeman. To make it clear to a policeman, an inspector, a coroner, a solicitor, a barrister *and* a judge, one after the other, that you and Hussar were so wrapped up in each other's conversation that you went into the wrong house without looking, would take about nineteen years, and then leave you just where you were at the start. Far, far better a life of exile.'

'Yes, *I* thought it would be difficult.'

'Impossible. Another anecdote of the Fenton family occurs to me. When I was a small boy I had an Aberdeen terrier. One day I lost it, and my father asked the local policeman to let him know if anybody found it. Next day the policeman came up to the house, saluted and said: "Sir, I have to report that the animal in question was last observed proceeding in the direction of Chorlton-cum-Hardy." If you can imagine to yourself the back-view of an Aberdeen terrier doing this, you will realize how very matter-of-fact we are in the police force.'

But it was not at an Aberdeen terrier proceeding in the direction of Chorlton-cum-Hardy that Jenny was looking; she was trying to see Derek as a small boy, unhappy because he had lost his friend...

'And now', said Derek, 'to business.'

'Business?' said Jenny, waking up with a start.

'Yes. What are we going to do?'

'I don't know. I thought perhaps you'd know.'

'Then let me think.'

Jenny let him think. She wanted to think, too. Just of how lovely it was to let somebody else think for you like this...

'Obviously the first thing', said Derek, 'is to find out what's happening in London. This afternoon, therefore, I shall be observed proceeding in the direction of Maidstone, where I shall get all the morning papers.'

'Oh!' said Jenny suddenly.

'Why "Oh!" ?'

'I've just remembered! I asked Nancy to write to me at the Tunbridge Wells post office.'

'Oh! Very well then, I shall proceed in the direction of Tunbridge Wells, and get all the morning papers.'

'And my letter?'

'And your letter.'

'Will they give it to you?'

'I hope so.'

'Couldn't I come with you?'

'Safer not. Sleuths may have tracked you to Tunbridge Wells.'

'I do look different. Really. I mean my hair—it makes a tremendous difference.'

Derek looked at her.

'I should know you anywhere, Jenny Windell, Gloria Harris, Naomi Fenton, Dryad, Naiad and Oread. No matter what you did to your hair.'

'Oh, *you,*' said Jenny, as if that were natural.

'Yes, me. Or, as Archibald would say, I. No, what you shall do is to give me a note saying that your brother Wilbraham Harris, of Wilbraham Harris Ltd., preserved fruit importers, is calling for a letter for you. I will bring the letter and the papers back here, and we will spend a long evening with them. That all right?'

'Yes,' said Jenny.

'Good. Now then, what about the Wattersons?'

'Oh, *please!*'

'However old they are, they must have noticed that you have left St. John's Wood.'

'Oh, I know. They must be anxious.'

'Well, they ought to be told that you're safe. Shall I ring Mr. Watterson up? Anonymously?'

'But then, wouldn't he go to the police? He's a solicitor, you know. He'd find out where the call came from—they always do—'

'Yes.' Derek thought this over. 'A telegram would be safer.'

'Oh, but they trace telegrams! Always! They get an authorization from the Postmaster-General—'

'What a lot you know, Naomi. All right, then, let's think of something else.'

He thought. Jenny frowned. Between them they were baffling the police...

'Where is Mr. Watterson now?' asked Derek. 'Office or Home?'

'He goes to the office every morning.'

'And gets home?'

'One o'clock. Regularly.'

'Sure?'

'Oh, but it used to be a joke how regular he was.'

'Then if I rang up the house now, who would answer it?'

'The cook. Mrs. Price.'

'Is she quick? Intelligent?'

'Not very,' smiled Jenny. 'Of course it might be Hilda, the house-parlourmaid.'

'You're sure it wouldn't be Mrs. Watterson?'

'It goes to the kitchen first, and then upstairs. Besides, she generally goes out for a drive at eleven.'

'Good.' He looked at his watch. 'Half-past ten. Mr. Watterson gone?'

'Oh, yes. He's at the office by ten.'

'Then I think that's fairly safe. Now listen. We go back to the house in a quarter of an hour, and at five minutes past eleven, you ring up.'

'Me?'

'You. Cook answers—or Hilda. Do you know their voices on the telephone?'

'Oh, yes, easily.'

'What do you call Mr. Watterson?'

'Uncle Hubert.'

'Right. Then you say, "Hallo, is that Mrs. Price?"—or Hilda, or whoever it is. Don't say who you are, but let her recognize *your* voice, and if she says; "Well I never, is that Miss Jenny?" you can say "Yes". But all you've really got to say is, "Will you tell Uncle Hubert when he comes back that I'm quite, quite safe?" And then you ring off quickly. And when Uncle Hubert gets the message two hours later, not all the Postmaster-Generals in the world are going to find out where the call came from. At least, not nearer than Tunbridge Wells. How's that?'

'Perfect,' said Jenny admiringly. And though Derek didn't think that it was perfect, he thought it was the best they could do, and not too bad at that.

II

Up till now the one love of Jenny's life had been Hussar. But just as many grown-up people prefer to concentrate their religious emotion on some material representation of their God, so the child Jenny had found that her passion for Hussar could most easily be worked off on the current governess. The expression of this passion took many strange forms, one of them being an earnest imitation of the handwriting of the loved one. It was with the pen of her fourth governess that she wrote a letter of authorization to the Tunbridge Wells post office.

> *'Please give the bearer any letters addressed to Miss Gloria Harris, Paste Restante, Tunbridge Wells. Gloria N. Harris'*

The fourth governess had been the most uncertificated of them all. She didn't really know anything. Not for her the Greek 'e', the modern script, the clerkly, undistinguished style. She wrote home to the vicarage in a round, rolling hand, full of Victorianly feminine curves and flounces, saying that she had a bedroom on the top floor, which looked quite homey now that all the photographs were up, and Jenny was a funny little thing, but sweetly pretty, and they were going to be great friends. Jenny had loved her dearly; and, while waiting for the day when she would save her darling Miss Withers from being run over, and be taken to St. George's Hospital and have her life despaired of, and be slowly nursed back to health by a more than ever devoted Miss Withers, who would now let Jenny call her Grace, she had occupied herself in adapting to her own needs all of Grace Withers that was accessible: her movements, her speech, her handwriting.

'Do you always write like this?' asked Derek.

'No,' said Jenny; 'look.' She wrote the message out again, this time in her own hand. Derek compared the two.

'There's nothing you can't do. It's marvellous. We really *ought* to murder Archibald between us. Think it over. We'd get away with it easily.'

Derek drove to Tunbridge Wells in his two-seater *coupé*, and parked his car opposite the Wesleyan Methodist Church. An earnest-faced, spectacled young woman was at the entrance to the post office as he went in. They got in each other's way, apologized, smiled at each other. For a moment he thought that he recognized her, but perhaps it was only because she seemed for a moment to recognize him. Then she moved away, and he went inside. The combination of Gloria Harris and Grace Withers brought complete conviction to the clerk, and the letter was given to him. As he turned to leave he seemed to feel, rather than to see, that the young woman was now inside thc post office, writing at the telegraph desk. He went out, and walked to the station for the papers.

A poster outside the bookstall said:

WHERE IS
JENNY?
STARTLING DEVELOPMENTS

'So it's like that,' said Derek to himself. 'What fun we're going to have.'

12

MISS PITMAN AT THE WELLS

I

In Lovely Lady, the novel of which he was ashamed, Mr. Archibald Fenton describes his heroine, Barbara Wilmot, in what he thought at the time were a few well-chosen words. She was at the threshold of life, standing with reluctant feet, as Mr. Fenton pointed out, where the brook and river meet, and already the slender lines of her figure indicated the gentle promise of womanhood. One could hardly put it more delicately. She had a vivacious, mobile face which lit up when she talked, and on one occasion, but fortunately only in the first rough copy, it went so far as to make a delicious little moue at Leslie Brand, the hero. This face was framed in a mass of unruly hair, stray tendrils of which escaped from time to time, and had to be pushed back beneath the hat where customarily they nestled. Whenever Leslie Brand let fall an epigram, and he seemed unable to let fall anything else, she either trilled or else bubbled with happy laughter. Altogether she seemed to be a delightful creature, and Archibald's engagement to Fanny a few days after publication came as a surprise to his friends.

It may have been because she reminded him of Barbara Wilmot that Mr. Fenton chose Miss Fairbrother, rather than one of the stouter and less mobile applicants, as his private secretary. Nancy hoped that this was so, because, in order to obtain the post, she had, in fact, modelled herself on Miss Wilmot. In the game which she played with life it was almost a necessity for her to model herself on somebody; so that, hearing of Mr. Fenton's need, it was natural for her first to wonder what sort of applicant would most appeal to him. Obviously one who had read all his books. She read them, and, as she read, looked out for further clues. The heroine of *A Flock of Sheep* was fair, and, in a nice sort of way, generously proportioned, but this was outside Nancy's range. The heroines of the two intermediate books (omitting, of course, the essays and the critical studies) were, in her opinion, much better left there. One of them had a pimple on her chin, which Mr. Fenton had described so lovingly and so often that he would certainly miss it; the other had a horselike face, which had so stamped itself on the man's mind, that nothing short of a horse (or, rather, a mare) could expect to awaken the necessary tender memories. Nancy made her personal application, therefore, as Barbara Wilmot, hoping that the sight of his first love would strike a chord in the Great Man's heart. Apparently it struck it, for she was engaged at once.

The post obtained, she dropped Barbara Wilmot, and became the Complete Private Secretary. This was a disappointment to Mr. Archibald Fenton. Gone were the trills, the bubbles of happy laughter when he let fall an epigram; Miss Fairbrother had nothing for him now but a prim 'Yes, Mr. Fenton'. If *moues* were still made, they were made behind his back, and, in any case, were no longer delicious. But the tendrils still escaped, the hair still was unruly. The face remained mobile, though its vivacity seemed to be gone. It may be that there is no vivacious way of taking down shorthand or clacking on a typewriter; it may have been that the poor girl had troubles at home which she hid from him. In any case no possible fault could be found with her work—nor with the slender lines of her figure. These, as Mr. Fenton noted from time to time, indicated the gentle promise of womanhood...

On this Thursday morning Mr. Fenton (thank the Lord) was out of the way, and Nancy was going to 'do something'. What it was she would do was not yet certain, but she had decided that it was Alice Pitman who would do it. Miss Pitman, it may be remembered, was good, earnest and slightly perspiring; half governess, half matron at a large kindergarten in South Kensington. What else? A little fuller in the figure than Nancy, which would mean padding of some sort. That would be uncomfortably hot in this sort of weather, but then Miss Pitman was always uncomfortably hot in this sort of weather, which would make it just right. Glasses? Glasses undoubtedly. And probably a white, full, silk petticoat, which showed a little...

At ten o'clock Miss Nancy Fairbrother entered Mr. Fenton's Bank, and cashed her cheque.

At 11.15 Miss Fairbrother returned to her flat with several brown-paper parcels.

At 12 Miss Alice Pitman looked at herself in Nancy's glass with a satisfaction which the real Miss Pitman could never have felt.

At 12.30 Miss Pitman left London for Tunbridge Wells. She was going to find Jenny.

'Now,' said Nancy to herself in the corner of a third-class carriage, 'let's think it out.'

Whatever Jenny was doing, she couldn't go on doing it without money. If she had had Nancy's letter, she would have written to give an address to which the money could be sent. Therefore, up to yesterday evening she had not had Nancy's letter. But she might have got it this morning. Obviously the first thing to do was to find out about this. If Miss Gloria

Harris's letter was still waiting for her in the Tunbridge Wells post office, and if she did not come for it today, then Jenny was not in the Tunbridge Wells district, and would have to be tracked.

How?

As far as her studies had gone, Nancy had learnt of only three ways of tracking. The first way was by following the spoor of the wanted person; which could really only be done over snow or sands, or (if one was an Indian) through trackless forests. Tunbridge Wells was obviously unfavourable ground for this. The second way was by showing a bloodhound some garment belonging to the fugitive; but even if she had had the garment with her, and could have bought a bloodhound in Tunbridge Wells, Nancy felt that this method was too public for her purposes. It did happen sometimes that, owing to the fact that the fugitive had accidentally stepped into some aniseed before starting out, the pursuit could be made with a less noticeable dog, but Nancy felt that it was unlikely that Jenny had done this. The third method was by asking questions in a roundabout way in the bars of public-houses. This method was clearly unsuited to Miss Pitman.

What was left?

'Well,' said Nancy to herself, 'let's see when we get there.'

'Care to look at the paper, miss?' said the young man opposite, seeing that she was now disengaged.

'Oh, *thank* you,' said Miss Pitman, instinctively gushing a little. 'That *is* kind of you. I quite forgot to *look* at it this morning.'

'Queer business this Auburn Lodge murder.'

'Yes, *isn't* it queer?'

'There.' He folded back the paper and handed it to her. 'See that? That's funny, isn't it?'

Nancy took the paper eagerly. Her heart beat a little more quickly under its padding. She was looking at a reproduction of her lettercard, and feeling as so many authors have felt when they first saw their own work in the press.

'What does it mean?' she asked. 'Renton Frers?'

'It tells you down below. Name of a boot-shop. French, you know, for Renton Brothers. It tells you there.'

'Oh, I see. Frères.'

'That's right. Brothers. Tell you what *I* think?'

'Oh yes, *do*, please.'

'I'll tell you. All this about White Slave Traffic—if you don't mind my mentioning it to a lady—'

'That's *quite* all right,' said Miss Pitman earnestly. 'I've just come back from Geneva as secretary to a gentleman—'

'That so? Well, you can take it from me that most of the talk you hear is just bunk. Bunk,' said the young man, making a discarding movement with his two hands. 'Nothing in it. D'you know the first thing I say, when I read about a murder?'

'No.'

'I say, who's *this* going to do a bit of good to? See what I mean?'

'You mean who's going to profit by it?'

'That's right. And the answer's plain. Jenny.'

'Oh, do you *think* so?'

'Well, she's Jane Latour's niece, isn't she?'

'Yes, but—'

'*And* only relation?'

'Yes, but—'

'Well, it really isn't quite fair of me talking like this, because I happen to be a bit in the know. But you can take it from me—'

'Oh, are you a detective? How *exciting!*'

'Well, yes and no. More in an amateur way, if you see what I mean. I've studied this sort of thing a lot. But it just happens that a friend of mine happens to be in with the Scotland Yard people, and he told me for a fact that they *know* in Scotland

Yard that it was the niece who did it. That doesn't mean that they can prove it, mind you. But they know.'

'Oh, but how awful to think of a young girl like that being a murderess! I still can't quite believe it.'

'Fact, I assure you.'

'Then does that mean she wrote this letter-card herself?'

'That's right. Put 'em off the scent.'

'Yes, but wouldn't it have been better if she hadn't said anything at all, and then everybody would have thought she was dead?'

'Well,' said the young man, after thinking this over, and finding that it was too much for him, 'you've got to look at it all round. See what I mean? I'm only telling you what they say at the Yard. Well, I get out here. Sevenoaks. Good morning, miss. No, that's all right, thanks, I've finished with it.'

Left alone, Nancy went back to the paper. She read her own contribution again, and then passed on to the inferior work of other contributors. Well, no; not so inferior. Suddenly the paper dropped out of her fingers, and she gave a whistle of dismayed astonishment, quite outside Miss Pitman's range. 'Lordy!' cried Miss Fairbrother. 'What do you know about that?' She had just discovered that they were looking for Jenny's watch...

What would happen? They would find the pawnbroker. The pawnbroker would reveal Mr. Fenton. Well, no need for that. Fenton would read the papers and recognize for himself that 'J' in diamonds. He would go to the police. The police would go to Elm Park Mansions... and in twenty-four hours the papers would be saying 'Where is Nancy?'

'Well, after all,' said Miss Pitman complacently, 'where is she?'

II

At Tunbridge Wells Nancy got out of the train, and put her bag in the cloak-room. Then she walked down to the post office.

So that was the post office.

It was half-past one. Should she go in and ask about Gloria Harris?

Yes...

No...

Obviously no. If Jenny had not called for her letter, then there was just the one chance of finding her. Hang about the post office until Jenny came. Sooner or later she was bound to come. But if Nancy asked about the letter now, and went away and had lunch, and came back again, then all through the afternoon while she was waiting, she would have the uneasy feeling that perhaps Jenny had come and gone in that luncheon interval, and that now she was waiting for nothing. For it would be quite impossible to make a second innocent inquiry about the letter.

She walked up to the High Street and lunched. She came back to the post office and went in.

'Good-afternoon,' said Miss Pitman, with a nervous but friendly smile. 'Is there a letter for me? Pitman. Miss Alice Pitman. You see, I'm camping, and I didn't quite—oh, thank you so much.'

The clerk had gone away to look. He came back to say that he was sorry, there was no letter for Miss Pitman. Miss Pitman looked disappointed.

'Oh!' she said. 'Oh, thank you.' She hesitated; and then, taking courage, gave the clerk another nervous smile, and said: 'I'm *so* sorry to trouble you, but I *wonder* if you would mind telling me if there are any letters for my friend Miss *Harris*'? We're camping together, you see, and she—'

'Have you an authority from Miss Harris to—'

'Oh, no, no, no,' interrupted Miss Pitman quickly. 'I didn't mean *that!* How silly of me! No, all I meant was, she's coming into the Wells to *tea*, but it's right the other side of the *town*, you see, and I *know* she talked of seeing if there were any letters for her, and I thought if I could tell her there weren't any, then it would save her all that walk, you see, and if there *were* any, then of course she would come for them herself. I knew I couldn't take them without an authority, of course, but I thought if I could just tell her, you see—oh, thank you so much.'

The clerk had gone away to look. With his back to her, he said: 'Any name or initials?'

'Gloria,' said Miss Pitman eagerly. 'Miss *Gloria* Harris. It *is* kind of you. It will save her all that *long* walk, and—'

'Miss Gloria Harris,' read out the clerk. 'Yes. There is.'

'Oh, thank you *so* much, then he *has* written. I'll tell her. Unless of course she may have started to walk in *earlier* than she said, but then I expect she'd come anyhow, but of course she *may* have changed her mind and not be coming in this afternoon at *all*, but it is nice to *know*, isn't it? Thank you *so* much, good-afternoon.'

So far, thought Nancy, so good. Now all she had to do was to hang about the post office until Jenny came.

All! It was enough. Up to now the adventure had been exciting, but there was nothing exciting in walking up and down outside a post office, lingering a moment here and a moment there, pretending to look in at this shop-window and at that. In books the hero always engaged a room opposite the house he was watching, and so gave himself a chance of sitting down, but in real life there was no reason why the owner of any house opposite any house which anybody happened to suspect should want to take in lodgers of a suspicious nature. It might be worth trying, of course; she would have to sleep somewhere; but she dare not begin to make inquiries until her vigil for the day was over. Three o'clock. She must not leave before six at the earliest. Six would be fairly safe. She continued to walk up and down...

With the idea of increasing the amenities of an attractive town the authorities have had the vision to place a demobilized Tank just outside the post office, where it serves equally as an inspiration to the young, a tender memory to the middle-aged, and a token of their faith to the elderly. After nearly an hour in its company, Nancy, a little capriciousry, began to feel that Tunbridge Wells was practically all Tank (all of it, that is, which was not post office) and she wished that Jenny had chosen some other town to escape to, one, for instance, which had been content to decorate itself with an odd howitzer here and there, or a handful of bombs. Then she felt ashamed of herself for thinking this, because, of course, a Tank was really a very beautiful thing, and it wasn't meant to be next to the post office at all, it only just happened to be there because they wanted to have it opposite the Wesleyan Methodist Church...

Next to the church were two hotels. At six o'clock, she would get her bag from the station, and take a bedroom in one of the hotels, and then tomorrow she would be able to sit down...

The bother was that she was now cut off from London. She had meant to send her address to Mrs. Featherstone, who 'came in' every morning, so that if Jenny wrote from some other town, the letter could be forwarded; but now it was impossible. WHERE IS NANCY? Definitely not giving the police an address at Tunbridge Wells. Let them find her there if they could.

She came to the post office again, looked idly in through the swing doors, and came out.

Bump!

'Oh, I'm *so* sorry,' said Miss Pitman, confused and earnest.

'I *beg* your pardon,' smiled the young man, taking off his hat.

For a moment they looked at each other, and with a sudden pleasurable shock Nancy recognized him.

His face was not very familiar, but to one who, hour after hour, as it seemed, had been eagerly looking out for a friend, and had seen nothing more responsive than a Tank, even the sight of a recognizable stranger was in some way reassuring. She had seen him in Bloomsbury once—twice, wasn't it?—he had called for Mr. Fenton and they had gone out to lunch together. She wasn't introduced. Secretaries weren't. He had just walked in, so she didn't hear his name. Archibald had been rather annoyed about it, and the other man had said, 'My dear Hippo, I assure you—', and had been hurried out, leaving Nancy to wonder whether Hippo was short for Hippolytus or Hippopotamus. Either way Archibald hadn't liked it. The other time was in the hall, as she was going out, and he had smiled and said 'Good-afternoon'.

There was no reason why he should have anything to do with Jenny, but on an impulse she followed him into the post office...

Nothing like being impulsive.

She heard him say: 'Have you any letters for Miss Gloria Harris?' She saw him hand over a piece of paper to the clerk... She followed him out.

He walked to the station. He looked at the posters outside the bookstall. He bought all the papers. He put five under his arm and stood reading the sixth. He went back to the car-park below the Tank, still reading. He dropped the papers into a blue *coupe*, and walked up to the High Street...

What did it mean?

The simple explanation (always the best, said the books) was that Jenny had settled down somewhere as Gloria Harris, and being unable, or afraid, to come into Tunbridge Wells herself, had asked some newly met acquaintance to call for her letter. By one of those odd coincidences he happened already to be an acquaintance of Nancy's. That was all.

Should she wait until he came back and then say 'I think we *have* met—' But they hadn't. She was Alice Pitman. Bother! Yet somehow she *must* get a message to Jenny. How?

In the days when Gloria Harris and Acetylene Pitt had been drummer-boys together in Wellington's army, it had been necessary for them to communicate with each other (or with Wellington) in code, in case, as Nancy pointed out to Jenny, their communications fell into the enemy's hands and gave away the position of the British forces. The code had been invented by Nancy, and would certainly have baffled Napoleon. Indeed, for a moment it had seemed as if it would baffle Jenny.

You wrote your message out thus:

'AM AT CASTLE HOTEL WITH MONEY FOR YOU ALICE PITMAN.'

Then you wrote do\th the number of letters in each word.

Thus:

2265453356

Then you took away the first letter of each word and put down the result thus:

MTASTLEOTELITHONEYOROULICEITMAN

You divided this up, however you liked. For instance:

MTAS TLEOT ELITHON EYORO ULIC EITM AN

You put in the figures in ones or twos between the groups, and on each side of the figures you put any letters you liked. Then, at the end, you added all the first letters. Thus:

MTASK22RTLEOTF6EELITHONS5BEYOROO
45EULICD33LEITM05QANW6EAACHWMFYAP

When Jenny first saw this, or something like it, at the age of eleven, she said 'Oh!' Nancy explained to her that it was very easy to uncipher, and that her uncle Mr. Pitt, the Prime Minister, thought it was clever.

'How do you *begin?*' said Jenny, frowning at it.

'I'll show you,' said Nancy. 'First you count how many figures there are, and there are ten of them, so you take away the last ten letters, but don't lose them because you'll want them directly. Then you make a circle round the figures and the letter on each side of the figures, and you don't bother about the circles any more, except for looking at the figures, and the first figure is 2, so the first word has two letters, and the first letter is the first of the ten you took away, so that's A, and the first word is AM, do you see, Jenny darling? And the next is AT. And the third has six letters, and it begins with C, so you take the next five, leaving out the circle, which is ASTLE, so it's CASTLE, d'you see, darling? It's easy, isn't it, and my uncle said Napoleon would never guess even if he knew English *perfectly*, so now we needn't *eat* messages any more, even when we get surrounded.'

'Oh, *I* see,' said Jenny suddenly. 'Where's a pencil, quick! I'm going to write *you* one.'

Now sometimes it was necessary that a message should be hidden in a secret place, and if you knew it was there you went and looked, and if you didn't, then you might miss it. To guard against this Nancy arranged that each of them should have a special sign, which meant: 'Look out for something from me,' and it had to be something which you could leave about, and other people wouldn't notice. They wondered about this for a long time, and Jenny thought their initials ought to come into it somehow, like monograms. And then Nancy said *I* know!

I'll have "Cap" because it ends in A.P., and you have "Bough" because it ends in G.H.' Jenny said: 'Do you mean leaving your tammy about, because you're always doing that?' and Nancy said: 'Well, I never will again, except when it's a Sign, and everyone will say: "How tidy the dear child is getting" and that will be a great joke between us, because I shan't be really.' Jenny said: 'Well, they won't think *I'm* getting tidy if I have to leave *boughs* about everywhere,' but Nancy explained that it need only be a *twig*. One day A.P. had been escaping from the licentious soldiery with the help of a pistol which really fired, and she had to hide a message for G.H. in the secret place, so she dropped one of the caps which they used for the pistol, and Jenny saw it and guessed at once, and found the message. So, after that, they both knew that, whatever happened, they would always be all right.

Would Jenny remember all this? Of course!

Nancy hurried to the station and bought a *Daily Mail*. This was the paper which the man had been reading: the paper, therefore, which he would be most ready to lend Jenny. Jenny, of course, would want to read everything she could about herself, and would almost certainly try to borrow all the papers, but, even so, it would be better if the secret message were in the paper which the man had already read, so that he would not be likely to see it. On the outside of the *Daily Mail*, then, she drew a cap, and in the margin of the page which said WHERE IS JENNY she drew another. Then, hidden away in the most uninteresting part of the paper, she wrote her cipher message MTASK22R ... It took her a little time to get this done, and she ran from the station waiting-room and down the street in panic lest the car should have gone, but it was still there, and she slowed down and looked about her, wondering just how to do what she had to do. Should she go boldly up to the car from the roadside, or secretly from the common?

As always, Nancy was for boldness. Be natural, she told herself, and, whatever odd thing you are doing, nobody will suspect you. Be unnatural, and the most innocent action looks suspicious. Nancy walked along the cars swinging her paper; stopped at the *coupe;* put her head and shoulders in at the window; dropped her *Daily Mail* on to the seat, and took away the one that was there; smiled, nodded and walked away, still swinging her paper, still smiling. She had recognized a friend in the car and had stopped to shake hands. That was all. Absurdly simple.

She went back to the station for her bag. At the Castle Hotel she engaged a room, tidied Miss Pitman up, and went off to the Pantiles for tea. Only one thing prevented her from being completely happy. From her bedroom window she could see that dreadful Tank.

13

FEVERISH ACTIVITY IN LONDON

I

'All right, all right,' said Cook damply from the scullery.

The telephone-bell went on ringing.

'*All* right, I'm coming,' Cook reassured it.

'Telephone, Mrs. Price,' said Alice helpfully from the kitchen.

'Well, I'm not deaf,' said Cook, coming out of the scullery still drying her hands. 'Shut the window, there's a good girl, there's so much noise blowing in—Hallo!... Yes... *Window*, Alice!... Yes?'

'Is that Mr. Watterson's house?' said a distant voice.

'Yes, madam.'

'Oh—is that Mrs. Price speaking?'

'Yes, who is it, please?'

There was a note in Cook's voice which made Alice come away from the window, and say—

'*H'sh!* ' said Cook, waving her back before she could say it. 'Yes, madam, who is it, please?'

'Oh, Mrs. Price, will you tell Uncle Hubert, please, when he comes in, that I'm *quite, quite* safe.'

'*Miss Jenny!*' shrieked Cook.

'Miss Jenny?' cried Alice.

'Here, what's the matter?' said Hilda, poking her head in from the hall. 'I say, Alice. I *wish* you wouldn't leave all your—'

'S'sh!' said Cook imperiously. 'Hallo... Hallo!... Hallo!... Miss Jenny!... *Hallo!*'

'What's it all about?' said Hilda. 'That Marigold again?'

'Miss Jenny on the telephone,' said Alice eagerly. 'What did she say, Mrs. Price?'

'Hallo!' said Cook, refusing to give in. 'Hallo!'

'Here, let *me*,' said Hilda, taking the telephone from Cook. 'Hallo!'

Mrs. Price sank into a chair.

'Well, I never,' she panted.

'Cut off,' said Hilda, putting back the receiver. 'P'raps she'll ring again. Sure it was her?'

Cook told them.

Alice nodded eagerly, understanding it all so well.

'And at that moment', said Alice, carrying the story on, 'the Leader of the Gang came in surrepshously, and put *one* hand over her mouth, and the *other*—'

'Queer,' said Hilda thoughtfully. 'Sounded like as if she was quite all right?'

'Well, I'm telling you. Those were 'er very words. "Tell Uncle Hubert when 'e comes in that I'm quite, quite safe." '

'And then, before she could say more, the Leader of the Gang—'

'Oh, *shut* up, Alice!'

'Now, now, Hilda,' said Cook, 'you don't want to take Alice up like that.'

'Well, what's she want to be so silly for with 'er silly gangs?'

'*You* wouldn't mind', said Alice, ''ow many gangs carried 'er; off.' She sniffed, and went on, 'I'm the only one as reely—'

'Now, Alice, we don't want to go into all that again. Those were her words, and if you ask *me*, she's quite safe, but doesn't want anybody to know where she is.'

'That's about it,' said Hilda. 'Gone off with somebody.'

'That I *won't* have said,' declared Cook firmly. 'Not in my kitchen. Miss Jenny's *not* the sort, as you know well—'

'Oh, isn't she? Well, look at 'er aunt!'

'What aunt?'

'Well, Jane Latour's 'er aunt, isn't she? 'Er reel aunt by blood. So it's in the blood, y'see, and what's born in the blood, as they say—'

'I s'pose voices 'aven't never been imitated before,' said Alice sarcastically to nobody.

'That won't do, Hilda. You might as well say that because your Aunt Lucy had the dropsy—'

'Never mind my Aunt Lucy,' said Hilda, a little shrill suddenly. 'If you think it's manners to bring up my Aunt Lucy, which I only told you about, talking in secret confidence about aunts—'

'I s'pose voices 'aven't never been imitated before,' said Alice on a slightly higher note.

'I'm not one to break a confidence, Hilda, as you know well. And if you overheard anything, Alice, about Hilda's Aunt Lucy having the dropsy, then you'll remember, please, it's a sealed book between us three. All I'm saying—'

'Then say it to yourself,' cried Hilda, and slammed the door on them.

Cook's lower lip was trembling, but she got possession of it again and said kindly to Alice:

'What was that you were saying, Alice, about voices?'

'Nothing,' said Alice, 'only I s'pose voices can be imitated, can't they?'

'This wasn't. It was Miss Jenny 'er very own self. I'll swear to that. 'Er own voice.'

'Well, hadn't you better ring up Mr. Marigold? He said to ring up if we heard anything.'

'Miss Jenny didn't say anything about any Mr. Marigold. She said "Tell Uncle Hubert", and if that's what she said, it isn't my place to tell anybody else. First thing he comes back I go out and tell him.'

But she didn't. At a quarter to one Mrs. Watterson came back, bringing her husband with her. Hilda was waiting for her, and hurried into the hall.

'Oh, madam,' she cried, 'oh, sir! Miss Jenny's rung up, and says she's quite, quite safe!'

'What's that?' said Mr. Watterson.

Hilda gave him the story at full length. It wasn't really her story, of course, but cooks who drag in people's Aunt Lucy's dropsies have got to be taught their place.

II

Mr. Bernard Morres, his story ended, twiddled his hat. Inspector Marigold continued to write. Sergeant Bagshaw continued to watch him writing. Mr. Morris looked at Inspector Marigold and at Sergeant Bagshaw, and decided that he didn't like either of them. There was something about policemen's faces that made an honest man sick.

'H'm,' said Inspector Marigold. 'And you think it was the actual watch?'

'Well, I'm telling you, aren't I? Holy Snakes and Ladders,' said Mr. Morris to the ceiling, 'what d'you think I came here for? Company?'

'I don't want comments, Morris. Just answer the questions. It had "J" on it in diamonds?'

'That's what I said. That's all I do say. I don't know who's milky watch it was, and I don't care. It had a "J" on it in diamonds. Standing for Julius Caesar, I dare say.'

'Now then, Morris,' put in Sergeant Bagshaw dutifully.

'And you say he pledged it with you, and then half an hour later redeemed it? Now I wonder why he did that?'

'Wanted to know the time per'aps,' suggested Mr. Morris unhelpfully.

'Cold feet,' said Sergeant Bagshaw, nodding at the Inspector.

'That's about it,' agreed Marigold. 'You took his name, of course?'

'I did. What d'you think?'

'Well, come on, let's have it.'

Mr. Morris searched for, and found, a dirty piece of paper in his waistcoat pocket.

'William Makespeak Thackeray,' he read.

'Ah! Think it was his real name?'

'Suffering Chorus-girls,' said Mr. Morris to Heaven. 'D'you think I looked at his passport, or asked to see the monogram tattooed on his chest?'

'Don't be a fool, Morris. You know well enough by now when a man's giving his real name or not.'

'Sweet Potatoes,' said Mr. Morris, '*how* many—'

Sergeant Bagshaw cleared his throat and looked self-conscious.

'After you,' said Mr. Morris courteously.

'It wasn't,' announced Sergeant Bagshaw.

'Wasn't what?' asked the Inspector.

'Wasn't his real name.'

'How do you know?'

'Because he's a northor.'

'Who is?'

'What he was saying. William Makepeace Thackeray.'

'Well, why shouldn't he be? Think a northor can't commit a murder as well as anybody else?'

'I mean he's a classic.'

'Who is?'

'William Makepeace Thackeray.'

'How d'you mean a classic?'

'Like Shakespeare.'

'That's right,' said Mr. Morris, thinking it was time he joined in again. 'Like Shakespeare.'

'D'you mean like Edgar Wallace?'

Sergeant Bagshaw considered this.

'Well, more like Shakespeare,' he said, wishing to get his values as accurate as possible.

'I told you so,' said Mr. Morris. 'We keep telling you. Like Shakespeare.'

'Look here, Bagshaw,' said the Inspector, 'where do you *get* all this?'

'I'll tell you. It was this way. I had occasion to speak to a gentleman—had to ask him his name. He said, "Thackeray". I said, "Thackeray, eh?" thinking of Charlie Thackeray, *you* remember, the forger. North Midland Bank Case. He said, "Know the name, what?" and I said, "I should think I do, sir"—well, considering everything. He says, "Some writer, eh?" and I says, "That's right, sir. What that Charlie Thackeray couldn't do with a pen—" and he says, "Charlie? To hell with Charlie. It's William." So I says, "Beg your pardon, sir, I ought to know, seeing as it was me—" and he says, "Bet you a fiver, Sergeant, it's William Makepeace Thackeray. You're thinking of Charlie Dickens." Well, then it all came out, as you might say, and it transpired that this William Makepeace Thackeray was a nothor like Shakespeare. What they call a classic.' He nodded at the Inspector. 'That's the way it was.'

'That's right,' said Mr. Morris, twiddling his hat. 'A classic.'

'Ah! Meaning it might be an *alias?*'

'A nom de pop,' translated Mr. Morris.

'That's right,' said the Sergeant.

'Might be,' said the Inspector judicially, 'and then again, might not be. He said it was his wife's watch, is that right, Morris?'

'Something o' that sort. I wasn't listening *too* 'ard.'

The Inspector turned back to Bagshaw.

'Is this William Makepeace Thackeray married?'

'I told you, 'e's dead.'

'He's lucky,' said Mr. Morris to the world.

'Like Shakespeare. Right off the map.'

'Ah!... Well let's have a description of him.'

Mr. Morris looked expectantly at Sergeant Bagshaw, and waited for a description of William Makepeace Thackeray.

'*You*, Morris, you fool!' shouted the Inspector. 'What was this man like?'

'Who's a fool?' said Mr. Morris, annoyed.

'You are.'

'Oh, am I? Well, 'ow did I know you weren't asking about this other feller?'

'What does it matter about this other feller if he's dead?'

'Well, what does it matter about him whether he's married or not?'

'Who said it did?'

'You did.'

'No, I didn't.'

'You asked *him*,' said Mr. Morris, indicating the Sergeant, 'and *he'll* bear me out, you asked *him* if this William Makepeace Thackeray was married or not. So naturally *I* thought—"

'Well, I didn't know he was dead then, did I?'

'Yes, you did. I'd just told you he was a classic. We'd both told you. 'Ow could he be a classic if—'

'Now, now, Morris,' said Sergeant Bagshaw pacifically. 'What was 'e like?'

Mr. Morris turned to him.

'I don't mind telling *you*,' said Mr. Morris with dignity, 'because you and I are educated men as knows what a classic is, and don't go calling each other names. Speaking as one college man to another, he was a short, stout feller with a little fair moustache.'

'Ah!' said Inspector Marigold coldly...

Five minutes later Mr. Morris was in the open again, breathing an air unpolluted by policemen.

'Hips and Thigh-bones,' cried Mr. Morris to High Heaven. 'And *that's* what has to catch our murderers for us! Why, they couldn't catch the measles in a Measle 'Ospital.'

III

Now all is set for the Inquest on Jane Latour. Now to the little court-room in Merrion Place the fashionable world comes streaming. Hither come the Leaders of Society; the Young Eligible Set, the Young Married Set, the Young Divorced Set. Hither comes the Marquis of Puddlehinton on behalf of his Sunday paper. Hither comes the ex-President of Canova's solicitor, just in case.

Mr. Ponsonby Wicks, the Coroner, opens the proceedings. He touches lightly upon a number of matters which have interested him during the last few weeks: the inefficiency of the League of Nations, the rising spirit of unrest among the working classes, the growing licence allowed to novelists and other so-called artists, the necessity for removing children's tonsils as soon as they become available. 'It is for you', said Mr. Ponsonby Wicks to the Jury, 'to decide how this poor lady met her death,' and went on to denounce the corruption in American politics. 'You will not', said Mr. Wicks, 'shrink from the responsibility,' and spoke coldly of the Trade Agreement with Russia...

The Jury retired and viewed what Dr. Willoughby Hatch had left of the body...

Mr. George Parracot gave evidence. He was wearing the Old Felsbridgian tie and (though these were not seen) the Old

Felsbridgian braces. He was, so it appeared at first, a bachelor, living at Auburn Lodge near the Brompton Road. He had been having a holiday at Eastbourne, and the house was empty. On the day in question he had left Eastbourne by an early train on his way through London to Cromer, and had looked in at Auburn Lodge in order to collect one or two things.

'What sort of things?' asked Mr. Wicks, feeling that all this would go better as a duologue.

'Oh, well, as a matter of fact,' said George carelessly, 'just one or two things. Brilliantine —and face cream—and—er—'

'Face cream?' said Mr. Wicks, frowning.

'Er—yes,' said George guiltily, realizing suddenly what he had said, 'as a matter of fact, yes.'

'Do you use face cream?'

Everybody looked at Mr. Parracot's face, which was now bright-red.

'Er—as a matter of fact, yes,' said Mr. Parracot doggedly.

'Why?' asked the Coroner, and the Young Eligible Set wondered if this was a new one which they hadn't heard about.

'For the face,' said George, after giving the matter careful thought.

Inspector Marigold whispered in the Coroner's ear.

'Arsting if 'e can't arrest 'im at once,' said the cheaper seats to each other hopefully.

'Ah!' said Mr. Ponsonby Wicks. And then to George: 'You are married, Mr. Parracot?'

'Well, yes,' admitted George reluctantly. 'Yes, as a matter of fact, yes.'

'And Mrs. Parracot was with you on your holiday, and called in at Auburn Lodge with you?'

'Well—er—yes,' admitted George, still more reluctantly.

'Then kindly say so. There's no need to be ashamed of it, Mr. Parracot, not even in these days.'

Everybody laughed; the Young Eligible Set loudly, the Young Divorced Set defiantly, the Young Married Set self-consciously.

'Go on, Mr. Parracot, please.'

Mr. Parracot went on. The cheaper seats were now distinctly hostile to him, and wondered if it would be safe to take the children to Cromer this year. The stalls looked at him admiringly. Everyone knew that that fellow Parracot was well known to Scotland Yard as a drug-trafficker, and now it seemed that he was mixed up in the White Slave Traffic too. Some lad...

Old Girl gave evidence. The cheaper seats felt sorry for Old Girl, married to a murderer. The stalls also felt sorry for Old Girl. I mean to say, darling, positively *nude* about the face, and simply *too* dairymaid altogether.

'You were not personally acquainted with the deceased, Mrs. Parracot?' asked the Coroner, and the stalls laughed at the idea of Toto knowing Laura...

Inspector Marigold gave evidence. The cheaper seats whispered to each other that this was one of the Big Five, but, when challenged, were uncertain who the other four were. The stalls looked at him with mixed feelings. He had the reputation of being a difficult man to bribe, and the less affluent of them had found this to be true. Also he had no sense of humour, and when the famous Baby's Bottle Party had overflowed into Merrion Place, and started playing Postman's Knock at three o'clock in the morning, he had been extremely stolid about it. But those of them who were running Night Clubs realized that Inspector Marigold had a human side which he did not allow the ordinary public, or his superiors, to suspect...

Dr. Willoughby Hatch was called, and the Court sat up hopefully. Dr. Hatch gave, fortunately without being too technical, the result of his researches into the more sequestered organs of the deceased, Mr. Ponsonby Wicks drawing him out with a well-placed question whenever the interests of Justice or the press-value of the organ seemed to demand it. Coming, a little reluctantly, to the external injuries, the Court learnt that these were caused by a blow on the head from a narrow sharp instrument of some nature.

'Not', said Mr. Wicks, surprised, 'by a heavy, blunt instrument?'

'No,' said Hatch.

Mr. Wicks hid his disappointment as well as he could, and got down to business. 'Now, Dr. Willoughby Hatch,' he said, 'have you formed any opinion as to the physical characteristics of the assailant?'

'I have,' said Hatch.

There was a tense silence. Everybody looked at Mr. Parracot, and wondered how one would describe him. Inspector Marigold whispered in the Coroner's ear.

'Well,' said the Coroner on a different note, 'we need not go into that. All we are concerned with today is the cause of death. We will keep to that if you please, Dr. Hatch. What can you tell us of the personal habits of the deceased?'...

And now Mr. Ponsonby Wicks is about to sum up. He looks through his notes, and sees that he has said nothing yet about Birth Control, Reparations, or the Sunday opening of Cinemas. He sums up...

The Jury retires to consider its verdict. The stalls chatter, and those of them who have not yet caught the eye of the Marquis of Puddlehinton hasten to do so, in order that my lord's Sunday readers shall not be defrauded. The cheaper seats look at Mr. Parracot hopefully, with their mouths open.

The Jury delivers its verdict. To the relief of Inspector Marigold, who is now looking for a short, stout fellow with a fair moustache, and does not want to have George on his hands again, it announces that deceased was murdered by some person or persons unknown. Everybody scowls at Mr. Parracot, who fingers his tie. The Court empties slowly...

INQUEST ON JANE LATOUR
SENSATIONAL EVIDENCE

cry the posters.

14

AFFRAY AT BASSETTS

I

The gentleman who had brought back a Rabelaisian robustness to the English novel loosened the cord of his pyjamas and sipped his early morning tea. It was good to be at Ferries again—without Fanny. Ferries (without Fanny) in the Garden of England, with the smell of hops, or something, drifting in through the open windows, was his true home. Here a man could write—God, how he could write! Already the slow loveliness of the place was inspiring him. Thoughts, flashing thoughts, which clothed themselves even as they lit up his brain in beautiful words, paraded for his approval, too quick for pen to record them. If only his secretary—Miss Fairbrother—had been here, alert to take them down in shorthand, just so, and only so, he might have kept pace with them...

But then if his secretary—Miss Fairbrother —Nancy—were here at this moment, in this room, would they—

Obviously not...

(Not shorthand.)

Nancy...

A new set of thoughts flashed into his mind, and were made comfortable there. Robust thoughts. Rabelaisian... Nancy...

No. Idiot. *Julia.*

Julia! That was why he felt so gay, so eager, so young this morning. After breakfast he was going to write to Julia.

He rose. He looked at himself in the Queen Anne mirror, and found that once again it had no alternative to offer him. He shaved. He went into the sunlit bathroom and turned on both taps. Through the open casement July came in with banners, and he decided not to weigh himself.

After breakfast he wrote to Julia.

> 'Julia, my dear, something tells me that it is your birthday tomorrow, which means that once again you are a year younger and a ftear more beautiful; for so it is, divinely, that you live among us poor mortals, for whom birthdays are ever-hastening, ever-lessening, milestones to the grave. Today you are twenty-five, is it not? Tomorrow, when this reaches you, you will be twenty-four. In the little token which I send you for a reminder of our friendship, I have set out these twenty-four years as one sets out candles for a child around its birthday-cake—'

('Perhaps I *had* better count them again,' said Mr. Fenton. He counted again the little diamonds round the face of the watch. Twenty-four.)

'—birthday-cake, for it is as a beautiful and innocent child that I shall always think of you.'

('An awkward approach', said Mr. Fenton, 'to the suggestion that she should spend the weekend with me. Also the English is a little careless, and leaves it uncertain which of us is the beautiful and innocent child.')

'—birthday-cake, and above them I have placed a "J"—'

('No,' said Mr. Fenton. 'Hardly necessary. She will naturally assume that "J" stands for Julia, and I really cannot keep on calling her attention to the diamonds.')

'—birthday-cake, and if I am wrong, and you are only twenty-three—'

('I mustn't overdo this,' said Mr. Fenton. 'Actually, I suppose she is forty, and looks thirty-two.')

'—birthday-cake, and sometimes when you—'

('Damn,' said Mr. Fenton.)

'—birthday-cake.'

July still called insistently to him. He dropped his pen, and wandered into the garden for inspiration. He walked among his roses, he blew cigarette-smoke at the greenfly, he picked a bud for his button-hole. No inspiration came... Birthday-cake... Curse... He went back to his room, tore the damned thing up, and began again.

> 'Dearest Julia, All my love comes with this trifle which I have designed for you for your birthday. It is your month, the most beautiful of the year, as it should be, and I have come down here to welcome it. Walking in my garden just now I wondered what it lacked of perfection, and the answer came at once—"Julia". If it could but have Julia for a little! Would you not drive down on Sunday morning and have lunch, and what else you will, with me? I am alone; we could talk; I could show you my garden. "You foolish man," I can hear you saying, "I have ten engagements for Sunday already!" Of course you have, but you will never sort them out properly, so let them go, Julia. You will? Thank you, my dear. And now give just a glance again at Julia's new watch, and say to yourself: "He is counting the hours until I come, from now on he is counting the hours"—and Come!'

Mr. Fenton read this through and was moderately pleased with it. Remained the signature.

What?

At their last meeting she had greeted him 'Hallo, Funny-face', but one could hardly sign a well-phrased letter of this sort 'Funny-face'.

Archibald? But nobody called him Archibald.

Archie, then? She had never called him Archie; she had never called him anything distinctive (unless Funny-face was distinctive); the occasional 'Darlings' which she had thrown at him, he shared with a hundred others. If he signed it Archie, would it define him in her mind? Probably not. And the address meant nothing to her.

Archibald Fenton, it must be. It lacked intimacy, but, after all, it was his signature, and in a sense made the letter more valuable.

Come! Archibald Fenton.

Mr. Fenton thought, and perhaps may be excused for thinking, that really, you know, '*Come! Archibald Fenton*[1] ought to be good enough for anybody.

II

Miss Emily Gathers, aged fifty-four, popped a small piece of barley-sugar into her mouth and returned the jar to its shelf. George Alfred Hickley, aged four, went out, clinging to a larger piece. 'Shut the door, Georgie, there's a good boy,' called out Miss Gathers. George Alfred Hickley shut it. He had always meant to do this, so that he could open it again and make the bell ring. 'No, Georgie, no!' said Miss Gathers firmly after the third ring, and George Alfred Hickley, thinking that perhaps she was right, left the door open, and came out into the sun again, with the air of a man who was having, one way and another, a good pennyworth. But there was still some small change to come. A car was rushing up, was stopping; a man was getting out, was taking a parcel into the shop. George Alfred Hickley sucked his barley-sugar and waited.

'Hallo, Tommy,' said Mr. Fenton genially.

George Alfred Hickley said nothing.

'Barley-sugar, eh?' said Mr. Fenton, and getting no reply added, 'Well, well,' and patted George Alfred Hickley's head in a kindly manner. Then, feeling that he had entered into the life of the village enough for one morning, he passed through the door, and closed it behind him. George Alfred Hickley opened it, so that Miss Gathers should know that somebody was coming...

'Why, bless my soul,' said Miss Gathers, hastily swallowing, 'if it isn't Mr. Fenton! Well, you *are* a stranger, Mr. Fenton.'

'Good morning,' said Archibald gaily, for it was indeed a beautiful morning, and Julia was getting nearer every minute. 'Registered, please.'

He handed over his parcel, and the Postmistress became professional...

'Quite a Gathering of the Clans,' she said archly, as she wrote.

'I beg your pardon?'

'Your brother is at Bassetts again, isn't he, Mr. Fenton?'

'Oh!' said Archibald coldly.

'*And*, your sister, I understand.'

'My sister?'

'Miss Naomi. She was in here telephoning. Quite romantic. Her friend spraining her ankle, I mean, and then finding that her brother was quite close.'

Miss Gathers held a sensible view of her responsibilities as a postmistress. She was the last person to betray a trust; but if she accidentally overheard a telephone conversation or glanced at a post card, or when, as was inevitable, she was taken into the confidence of a telegram, she looked at the matter all round in a broadminded way. For example: when Mrs. Trevor from the Round House went up to the nursing home in London (and not a moment too soon), and the telegram came: '*Diana Mary arrived safely this morning all well'*, and when, five years later, Diana Mary came in with her nurse and asked for a pennyworth of bulls'-eyes, one couldn't refuse to serve the child on the ground that one had heard of her existence officially, and under the pledge of secrecy. Pursuing this line of reasoning to its logical conclusion, one realized that if Miss Naomi Fenton, or anybody else, telephoned to Mrs. Bassett, or anybody else, and if Mrs. Bassett, or whoever it might be, was one's intimate friend (as she was) and quite certain to reveal every detail of the conversation at their next meeting, whenever this should happen to take place, then for practical purposes, and looking at the matter all round in a broadminded way, this could not be regarded as knowledge which had come to one in an official capacity, but as knowledge which would naturally come to one as a friend of Mrs. Bassett's, and of course if it had been two strangers telephoning it would have been different.

'Quite romantic,' said Miss Gathers again. 'But I expect you've heard all about it from them by now. That will be eightpence exactly, Mr. Fenton.'

Mr. Fenton had not heard anything about it. He had not even seen the original telegram *'Gloria Naomi arrived safely this morning all well'* which should have told him that he had a little sister. He was interested.

'No, I hadn't heard,' he said. 'When was this?'

'Yesterday. About lunch-time.'

'And she's staying there?'

'So I understand, Mr. Fenton. So,' said Miss Gathers, anticipating a little, 'Mrs. Bassett informs me.'

'I must go over and see them,' said Archibald firmly.

'Well, I'm sure that would give them great pleasure, Mr. Fenton.'

Archibald was not so sure. Indeed, he hoped it would give them no pleasure at all. Sister! Ha! And this was the moral

Derek! He would go over this afternoon and see them... and watch the moral Derek trying to carry it off. *Sister!*

'Thanks,' said Archibald, receiving his change. 'Well, good—morning, Miss—er—' What was the damned woman's name?

'Good morning, Mr. Fenton.'

As Mr. Fenton came out, his electric motor-horn, which had been silent too long, gave a sudden welcoming cry. Removing George Alfred Hickley at the very peak of endeavour from the off side running-board, Mr. Fenton climbed into the car and drove off. What seemed to be the greater part of George Alfred Hickley's barley-sugar went with him.

III

It was summer afternoon at Bassetts, but rain was coming. 'P'raps not Friday, p'raps not Sat'day, but 'tis coming.' Farmer Bassett felt it in his bones, and in the autocracy over which he ruled the authority of his bones was acknowledged. To the last man, woman and child his subjects were in the fields, making hay while the sun still shone.

Jenny, an opened book on her lap, sat alone in the cool of the little parlour, delightfully postponing sleep. She felt restful, at ease, well cared for. Derek would be coming back to her soon, but she was in no hurry for him. When he came back, they would have to talk things over again, make some new plan together. That would be fun, making plans with Derek; but the lazy content which enveloped her, the consciousness of being wholly and perfectly herself, was a happiness which no other could share, or by his presence intensify. She was Jenny. Jenny was good, Jenny was beautiful, Jenny was clever. Now Jenny was going to sleep...

There was a sudden knock on the door, sudden and alarming to one who seemed to have the quiet afternoon so completely to herself. Jenny was on to her feet, her heart ridiculously beating. She tried to say that it was a friend of Mrs. Bassett's, a tradesman, a passerby in quest of something, but absurd little fears were creeping into her mind, and growing there, and taking well-recognized shapes: Tramps at Lonely Farms, Policemen Effecting Arrests: Law and Violence now equally her enemies. Jenny, Jenny, pull yourself together! This is childish, and you are so brave.

'I know!' she thought suddenly, and, holding her breath, she tiptoed into the passage and past the slender barrier of the door, and so up the stairs to her room. From behind the curtains she peeped at the unknown.

Not a Tramp, not a Policeman. Just a man from a car, well dressed, short, stout, reassuring.

'I'm an idiot,' laughed Jenny to herself, 'but I shan't be an idiot again'; and to make sure that she should not be an idiot again, she took from its drawer Watson's Wonderful Combination Watch-dog-and-Water-pistol and the two pink garters. With Watson in his place she went downstairs light-heartedly, almost wishing now for adventure.

She opened the door.

'Oh, good-afternoon,' said Mr. Archibald Fenton, and registered an immediate impression that Derek was doing himself well.

'Good afternoon,' said Jenny. 'Did you— Mrs. Bassett—everybody's down in the fields, getting the hay in. Did you—'

'Ah! Forgive me, but have I the pleasure of speaking to Miss Naomi Fenton?'

'Er—yes,' said Jenny.

It was not her fault that she did not recognize him. She had never seen him; and the many impressions in the papers of the famous Archibald Fenton, showing him to be a slender, good-looking young man of twenty-three, as indeed he had been for a few moments, and in a favouring light, twenty years ago, had not prepared her for the present authorized edition, as to which Nancy had never let fall any more enlightening word than 'catastrophic'.

'But, darling, what do you mean, catastrophic?' Jenny had asked.

'Well, wait till you see it, the whole thing's a disaster, that's all.'

Now she was seeing it.

'I heard in the village that you were paying your brother a visit,' said Archibald, enjoying himself extremely, 'and I ventured to call.'

'Oh! Oh, how nice of you. Won't you come in?'

'May I? Thank you so much.'

He followed her into the little parlour, and looked round him complacently, feeling sure of its secrets.

'I'm afraid Derek's out. He had to go into Tunbridge Wells. Do sit down, won't you? And smoke.'

'Thank you. Won't you—' He held out his case. She shook her head.

'So Derek's in Tunbridge Wells,' said Archibald, lighting a cigarette. 'And you're all alone. Poor little girl.'

'Why?' said Jenny.

Archibald had called a good many people 'Poor little girl', but never been asked 'Why?' before.

'I was sympathizing,' he said stiffly.

'Yes, but why? I don't mind being alone, do you?'

'It depends whose company I am missing. Just at the moment, my dear Naomi, I am very happy not to be alone.'

Jenny began to feel a little bewildered.

'Who are you, please?' she asked. 'Are you a friend of Derek's?'

'You might say so, yes. I have known him a very long time.'

'Oh!'

'He has often talked to me about you.'

'Oh!' said Jenny again.

'His little sister Naomi. You've no idea how proud he is of his little sister Naomi.'

'Oh!' said Jenny for the third time.

He had never taken his eyes off her. There was a look in his eyes, amused, appreciative, possessive, which she hated. He seemed to be sharing some secret with her. What did it mean? Did he know that she was a fraud?

'Even when little Naomi was a child,' the voice went on, 'he used to tell me of the amusing things she said. They were not very funny,' admitted Archibald, 'but then the things which children say never *are* very funny, are they? But Derek used to assure me that if I could have heard the dear little mite saying them—dear little Naomi—' He broke off and puffed at his cigarette, still keeping his amused eyes on her.

How much did he know? Perhaps—sudden brilliant thought—he knew nothing. Perhaps there had been, or was still, a real Naomi Fenton of whom Derek had spoken, a sister who had died or been married.

'You haven't told me your name, have you?' she said, trying to smile brightly. 'Perhaps Derek has talked to me about *you*'

'I'm sure he has,' said Archibald blandly.

'Oh?'

She seemed so innocent that for a moment his complacence was disturbed.

'Look here,' he said a little anxiously, 'I'm not making a mistake, am I? You *are* Derek Fenton's sister?'

'Y-yes,' said Jenny.

'Good. So you're Archibald Fenton's sister too, of course?'

Jenny nodded.

'Then,' said Archibald, getting up, 'I really must have one.'

He came over to her chair, and Jenny jumped to her feet.

'What do you want?'

'A kiss,' he said gaily. 'Just a kiss. Because you see, Naomi darling, I am your long-lost brother Archibald.'

'Oh!' cried Jenny. 'How awful!' She stared at him.

She thought: No wonder Derek hates him. No wonder Nancy says what she does about him. What am I going to do? Why doesn't Derek come back? Who shall I say I am? I think he's hideous. Fancy if he *had* kissed me! What *are* we going to do? He's not a bit like Derek. The funny thing is I did rather like A *Flock of Sheep.* I think I'll say nothing.

'Well?' said Archibald, still smiling, and coming a little closer.

Jenny went back a step and said breathlessly. 'Your brother will be here directly. Won't you sit down and wait for him? He will tell you anything you want to know.'

'*Our* brother, isn't it, Naomi?'

'*He* will tell you why I—who I—how it is—'

'Oh, but I think I know how it is, don't I?' smiled Archibald.

Jenny gasped.

'Do you mean you know who I am?'

'Of course I do, my dear child.'

'Let's have the worst,' thought Jenny.

'Who?'

'Not', said Archibald, 'Derek's—sister.'

Instinctively she moved away from him, and in moving knocked, her leg against the corner of the chair. Ah! How silly to have, forgotten! The faithful Watson! Now she was quite cool again.

'Please go away,' she said firmly.

Archibald shook an indulgent head.

'Not till I have had that kiss.'

'Please go away at *once*'

'Oh, come, my dear, don't be silly. What's a kiss more or less to a girl like you?'

Jenny stooped for a moment and stood up again.

'If you don't go at once, I shall fire,' she said. Almost unconscious she spoke in the voice of one who had had to do this sort of thing a good deal lately, and Archibald, recognizing the note, moved hastily back.

'Please go,' said Jenny.

The famous novelist recovered his poise.

'You've been going to the pictures a good deal, haven't you?' he laughed. 'What is it? A water-pistol?'

He was so nearly right that Jenny lowered her protector hastily lest all its secrets should be revealed. This was enough for Archibald, who jumped hurriedly for his kiss. A more active man might have reached her, but he was a stout mover, and Jenny's arm came up just in time. There was a flash which seemed to fill the room with sound. As instinctively he closed his eyes to it, something stung him sharply on the temple. Vaguely he felt for the place with his hand. The hand came away wet and horribly, horribly red. Vaguely he looked at the hand, as if trying to read its message. Then, suddenly realizing it, he dropped to the floor, and lay there...

It had all happened so quickly, it was all so utterly realistic, that Jenny could only stand there stupidly, looking at the pistol in her hand, as if to make sure that it was indeed the toy which Mr. Sandroyd had sold to her, and not some monstrous changeling. Perhaps Mrs. Bassett kept a real pistol in that drawer, she thought. Perhaps I'm going mad. Perhaps it's all a dream. Then she thought: I'm being a little fool, he just fell down.

'Please get up,' she said, 'it's quite all right.'

Mr. Fenton did not move.

'It *is* a water-pistol really, only I filled it with red ink. That was what frightened you, I expect.'

Mr. Fenton said nothing.

'That and the bang. It bangs too. That's really why it's so good. I bought it at Tunbridge Wells.'

Even so, Mr. Fenton did not move.

'*Really* you aren't hurt,' pleaded Jenny. 'It's only because I used red ink. I bought a bottle in the village.'

Even so, Mr. Fenton remained silent.

'Oh, dear! Perhaps he has bumped his head.'

And suddenly she began to pray that he *had* bumped his head; for an apprehension slowly filled her mind of all the vague tales she had heard of people being frightened to death; tales told her in childhood of men pretending to be ghosts, and of mock executions; and she remembered Aunt Caroline's warning to her once when she had jumped out at Cook: 'Never try to frighten anybody, Jenny. At the best it only causes justifiable annoyance, and at the worst it may have very serious effects.' Which was this?

'Oh, God,' prayed Jenny, 'let it be a justifiable annoyance, and *not* a very serious effect.'

Before any decision could be taken in the matter, the door opened, and Derek was there.

IV

When Derek had dropped his newspapers into the car and gone up into the High Street, his intention had been to buy two or three of the better-class milliner's shops for Jenny; for he knew that so charming a girl could not live charmingly for long on nothing more embellishing than one knapsack and a loan of Mrs. Bassett's wedding-dress. But on looking into his notecase, and finding that he had only thirty shillings with him, he realized that the dangers of choosing a wrong shape or an unfashionable shade were so outstanding that it would be kinder to Jenny to limit himself on this occasion to a box of chocolates, a basket of cherries and a flask of eau-de-Cologne. Having then no more than five and sixpence over, he rejected a passing thought about champagne, being in any case fairly sure that this was either the hour when you could buy a bottle but were not allowed to take it away, or the hour when you could take it away but were not allowed to buy it. Champagne, he felt, might have helped them to come to a wise decision on some of the important problems which would face them tonight; or perhaps not; but anyhow it would have been pleasant...

How brave Jenny was...

How beautiful...

How sweet...

How entirely idiotic.

Tonight they must really go into the matter seriously, and decide what was to be done...

He came into the parlour, one half of his mind still with Inspector Marigold in London, the other half on this new difficulty of opening a door without dropping one of his six newspapers and three parcels; and almost before he could straighten himself, Jenny was adding to the confusion in his arms.

'Oh, *Derek*,' cried Jenny, 'I've killed somebody!'

'Not *again?*' said Derek, surprised. 'Here, wait till I get these things out of the way.'

'He says he's your *brother!*'

'Oh, well, that's all right.'

He put the parcels on the table, Jenny moved out of the way... and there was Archibald.

'Good lord,' said Derek, 'so you have.'

Jenny, holding her breath, watched him as he knelt by the body.

'Is he dead?' she ventured at last.

'No,' said Derek. 'But he's much too fat.'

Jenny gave a deep sigh of relief.

'What happened?' he asked.

She explained it all...

'I see. Well, now you know why I like him so much.'

He was angry. She loved him for being angry.

'It must have been rather funny, though,' said Derek, beginning to laugh.

Now he was amused. She loved him for being amused.

'Has he fainted?' she asked.

'Yes. When he comes round, he'll say, "Where am I?" What does one do? Their knees have to be higher than their head, don't they? Or is it lower? At present the only part of him which is quite insistently higher than anything else—'

'Aunt Caroline used to faint sometimes.'

'Ah! What happened then?'

'Well, we used to loosen her stays.'

Derek regarded his brother's outline thoughtfully.

'Would you say he was wearing stays?' he asked.

'Well, I think you ought to loosen his collar.'

'That's a good idea. And, while doing it, we could throw away his tie.' He removed the tie and held it up to Jenny. 'There's a wastepaper-basket just behind you. Do you mind?'

Obediently she dropped it in the basket without quite knowing why. But she supposed that Derek disliked it for some reason; and indeed its colours, red and yellow stripes, assorted ill with the rest of Archibald, and were not wholly at ease among themselves.

'Club colours of the Royal Society of Literature,' explained Derek carelessly over his shoulder.

'Oh, I see.'

'We won't take his watch,' he went on, still busy at the body, 'because it wouldn't be fair, but we must think seriously about his eye-glass. How do you feel about that?'

'Oughtn't we to do something to revive him? With water or something?'

'Yes. Now wait a moment.'

He began to wonder what would happen when his brother came back to life. How were they going to behave, the three of them? Were they all going to talk together at the tops of their voices, arguing, recriminating, losing their tempers? Or were they all going to be perfect ladies and gentlemen, pretending that nothing had happened? Or were they—

'Yes. That's the way. Now listen.'

'Yes, Derek?'

'Fly up to the bathroom. You'll find a baby sponge there, which I use for cleaning tennis-shoes. Rinse it out a bit and bring it down, wet.'

'Yes, Derek.' She turned to fly.

'Wait. In the little cupboard there's a roll of bandage—or was Bring it down.'

'Yes, Derek.'

'Wait. There's a small bowl in my room, or perhaps it's in the bathroom, or anyhow there must be a small bowl somewhere. Is there any red ink left in your bottle?' She nodded. 'Well, fill the bowl with water, and put some red ink in to give it a little local colour, and bring bowl, sponge and bandage down here. Quick!'

She was very quick ...

'Good girl. Now then, take all those parcels—they're yours—and the papers— Oh, and here's your letter—and go up to your room, and read and enjoy yourself, and leave everything else to me.'

He opened the door for her.

'Are you sure—'

'Quick! Fly!'

She flew. He hurried back to the body.

V

When Archibald came to himself, he was lying on the sofa, his head heavily bandaged. At the table by his side was a bowl of what had once been water, but now was dyed ominously red.

'Where am I?' said Mr. Archibald Fenton.

'With friends,' said Derek soothingly. 'How are you feeling now, old boy?'

Archibald put his hand to his head and knew that it was not a dream.

'She shot me,' he said weakly.

'That's right. You were making advances to her.'

'I wasn't.'

'Well, making something.'

'All I—I just said—Anyway, she had no business to shoot me.'

'She didn't know what else to do. It was all so sudden.'

'You can't go shooting people like that,' said Archibald sulkily. 'She might have killed me.'

'I'll tell her. She thought you were making advances to her, that's how it was.'

'Well, I wasn't.'

'I'll tell her.'

'She said she was my sister, and naturally I asked her for a kiss. And then she shot me. I say, am I—'

Derek gave him a surprised look.

'How do you mean she said she was your sister?' he interrupted.

'How do you mean, how do I mean she— I'm telling you. Oh, gosh, I feel sick. She said she was my sister. Our sister, Naturally—'

'Who did? Miss Benton?'

'Miss who?'

'Benton.'

'Who's Benton? I'm talking about this girl who calls herself Naomi Fenton.'

'Naomi Benton, that's right.'

'No, *Fenton!* I tell you she said you were her brother.'

'Not me. Benton. You've got it muddled.'

'I tell you—'

'Don't talk too much, old boy. Not with a head-wound. It's dangerous.'

'I said "Then you're Archibald Fenton's sister too," and she said "Yes," and I said "Well, I'm Archibald Fenton," and she said "Oh!" and I said "Well, if I'm your brother—" '

'You're not *her* brother, old boy, you're mine. It will all come back to you soon. You're Archibald Fenton.'

'Look here—'

'So you couldn't be Miss Benton's brother. Cousin, yes. Brother, no. But I'll explain about that when you're stronger. How are you feeling now?'

'You fool, I never thought I—I say, am I badly hurt?' He saw the bowl suddenly. 'I say—'

Derek patted his shoulder reassuringly.

'Nasty scalp-wound, that's all. Miss Benton has tied it up for you. She knows all about that sort of thing. She's a nurse.'

'Oh, is that what she calls herself?'

'Yes.'

'And what,' said Archibald sarcastically, 'is this so-called Miss Fenton who now calls herself Nurse Benton doing here?'

'You mean what is this so-called Nurse Benton who you thought called herself Miss Fenton doing here?'

'What's she doing here?' shouted Archibald.

'Steady, old boy. Not with a head-wound. Miss Benton particularly warned me—'

'Who is she? What's she doing here?'

'But why shouldn't she be here? You remember Molly Bassett, don't you? The red-haired one who married John Benton from Five Ashes? Well, John Benton has a sister, and this sister—'

'Oh!'

'Exactly. And what happens?' said Derek reproachfully. 'You make advances to her.'

Archibald was silent, thinking.

'Don't think too hard,' said Derek anxiously, 'because of what I said just now about head-wounds.'

'I don't care who she is,' announced Archibald. 'She said she was your sister.'

'Not mine. Benton's.'

'*Yours*, damn you!'

'I knew a man, an accountant by profession, who had a nasty head-accident in Piccadilly, and when he came round, and they asked him how it had happened, he said that his sister had pushed him off the rocking-horse. It seems that in these cases one's memory often goes back to the last time one has fallen on one's head, and naturally—'

'Oh, damn you, shut up.'

'Right. Take it easy, that's the way. Do you mind if I smoke?'

'I don't care *what* you do.'

'That's right. Just lie there quietly, and don't bother about me.' Archibald Fenton lay there quietly, but he was not taking it easy. He was thinking. *Could* he have got it muddled? The whole business had been so sudden, so surprising, so confusing that it was difficult to be certain of anything. And then with a nasty head-wound like this—and feeling rather sick—

'Ah!' said Archibald triumphantly. Now it had all come back to him.

'What?'

'That woman at the post office said she was your sister!'

Derek shook his head.

'I have no relations in the post office,' he said simply. 'I have', he added, hoping to strike some chord of memory, 'a brother in Bloomsbury. A novelist.'

'You fool, I don't mean she said *she* was your sister, I mean she said Miss Fenton was your sister.'

'It is true', admitted Derek, 'that, if I had a sister, she would be Miss Fenton. Undoubtedly. But I haven't. We haven't. Don't you remember how you used to say to me with tears in your eyes: "Oh, if only I had a little sister!" and I used to say: "But you've always got *me*, Hippo," and *you* used to say—'

'My God!' said Archibald Fenton.

'Well, not quite that, but something like it.'

'I've had enough of this. I'm going.' He took his legs off the sofa, and tried to stand up.

'Steady,' said his brother, hurrying to his help. 'Just sit like that for a moment. That's right.'

'I say,' said Archibald, a little frightened suddenly, 'I say, how bad am I? I feel pretty rotten. Oughtn't I to see a doctor?'

'Honestly, if you go to bed as soon as you get home, and keep that bandage on till tomorrow, you'll be all right. You can let your housekeeper have a look at it in the morning. Miss Benton has taken every precaution, I assure you.'

'If she'd taken the elementary precaution of keeping her finger off the trigger—'

'I thought I'd explained that. You see, you made advances to her—'

'Ordinary people don't get shot just because they ask a pretty girl who says she's their sister to give them a kiss.'

'Ah, but then you're not an ordinary person, my dear Archie. But listen. That's what I want to talk to you about. You don't want to tell your housekeeper that you tried to assault a complete stranger, and got shot for it—'

'I tell you I didn't. I mean I didn't try—'

'And Miss Benton naturally doesn't want to get into trouble for shooting you. So what about all of us agreeing that you had a nasty motor accident on the way here to see me, and—and so on?' He made a circle in the air with his pipe to indicate the subsequent course of the story.

'She ought to be prosecuted.'

'Yes, but the Jury might think that you ought to have been shot.'

Mr. Fenton considered. Nobody took a more broad-minded view of publicity than he, and he had often thought that to be mixed up in a murder which one hadn't committed might be extremely good for trade, if one's publishers handled the affair properly; but this was not so good. In a sense not dignified. And only Heaven knew what lies Derek and this girl would tell in the witness-box.

'Oh, all right,' he said.

'Good. I'm sure you're wise. And now, how about getting home? Shall I drive you? You're a bit shaky still, I expect. It would hardly be safe—'

'Oh—thanks,' said Mr. Fenton grudgingly.

'Come on, then. And I'll bring your car over in the morning. Put your arm round my shoulder.'

Lovingly the two brothers walked to the door, and out. Tenderly Derek helped the wounded man into the car.

'All right? Good.' He climbed in and started the engine. 'Now then,' he said, as he rocked into the mainroad, 'we must think of an accident for you. What sort of accident would you like?'

15

MIXED EMOTIONS IN KENT

I

Jenny thought, going up to her room: How lovely to have Derek to leave everything to. I'm glad that horrid man isn't dead. Of course there's no reason why brothers should be alike, really. And then she remembered something which her fourth governess had told her, which was that every seven years you became a completely different person, all your skin and everything was different; so that, as Derek was at least ten years younger than his brother, it really meant that they had had quite different fathers and mothers, so that there was no danger that when Derek got older, he would get at all like Archibald Fenton, because in a kind of way they really belonged to different families. Besides, look at Nelson and Shakespeare and Joan of Arc, who can't have been a bit like their relations, and look at Aunt Caroline and Aunt Jane, well you couldn't have more unlike people than Aunt Caroline and Aunt Jane, and they were sisters—well, that really did show ...

She sat down on her bed, dropping her parcels around her; and then, remembering, but without any conscious effort of memory, Aunt Caroline's disapproval of this as being in some way slovenly, and in any case bad for the bed, she took the papers over to the little table in the window, and sat down there. Should she read the papers first, or Nancy's letter?

Before she could decide, she found herself thinking again: Fatness. Of course, fatness is quite different from character. Fatness does go in families. And looking at Nelson and Hereward the Wake and Garibaldi isn't really any good, unless you know for certain that their brothers weren't fat. And then she thought suddenly that of course *all* fatness can't be descended, because somebody must have started it some time, and perhaps Archibald Fenton was the one who was starting it in the Fenton family. Which would be quite all right, because then it needn't have anything to do with Derek at all...

Absurdly happy now, she felt that no luxury of happiness must be missing. Little idiot so nearly to have forgotten! She flashed across to the bed and tore open the parcels. Oh, *Derek!* Then, holding Nancy's letter in the left hand, and feeling absently for cherries with the right, she got into touch again with London...

But at first she didn't seem to be quite in touch. Who were the 'two new exhibits' who had joined the 'menagerie'? Who was Bertha Holloway? 'Did you see her that time you came?' Which time? Jenny wrinkled her forehead, and went on reading, but now a little doubtfully. What had happened to Nancy? 'The Jenny the police are looking for is not her illegitimate daughter.' Well, of course she wasn't. How could Nancy possibly—She took another cherry, and read again: 'The Jenny the police are looking for.' Then the police *were* looking for her. She thought: I'm glad to know that. I'm glad Nancy told me that. That's really what I wanted to know. That and the clothes. She looked down the page and saw the word 'georgette'. Ah! She read on very quickly, in case Nancy had minded about the clothes... Nancy hadn't... She read very slowly...

Now she understood. How clever of Nancy to have written like that. A thought leapt into her mind, and was followed in a flash by another, and the two thoughts, as it were, faced each other challengingly, and then turned their backs on each other and slunk away, refusing the combat.

How lovely if Nancy and she—

Derek and Nancy... and she.

Jenny sighed and stood up, and went round the table so as to lean out of the window; and she leant out of the window, her chin in her hands, and thought: How everything changes. Where shall be when autumn comes? I wish I could die now, while everything is so beautiful.

I suppose he'll never see that green georgette now. It's funny how nothing is ever the same as anything else, but only better or worse. I wonder where I shall be in ten years' time. I think dark people are prettier, *really*. Then she came away from the window, and suddenly a headline from one of the papers screamed at her 'WHERE IS JENNY?' Little idiot, she thought, why, I'd forgotten all about the papers. She snatched eagerly at one of them, and began to read...

Oh, dear!

Oh, Derek!

Oh, how awful!

Now she read Nancy's letter again; and, reading it now, she could translate it into all that Nancy had not said. But Nancy's letter was written on Tuesday evening. It was old news by now. She went back to the papers and read them slowly ...

'Renton Frers in shose.' Now who *could* have known that? Because she'd always got her shoes at Winthrops, until the other day, when she had found herself looking in at Renton's window and remembering what that girl at Norah's had said. About being the best place for shoes. Of course they would know at home, but then, why send a letter-card—

Silly! Why, of course it was Nancy, who had the shoes in her flat now. But *why?* Oh, I see, said Jenny, nodding to herself, it's so as Uncle Hubert shouldn't be anxious. How funny that Nancy and she should both think of that at the same time.

No, not funny. Weren't they Gloria and Acetylene, and didn't they always think of things at the same time? Like that day when they were driving the French out of the Peninsula, and they both thought of sending a message by the other to Wellington, saying that the Portuguese weren't feeling very well on the right, and could he reinforce them strongly...

She used to leave a twig about, and Nancy used to leave her tammy. Or any sort of cap. A cherry-stalk would make a good twig. Jenny put another cherry in her mouth, and thought: I don't believe we ever used cherry-stalks. I wonder why not. Nancy made a paper cap once... and we had that pistol-cap... and...

Jenny stopped a cherry half-way to her mouth, and stared down at the table. On the outside of the *Daily Mail* somebody had drawn a cap—in just the way Nancy always used to draw a cap when she was signing a document secretly so that only Wellington knew. Could I have drawn it myself, wondered Jenny, without knowing? She looked at the table, shook the papers and looked beneath them, but there was no pencil there which she might have picked up unthinking. Then Derek must have drawn it.

It was funny that Derek and Nancy should draw caps in exactly the same way. Perhaps they did a lot of things in exactly the same way. Perhaps they were sort of made for each other. I suppose, she thought, dark people *are* prettier, I mean *really*.

She got up and looked at herself in the wardrobe glass.

She thought: Of course my hair is awful like this. It isn't fair. I mean (and she smiled at her reflection, because she was making a kind of joke) it isn't *fair* anybody seeing me like this. I'm quite different really. Even the photographs in the papers look more like me—She felt suddenly that she must look at all the photographs again, because she wasn't so very hideous in some of them, and it was sort of helping her to escape if she looked at the photographs again, to make quite sure that she had disguised herself properly. . .

Another cap! And in the same paper, and on the 'Where is Jenny?' page! It *must* mean something! Eagerly she rustled through the other pages... and there in the margin among the advertisements she found the message.

MTASK2 2RTLEOTF6EELITHONS5BEYOROO
45EULICD33LEITMO5QANW6EAACHWMFYAP

Nancy! Nancy!

Now how did one uncipher it? She hardly dared to begin. If she began and then couldn't do it! If she tried to remember and found she had forgotten! She walked up and down the room saying to herself: 'I can do it, I know I can do it. As soon as I begin to think, I know I shall remember it. There's nothing to be afraid of, because I haven't begun yet.' But dared she begin? If she looked in her mind and found nothing there! Voices and the noise of a starting car came through the window. She peeped out. There they go, she thought. He's alive, and Derek's driving him home, so it's all right. Now if only I can do this—Oh, Nancy! Oh, darling! *You* remembered, so surely *I* can! I'm not thinking yet, I'm not trying to think. I'm just going to have one of those chocolates first... and I've got a clean handkerchief still, so I'll just try the *eau-de-Cologne*... Lovely... Now where's a pencil (I'm not thinking yet), I know I saw one —oh, there it is, and paper and everything. Now then. Now I'm going to begin to think. Oh, please let me do it. Now then...

AM AT CASTLE HOTEL WITH MONEY
FOR YOU ALICE PITMAN

II

Derek and Archibald had little to say to each other on the way to Ferries. Derek was wondering what was to be done about Jenny. Archibald was telling himself for the hundredth time that all relations were a curse.

This business about brothers. All wrong. Look at the animals. Mother-love, yes. The tiger defending her cubs—charming. Love between the sexes, by all means. Two turtle-doves on a spring day, two—well, two anything on a spring day. Nobody could object to love between the sexes. It was natural... so long as one didn't clutter it up with ecclesiastical tradition. But whoever heard of two rabbits from the same litter being expected to keep in touch with each other through all the exigences of a rabbit's career, or two frogs assuming a friendliness which they did not feel, simply because they had been eggs in the same spawn. Ridiculous.

'Let brotherly love continue.' But why should it ever have begun? He hadn't chosen Derek; he hadn't wanted him. From their very first meeting Derek had had an offensive way of looking at him, and as soon as the kid had had any eyebrows to raise, it had started raising them. And now that one of them was a famous man and the other one wasn't, what happened? Derek still went on raising ironical eyebrows...

Cousins, brothers-in-law, aunts—God, what a crowd. All trying to borrow money or asking him to use his influence. At least there was this to be said for Derek: he had never tried to borrow money...

The thought flashed into Archibald's mind and was hurried out again, that really the most offensive thing about Derek was that he had never tried to borrow money...

'Here we are,' said his brother suddenly, 'actually turning into carriage-sweep, and still no story for your housekeeper. What do we say?'

'I expect I shall think of something,' said Archibald stiffly.

'Well, but—'

'I must really remind you, my dear Derek, that for twenty years I have been earning my living by making up stories, and I am quite capable of making up one for Mrs. Pridgeon now.'

'You don't want a collaborator?'

'Frankly, no.'

'Right. Well, what is the story?'

'As I say, I expect I shall think of something.'

'Just as you like, Hippo. But don't look to me for corroborative detail on the spur of the moment, if you leave me in the dark like this.'

'I don't see—'

'I haven't your quickness of invention, and it makes all the difference to me to know beforehand whether we are talking about a bicycle accident or about something with a traction-engine in it. When Mrs. Pridgeon—'

'There is really no need for you to see Mrs. Pridgeon.'

'Not when you ring for drinks?'

'Oh!... Do you want a drink?'

'Obviously not now. No.'

'You can have one if you like,' said Archibald grudgingly.

'No thanks, I'm a teetotaller.'

'If you think I'm going back on what we agreed—'

'That's just the trouble, we haven't agreed.'

'We agreed to pretend that I had had an accident, and we agreed not to say anything about the deliberate attempt at murder—'

'No, I don't think we had better say anything about that.'

'Well, I have given my word not to, and that's really all that concerns you. There's no need for you to hang about in order to see if I keep my word.'

'Right. Then all I say to anybody is that you were driving over to see me, and had a bit of a smash, and that we tied you up, and helped you home?'

'Exactly.'

'Good. Then I have a free hand as to how much I smash up your car?'

'What's that?' said Archibald.

'Quite rightly in the case of a head-wound, you are exerting your brain as little as possible. But you do see, don't you, that if one has a bit of a smash when driving a car, both the driver and the car have the bit of a smash.'

'Oh!' said Archibald.

'I'm not worrying about the wind-screen, because of course that must go anyhow. That's all right, I can do that with a niblick. And dents in the mudguard, obviously. But when we get down to the finer details—'

'I'm damned if I'm going to let you smash up my car.'

'Entirely for you to say, Hippo. Only do let's have a story that hangs together. Like', he added kindly, '*Lovely Lady* or any of your major works.'

Archibald grunted. The car stopped.

'Well, here we are,' said Derek. 'Do I come in and help you with the story?'

'All you've got to do is to leave my car alone. Do you understand?'

'Perfectly. I won't even clean it.'

His brother was silent for a moment, and then said, as if grudging the information: 'I was standing in the road when I was knocked down by another car.'

'What were you standing in the road for?'

'Anything you like,' said Archibald impatiently. 'What the devil does it matter? The engine was missing, and I'd got down to look at it.'

'Would you do that just outside the house you were going to stop at? You know, this is what *The New Statesman* complained about when it said that Mr. Fenton seemed to have no idea of probability.'

'Hell, how can I think with a head like this?'

'Then let me suggest that the gate into Bassetts was shut, and you had got down to open it.'

'Oh... All right...Anything you like.'

'Thank you. Then that will be all today. Goodbye.'

As he drove away Derek's thoughts were back again with Jenny. Only once did Archibald come into his mind; and that was when he wondered vaguely, and in no particular connexion, whether weddings were ever so quiet that brothers didn't get invited to them.

III

He stopped the car and called up to her bedroom.

'Naomi!'

Her head came out of the window.

'Derek!'

'I say, have you had any tea?'

'Mrs. Bassett left it all ready, I've got the kettle on.'

'Good. I'll just put all these cars away and join you.'

'Was he all right?'

'Perfectly. I left him sipping a whisky and soda, and telling his housekeeper how he won the battle of Waterloo.'

'Why did you—'

'I know what you're going to say. Why didn't I drive him down in his own car?'

'Well, I wondered.'

'The answer is that I didn't want to walk back all by myself. *And* I wanted my tea. Do you really think you were prettier before you cut your hair?'

'Before I—? Oh! Oh, but it's cut so frightfully. It looks awful.'

'If you could see it from down here, you wouldn't think so. Are you alone in the house?'

'Yes. Why?'

'Jenny.'

'Yes.'

'Just Jenny, Jenny, Jenny. I'm practising. In a little while I shall have to think of you seriously as Jenny. It's much the best name we've had so far.'

'Oh, Derek.'

'Now I'd better go back to Naomi again, I suppose, in case we get overheard. It's very confusing. Well, Naomi, did you read the papers?'

She nodded.

'Exciting, aren't they?'

She nodded again, smiling mysteriously.

'What does that mean?'

'One of them's *very* exciting.'

'Oh? They all seemed to hold the attention quite comfortably. Well—' he switched on the engine—'let's have tea. Farewell, Miss Jenny Windell. If I had been trained in a circus, I should now drive these two cars off simultaneously, a foot on either running-board. As it is, I shall take the safer, if less spectacular course, of driving them one by one. Make the tea, there's a good sister.'

Jenny went downstairs and made the tea. She carried it into the apple orchard, thinking as she went: I might have been in London now. If I hadn't hidden behind the curtains, I might have been pouring out tea for Uncle Hubert. She looked back through a lifetime of growth, of experience, of knowledge, to the child who had knelt behind the curtains two days ago. When she had arranged the table, she went upstairs and gazed earnestly at herself in the glass. Why did he like her hair so much? She thought: I shall never know what I really look like. I suppose I *am* pretty in a way.

With his first cup Derek said: 'Well, what's the news? I mean the very exciting news.'

'I've heard from Nancy! I mean again.'

'Again? But how does she know you're here?'

'I don't know. It was in the paper. Look!'

Derek looked, and naturally asked: 'Meaning what?'

'Am at Castle Hotel with money for you Alice Pitman,' translated Jenny.

'But however—You're sure Alice Pitman is Nancy Fairbrother?'

'Must be, mustn't she?'

'You would know, Miss Windell-Fenton-Harris. But how could she write in *my* paper?'

'You didn't stop and talk to anybody—or anything?'

'No. Except the hairdresser. You like my hair like this? Good. Oh, but wait a moment. I bumped into somebody when I was asking for your letter. She must have heard me...and then...still I don't see—Oh well, never mind.'

'*Is* there a Castle Hotel at Tunbridge Wells?'

'Yes. I suppose we'd better collect her, and then she can tell us all about it.'

Jenny said: 'Oh, I never thanked you for all those lovely things. Oh, *thank* you! It was lovely of you.'

'I meant to get a lot of other things, and then I hadn't any money.'

'I do want—well, one or two things. And now Nancy's got some money for me, so could we perhaps—I mean I haven't even got a hairbrush.'

He looked across at her and said: 'What do you want a hairbrush for? I thought I told you—'

'Oh, but one *must!*'

'All right, you shall have a hair-brush.'

'You see I *have* got some money now, I mean when I see Nancy, because of my watch. Why are you frowning so?'

The frown went as Derek began to laugh.

'You *are* a couple, you two. You realize that the police know all about your watch, and are now looking for the young woman who pawned it?'

'I expect she's disguised all right,' said Jenny confidently.

'Alice Pitman.'

'Yes. But she really would be Alice Pitman. She's wonderful like that.'

'And you think the police will never find her?'

'Nancy? Of course they won't,' said Jenny scornfully. Was this not the girl who had baffled Napoleon himself on more than one occasion?

Derek laughed again, and said: 'Shall we go and help with the haymaking after tea?'

'Oh, do let's.'

'I'm thinking of that fellow Parracot. If the police are really after him—but we shan't know that till tomorrow. I mean the inquest. I'll ring up Miss Pitman tonight, and tell her to expect me tomorrow morning, and we'll come back with the papers, and when we've read them, we'll decide what to do. Which gives us the rest of the day to ourselves. So let's make hay while we can, because by tomorrow we may all be in prison.'

'Yes, Derek,' said Jenny happily. There was a prison at Maidstone, and she seemed to remember that, in touching upon this aspect of life there, her third governess had mentioned casually that the Maidstone prison was a mixed one.

IV

Miss Pitman went into the book-shop in the High Street, and asked one of the assistants for a nice book.

'Yes, madam. Any particular sort of book?'

'A nice one,' said Miss Pitman patiently.

'Certainly, madam.' He looked round the crowded shelves in a bewildered sort of way. 'Have you any particular—'

'Is this nice?' asked Miss Pitman, picking up *The A.B.C. of Horsemanship*.

'That's very good,' said the assistant, brightening. 'But I have another very good book just come in, if you are interested in the Horse—'

'Not specially,' said Miss Pitman. 'I like a *nice* horse,' she added.

'Now this is really the latest text-book on the care and management of Horses—'

Miss Pitman fluttered the pages, and said, 'It doesn't look very exciting. Are all your books about horses?'

'But I understood you to say, madam—'

'Haven't you anything not about a horse at all?'

'Certainly, madam.' He handed her a book with a flourish. 'Archibald Fenton's masterpiece.'

Nancy opened A *Flock of Sheep* at page 576 and read the top paragraph.

'Is this nice?' she asked.

'Oh, very, madam. That is his last published book. His new book is not out until next week, but if you haven't read that one, you should certainly read it first, because many of the characters—'

'Haven't you anything smaller?'

'Smaller?'

'I really want something small to read at dinner,' said Miss Pitman earnestly. 'Propped up against the cruet. You see, I'm all alone in a big hotel, and one gets so tired of reading the wine-list. Have you any book which you could prop up—'

'We have the small cheap editions, naturally, madam.' He pointed to a row of shelves. 'Perhaps you would care to choose something for yourself—'

'Oh, thank you! Then I can tell the size, can't I?'

She chose a detective story which she had read happily when it first came out, but since forgotten, and went back to her hotel. 'Of course,' said Nancy to herself, as she came in sight of the Tank again, 'Miss Pitman is not really such a fool as that, but a girl must amuse herself somehow.'

She dined, as she said, alone. The headwaiter handed her the wine-list, opened, but not very hopefully, at the champagnes. Miss Pitman studied the champagnes carefully; asked if Perrier Jouet 1923 was nice; hesitated long and earnestly between that and Bollinger 1921; and finally chose water. 'Really,' thought Nancy, 'the woman's being a perfect idiot. I shall lose all control of her directly.'

She was finishing the caramel pudding and the second chapter when the message came.

'Miss Pitman?'

'Yes?'

'Mr. Derek Fenton would like to speak to you on the telephone.'

'Uncle Derek!' said Miss Pitman joyfully, and hurried out. 'So *that's* who he was,' she thought. 'Fenton's brother.'

'Hallo!'

'Miss Alice Pitman?' *(Better be careful, thought Derek, in case Miss Gathers is listening.)*

'Speaking.' *(Better be careful, thought Nancy, in case the girl is listening.)*

'This is Derek Fenton.'

'Oh, is that Uncle Derek?' *(Bother, thought Nancy. I haven't really given my mind to this. Now I'm Archibald's illegitimate daughter.)*

'Er—yes.' *(I seem to be collecting relations, thought Derek. This may be awkward.)*

'How *did* you know I was here?'

'Naomi told me.' *(Now, will she get on to that or won't she?)*

'Who?'

'Na-om-i.'

'Naomi? Is *she* with you? How lovely!'

'Staying with me for a few days.' *(You angel!)*

'I say, you didn't really mind my calling you Uncle Derek? You sounded a bit as if you did. Naomi and I call you that for a joke sometimes. *(Good. Now I'm legitimate again.)*

'Delighted and honoured to be your uncle, Miss Pitman. And, after all, I suppose I *am* too much of the elder brother to Naomi.'

'Oh, she only does it for a joke. She's very fond of her brother really.'

'Good.' *(She's just like lightning, this girl.)*

'How *is* Naomi?'

'Splendid. And are you all right again?'

'Yes, thank you.' *(Again?)*

'Naomi told me about your ankle. Rotten luck.'

'Wasn't it rotten?' *(The man's drivelling.)*

'Is it all right again now?'

'Well, I have to be careful.' *(And I certainly am being.)*

'Well, look here, what I rang up for was—could you come over tomorrow morning and spend the day with us? I'd call for you at ten o'clock. Would that be all right?'

'Lovely!'

'That's splendid. Ten o'clock then?'

'Thank you so much. Goodbye—*Uncle* Derek.'

'Goodbye—Alice.'

'Give my love to your sister. Tell her I'm longing to see her again.'

'I will. Goodbye.'

'Goodbye.'

They hung up their receivers.

Derek thought: So that's Nancy. What a girl! The vexed question of who writes Archibald's books for him is now explained.

Nancy thought: Well done, Jenny darling. I knew you'd do it. The man seems quite intelligent. This must be celebrated in some way.

She went back to the dining-room, and ordered a *crème de menthe* with her coffee.

'It *is* good for the digestion, isn't it?' she asked the head waiter. 'I mean, quite medicinal?'

The head waiter assured her that it was.

V

A similar conversation, but with reference this time to a double brandy, was taking place in the best bedroom of Ferries.

'Not if it was me, I wouldn't,' said Mrs. Pridgeon.

'Why, my dear Mrs. Pridgeon, brandy is the first thing that a doctor orders in the case of shock. As a matter of fact, it's the only way of getting it when the pubs are closed.'

'Just as you say, Mr. Fenton. And sees that they drink a whole bottleful of Burgundy first, I dare say.' She held the bottle up to the light to make sure that Mr. Fenton had obeyed the doctor's orders.

'Oh, come, there's no harm in Burgundy.'

'That's what we'll know tomorrow, one way or the other. Anything else you'll be wanting?'

'No, thanks.'

'Well, don't sit up reading too long. You want to give your head a rest, *I* should have said.'

Archibald screamed to himself, 'For God's sake go,' and said aloud, 'It shall have it.'

'Then I'll leave you.'

'Good night, Mrs. Pridgeon.'

'Good night.'

Mr. Fenton was left alone with Plato. Six months ago he had been invited, by somebody who preferred that somebody else should do his writing for him, to contribute to a symposium entitled *Books Which Have Influenced Me.* Having mentioned *The Republic* as the principal one of these, Mr. Archibald

Fenton had now got into the habit of taking it to bed with him (when alone) with the intention, one night, of seeing if it could justify the distinction which he had given it. Now, propped on pillows, with the last rays of the setting sun lighting up the bandage round his head, heroically he began to read:

'I went down yesterday to the Peiraeus with Glaucon the son of Ariston, to pay my devotions to the Goddess...'

Grand stuff!

If only his publisher could have seen him...

Friday

16

CLOSE-UP OF MISS JULIA TREHERNE

I

It was Miss Julia Treherne's birthday. She was thirty-nine. She sat up in bed, a tray by her side, letters and parcels, some opened, some unopened, on her lap. She looked adorable.

She felt lazy this morning, being thirty-nine, and proposed to stay in bed until it was time to get ready for a luncheon engagement. Getting ready was always a protracted, if fascinating, business. Half an hour in the bathroom; half an hour in front of the mirror; half an hour deciding upon, and putting herself into, the privileged costume. Luncheon was at one-thirty. She need not get up until half-past eleven. It was only just ten. O blessed bed!

She was thirty-nine, and owed it to her toilet-table that nobody believed it. For it is one of the disadvantages of the New Cosmetic Era that the search for youth, however successful, never fails to suggest a corresponding need for search. In her natural purity, as seen only by her husband and her maid, Miss Treherne looked no more than thirty. Made-up for the early twenties, to which, from her professional record, she could not possibly belong, she immediately suggested the middle forties. But the bones of her face were so good that nothing could hide its beauty.

There was a tap at the door. She picked up a hand-mirror from the bed, pushed at her hair and called: 'Oh, Henry darling, come in.'

Her husband came in.

'Hallo, sweetheart, just off?' said Julia, pitching her voice to reach the upper circle, and giving in this way an air of increased spaciousness to her bedroom. 'Did you get your scrambled eggs as you liked them this morning?'

'Yes, splendid, thank you.'

'Because I can easily talk about them again.'

'Thank you for talking about them once. It was marvellous of you to remember.'

'Well, darling, if I'm not a good wife, what am I?'

'An angel.'

'No, there you're wrong, sweetheart. Angels are definitely not good wives. They lack just that something. Or so', said Julia, fluttering her eyelashes, 'I have been told.' The eyelashes which she would flutter at Our Theatrical Correspondent over the luncheon-table would be longer and of a different colour, but she would flutter them as skilfully.

'Enjoying your birthday?'

'Look!' She held up the back of a hand to him, and waggled the fingers.

'Like it?'

'Adore it. Thank you, my sweetheart. Come and kiss me.'

'Yes, I think I will.'

Five minutes passed, and Julia said: 'One of our longer kisses. Won't you be late?' She picked up the mirror to see what was left of her.

'Probably. When do I see you again? Come up and lunch with me in the City somewhere. Do. Why not?'

'Sorry, darling. I'm lunching with Bertie.'

Once again that curious tightening of the mouth was visible, which was the instinctive reaction in so many husbands when Bertie's name was mentioned.

'Must you?' he asked.

'Afraid so. It's a date.'

'What I meant was—'

'I know what you meant, darling.'

'Oh, all right,' said Henry with a shrug. 'We'll have supper somewhere after the show if you like.'

'You know you hate it.'

'As a habit. Not on special occasions.'

'Darling, I've promised to have supper with O.D.'

'That swine?'

'That one.'

'I wish you wouldn't.'

'Darling, as long as I know that he's a swine, it's all right, isn't it?'

'What's he after?'

'Shakespeare at the moment. And a very long way after, I suspect, unless I keep an eye on him.'

'Why choose your birthday of all days?'

'Good Heavens,' cried Julia, throwing up her arms to them, 'if I mayn't begin to arrange to play Juliet for the first time on my thirty-ninth birthday, when may I begin?'

'Oh, I see... You've got lovely arms.'

'I know. So had Juliet. "Arms, take your last embrace!" Oh, no, that was Romeo. Damn, I've upset the milk. Darling, take the tray away before it leaks, and then take yourself away. And we'll have an early dinner together if you like, but I know you hate that.'

'No, let's. Somewhere near the theatre. I'll be back by six. Goodbye, darling.'

His arms took their last embrace, Julia said: 'Oh, Henry, not again,' and felt for the mirror. Henry went out.

There were three parcels yet unopened. One was a book. John. Not really a birthday present, because he'd promised it to her anyhow. The next—oh, dear! The Ermyntrude child again. Real name: Gladys Walker. Age: nineteen. For nine years Gladys had had a passion for Miss Treherne, and on every birthday she sent the beloved one something of her own making. It was time, thought Julia, that she married some good, strong man and went to live in India.

The third parcel was registered. Now whoever's this, wondered Julia. This is rather exciting. Endover. Never heard of it. Who writes like that? Somebody.

She cut the string and discovered a letter and a box. Should she open the box and see what somebody had sent her, or should she read the letter and see who the somebody was? She lit a cigarette, picked up the mirror and looked at herself again. Was that a spot coming on her chin? Curse all spots. No, nothing. She dropped the mirror on the bed and opened the letter.

Archibald Fenton. Well! She read the letter. Well! (What *was* she doing on Sunday?) She opened the box. *Well!*

She looked at the watch with 'J' in little diamonds for 'Julia', and began to think how sweet it was, and how nice of him—(he *was* the tall thin one, wasn't he?)—and of course he oughtn't to do a thing like that really, and she tried to disentangle him in her mind from all the other hundred men who might have given her watches with little diamonds on them, but hadn't. She found this difficult, because to Julia all men, save her husband, were the same; just men; who said amusing things and complimentary things and paid the waiter and were called 'Darling'; and if they had characters of their own, as she supposed they had, and souls, and aspirations, somehow she had never found time to explore them, nor they the impulse to reveal them. Perhaps it was because one didn't at lunch, or at supper, or when dancing, or in a dressing-room, or at cocktail-parties, and these seemed to be the only times which she had. It was easy to know about women, to know one woman at a glance from another, but a dozen men trying to make a good impression were the same man, with nothing but their faces for remembrance.

All the time that she was thinking this, and playing with the watch, another part of her mind was wondering what it was which had happened before like this. Where had she seen a watch like this? Who else had given her a watch like this? To whom else had Archibald Fenton given a watch like this? Surely somehow, somewhere...

'My God!' said Julia, and picked up the mirror, and looked at herself to see how surprised she was. 'Clara!'

'Yes, madam?' said Clara, putting a head hastily in at the door.

'Have you got last night's paper in the kitchen? And the morning ones, too. Bring them all. Hurry!'

Three minutes to study the papers, two minutes to make her plans. She was always a quick worker.

'Bertie, is that you?'

'Hallo!'

'Julia. Listen. I want you to be at Scotland Yard at—I must be quick, that's all—at half-past eleven, and wait for me.'

'At *where?*'

'Scotland Yard. S for Scotland, Y for Yard.'

'I say, are you being arrested?'

'Keep the jokes for afterwards, Bertie. This is business. Now listen. Have two cameramen ready. Miss Julia Treherne entering Scotland Yard. Got it?'

'May I ask what it's all about?'

'I'll tell you later. What time do the evening papers go to press?'

'All day.'

'Of course. Silly of me. Oh, well, that's all right.'

'You can't give me an idea of what's on?'

'Well, listen. This is utterly private until I say. Bertie, it's the Auburn Lodge murder!'

'Thank God for all his mercies! I'd been wondering if we couldn't get you into that. My dear, we can work this—'

'No, but listen. I'm not absolutely certain if it's—'

'You aren't Jenny, are you?'

'Idiot, Jenny's eighteen.'

'That's what made me ask.'

'Sweet of you, angel. Now is that all right? I'll see you when I come out, and tell you if we can use it.'

'You're sure you *will* come out? They haven't got anything on you?'

'Good Heavens, no, I'm all right. I'm giving important evidence—'

'My dear, this is too marvellous. You'll be a witness at the trial—'

'*Listen*, Bertie. Not a word till I tell you. I may be wrong about it all, but I don't think I am. Now we don't want a mistake. Is there a main entrance to Scotland Yard, or are there a whole lot of little entrances, or only one or what? And how far can you drive in? I shall come in a taxi, and—'

'None of that. I'll call for you.'

'Oh, but—'

'I'll arrange for the photographers now, and decide where to put them—I rather see you making inquiries of a policeman outside the gates—'

'That's good, Bertie. Get a *big* policeman if you can. A big, fair one.'

'I expect we shall have to take what's provided. And then I'll come and fetch you, and explain the words and business to you on the way. Eleven-fifteen. That all right?'

'Well, I shall have to hurry. My God, I *shall* have to hurry.'

She hooked up the receiver, took one look at herself in the hand-mirror to see if she had altered, and jumped out of bed.

II

'Now,' said Inspector Marigold, curling his moustaches symmetrically with both hands, and gazing at the wall in front of him, 'let's see where we are. I'm going to run through what's in my mind, and if there's anything that isn't quite straightforward, you say so. Right?'

'Right,' said Sergeant Bagshaw.

'Right. Now then. The murderer is a short, stout feller of sedentary occupation. We know that because Hatch tells us so. Right?'

'Right,' said Sergeant Bagshaw.

'Right. The man who pawned Jenny's watch was also a short, stout feller, but whether of sedentary occupation or not has not yet transpired. Right?'

'Right,' said Sergeant Bagshaw.

'Right. For working purposes we may assume that there's not going to be two short, stout fellers mixed up in the same case. Right?'

'Right,' said Sergeant Bagshaw.

'Now follow me closely, Bagshaw. I therefore deduce that the murderer is a short, stout feller with a fair moustache, because the short, stout feller who pawned Jenny's watch had a fair moustache, and we have established, owing to there not being two short, stout fellers in the case, that he is the same short, stout feller as the other one. Right?'

'Right,' said Sergeant Bagshaw.

'Now then. The man who pawns Jenny's watch gives his name as William Makepeace Thackeray, thus using the name of a well-known literary classic. The natural deduction is that he himself is a literary man, as being conversant with the literary works of the said William Makepeace Thackeray. Right?'

'Wait a moment there,' said Sergeant Bagshaw, holding up a large hand. 'What about me? *I* knew about Thackeray and I'm not a literary man.'

'*You* knew about him from information received in the course of duty. That's different.'

'Ar, that's different,' agreed Bagshaw.

'Very well then. On the one hand we see that the man who pawned Jenny's watch is of literary habits, on the other hand we see that the man who murdered Jane Latour is of sedentary habits. Putting two and two together, we deduce that the murderer is a short, stout feller with a fair moustache of the sedentary occupation of literary work. Right?'

'Right,' said Sergeant Bagshaw.

'Right. We get further proof of this, if further proof were necessary, by reason of the fact that the murderer may be presumed to move in the same circles as his victim, who was an actress, and as such likely to move in the same circles as a short, stout feller of literary habits. Right?'

'Right,' said Sergeant Bagshaw.

'Right. We pass on. Leaving aside the question for further consideration whether the girl Jenny is victim or accomplice, we have the fact that two communications have transpired which may be assumed as coming directly or indirectly from the murderer, one, by letter-card from the neighbourhood of Bloomsbury, the other, by female voice, from the neighbourhood of Tunbridge Wells. Furthermore, we have been informed by Doctor Hatch that the murderer was undoubtedly left-handed. So,' said Inspector Marigold to Sergeant Bagshaw, 'summing the whole matter up, we come to this conclusion. What we want is a short, stout, left-handed author of fair moustache and literary occupation, who lives in Bloomsbury and has a place in the Tunbridge Wells district where he could take a girl. See what I mean?'

'That's right,' said Sergeant Bagshaw.

'Well,' said the Inspector, after an interval of silent moustache-curling, 'now we've got to find him.'

'That's right,' said Sergeant Bagshaw again.

Vague pictures formed themselves in the Sergeant's mind. He saw himself, disguised down to the boots as a literary man, moving in the literary circles of Bloomsbury, and keeping his eyes open for stoutness, and his ears alert for mention of William Makepeace Thackeray. The prospect did not please him; for, being unaware that the two main schools of fiction were the Beer School and the Gin School, he saw himself condemned to a long course of the barley-water and health-biscuits with which, for some reason, he had always associated literature. One day, p'raps in the British Museum Refreshment Room, he would meet a short, stout feller with a fair moustache, and they would get talking about Thackeray together, and then he would ask the feller to have a barley-water with him, and order two small b-w's, and the feller would pick his glass up with the *left* hand, and then at last, he'd KNOW.

But it was a dreary prospect for an ordinary human being. Sergeant Bagshaw blew out his cheeks in a sigh, and thought wistfully of the Edmonton murderer, who had taken him round gallantly to one Spring Meeting after another, before giving himself up, in sheer embarrassment, at Epsom.

'Show her in,' said the Inspector down the telephone. The Sergeant came out of his nightmare and looked up.

'Sent round from Scotland Yard,' explained the Inspector. 'Julia Treherne, the actress. Something to tell us. Friend of the Latour woman probably.'

Julia made a beautiful but extravagant entry. The cameramen were down below waiting for her to come out.

'Miss Treherne?' said the Inspector, rising. 'Pray take a seat. Er—your husband?'

'Lord, no,' laughed Julia. 'This is Bertie Klink.'

'Oh—er—?'

'Come to take care of me. D'you mind?'

'You're quite safe *here*, Miss Treherne,' said Marigold with a gallant bow.

'I'm never safe with a really handsome man, Inspector. Two really handsome men,' she corrected herself, giving Sergeant Bagshaw a gracious smile.

The Inspector, feeling a little annoyed at the inclusion of Bagshaw, and wishing to dissociate himself from his inferior, said: 'Let me see, Miss Treherne, the last time I had the pleasure of seeing you on the stage was in *The Bing Boys*, I think.'

Miss Treherne's smile faded into coldness as she said: 'Bertie, explain the difference between me and George Robey to the gentleman.'

Bertie explained. The Inspector coughed officially, and asked Miss Treherne if she would be kind enough to state her business.

Julia stated nothing. Very slowly she opened her bag; took from it a box; opened the box and produced something in tissue paper; removed the paper and placed a little diamond-studded watch in front of the Inspector. 'Remind me at lunch to tell you a funny story about a small child at the Zoo,' she said in a stage whisper to Bertie. 'I've just remembered it.'

Inspector Marigold had no time in which to wonder why the Zoo. He stared at the watch; then turned it over and stared at the back of it.

'Where did you get this, madam?' he asked.

'A friend sent it to me today. It's my birthday.'

'Miss Treherne's thirtieth birthday,' explained Bertie.

'May I have the name of the friend?'

'Archibald Fenton,' said Julia with something of an air, for even among the many famous people she knew, Archibald Fenton was not least.

'Occupation?'

'I beg your pardon?'

'What is Mr. Fenton's occupation?'

'How do you mean?' said Julia, rather bewildered.

'What does he do for a living?'

Julia raised her eyebrows at Bertie, who said, with the careful articulation due to a deaf foreigner: 'He writes.'

'He wrote *The Sign of the Cross* and *Huckleberry Finn*,' explained Julia.

'And *The Bride of Lammermoor*,' added Bertie.

'But *not*,' said Julia, 'the poem beginning "There are fairies at the bottom of the garden".'

The Inspector and the Sergeant exchanged nods. Then the Inspector, caressing his moustache with trembling fingers, said: 'Should I be correct, madam, in saying that Mr. Fenton is a short, stout gentleman?'

'Oh, *no!*'

'*Not*, madam?' said the Inspector, amazed.

'Well, how would *you* describe him, Bertie?' asked Julia, wondering if she could possibly have got them muddled.

'Near enough,' said Bertie. 'Short and fat.'

'Ah!' The Inspector was triumphant.

'*Then who's the tall, thin one?*' whispered Julia, frantically.

Bertie, misunderstanding her, said behind the back of his hand: 'One's an Inspector and the other's a Sergeant.'

'Oh, never mind,' said Julia impatiently.

'And should I be right in saying, Madam, that he had a fair moustache?'

Now she remembered him.

'Oh, that one! Yes, that's right, a fair moustache.'

'And left-handed?'

Julia wasn't so sure of that. All she could say for certain was that he shook hands with the right. 'Well, you know what I mean, Bertie, I've never seen him throw or play tennis or anything like that.'

'And now, madam, if you could tell me a little more about the circumstances of the gift. Was it presented to you personally or—'

'Oh no, by post.'

'Did a letter accompany it?'

'Of course.'

'May I see it?' asked the Inspector, holding out his hand.

'I'm afraid not,' said Julia, shaking her head, but smiling sweetly at him. 'It's rather private, you know.'

'I'm afraid I must insist, madam.'

'What nonsense! I've never heard such nonsense. Bertie, have you ever heard such nonsense?'

'I don't think Mr.—'

'Klink. You know Bertie Klink? Bertie, I thought all the police knew you.'

'I don't think Mr. Klink's opinion is going to help us. May I see that letter, madam?'

With a shrug of her shoulders Julia opened her bag, took out Archibald's letter, and pushed it down the front of her dress. 'It's going to be *very* uncomfortable down there all through lunch,' she said reproachfully. 'I shall probably crinkle every time I swallow, and people will think that I have some most irregular disease. Bertie, you'll have to explain to them.'

The Inspector stood up. So did Bertie.

'Bertie,' said Julia delightedly, 'he's going to assault me.' The Inspector sat down again. So did Bertie.

'I must warn you, madam,' said Marigold sternly, 'that your conduct is calculated to defeat the ends of justice—'

'What nonsense!'

'It is essential that I should know from where that letter was written.'

'Well, my dear man, why didn't you say so? Now I've got to—do you mind all looking at the ceiling while Bertie counts ten? It's really gone down much farther than I meant.'

At 'seven' Julia said: 'Ferries, Endover, Tunbridge Wells', and the two policemen exchanged triumphant nods.

'Have you any idea, Miss Treherne, how this watch came into his possession?'

'Well, I suppose he saw it in a pawnbroker's, and thought the "J" would do for "Julia". It's Jenny's, isn't it?'

'But he's in the country?'

'Oh! Well, perhaps—' She stopped powdering her face, and turned to him excitedly. 'I say, you don't think—'

The Inspector said to Bagshaw: 'Ring up Mr. Watterson's house and get somebody to come over and identify it.' Bagshaw went out.

'Bertie! Have I been made love to by a murderer?'

'Looks like it. Have you ever been photographed with him?'

'No.'

'A pity,' said Bertie sadly.

The Inspector stood up.

'Well, thank you, madam. I shall have to keep this, you understand?'

'Well, of course, if it's Jenny's.'

'Thank you. Good-day.'

'Goodbye. And give my love to that nice—I mean say goodbye to that—'

'Come on,' said Bertie, clutching her arm.

They went out. As they came to the entrance into the street Bertie whispered to her, and stopped to do up his shoe-lace. Julia went out alone with an air...

MISS JULIA TREHERNE LEAVING MERRION PLACE POLICE STATION

17

TRANSFORMATION OF JENNY

I

Nancy sat in the lounge of her hotel, reading the latest allocution from Smilax Beauty Preparations, entitled: How I Keep my Face Clean and Free from Blemish—by Julia Treherne. In this respect she was having the advantage of Miss Treherne.

'I don't mind what I'm supposed to say about it,' Julia had explained to Bertie, 'as long as I needn't read it, and haven't got to use the stuff.'

'Well, of course not,' said Bertie. 'Give it to Clara.'

So this was done; and Nancy struggled on, unaware that she was reading: *How I Keep my Face Fairly Clean and Free in one or two places from Blemish—by Clara Watkins.*

Derek came down the hill from the top of the common, in his pocket a list of things which Jenny wanted. This included certain Smilax beauty preparations. Jenny's face was absolutely clean and entirely free from blemish, but naturally she wished to keep it so.

He parked his car opposite the hotel, and went in. He shook hands with Nancy.

'Ah!' he said. 'It *was* you.'

'You mean at the post office?'

'Yes. I want to hear all about that.'

'I want to hear all about everything.'

'You shall. Are you ready?'

'Yes.'

'Come on, then.'

They went outside together.

'Now then,' said Derek, when they were sitting in the car, 'we can talk safely. First of all, you *are* Nancy Fairbrother, aren't you?

'Undoubtedly.'

'So am I. I mean I'm quite genuine too. With all these detectives about, one has to be careful. Now, Jenny wants a lot of things. Here's the list. Just look at it, and tell me what you feel about it.'

Nancy glanced at the list and said: 'How do you mean feel? There's nothing difficult.'

'Well, have you got enough of Jenny's money?'

'Lord, yes.'

'Good. And do you want me to come with you and carry the parcels, or would you rather be on your own?'

Nancy looked at the list again.

'I think Jenny—I think I shall be quicker alone. Besides, if you're there, I shall be saying "Jenny" by accident.'

'That would be fatal. We should be arrested at once. Well, I'll walk up to the High Street with you, and leave you to it. What do you want, about half an hour?'

'Three-quarters.'

'Good Heavens, are you sure you've got enough money?'

'Quite. I may be an hour.'

'Then I shall get my hair cut again.'

As they walked up to the shops Nancy said: 'You realize that I don't even know yet why Jenny ran away, or what she saw anything?'

'You shall hear it all as we go back.' He was silent for a little, and then said: 'I like your Jenny, you know.'

'So do I, you know,' said Nancy.

So she heard all about it on the way back to Bassetts, and the story was finished just as they came in at the gate. Then she and Jenny were in each other's arms.

'Oh, Jenny! Oh, darling!'

'Oh, darling! Oh, Nancy!'

Derek decided to leave them to it. After all the terrible adventures which they had been through, they would have much to say to each other. They said it.

'Darling, your hair!'

'I know! Isn't it awful?'

'Did you do it yourself?'

'Well, I had to. Nancy, did you get my things?'

'I rather like it. Turn round and let's have a look.'

'Oh, *darling!*'

'Sort of wind-swept.'

'Well, I did wonder about that. I mean getting a proper windswept when I went back. Did you get my things?'

'Rather. I don't think it's bad, that skirt. Turn round again.'

'Oh, but it *is* short.'

'Jenny darling, you do look funny in my clothes. I can't tell you how odd it is.'

'Darling,' gurgles Jenny. 'If you could *see* Miss Pitman! What *have* you got underneath? Did you get *all* the things?'

'Of course. Yes, it is a bit short. You ought to have had the other.'

'Oh, but I couldn't! Did you get the dress?'

'Out in the car. Yes, I do like the hair, Jenny.'

'Oh, darling! But, darling, could you *get* a washing-silk in green?'

'I mean in Tunbridge Wells? How wonderful of you.'

'Not in green. I simply couldn't, darling. And of course with your Derek getting his hair cut over and over again, and looking at his watch every five seconds, and comparing it with the nearest policeman's—'

'Nancy! He had his hair cut yesterday!'

'I know. It's getting a mania with the man. So you see, Jenny darling, I had to take what I could get. It's white, and—'

'Oh, Nancy!' said Jenny tragically.

'Yes, but listen, darling. It's got a green belt, and a little turndown green collar, and little green buttons all down the front which give a most unsettling effect. Really sweet, Jenny.'

'Oh, how lovely! You angel! Is it in the car?'

'And I got some green sandals—quite cheap—six and eleven—'

'Did you really?' cried Jenny, seeing them.

'And it has an absurd little pocket over the chest, so I got a little green handkerchief to put in—two in fact—one to dangle—'

The thought of the little green handkerchief to dangle was too much for Jenny. She took a sudden heroic decision.

'Nancy darling,' she said, 'I wish you hadn't got to be Miss Pitman. Couldn't we *both* change now, and you could wear your own things, and I could wear the washing-silk, and you could take off the spectacles and all the *layers* you must have underneath, and be Nancy again. I hate to think of Derek not really seeing you.'

'Shall I?' said Nancy eagerly. Wavering.

'Come on, darling, let's get the things out of the car, and take them up! You got the stockings, didn't you?'

'Jenny?'

'Yes?' said Jenny nervously, knowing what was coming.

'Look me in the face.'

'Yes.'

'Hand on heart.'

Jenny put a hand on her beating heart and held it still.

'Now then, say it.'

A little girl again in Nancy's nursery, Jenny said meekly:

'Cross my heart, and let me die,
If ever I tell my friend a lie.
Cross my knees and waggle my toes—
When *I* know anything, Nancy knows.'

'Well?' said Nancy.

Two large eyes looked out pleadingly from Jenny's burning face.

'All right, darling, I think I know.'

'Oh, Nancy!'

'Come on and let's get the things. What larks.'

Clutching the precious parcels they went up to Jenny's bedroom.

For an hour they stayed there... and along the remotest backwaters; of Bassetts Farm the ripple of their chattering voices played unceasingly.

II

'Derek, this is Nancy,' said Jenny proudly.

Derek looked at Nancy, and then said: 'Who's the other one?'

'Jenny,' said Nancy.

Derek looked at them both as they stood there, hand in hand, and nodded to himself.

'Right. It's a bit confusing just at first. Now then—oh, by the way, Miss Fairbrother, we have a good deal to settle, and saying "Miss Fairbrother" won't make us any quicker, if you see what I mean.'

'Quite, Mr. Fenton.'

'No, no, that's what you say to Archibald. My name's Derek.'

'I'll make a note of it, Derek.'

'Good. Let's take a cushion or two outside where nobody can hear us.'

They made themselves comfortable at the far end of the orchard. Jenny thought: I wish we could just sit here, me in this dress, and not bother about *doing* anything.

'Now, then,' said Derek, 'what are we going to do? I've been reading about the inquest. They aren't arresting Parracot, so we haven't got *him* on our hands yet. Nancy, you're the latest from London—who does the average Man about Town, West-end Clubman or Man in the Street suspect?'

'The Man in the Train—'

'That'll do. Well?'

'Jenny. He told me he knew it for a fact.' She gave a quick impression of the Man in the Train knowing it for a fact. Derek laughed. Jenny, feeling completely right and envious of nobody in the new washing-silk, smiled happily to herself to think that this was her friend, who had made Derek laugh.

'Yes, but now what about the watch? Or is that going to make it still worse for Jenny? I mean, will people think that just because a woman—of course you aren't a bit alike really—'

'Oh, but I didn't pawn it.'

'Nancy!' cried Jenny. 'Then where did all that money I've been spending—Darling, you haven't been—'

'No, I mean, Mr. Fenton pawned it for me.'

'Archibald?'

'Yes. So you see, as soon as he saw the papers, he'd write to Scotland Yard, and tell them it was me. So the pawnbroker wouldn't come into it at all, and I couldn't be mistaken for Jenny.'

'But Archibald is here!'

'I know. At Ferries. That's how I could get away.'

'But, my dear girl, we don't get papers down here.'

'Oh!' said Nancy, astonished. 'Why not? Are you afraid', she asked earnestly, 'that the locomotives will frighten the cows, or is education not spreading as much as one thought?'

'When I say we don't get papers, I mean that we don't buy them in the village shop as we buy cigarettes and nutmeg-graters. There *is* a way of getting a paper delivered, which I haven't quite mastered yet, but anyhow it takes a little time to get it into motion. How long has Archibald been down?'

'Wednesday evening.'

'Did he come suddenly?'

'Very.'

'Then he hasn't the slightest chance of seeing a paper until next Monday. Unless of course he goes into Tunbridge Wells or somewhere.'

'He wouldn't do that. He's working very hard.'

'Well,' said Derek, 'not so hard but what he's found time to pay us a call.'

'Jenny!' cried Nancy. 'Did you see him?'

'Not only saw him, but shot him,' said Derek.

'Darling!'

(There was an interval while the story of Archibald's visit was told to a delighted Nancy.)

'So that was that. Well now, how do we stand? The pawnbroker comes in very strongly now with a description of Archibald. Is it on all the hoardings of London? What a glorious thought!'

The little sleeveless washing-silk with the green belt and little turn-down green collar and the green buttons down the front and the green handkerchief peeping out of the absurd little pocket felt very, very good to Jenny, so good that she was sorry suddenly for all the poor people who were not wearing such a darling dress; and as these undoubtedly included Mr. Archibald Fenton (who, indeed, would have been ill-suited by it), she felt sorry for Mr. Fenton, and the more so because at any moment he might be wrongfully hanged.

'Derek,' she said shyly.

'Yes?'

'I think I'm going to give myself up.'

'I'm dashed if you do.'

'Darling,' said Nancy, 'wait till—Derek, *when* did you say the village would be reading all about last Thursday's weather?'

'You misunderstand me. What I said was that Archibald would be reading next *Monday's* paper on Monday.'

'Well, then, wait till Monday, and I'll give myself up too.'

'And so will I,' said Derek. 'Accessory after the crime. We all will.'

'But we can't let poor Mr. Fenton—'

'How would it be', said Nancy, 'if I went to Ferries this afternoon to spy out the land?'

'Just how does one spy out land? Spy out a bit here to show us.'

Nancy went through the exaggerated movements of a bloodhound looking for its collar-stud.

'Yes. Well, you *could* do that, of course. And then we could do something helpful afterwards.'

Nancy waved him into silence.

'*Having* done that,' she said, 'or not, as the case may be, I then ring the bell and ask for Mr. Fenton. I say that I'm spending my holiday in Tunbridge Wells, and came over to see if I could do anything for him. That's all quite natural, and he'd want to know my address anyway. He is delighted to see me, gives me three autograph albums to return, and asks me how to spell "disassociated".'

'Can you?'

'No. But he wouldn't know that. Then we get talking, and I find out how much he guesses, and if he's read the papers, and so on.'

Derek looked inquiringly at Jenny.

'What do you think? Not bad, is it?'

'Oh!'

'What's the matter?'

'I've just remembered. We've still got his car.'

'Oh, Lord, yes, we've got to get that back somehow.'

'Well, why couldn't you drive me down in it?' suggested Nancy.

'Good idea!' said Derek eagerly. 'And then we leave you and the car, and Jenny and I walk back and collect mine, and drive down again, and—'

'Wouldn't your brother recognize his car, and wonder how Nancy came in it from Tunbridge Wells?' said a lazy voice.

Derek broke off and stared at Jenny. Then he turned to Nancy with a look of patient suffering.

'*Stupid* idea,' he said, shaking a reproachful head at her. '*Why* do you make these idiotic suggestions, Miss Fairbrother?'

'Sorry. I'll try again. How would it be if I ran both ways?'

'It would be hot,' said Derek simply. 'But', he added, 'we could lend you a bicycle.'

Nancy turned on him a look of patient suffering which bettered his own.

'And suppose your hawk-eyed relations recognized it, and saw at once that it had started from Ipswich?'

'They wouldn't. This is an anonymous bicycle.'

'Any particular sex? Or is there a pair of trousers which goes with it?'

'There's a—'

'It would be better the other way round,' said Jenny thoughtfully.

'You mean facing the back-wheel, darling?'

'Thus,' said Derek, 'giving the false impression that one was travelling *to* Tunbridge Wells—'

'*From* Ipswich. Ingenious,' said Nancy, 'but tiring.'

Jenny, smiling lazily at the foolish pair, said:

'The best way would be for us to take Nancy down in *Derek's* car, hide it somewhere, and walk back here for the other. Then when we got to Ferries again, it explains why we're there—to return Mr. Fenton's car—'

'Listen to this, Miss Fairbrother. This is the real thing.'

'And we can walk in, and be introduced properly to Mr. Fenton's secretary.'

Nancy blinked rapidly at Derek, and said brightly to Jenny: 'Your brother, Mr. Fenton? Really? So you have a brother? I thought you only had a mother.' And then to Derek: 'Isn't it amusing, Mr. Fenton, that I am also a brother, a Fairbrother, and you are a dark brother, ha-ha, very amusing, I often say things like that to your brother and then he uses them in his novels, no, he doesn't pay me, but I'm allowed to see the press cuttings.'

This was the sort of thing that Nancy did so well; spontaneous, unaffected: as it seemed inevitable, when you had touched the right button and set her off. Derek laughed wholeheartedly; Jenny smiled a little wistfully.

'Well, anyhow,' said Derek at last, 'let's do that. Starting about three. Agreed?'

'Agreed,' said everybody.

Lying there in the half-shade of the apple-orchard they drifted lazily into their own thoughts.

Derek thought: She's heavenly, this girl. We must see a lot of her when we're married...

Nancy thought: He's up to the ears, this man. I shall be chief bridesmaid...

And Jenny thought: They're lovely together. They just suit each other.

She felt glad and proud about this, not sorry; because the day was beautiful, and, whatever might happen in the future, this one hour was assured to her, when she and Derek would walk back from Ferries together, she bareheaded and in her new washing-silk.

18

PORTRAIT OF THE ARTIST

I

Mr. Fenton stared at a patch of sunlight on the wall and began to think about Chapter Five...

Chapter Five...

Tomorrow he would be getting ready for Julia. On Sunday Julia would be here, and there would be no time for anything but Julia. Yesterday, apart from getting shot, he had done nothing. Supposing Julia stayed the night, then he would do nothing (nothing, that is, literary) on Monday. Certainly, then, he must work today.

Chapter Five...

The curse of being a writer was that one was never comfortable when not writing, and the curse of being a successful writer was that one was offered so many delightful alternatives to writing. Another perfect day, and a perfect garden in which to enjoy it... who cared what happened to Eustace Frere?

Chapter Five...

The real curse of writing was that one was always looking forward to some particular scene in the book and having to hold oneself in check until one came to it. In Chapter Seven Eustace Frere was to sail for America (whence Archibald

Fenton had lately returned), and never was a visit to America so eagerly anticipated by the man chiefly responsible for it. Mr. Fenton had had America docketed in his mind for months. Thus:

CHAP. 8: *The First Day Out*
CHAP. 9: *The Second Day Out*
CHAP. 10: *The Third Day Out*—(it was one of those long books)—
CHAP. 11: *Mid-Atlantic*
CHAP. 12: *Landfall*
CHAP. 13: *'Ilion like a mist rose into Towers'*
CHAP. 14: *Settling Down*
CHAP. 15: *'You're Welcome'*...

Once away from Southampton the book would swing him along from chapter to chapter. Frere, travelling on his cuff-links, would naturally be among the third-class passengers; but from his lordly upper deck Archibald had watched them sunning themselves, and had felt himself made free of their lives too. Even now, on the sunlit wall in front of him, he saw Eustace and the little sempstress, Stella, emerging, heads bent, from the hatchway into the morning, and sitting with their backs up against a bollard... bollard?... bollard, but Miss Fairbrother had better just make sure... wondering what the new world had in store for them...

Meanwhile—Chapter Five...

Of course it was idiotic to try and work in the afternoon. After lunch. After steak-and-kidney pie. After one of Mrs. Pridgeon's steak-and-kidney pies. And a tankard of beer and one's own new potatoes. Yet, after wasting the morning, what could he do but try? It was that damned girl's fault for shooting him. For not shooting him. How could anybody have worked in the morning when he was in complete uncertainty as to whether he had been shot in the head or he hadn't?

'Well, how's the head?' Mrs. Pridgeon had asked, when bringing him his morning tea. 'Kept you awake all night, I expect?'

'No, no, I got a little sleep, thank you,' said Archibald.

'Better let me dress it again. You probably got a bit of gravel in it or something.'

'It's all right, thanks. It was washed very carefully.'

'Sometimes a bit of gravel or something gets left in. Anything like that left in sets up mortification, and before you know where you are—'

'Quite. But this was attended to by a hospital nurse.'

'Oh well, you know best. Only you want to be careful not to leave a bit of anything in. Same as when I got a bit of glass left in me elbow, bit of broken ginger-beer bottle the doctor said it was when he got it out. What's happened once can happen again, I always say, and if there's anything like a bit of broken ginger-beer bottle left in, it's much better out. I've got your marmalade for you this morning.'

'Oh, good. Then I'll be getting up.'

Archibald was not anxious that Mrs. Pridgeon should examine his head. The bullet, he was beginning to think, could only have grazed the scalp. He had pressed his fingers, lightly at first, then more heavily, on what he supposed was the actual wound, and felt no serious pain. Probably in Mrs. Pridgeon's opinion, a piece of sticking-plaster was all that was now wanted. Archibald preferred a bandage. Any man about to be visited by, and make love to, a charming woman would prefer a bandage. Archibald, having seen his bandage in the mirror, had every intention of keeping his bandage on until Sunday... and then bravely making light of it.

He got out of bed and looked at it once more. Curiously effective, anything round the head. All the same he might just have a glance at the place. He could tie it up again afterwards just as effectively... perhaps more effectively.

He began unwinding, gingerly. However slight the wound, there would be a nasty moment at the end, when the bandage stuck... Careful...

Nothing stuck. There was no nasty moment. Odd.

He looked at the bandage in his hand. Signs of blood, but nothing more. A very clean wound. He felt the wound; it didn't seem to be there. He examined it in the glass ... in several glasses held at several angles ... it didn't seem to be there. And yet there was blood. Most odd.

The oddity of it pursued him through his dressing, his breakfast, his first struggles with Chapter Five. A moment's escape sent his hand to a tray of pencils in front of him; now he could begin. But he did not begin. He found himself staring at a bottle marked RED INK.

Mechanically he unwound the bandage from his head; stared at the blood-marks; stared at the bottle. Mechanically he took the cork from the bottle, and poured a little more blood on to the bandage. A detective would have seen at a glance that it was the same blood.

'My God,' said Archibald coldly.

Well, who could work after that? And then, to spoil the morning completely, came the telephone call.

'Is that Mr. Archibald Fenton's house?'

'Yes.'

'Can I speak to Mr. Fenton?'

'Speaking.'

'Oh.' Silence. A dimly heard whispering. Then: 'Will you be in about four o'clock this afternoon, Mr. Fenton?'

'I expect so. Why?'

'That's all, thanks.'

'Who is it?'

No answer. End of telephone call. Who? Why?

II

Mrs. Pridgeon came in, said 'Oh, he's working,' went out, knocked and came in again.

'Yes?'

'There's a lady come to see you. Calls herself Miss Fairbrother. What shall I do with her? I've got her in the hall.'

'Miss Fairbrother?' repeated Archibald, surprised.

'Sounded like. Shall I ask her again?'

'No, that's right, it's my secretary. Show her in.'

Mrs. Pridgeon came out to Nancy, said 'In there' with a jerk of the head and returned to the kitchen. Nancy went in and found the author hard at it.

'Hallo, Miss Fairbrother,' said Archibald's back, 'sit down, I shan't be a moment.' He wrote 'CHAPTER FIVE' slowly and thoughtfully, underlined it twice, and turned to her.

'Oh, good afternoon, Mr. Fenton. I just—Oh, good gracious, have you hurt yourself?'

'What? Oh! Oh no, it's nothing.'

'But, Mr. Fenton!'

'It's nothing, really. I very stupidly got knocked down by a car—'

'Oh, but how awful!'

'Well, it was my own fault really. I—er—'

Various romantic ways of being knocked down by a car offered themselves in rehearsal for Sunday, but were firmly rejected. One mustn't get carried away.

'I believe', said Nancy, looking at him with awe, 'you were saving somebody's life!'

Of course if the girl insisted—'Well, hardly that,' he said with a shrug. 'Even if I hadn't been there, I don't suppose—Well, never mind that. What are *you* doing in this part of the world? I thought I told you to take a holiday?' He smiled genially, paternally.

'Well, I am, you see, only I'm in Tunbridge Wells, you see, so I thought I'd come over in the 'bus to see if you wanted anything, and take back any letters you had for me.'

'Well, that's very charming of you. As it happens, there *was* something—I'd made a special note in my mind—What was it? Oh, yes—what's a bollard?'

'A what?'

'A bollard.'

'Isn't it something you do to a tree?'

'No,' said Archibald, 'it isn't anything you do to a tree.'

'Oh, *bollard*!' said Nancy. 'How silly of me! Weren't they followers of Wyclif?'

Archibald said that the ones he meant weren't so much followers of Wyclif as things you hitched a rope to on a pier, and what he really wanted to know was whether they were also things you hitched a rope to on a liner, and if so, whether you could lean against them. Miss Fairbrother, frowning to herself a good deal, said she was almost certain you could.

'Yes, you're not really being very helpful about bollards, Miss Fairbrother.'

'I'm sorry, Mr. Fenton, I'm afraid my brain all seems to go when I get away from London. I'll find out for you, of course.'

'That's very kind of you.'

'Oh, Mr. Fenton, I wanted to say how very kind it was of *you*— about the watch, I mean. It *was* kind—and *such* a lot. I don't know *what* Joyce will say.'

'Oh, you got that all right? Good. Joyce does understand that I sold it, not pawned it? Probably', said Archibald, 'it's in somebody else's possession by now. A good watch like that soon gets snapped up.'

'Oh, that's quite all right, thank you. Oh, there's one thing I meant to ask you. Did you do anything before you left London about having *The Times* sent on to you? Or shall I write to have it stopped while you're away? I thought perhaps if you didn't get any papers down here, you might like—'

'Yes.' Archibald considered. 'You might do that. Write to the newsagent and tell them to send it here until further instructions. Oh, by the way, you didn't telephone to me this morning? Asking if I'd be in this afternoon?'

'No,' said Nancy, wondering.

'I had a mysterious message. Probably some reporter or other—'

'Somebody wanting to know about the new book.'

'Yes. Look here, you'd better stand by. I may want to turn him on to you, if—'

'Quite, Mr. Fenton,' said Nancy sedately, the complete secretary again. Miss Fairbrother, obviously, was the right person to be enthusiastic about the new book.

'Good.' He got up. 'You've never seen Ferries, have you? Come and have a look at it.'

They went out and had a look at it. Nancy, not on duty for the moment, was a charming little thing. He liked showing her Ferries.

III

It was not a reporter.

At five minutes to four Mr. Fenton returned to the house, leaving Miss Fairbrother in the garden. 'This fellow will be here in a moment,' he said. 'I'll send for you if I want you. And then we'll have tea.'

'Oh, but I—' What about Derek and Jenny, wondered Nancy. He would hardly want to give them tea too, with that ridiculous bandage round his head.

'That's all right,' said Archibald, and was gone... Five minutes later Inspector Marigold arrived.

'Two gentlemen to see you,' announced Mrs. Pridgeon. 'Says a they've rung up and it's very important. Here you are.'

Here they were. Reporters? Reporters didn't come in couples, as a rule. Still, one couldn't afford to take risks. Archibald rose courteously, motioned them with an old-world gesture to a sofa, and asked what he could do for them.

The visitors remained standing. Inspector Marigold glanced swiftly round the room with the air of one whom nothing escapes, If Jenny had been there, he would probably have seen her; but she wasn't. However, he noticed that Mr. Fenton was wearing a bandage round his head. Suspicious.

'Yes?' said Archibald.

'Mr. Archibald Fenton, the author?'

'Yes,' said the author modestly.

The Inspector handed over his card. Sergeant Bagshaw looked stolidly out of the window. His Hyde Park days were over, and the two pigeons on the stable roof who were rendering themselves liable to summary arrest roused no emotion in him...

Definitely not reporters.

'Well,' said Archibald, with a note of reserve in his voice, 'and what can I do for you, Inspector?'

'You've had an accident, sir,' said Marigold, deducing from the bandage that this must be so.

'Well?'

'May I ask how it happened?'

'No,' said Archibald, 'you mayn't.'

'You don't wish to make a statement on the subject?'

'No,' said Archibald, very naturally, 'I don't.'

'Ah!' said the Inspector. His suspicions were now certainties. Evidently there had been more of a struggle at Auburn Lodge than he had supposed. He looked across at the Sergeant, who brought out his notebook, and thumbed over the pages.

'But I will tell you this, Inspector. I'm a very busy man.' To indicate the nature and volume of his business Archibald gave a meaning glance at the words 'CHAPTER FIVE' on his desk, and added kindly: 'If you are collecting for the Police Orphanage, my secretary will attend to it.'

'No,'—said Marigold, with all the sarcasm he could get into his voice, but he was not very good at it, 'we are *not* collecting for the Police Orphanage.'

'Then', said Archibald, 'what *are* you collecting for?'

He was beginning to enjoy this. After all, he was Archibald Fenton. He knew the Home Secretary, the Public Prosecutor, the Editor of the *Sunday Sentinel*, three Judges of the High Court, five Police Court magistrates and, as it seemed to him sometimes at the Club, the whole of the Bar. He met them frequently. He had also met, but not so frequently, one of the Princes. An ordinary man, faced suddenly with an Inspector who was *not* collecting for the Police Orphanage, would have been vaguely apprehensive, wondering if he had run over some silent old lady at the crossroads last week, or left the bath-tap running. Even if his conscience was clear on these and all other matters, he would still wonder if they had found out about his Income Tax. But Archibald Fenton was not an ordinary man. He was *the* Archibald Fenton, whom only reviewers frightened. Inspector Marigold meant nothing to him. He was much more concerned with Sergeant Bagshaw, who, from the way he was licking his pencil, looked as if he might be the Literary Critic of the *Police Gazette*.

'I am not', said Marigold with extraordinary dignity, 'collecting; for *any* charity.'

'Then why', asked Archibald reproachfully, 'are we talking about them?'

The Inspector had no idea. All this came, he felt, from being mixed up with literary people. He decided to get down to what he thought of as brass tacks.

'Have you ever seen *this* before?' he said.

Archibald took Jenny's watch from him, and stared at it.

'Where did you get this?' he asked sharply.

'Never mind that, sir, I'm asking you have you seen it before?'

'Never mind that,' said Archibald, 'I'm asking you where did you got it?'

The Inspector wanted to say 'I asked you first,' but thought it would be undignified.

'That watch', he said, 'was handed to me this morning by Mis Julia Treherne, who informed me that you had sent it to her.'

It is annoying to send a birthday present to a lady, and find that she has immediately handed it to a rival in the police force. Archibald was annoyed.

'If Miss Treherne says I gave it to her, I did.'

'Ah! You notice that there is a "J" on it in diamonds?'

'As I put it there, naturally I notice it.'

'You put it there?'

'Had it put.'

'And what, may I ask, does "J" stand for?'

'It was meant to stand for Julia. Apparently Miss Treherne thought it stood for James.'

'Would it surprise you to hear that "J" stands for Jenny?'

'Not at all. It could stand for almost anything beginning with J.'

'And that this is Jenny's watch?'

'I gathered that it was yours.'

'That it has been identified as Jenny's?'

'Indeed? And who is Jenny?'

It was the question which the whole of England had been asking two days ago, but now it seemed to the Inspector an unnecessary one. 'Jenny Windell, of course,' he said sharply.

'And who is Jenny Windell?'

'Come, come, Mr. Fenton, don't play with me.'

'My dear Inspector, do we look as if we were playing together? I appeal to your literary friend. Am I', he said to Sergeant Bagshaw, 'playing with the Inspector? And if so, what?

On the contrary, I am trying to work, and being continually interrupted.' He turned to his manuscript and drew another line under CHAPTER FIVE.

'Now I warn you, Mr. Fenton. This will only get you into trouble.'

Archibald Fenton gave a sigh of exasperation.

'Can you begin from the very beginning and tell me what you're talking about? All we have arrived at so far is this: You deny that you are collecting for the Police Orphanage Bazaar, and yet you tell me that Miss Treherne has just given you a diamond-studded watch for it. As one man of letters to another,' he said, turning to Sergeant Bagshaw, 'I ask you, does not this call for explanation?'

The Inspector knew what it called for, and what in any other country it would get. Denied the natural expression of a policeman's feelings, he said in a cold official voice:

'On the 29th *ult.* the woman Jane Latour was found murdered in the drawing-room of Auburn Lodge. Incontrovertible evidence proves that her niece Jenny Windell was present at the scene of the crime. This young woman has since completely disappeared. On the 30th *ult.* a watch belonging to the said Jenny Windell is pawned, and subsequently re-purchased, by a man giving the assumed name of William Makepeace Thackeray, and answering to your own description. On the 1st *inst.* this watch is sent to Miss Julia Treherne, admittedly by yourself. I am now asking you if you wish to give any explanation of these facts.'

Archibald's immediate explanation was an amazed 'Good lord!'

So that was what it was all about! He had seen the papers on the Wednesday before he came away, and knew that the Latour had been found dead. He remembered now that there had been some talk of a Jenny who was missing. And it was his secretary, Nancy Fairbrother, now sunning herself in his rose-garden, who had given him the missing Jenny's watch, with an entirely made-up tale of a little sister Joyce! Good lord!

'Well,' said Mr. Fenton...

'It was really like this,' said Mr. Fenton...

'What actually happened—'

'Don't be in a htuhy, sir,' said Marigold. 'And', he added kindly, 'if you like to explain at the same time how you hurt your head, then we shall know *all* about it.'

Mr. Fenton was not an Old Felsbridgian; and though, as a boy, he had passed through Eton on a bicycle, he was not, strictly speaking, an Old Etonian. But he had been at Harrow for a few terms, and even if the school motto, *Stet fortuna domus*, had never been a real inspiration in his life, he did realize that there were some things which no decent man could do. He could not give away a charming little thing who was just going to have tea with him.

'Are you seriously suspecting me of murdering Jane Latour?' he asked, with as careless a laugh as he could manage.

'That I shall know, sir, when I have heard your explanation.'

'Well, I'm not sure that you're going to get one.'

'It's only fair to warn you, Mr. Fenton, that there is a great deal of evidence pointing in your direction already, and that your refusal to give a reasonable explanation—'

'You mean you're going to arrest me?'

'Well, sir, as things are, you're practically asking for it?'

'Got the handcuffs?' sneered Archibald.

An accidental clink came from the direction of Sergeant Bagshaw, as he put his notebook back in his pocket. The Sergeant gazed stolidly out of the window at the pigeons. Still at it.

Archibald thought quickly. He did not tell himself that an innocent man could not be hanged in England, because he had every reason to believe that he could; but he did tell himself that an innocent Archibald Fenton, who knew the Editor of the

Sunday Sentinel, the Home Secretary, the Public Prosecutor, three Judges, five Police Court magistrates and practically the whole of the Bar could not possibly be hanged. He also told himself that his new novel was coming out next Tuesday...

After all, one must do something for one's new novel. In the old days he had given it a cocktail party, to which had been invited such literary friends of his as might conceivably review it, together with such fashionable acquaintance of his as might conceivably make the invitation attractive. Himself and the latest Lovely had held the book rigidly between them, in the manner of two members of a jury taking the oath, and the press photographer, who had accidentally found himself there, nobody quite knew how, had said: 'Now keep it cheerful, Mr. Fender, we don't write a new book *every* day,' and, Mr. Fender keeping it cheerful, the *maître d'hôtel* of the moment had christened it (to use again that strangely inappropriate word) with a gin and vermouth, most of which was trickling up Mr. Fenton's (or Fender's) sleeve as the camera clicked. Archibald had liked these parties, for he felt that some such spontaneous expression of gaiety was natural on these occasions. But now the thing was becoming ridiculous. The dignity of letters was in danger when authors of whom one had never heard gave christening parties for books of which one never wanted to hear, and got more publicity in the illustrated papers than one did oneself, simply because they had scraped acquaintance with still more members of the peerage.

So there was to be no party for the new book; no fuss; simply the bare announcement in the papers: 'Mr. Fenton was much the least concerned man in London yesterday when his long anticipated new novel was at last published. I found him sitting quietly in his library, reading the *Odes* of Horace...' and so on, with, of course, a photograph of Mr. Fenton doing this. Perhaps now it would be 'walking in his garden at Ferries, his country seat in the heart of the Hop district, and apparently much more concerned over the shaping of a new rose-bed than over the sensational success of his new book'. That was all. Unless...

Arrested for murder!

What an advertisement!

'Well,' said Inspector Marigold, 'are we going to have that explanation, or aren't we?'

'No,' said Archibald firmly. 'I shall say nothing until I have seen my solicitors.'

With an air of great dignity he put his wrists together, and held them out to Sergeant Bagshaw. The clinking noise this time was louder.

19

SIX MEET AT FERRIES

I

As they drove back to Ferries in Archibald's car Jenny was singing. From time to time Derek's hand left the wheel and found hers, and said to hers 'I love you, I love you, I love you', and went back to the wheel again; because this was a strange car, and the one terrifying thought in the world now was that there might be an accident in which Jenny, just found, was lost to him. But Jenny thought of nothing. She was enfolded in a dream of happiness, and hardly knew that she was singing.

'There's Nancy,' said Derek. 'May I have my hand, darling? I want to stop.'

Nancy was waiting for them outside the gates. She came up to the car eagerly.

'I say! The police are here!'

'Good lord! Have you seen them?'

'Saw them come. I talked to your brother. He didn't know anything about anything. All quite innocent. Then we went round the garden and did the Ruth Draper business, and somebody telephoned to say they would be there at four, so he went in so as to be ready for them, and I spied round the bushes and it was the police.'

'D'you hear that, Jenny?'

'Did I?' said Jenny vaguely.

'How long ago was this?'

'About ten minutes ago. He's probably just being arrested, and clapping a white tablet to his mouth, and the Inspector is leaping forward and saying "Not that way, sir," and Mr. Fenton is saying "You fool, it's a soda-mint," because he always carries them about with him, and—'

'Quite so. Hadn't you better get in?'

'I'm all right here,' said Nancy, standing on the running-board. 'Hallo, darling.'

Jenny smiled vaguely and went on singing.

'I don't mind telling you,' said Derek, 'that just at the moment I'm not afraid of twenty policemen.'

'Actually there are two.'

'Good, then I'm eighteen in hand. Now we'll just go in as if we were paying an ordinary call, and see what the position is. We shall have to do a whole lot of explaining some time or other, but don't let's be in a hurry. The great thing is to see how the conversation goes, and come in at the right moment.'

They came in at the right moment. The arrest had just been effected. This was how the conversation went.

'Hallo!'

'My God, you again!'

'Excuse me, sir; excuse me, ladies. Now then, sir, if you're ready.' Inspector Marigold's party, Archibald in the middle, began to move towards the door.

'Are you being arrested, Hippo?'

'I'm afraid, sir, I cannot allow any conversation with the prisoner—'

'Oh come, if an intelligent man sees his only brother knocked on the head and hauled off in chains by two obvious policemen, the least he can do is to say "Are you being arrested?" Anything less would be—'

'I cannot allow that statement to pass, sir.'

'Which one?'

'That the prisoner has been knocked on the head by the police. The prisoner himself will tell you—'

Sergeant Bagshaw hurriedly got his notebook out again, in case the prisoner made a statement.

'What the devil are you doing here anyhow?' said the prisoner.

'Brought your car back. And now that we're all together—'

'Now then, sir, *if* you please.'

'Look here, you can't seriously mean to arrest Archibald Fenton? Not old Hippo?'

'*Alias* Hippo,' wrote Sergeant Bagshaw in his notebook.

'I should advise you, sir, not to interfere with the police in the execution of their duty.'

'But he's absolutely innocent. As innocent as a—'

'Newborn babe,' prompted Nancy.

'As innocent as a—well, as a matter of fact I was going to say a "babe unborn". I don't know that there's much in it.'

'Babe unborn,' said Nancy. 'Much better. Sorry.'

'Thank you. As innocent, Inspector, as a babe unborn. And you know how innocent *they* are. I tell you, the whole thing's ridiculous.'

'Oh, shut up!' commanded Archibald, seeing his advertisement slipping away from him.

'Indeed, sir? And may I ask of *what* he is so innocent?'

'Yes,' admitted Derek thoughtfully, 'that's a nasty one.'

'And how you know what he's being charged with?'

'Don't rub it in. I see your point.'

'The fact is,' said Nancy, 'I happen to—Ow!'

'Look at it this way, Inspector,' said Derek, removing a warning heel from Nancy's instep. 'I don't know if you have any brothers— or you, sir,' he added courteously to Bagshaw—'but if you have, you will realize the impossibility to a brother of—'

'Yes,' said Inspector Marigold, curling his moustache at the three of them, 'I think perhaps I *should* like to know a little more about you all. Sit down, please, ladies.' He turned to Archibald. 'If you would like to sit down, sir—'

'Mayn't he take his cuffs off?'

'Certainly not,' said Archibald with dignity. 'It would be most irregular.'

'Now, sir.'

'May I sit down too?' asked Derek, and, taking the Inspector's permission for granted, sat down on the sofa between Jenny and Nancy.

'Name, please?'

'Derek Peabody Fenton.'

'Peabody?' said Nancy, surprised.

'Yes. Why not?'

'Oh, I don't know.'

'Profession?'

'What's the matter with Peabody?'

'Oh, nothing. It just seemed rather funny.'

'Profession?'

'Well, it's really more of a business. I'm in the wine-trade.'

Nancy's quick look behind his back at Jenny said 'Oh, is that what he is?' and Jenny's answering look made it clear that he had nothing to do with the bottles but only with the grapes. More a gentleman-fruit-farmer, sort of, said Jenny proudly, and Nancy allowed that that made all the difference and that, when you were as nice as Derek, it really wouldn't have mattered if you were the man who licked the labels.

'And you, madam?'

'Nancy Slade Fairbrother.'

'Slade?' said Derek, surprised.

'Yes. Why not?'

'Oh, I don't know.'

'Married or single?'

'What's the matter with Slade?'

'Oh, nothing. It just seemed rather funny.'

'Married or single?'

'Single.'

'Any occupation?'

'Secretary to Mr. Archibald Fenton, the author.'

'Ah!' said the Inspector meaningly. Now the whole case was getting linked up.

'Mr. Fenton and I', explained Nancy, unlinking it, 'were together in his house at Bloomsbury throughout the whole of Tuesday morning. He was dictating to me Chapter Four of his new novel *Parallel*'

'One "r", two "ls",' said Derek behind his hand to Sergeant Bagshaw.

'Three,' said Nancy.

'Three,' corrected Derek. 'A little one at the end.'

'You can make a statement later if you wish, Miss Fairbrother,' said the Inspector coldly. 'Now, madam. You?'

'Jane Windell.'

'Married or single?'

'Single.'

'But about to be married,' explained Derek.

'Jenny!' cried Nancy. 'Darling! *Really*, darling?'

Jenny nodded happily.

'Oh, Derek!' cried Nancy.

'I know, isn't it marvellous?'

'Oh, I *am* glad. When did you—'

'Please, *please!*' said Inspector Marigold.

'Really,' said Archibald, disgusted to find himself no longer in the foreground, 'this is almost too crude.'

'Sir!' implored the Sergeant in a loud aside.

'Occupation, if any?'

'Inspector, how can you ask,' said Derek reproachfully, 'when I've just told you we're engaged?'

'Sir!'

'Well, well, what is it?'

'Windell! Jane Windell! *Jenny* Windell!'

'*What?*'

'I say, look here,' said Archibald, 'we can't have this sort of thing.'

'Are you Jenny Windell?'

'Yes.'

'Ah!' The Inspector drew a deep breath. Unaided he had tracked her down.

'Really,' said Archibald, 'these hysterical females will call themselves anything. Psychoanalysts—'

'Just a moment, sir. Now then, Miss Windell. Carry your mind back to the morning of the 29th *ult.*'

'He means where were you on Tuesday, darling.'

'Were you in the company of the prisoner—'

'No,' said Archibald.

'I have already told you that Mr. Archibald Fenton was with *me*,' said Nancy. 'Dictating the fourth chapter of his new novel *Parallel.*'

'One "r" and *three* "ls",' whispered Derek to Sergeant Bagshaw. 'We got that wrong last time.'

'Never mind that,' said Archibald, feeling that it was time he asserted himself. 'Never mind where I *was*; the point is, where am I now? I have been arrested at a very inconvenient moment when my new book *Waterfall* is just coming out. I have—'

'*Waterfall?*' said Sergeant Bagshaw, scratching his head. 'I've got it down *Parallel*.

'Oh, my dear Sergeant,' said Archibald, clinking his handcuffs irritably, 'do use your intelligence. My new novel which is being published on Tuesday at eight-and-sixpence is called *Waterfall.* The one which I am now writing, and shall not finish until next year—'

'Now please, please, *please!*' implored the Inspector. 'Let us get things in order. Miss Windell, I am asking you—'

'All I am saying is that, having been arrested in this summary manner, I naturally wish to get in touch with my solicitors. Sitting here and listening to the life-story of a young woman who may or may not be Jenny Windell, who I have very grave—*whom* I have very grave reasons to suspect of not being Jenny Windell, of, in fact, going about the country—'

'Come to think of it,' said Marigold thoughtfully, 'you aren't much like the photographs in the papers, miss.'

'How right you are, Inspector,' said Derek. 'But then, how rarely photographs in the papers do one complete justice. Now take your own case. I pictured you—it is the famous Inspector Marigold, isn't it?'

The Inspector curled his moustache, and inclined his head.

'Exactly. But who would have known from those photographs of you that the handsomest man in the police-force—'

'*Have* I been arrested, or have I not?' shouted Archibald. 'That's all I want to know. If I have, then my natural desire to get in touch with my solicitors—'

'Shall I ring them up, Mr. Fenton?' said Nancy.

'No. Ring up the Home Secretary. He'll be at the Club. He always goes there for tea. Tell him that Mr. Archibald Fenton—'

'Well, Mr. Fenton,' said Marigold hastily, 'I did ask you to explain about the watch. Even now, if you care to give me an explanation, I shall be only too glad—'

'Jenny's watch? Why, of course, *I* gave him that.'

'*You*, miss? What did you say your name was?'

'Nancy Fairbrother. I—'

'Nancy *Slade* Fairbrother,' corrected Derek. 'Do let us stick to the facts.'

'I gave it to her,' said Jenny, 'so as she could sell it.'

'And Mr. Fenton very kindly offered to sell it for me. And—'

'Is that right, sir?'

'I have already told you', said Archibald with dignity, 'that I have nothing to say until I have seen my solicitors. Hardcastle and Hardcastle. In any case I have no intention of sheltering myself behind these two ladies. As it is, I ask myself what the police-force of this country is coming to. In America an arrest like this would have been conducted with a simple formal dignity. Having been photographed in his handcuffs for the principal daily papers, the accused would have made a short statement for publication—'

'Haven't you got a camera here, Hippo? We'll take one now.'

'No, no, sir, I can't allow that.'

'Indeed?' said Archibald coldly. 'Are you presuming to tell my brother which of the family he may photograph? There's a camera on the shelf over there, Miss Fairbrother. If you wouldn't mind getting it—'

'Here, give me that key,' demanded Inspector Marigold of the Sergeant. The Sergeant gave it to him.

'What are you going to do? Go away! No, look here, you mustn't do that!'

'No violence, please. There!' The handcuffs came off.

'That', said Archibald bitterly, feeling in his pocket for his cigarette-case, 'constitutes an assault.'

'Forcibly depriving a gentleman of his cuffs,' nodded Derek.

'You cannot have it both ways. You cannot go on handcuffing and unhandcuffing a man just at the whim of the moment. If I was legally arrested before, then I have now been illegally de-arrested. If on the other hand—take a note of this, Miss Fairbrother—if on the other hand—'

'Which hand would that be, Mr. Fenton?'

'If I was legally de-arrested, then it follows—'

'Sir, sir!'

'What is it now, Bagshaw?'

'He's lighting his cigarette with the left hand!'

The Inspector gazed, open-mouthed.

'If', said Archibald, blowing out the match, 'I was legally—'

Legally or illegally Mr. Archibald Fenton was then arrested again.

II

Jenny was in the living-room with Nancy, telling her all about it; Archibald was in the rose-garden with Sergeant Bagshaw, taking exercise; Derek was in the dining-room with Inspector Marigold, giving him a drink.

'This is very charming of you, Inspector,' said Derek. 'Say when. Oh, come, it's a warm day. Soda or plain? Quite right, we mustn't spoil the colour. Well, now—'

'Your health, sir.'

'Thank you, Inspector, that's very—'

'Course you do see, sir, I got my duty to do.'

'Absolutely. Have another.'

'Well, sir— That's enough, sir, thank you.'

'What? Oh, sorry.'

'P'raps I was a bit hasty that second time—Your health again, sir.'

'That's very kind of you. I think I'll join you.'

'That's the way, sir. No, no more for me— oh, well, thank you, sir.'

'Your very good health, Inspector.'

'Thank you, sir. What I was saying. Short, stout, left-handed man of sedentary occupation. Now, sir, is that your brother, or isn't it? I ask you, man to man.'

'Undoubtedly. How does this whisky strike you? It's pre-war.'

'First-rate, sir. Capital. What I was—'

'Just a spot more.'

'What I was saying. Dr. Willoughby Hatch's diagnosis of the murderer is of a short, stout, left-handed man of sedentary occupation. No, sir, you shouldn't have done that.'

'Between ourselves, Inspector, I always regard a really good whisky like this as more medicinal than anything else.'

'Well, sir, there *is* that to it. What I was saying. Dr. Hatch tells me I'm looking for a short sedentary feller of stout occupation. And that's the man I see. But is he left-handed? Who knows? And then, right in front of my nose, as cool as brass, out comes his match-box, and—well, p'raps I lost my head a little. Who wouldn't?'

'Who indeed?'

'Mind you, I don't say I've made up my mind, but what I do say is I can't afford to take risks. That's why I'm listening to you now in this informal way, because I can see you're a gentleman who understands how these things have to be done.'

'That's very gratifying.' Derek looked cautiously round the room, and then said in a lowered voice: 'Quite between ourselves, Inspector, do you believe *everything* which Dr. Hatch tells you?'

'Well, sir, that's one way of putting it. I see what you mean, sir, without going so far as to—Well, let's put it this way. Supposing I didn't believe everything a certain gentleman says? Supposing sometimes I found myself thinking "Ho! And who told *you* I should like to know, Dr. God Almighty Hatch?" Well, I shouldn't say it, that's all. Not even to you, sir. Your very good health, Mr. Fenton.'

'You know,' said Derek, absent-mindedly tilting the bottle, 'I sometimes feel that if Dr. Hatch said that a short, stout, left-handed man had committed a murder, the really sensible thing to do would be to look for a tall, thin, right-handed man who had committed suicide.'

'Ha-ha-ha! That's good, sir. That's very good. Witty. Your health, sir. I see what you mean, and I know you understand my position, sir. And you understand—What I mean when I just put it like that. Witty. Well, p'raps I will, sir, it's thirsty work, keeping a guard on yourself so as you don't say more than you ought to.'

'Exactly. Well now, Inspector, I want to tell you just what happened at Auburn Lodge which a certain medical friend of ours didn't happen to notice.'

'That's good, sir, I like that way of putting it.'

'It's a story which Miss Jenny Windell—a charming girl, Inspector?'

'Very natty. Her health, sir. Well, just up to the—thank you, sir.'

'As you know, Miss Windell was born and brought up at Auburn Lodge, and all those happy childhood memories which mean so much to us, and have such an influence on our lives—'

'That's right, sir. I remember a buck-rabbit I had in nineteen-owe-one—'

'All her happy memories were bound up in this house, Auburn Lodge, now let furnished to these strangers to her, the Parracots.'

'That's right, sir. Handsome woman, Mrs. Parracot. Nineteen-owe-two it would be.'

'Miss Windell had in her possession—after all, it was her house—a latch-key to Auburn Lodge, and last Tuesday morning she had a sudden urgent desire to re-visit, just for a brief moment, the home of her youth. We can understand that, can't we, Marigold? We don't blame her, Marigold?'

'We don't, sir. Very natural. I remember this buck-rabbit o'mine—'

'After all, what harm in it? She knew that the Parracots were away, that the house was standing empty. It may be—she hasn't actually told me this yet—but it may be that she wished to look again upon some of the photographs of her family, standing in silver frames upon the grand piano, which meant so little to these strangers, the Parracots, and so much to her. That I think, Marigold, would be a natural, almost a laudable wish? A pretty thought, Marigold?'

'Very laudable, Mr. Fenton. Very pretty. And borne out by the facts of the case. I made a particular note of those photos. All solid silver. A fine show.'

'And then, in the drawing-room of Auburn Lodge, she finds the dead body of her aunt.'

'Is that so, sir? *Found* her there. Dr. Hatch said— Quite so, sir.' The Inspector chuckled, watched his glass being re-filled, and gave the toast: 'Dr. God Almighty Hatch!'

'Apparently Miss Latour had slipped on the polished boards—'

'Well, they certainly were that, sir. I nearly—'

'—and struck her head against a curious brass ornament.'

The Inspector struggled out of his glass.

'Is this Miss Windell's story, sir?'

'Yes.'

'Well, sir, I'm bound to tell you—'

'Wait a moment, my dear Marigold. Without thinking what she was doing, Miss Windell picked up this brass ornament, wiped it, and restored it to its place upon the grand piano.'

'Stop there, sir,' said Marigold, holding up his hand. He closed his eyes. Derek watched him anxiously, wondering if he had decided to go to sleep, and appalled at the thought of having to begin all over again, when, and if, he woke up.

'A piece of brass,' said the Inspector slowly, still with his eyes shut, 'representing as it might be the effigy of a castle. Am I right, sir?' He opened his eyes, and waited expectantly.

'Are you right?' cried Derek. 'My dear Marigold, you're a marvel. Nothing escapes you. You must have another.'

'No, no, sir.'

'Yes, yes, I insist.'

'Well, sir, if you—thank you. Your health, sir, *and* the lady's. Yes, I remember that castle. In brass it was. Ornamental.'

'Conway Castle.'

'Is that so, sir? Well, I didn't notice that. But I'll tell you what I did think was funny, Mr. Fenton.'

'What was that, Inspector?'

'Why, being on the piano at all. Because, rightly speaking, it was what they call a door-stop, what people use to keep doors open with when serving food and coming in and out.'

'Marigold,' said Derek, gazing at him with awe, 'this is almost unbelievable. This must be celebrated. I know! You must have a drink with me.'

'I couldn't do that, sir. I never as you might say drink, not to say drink, at this time of day. Not till after supper's always been my rule.'

'I don't care. You must break your rule for once.'

'Well, thank you, sir. That's enough, sir. Thank you.'

'You've solved the problem, Marigold.'

'Is that so, sir?'

'You see how the pieces of the jig-saw fit themselves together?'

'Your very good health, sir. And the lady's.'

'Thank you, Marigold. You are a good man.'

'What you were saying, sir, about the pieces of the jig-saw—'

'Exactly. The Parracots, knowing this ornament for what it was, a door-stop, kept it on the floor. Miss Windell, whose childish memories are of a castle, instinctively picks it up, and puts it back on the piano where she had always seen it. Isn't that what happened?'

'Looks uncommonly like it, sir. Yes, that's about how I should figure it out. All the same, sir, you know as well as I do that she had no business to touch it.'

'Absolutely right, Marigold. But—a young girl like that, a—what was it you called her?—a charming young girl like that—'

'That's right, sir, very natty.'

'You and I are experienced men of the world—'

'Well, sir, we're certainly—'

'You're younger than I am, of course—'

'Well, I wouldn't say that, sir.'

'Nonsense, you're not a day more than thirty.'

The Inspector curled his moustaches and said: 'What would you say if I told you that I shouldn't see forty again?'

'You don't mean that?'

'It's true, sir.'

'Then you must have another drink. I haven't liked to press you before, but if you say you're forty, then you're just at the age when one really begins to want it. How's that?'

'Thank you, sir, that's plenty.'

'Well now, you know women, Marigold. It isn't many that do, but—'

'Well, sir,' said Marigold complacently, 'I won't say—'

'And the first thing you'll tell me, as a man of real experience, is that women are impulsive. Aren't I right?'

'That you are, sir.'

'Then do you blame Miss Windell that she acted on a sudden feminine impulse? I don't like these manly women, Marigold.'

'No more do I, Mr. Fenton. A man's a man and a woman's a woman, just as God made them. This buck-rabbit o' mine—'

'Do you blame her that, hearing the Parracots arriving and knowing that she had no business to be there, she fled? Do you blame her that she wandered about the country in a dazed manner for two days before I found her? Do you blame her that, when at last she realized what had happened, she decided to come to my brother for advice, knowing that he was an intimate friend of the Home Secretary, the Public Prosecutor *and* the Chief Commissioner of Scotland Yard?'

'Is that so, sir?' said the Inspector thoughtfully.

'You do blame her, Marigold? Well, perhaps you are right. Dr. Willoughby Hatch would certainly blame her. Your

Sergeant, excellent man as he is, but, if I am any judge, entirely ignorant of women and wholly lacking in imagination, your Sergeant would blame her.'

'Bagshaw's a fool, sir.'

'Hallo, there's still some in the bottle. Just a spot more—'

'Well, I oughtn't to really, sir—Thank you. Your brother seems to know a good many people, Mr. Fenton.'

'Archie? But, good lord, everybody knows Archie Fenton. I tell you, Marigold, we're in the wrong job. These popular novelists—'

'Course it's easy to me now to see how the whole thing happened.'

'As soon as you put your finger on that point about the doorstop, you'd got it. Very quick that, Marigold. Very subtle.'

'Course I shall have to ask the ladies a question or two. Just for corroboration.'

'Of course. I say, we haven't quite finished it, after all.' He turned the bottle upside-down.

'Thank you, sir. I shan't worry them, Mr. Fenton.'

'That's very nice of you, Inspector. I was sure of it.'

'Well—good health, sir.'

'Good luck.'

Inspector Marigold wrung out his moustache, curled it back into shape, and marched to the door. Derek looked at the empty bottle, and then at the open door through which the Inspector was walking so straightly. The echoes of a perfectly articulated 'corroboration' were still ringing in his ears. Once again he marvelled at the efficiency of the London Police Force.

20

HUSSAR SAYS GOODBYE

It was naturally a disappointment to Archibald to learn that he was a free man again; but he agreed, gracefully enough, that he could not insist on being charged with a murder at which he had not been present, and which, in fact, had not been committed. Indeed, he became quite genial, and suggested that the police officers should have a drink before leaving for London.

'It's very kind of you, sir,' said the Inspector firmly, 'but it's against orders to drink while on duty. I won't say but what if Sergeant Bagshaw was to slip off to the kitchen for a glass of beer while I was looking the other way—no, thank you, sir, nothing for me.'

So Sergeant Bagshaw slipped gratefully off, and Archibald Fenton, much touched by the Inspector's sense of duty, and no less by the humanity which softened it, wondered if he would care to be photographed under the Elizabethan window, which was a feature of some historic interest. Whereupon Mr. Fenton and Inspector Marigold were so photographed; and, some days later, when it transpired that it was not generally known that the clearing up of what had been termed the Auburn Lodge Mystery was in large measure due to the activities of the famous author of *A Flock of Sheep*, whose new book *Waterfall* was so much in demand, and who had taken an active interest in what had at first promised to be a sensational case—when all this came out, it was discovered that, by a happy accident, a photograph of Inspector Marigold and Mr. Fenton in consultation at the latter's country seat, Ferries, was available for publication. Which was very gratifying to all concerned.

By and by Sergeant Bagshaw came round the corner drying his moustache, and the Police climbed into its car and drove off. 'This', thought Marigold, 'will make a sensation in the papers tomorrow, and be one in the eye for G. A. Hatch.' But it was not so. For at that very moment Miss Innocent Home (*nee* Winkelstein), the famous film star, was stepping down the gangway and calling over her shoulder to her manager: 'Say, what's this darned burg anyway?' and her manager, who had previously assured her that it was *not* London, was now explaining that it was actually called Southampton. But in a little while she would be in London; and in readiness for her the route from Waterloo to the Carlton Hotel had been sanded, and lined with policemen. And fighting madly for a glimpse of her, were a hundred thousand women who had seen Innocent Home on the screen, but much preferred Ronald Colman, and a hundred thousand women who had never heard of her, but wanted to see what the other women were looking at, and ten thousand men who would otherwise have been distributed among the more exciting street accidents of the moment. Was it any wonder that the Press, with its fingers on the public pulse, should decide that, in comparison with Innocent Home's front page and shouting streamers, Jenny's claim on the attention was now met by six lines among the Bankruptcy notices beneath the modest heading 'Miss Jane Latour'?

And so Derek and Jenny, Archibald and Nancy were left alone at the front door. Then Jenny did a very brave thing. Knowing that this was going to be her brother-in-law, she turned to Archibald and said meekly: 'May I have that kiss now?' So

Archibald, looking a little pink, kissed her, and somehow, in the embrace, his bandage fell off, and they all moved casually away and left it there. Really, thought Archibald, she's rather a nice little thing, though I must say I prefer Miss Fairbrother; and just for a moment he wondered whether it mightn't be a good idea to have a double wedding, he marrying Nancy, and Jenny, Derek. Then he remembered that he was married already, and had six children. So, instead, he suggested that they should all stay to tea and dinner, and he would drive Miss Fairbrother back after dinner to her hotel. Derek, who wanted to be alone with Jenny, was a little gloomy about this; but he brightened up when Archibald said that, if they could possibly find something to do, he did rather want to work after tea, and perhaps Miss Fairbrother would be kind enough to take some dictation, as he suddenly felt in the mood. And at dinner Archibald produced a Perrier Jouet 1923, which Nancy recognized at once as a good wine, and healths were drunk.

At last Jenny and Derek drove off together, but not until Derek had told his brother several times that he didn't want a whisky before he went, and Archibald had assured him several times that he had one bottle left of absolutely pre-war if only he could find it. They said loving goodbyes to Nancy, and promised her that they would come to see her tomorrow; they interrupted Archibald's monologue in the cellar, and left him at the front door still muttering that it was a damn funny thing about that bottle; they waved once more as they turned the corner... and then they were out on the road together, hand in hand (since it was now Derek's car) with Hope and Inexperience for guides, and the world in front of them.

The night was very still. Jenny lay in bed with her eyes shut, and whispered:

'Hussar?'

'Hallo, Jenny.'

'Darling, I thought of getting married. You don't mind, do you, darling?'

'Well, that's very funny, because I was just thinking what a good idea it would be.'

'Darling, were you really? How lovely of you!'

'Who were you thinking of marrying, Jenny?'

'Well, I was wondering if you could think of anybody?'

'Do you mean a soldier, or something like that?'

'Oh, dear! Oh, *darling!*'

'As a matter of fact, Jenny, I don't think a soldier. Soldiers aren't what they were.'

'Just as you like, darling.'

'I thought more like somebody as it might be in the wine-trade.'

'Oh, Hussar, isn't it funny? I do just happen to know somebody in the wine-trade! Do you think that would be a good idea?'

'I think it would be a lovely idea, Jenny.'

'All right, then, I will. Thank you, darling.'

'Goodbye, Jenny.'

'Goodbye, darling, *darling* Hussar,' said Jenny, knowing that now it was really goodbye.

Then she curled up and went to sleep.

For more details and a full list of titles:

visit https://www.hachetteindia.com/home/yellowbacks

HODDER AND STOUGHTON

WELCOME BACK TO THE GOLDEN AGE